# ACCLAIM FOR RACHEL HAUCK

Powerful and relevant, *Once Upon a Pr*... ... pages flew by. This is classic romnace ... ... Hauck for creating a story that's sure to touch hearts and souls.

DEBBIE MACOMBER, #1 *NEW*
*YORK TIMES* BEST-SELLING AUTHOR

*The Wedding Dress* will capture you from page one with a story only Rachel Hauck could weave.

—JENNY B. JONES, AWARD-WINNING AUTHOR OF
*SAVE THE DATE* AND *THERE YOU'LL FIND ME*

*The Wedding Dress* is a seamless tale of enduring love that weaves the past and present in an intricate, wedding dress mystery. Hauck again manages to mesmerize for well over 300 pages with quirky characters, a compelling plot, and a satisfying happily-ever-after. Highly recommended!

—DENISE HUNTER, BEST-SELLING AUTHOR OF
*THE ACCIDENTAL BRIDE* AND *BAREFOOT SUMMER*

The talented Rachel Hauck has given us a contemporary love story enmeshed in a fast-paced mystery. Juggle your reading list, y'all. Brimming with the twin themes of redemption and grace, *The Wedding Dress* deserves a spot at the top!

—SHELLIE RUSHING TOMLINSON, BELLE OF
ALL THINGS SOUTHERN AND BEST-SELLING
AUTHOR OF *SUE ELLEN'S GIRL AIN'T FAT, SHE*
*JUST WEIGHS HEAVY!*

Rachel Hauck's writing is full of wisdom and heart, and *The Wedding Dress*, as artfully and intricately designed as the most exquisite of bridal gowns, is no exception. This novel tells the story of four loveable women, miraculously bound by one gown, whose lives span a century. Their mutual search for truth and love—against the odds—will most certainly take your breath away.

—BETH WEBB HART, BEST-SELLING AUTHOR OF
*SUNRISE ON THE BATTERY* AND *LOVE, CHARLESTON*

From the moment I heard about this story, I couldn't wait to get my hands on it. A wedding dress worn by four different women over 100 years? Yes, please! I loved the story of these women . . . and their one important dress. For anyone who's ever lingered over a bridal magazine, watched a bridal reality show, or daydreamed about being a bride, Rachel Hauck has created a unique story that will captivate your heart!

—MARYBETH WHALEN, AUTHOR OF *THE MAILBOX*,
*SHE MAKES IT LOOK EASY*, AND *THE GUEST BOOK*

A tender tale that spans generations of women, each a product of her time and ahead of her time. A beautiful story laced together with love, faith, mystery, and one amazing dress. Rachel Hauck has another winner in *The Wedding Dress*!

—LISA WINGATE, NATIONAL BEST-SELLING
AND CAROL AWARD-WINNING AUTHOR OF
*DANDELION SUMMER* AND *BLUE MOON BAY*

Once Upon a
PRINCE

## ALSO BY RACHEL HAUCK

The Wedding Dress

Lowcountry Romance novels
Dining with Joy
Love Starts with Elle
Sweet Caroline

Diva Nashvegas
Lost in Nashvegas

## With Sara Evans

Sweet By and By
Softly and Tenderly
Love Lifted Me

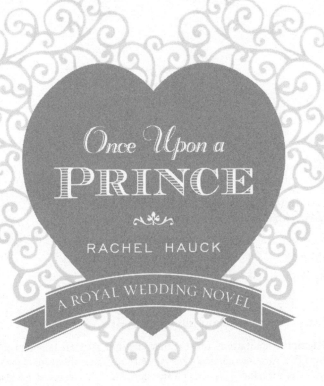

# Once Upon a
# PRINCE

### RACHEL HAUCK

A ROYAL WEDDING NOVEL

**ZONDERVAN®**

ZONDERVAN.com/
AUTHORTRACKER
*follow your favorite authors*

Zondervan

Once Upon a Prince
Copyright © 2013 by Rachel Hayes Hauck

This title is also available as a Zondervan ebook.
Visit www.zondervan.com/ebooks.

This title is also available in a Zondervan audio edition.
Visit www.zondervan.fm.

Requests for information should be addressed to:

Zondervan, Grand Rapids, Michigan 49530

Library of Congress Control Number: 2013933466

Editorial: Sue Brower, Becky Philpott, Bob Hudson, Linsey DeVries

Printed in the United States of America

13 14 15 16 17 18 19 20 /RRD/ 20 19 18 17 16 15 14 13 12 11 10 9 8 7 6 5 4 3 2 1

Dedicated to:

Kendall Alexis
Elizabeth Grace (Gracie)
Suzanna Rae
Avery Lillian
"Grow up to be women of God where
royalty is guaranteed."

Part One

The Prince

# ONE

What did he say? The storm gusts moving over the Atlantic must have garbled his words.

*"I can't marry you"*?

Susanna stopped, flip-flops swinging from her fingertips. She'd misunderstood, right? Sand washed out from under her feet as the afternoon tide pulled the waves back into their ocean boundaries.

Adam walked on, failing to notice she wasn't with him.

"Hey, wait . . ."

On the northern horizon, spikes of gold broke through mustang-blue storm clouds and ignited the dark afternoon with light.

"Adam, what did you say?" Her feet slapped the wet sand where his footprints were already fading.

"This isn't easy, Suz," he said, taking one last step, a low breeze nipping at the hem of his cargo shorts.

"What's not easy?" The man had fought battles in Afghanistan; how could anything on a St. Simons Island beach be difficult?

Her hair blew around her face as she stared toward the dispersing rain clouds. This wouldn't be the first time a storm had brewed in Adam Peters after he'd returned from a Middle East tour, jammed up and bothered. She'd weather it with him. Again.

Susanna dipped her head to see his averted gaze. "Come on, what's bothering you? Being stateside? Leaving your men? You've done four tours in six years, Adam. It's okay to do something for yourself." She wiggled his arm, teasing him, drawing him out. "You're an amazing marine. Stateside or fighting the front lines."

"Suz?" His tone and the way he collapsed his marine-muscled shoulders made her heart seize. "It's this." He motioned to her, then to himself, exposing the tip of his red-and-blue *semper fi* tattoo hidden beneath the sleeve of his white T-shirt.

"This?" She glanced around. "Walking on the beach?"

He made a face. "No, Suz. Why would I not like walking on the beach?"

"I don't know. You started this." Impatience. A sign of a brewing argument. "Excuse me if I can't read your mind . . . What's bothering you? Did something happen on the tour? Before you came home?" She tossed softballs, trying to get him to swing, to hint at the emotion he was struggling to articulate.

She had twelve years of history to back her up. Twelve years of friendship. Of an ebbing and flowing romance. Of drives up to Quantico when he was in officer candidate school. Of weekends in Atlanta, where she had launched her landscape-architect career. Of four shipping-outs to the Middle East. Of four homecomings.

Susanna had twelve years of letters, emails, phone calls. Twelve years of walks on the beach, of laughing on the Rib Shack's deck while eating ribs under the swinging strings of light, barbecue sauce slipping down their chins.

Of ups and downs, disappointments, postponements, arguments, and apologies.

All melded into her heart by memories, all a part of the bigger picture. The promise of something more. Commitment. Marriage. Growing old in a St. Simons cottage.

This was Adam's third day home on leave and he'd been mostly sleeping since he arrived. So when he called her at work this afternoon and asked her to meet him behind the Rib Shack, she'd dashed out. Didn't even tell her boss she was leaving.

A special call to meet him on the beach? It was romantic rendezvous enough for her. Enough to awaken her hopes for declarations of love, a marine on bended knee, and a diamond ring.

Okay, so she'd always dreamed of getting engaged under Lover's Oak, but far be it from her to nitpick. If Adam was proposing, she was accepting. Any place, any time.

But he wasn't proposing, was he? He barely looked at her. She surveyed his tense stance, his off-kilter, dark, and morose mood.

"Adam, talk to me. What happened over there?"

"I told you, this isn't easy." Adam tipped his head back, squinting up at a circling seagull. "I don't know, Susanna . . ."

"What don't you know?"

"Looks like it's not going to rain after all." He pointed toward the sun's breach through the dark-bottomed clouds and walked forward again.

"Adam, stop . . ." His demeanor awakened all of her dormant insecurities. The kind she had befriended as a girl hiding in her room while her parents fought, smashed Walmart dishes against the kitchen walls, and yelled four-letter words Susanna dared not repeat. "Stop walking away."

She reached for his arm again, a realization setting in that the wind had *not* garbled his words at all. What troubled him was her, their relationship. Not Afghanistan. "You said you couldn't marry me, didn't you?"

"I've rehearsed what I wanted to say." He peered down at her through narrowed eyes, cloaking his warm-chocolate irises. "You're pretty amazing. You know that, don't you?"

"I guess." The confession raised her suspicions more than eased them. Where was he going with this? He was hard to read when his soul was shuttered.

Adam lowered himself down to the beach, hooking his arms

around his raised knees. "I missed the ocean. A couple of my buddies and I made makeshift surfboards and drove way out in the desert to surf the dunes." He shook his head, angling his hand through the air with a whistle, then a mock explosion. "Crash and burn. We had sand stuck in places we didn't even know we had places."

"Sounds fun." With her gentle response she gave him room to talk, let him figure out words for his internal turmoil. Susanna picked a spot next to him, sat, and dug her heels into the sand, letting the stiff breeze braid her hair across her eyes. "You were saying something about me being amazing?" She nudged his arm with her shoulder.

He'd not said he loved her since he had returned, but after twelve years, some of their affection had dulled. But if he thought she was amazing . . .

"I don't know of a guy who had a girl wait for twelve years. Through college, officer training, back-to-back tours. Four in six years." Adam reached out and captured the floating ends of her hair with his fingers, letting the strands weave in the spaces between.

"It's not like I was sitting around, Adam. I graduated from college, worked for a big fancy Atlanta architecture firm, started my landscape career, and—"

"And now you work for Gage Stone."

"Oh, come on." She regarded him. "That can't be what's bothering you. That I work for Gage?" Susanna and Adam had gone to high school with Gage. Been good friends until time and distance pulled them apart. "I moved home to work for Richard Thornton, *the* most prominent landscape architect in the South. It wasn't my plan for him to die a month later."

She'd never have returned to the island if Richard Thornton hadn't pursued her. But an architect mentored by him could write her own ticket.

"Guess death wasn't part of the equation."

"No." Aneurysm. At the age of sixty. Died at his drafting table. In her grief, his wife closed the office and liquidated everything. And Susanna received her first and last paycheck.

"Why didn't you go back to Atlanta?"

She peered at him. "Do you even listen to our conversations, Adam? We talked about this."

"Yeah, yeah, I guess we did. You liked being home, right?"

"Once I got here"—she scooped up a handful of sand and let it sift through her fingers—"I felt like I was supposed to be here."

The day of Richard's funeral, Mama put Susanna on the Rib Shack schedule. Said it was a family business and Susanna shouldn't hesitate to take her rightful place. It was Mama's way of giving her a job without making Susanna ask. She'd made a big stink about going off to college to get *away* from waiting tables and mopping floors. But she welcomed the job while figuring out her next move. Then, a month after Richard died, Gage returned to the island and hung out his architect shingle.

"How's it going with Gage, Suz?"

"Struggling. He chases every possible job like a dog on the hunt, but with the economy the way it is, people hold on to their money. My shifts at the Rib Shack pay the bills."

Adam laughed. "I know your mama's loving that . . . having you back at the Shack."

"She knows it's temporary." Emphasis on *temporary*. The on-ramp to talk about their future couldn't be any wider. There was nothing keeping her on the island. She was only waiting on Adam to finish this tour and propose.

"Suz." He cleared his voice. "I've accepted an assignment with a new task force in DC."

"DC? Okay . . ." She could do DC. "I have a connection in Virginia. One of the architects I interned with works for a firm there." She slipped her phone from her shorts pocket. "I'll make a note to call her tomorrow?"

He cupped his hand over hers. "I can't give you what you want."

"I don't know what you mean." Her eyes blurred. "W–what do you think I want?"

"To get married."

"Not just *to get married*, Adam. Married to *you*." She blinked her eyes clear as she gazed at him. Marriage was the plan. Since their sophomore year of college.

He sighed and shifted in his sandy seat. Anxiety fueled Susanna's heart.

"Earlier you asked me what happened in Afghanistan." He reached for his shoe, slipped it off, and let the sand run out. "I met someone." His voice faltered, his boldness waned. "Actually, we met in OCS."

"Y–you met someone?" Seven years ago?

"She was dating a guy, I had you. But we were always good friends. Then we were assigned to the same intel unit on this last tour." For a moment, he postured himself like a combat marine. Shoulders square, eyes alert, confident. But in the next second, he seemed every bit like a guy breaking up with his girlfriend and hating it.

"There's . . . you met . . . someone else?" Susanna said, low and soft, weighing his confession through a sheer déjà vu veil. Did she dream this?

A blush of rain-scented wind cooled her hot skin and burning eyes.

"Her name is Sheree. We—"

"And you didn't tell me?" She shoved around the coarse granules of sand with her toes. "Adam, battlefield romances rarely succeed. You told me so yourself. You and I . . . we succeed." She tempered the desperation out of her voice. "You just said no other marine had a girl who stood by him for twelve years."

"I know, and it's true, but come on, Suz, did you ever think twelve years was a long time to date *and* wait for someone? Even for a deployed marine?"

"Yes, but we had a plan." Susanna liked plans. They made life easier, simpler. They made life run smooth. Even a *stupid* plan like waiting until Adam finished his tours before getting married was still a plan.

But he wanted to make captain so he kept volunteering for tours. The plan revolved around Adam's career and sense of duty. But Susanna didn't mind. She didn't. She was in love and love was patient. Right?

"The plan. Forever in perpetuity," he said with a heavy exhale. "Suz, did it ever occur to you that the plan needed to change . . . because we've changed? Did you ever wonder if we'd only stayed together because we were comfortable? That we liked the *idea* of us more than we actually liked us?"

"The *idea* of us?" Where was this coming from? "Yes, I like the *idea* of us. But it stands to reason that if I like the *idea* of us, then I like *us*."

"You're in love with the plan, Susanna. Not me." His words fired silver bullets straight to her heart.

"In love with the plan? Don't talk crazy." She jumped up and dusted the sand from her shorts. "If you want to break up with me, don't blame me or the plan. What kind of girl waits twelve years"—oh, those years suddenly felt like an eternity—"because she loves a *plan*? She'd have to be insane."

But what was the value of a plan if she didn't stick to it? By gum, it's why she waited for Adam. How she survived childhood. How she worked her way through college.

The plan.

She started walking up the beach toward the widening pinwheel of sunlight, Adam's words spinning around her heart.

Did she love the plan more than him?

The fragrance of Adam's skin chased her. His voice came

softly over her shoulder. "I understand the plan. You didn't want to be like your parents, fighting, divorcing—"

"And remarrying." Glo and Gibson Truitt were local celebrities among the church crowd. Once a year, they testified in church about their "failed divorce."

They still snipped and fussed, but they loved each other. Jesus had done some fine work in her daddy and mama.

"But not before you learned to wake up braced for anything. War or peace. You hated waking up in the morning not knowing what kind of day you'd face so you became a planner. Even as a kid."

"Do you blame me?"

"No, but I'm saying . . ." He slipped his hand around her arm. "Maybe that's why you clung to our plan. It makes you feel safe."

"Did you take a pop psych class in Afghanistan?"

He released her and stepped back. "Remember last New Year's when my dad pulled me aside?"

"I remember."

"He said if I was going to marry you, I'd best get with it. It wasn't right to make you wait any longer."

"I love your dad." A true, blunt confession.

"So I took a little hop across Europe on my way to Afghanistan—London, Paris—searching for a unique engagement ring. I must have looked at a hundred before I finally found one in a little shop outside Paris."

"Wait . . . you bought a ring . . . for me?" She took a hesitant step toward him.

"I did," he said, with a slow, contemplative nod. "Slapped down my credit card, but when the man asked the name of my *amour*, my mind went blank. I couldn't remember."

"My name? You couldn't remember my name?" Sadness butterflied in her heart.

"Blank." He tapped his forehead with the tips of his fingers. "I was distracted, thinking about getting my boots on the ground in Afghanistan, feeling like I was working off a checklist rather than buying a ring for my *amour*."

"That's it? You city hop your way over to Afghanistan, and when buying a ring feels like a chore, you decide I'm not the one? That the plan has drained you of love?" She shifted her stance, balancing on a narrow beam of peace and dread, one foot to the other. What happened to her sensible Adam? "Was Sheree with you?"

"No, Suz. Come on. Sheree and I?" Hands on his hips, he looked everywhere but at her. "The moment I pulled out my credit card, I knew I'd found the right ring but not the right girl." His glistening gaze landed on her face. "Sheree and I didn't reconnect until a few months ago."

"You found the right ring but not the right girl?" She crossed her arms, locked her hands on her elbows, squared her back, and raised her chin. "How can you have the right ring if you have the wrong girl? That . . . that makes no sense."

"I just knew I'd found a ring I'd love to give my fiancée someday, but"—he paddled hard against the conversation stream—"I . . . for the life of me, I couldn't see myself giving it to you."

"Adam, you went to Afghanistan seven months ago. You're just now telling me? We've been emailing, talking?"

"I had second thoughts. Maybe it was just cold feet or something. Besides, I didn't want to break up long-distance. You mean a great deal to me. Twelve years deserves more than a 'Dear Susanna' email or hey, 'Oh by the way,' on a phone call."

"Twelve years." She whirled back toward the Rib Shack. "Twelve years I waited for you, and I get 'I found the right ring but not the right girl'?"

"Suz, I'm being honest." Adam ran backward in front of her, his knees high, his form perfect. "If you stop and think, you'll realize you feel the same way."

"Don't tell me how I feel, Adam. Just don't." She tried to sprint around him, but he switched directions and kept in step with her. "Try to make yourself feel better by roping me into your wild decision."

*Not the right girl*... His words reverberated through her, to her very core.

"You know I'm right."

His words, his tone, a clarion bell to her heart. Oh mercy, how could it be? Yes, he was right, he was right. And it galled her. "I don't know what to say to you right now." Susanna maintained her march toward the Rib Shack's beachside deck. How had she not seen it? Was she so stuck and stubborn?

"Susanna, the last time I was home, we only saw each other six times. You never came up to Washington."

"I was working. I have a job." She lengthened her stride. "I didn't see *you* hightailing it home."

"You were working at the Rib Shack." He made a wild one-arm gesture toward the restaurant. "You could've taken off anytime you wanted."

She exhaled and stopped midstride. "If you want to break up with me, then do it. But don't you dump your guilt on me."

"No guilt dumping here. Just making observations. Suz, you know I'm right. We aren't each other's true loves. We were a high school romance that somehow got away from us."

"Got away from us? Who plans marriage like that?" Susanna pressed the heel of her hand to her forehead and turned for the edge of the Atlantic where the evening tide was rolling in. With each swoosh of the foam against the sand, realization washed over her. How had she not seen it? Truth awakened in her thoughts, her heart, and the edges of her senses.

"We were both comfortable. Our relationship was good. Safe. We do like each other, Suz. A lot."

She peered at him. "I'm twenty-nine, Adam. I want to get married. You're the only man I've dated since I fast-danced with

Bobby Conway at the seventh-grade fall dance." She flung her arms wide. "Now what? You're done with tours, ready to settle down, make a life for yourself in the States, and suddenly I'm not the right one?"

She rehashed what her heart already knew because it was how she processed. She fought because her dignity demanded it. But the fire of her vehemence never truly flared.

"What? You want me to marry you just *because?*" He looked incredulous, sounding half terrified.

"Yes, Adam, yes. I do." Her inner fight tumbled over the ravine of her resolve. She wasn't going to just walk away from twelve years with an, "Okay, sure, I'm jiving with you. Glad we cleared this up. Have a nice life."

"You don't mean it."

"We've said 'I love you.' We've planned a future together." She poked his chest with her forefinger to the rumble of sudden, low-passing thunder. Grit rose in her soul. "We. Had. A. Deal."

Adam gripped her finger. "I love Sheree. Reconnecting with her was when I really knew you and I didn't love each other in a husband-wife kind of way. If you'd met the right guy and I came home to propose, you'd be the one standing here telling me the ring was right but I was all wrong. You'd know you don't love me as a woman should love the man she's going to marry."

"Stop telling me how I feel." She gripped her hands into fists. He was such a commander—of men, of her feelings. This habit of his had spiked many of their arguments.

"Then look at me." He motioned to her with two fingers, then swung them around to his sharp unwavering gaze. "Look here. Tell me you love me like a woman should love a man she's going to marry."

"I don't even know what that means. Love is love."

"I could break into song over Sheree."

"Ha, song. Has she heard you sing?"

"Yes, and she lets me sing anyway."

Susanna folded her arms with a sigh. Any defense she might muster weakened in her heart. "But you don't want to break into song over me."

"I don't. I'm sorry." His gaze spoke of his regret.

"Yeah, well, me too." She started up the dunes toward the Rib Shack. Mama, her baby sister, Avery, everyone was waiting inside for the news.

*Engagement news.*

"Suz?"

She glanced over her shoulder at Adam. "I'm fine." She didn't wait for his response, just skirted around the sea oats and up the path to the deck.

Slipping on her flip-flops, she avoided the kitchen and the hovering expectations by heading for the parking lot.

She'd never been into romance, fairy tales, knights in shining armor, or handsome princes riding up to save the day. Just a happily ever after with her strong hometown marine. Now what was the plan for the rest of her life?

# TWO

*I*'m going out." Nathaniel glanced to the dining-room table for the keys to the motorcar, the rented black SUV. He thought Liam had deposited them there after he'd returned from his daily breakfast errand.

"Going where?" Jonathan, Nathaniel's aide, crossed the living room with his iPad in hand, concern creasing his face.

"Nowhere. Just out." Where were those blasted keys? Nathaniel lifted the newspaper Liam had been reading. *Aha...*

"Liam's gone for a run." Jonathan returned his attention to his iPad, tapping the screen, scrolling through his emails, no doubt. "Wait for him to return."

"I don't need Liam."

The aide snapped his attention to Nathaniel. "You're not going alone."

"I don't need a security officer with me on this small island. No one even knows I'm here."

"Mrs. Butler knows you're here."

"Yes, but I'm her surprise guest at the benefit, so I'm sure she's not made my presence known. Besides, Americans love the British princes. Us Brighton lads go virtually unnoticed."

"The Crown will have my head if anything happens to you."

"Shall I send a note, tell them I'm choosing to wander about on my own, absolve you of all responsibility?"

"Now you patronize me."

"And you worry too much, Jonathan." Nathaniel turned, signaling the end of the conversation. He was going for a drive—alone.

Having been on the island for three days at the family's American holiday cottage, Nathaniel had seen nothing except the beach, which was beautiful, the pinched expression of his aide and solemn countenance of his security officer, both of whom were fine friends but *not* beautiful to behold.

Three grown men on holiday, lounging in a hundred-year-old cottage, watching movies and playing an ancient Brighton card game, made Nathaniel restless.

Technically, though, he'd traveled to America on business, not for a holiday. The king's business, to be exact. So the kingdom of Brighton *owed* Nathaniel a true vacation. One with sun and surf and perhaps the company of a pretty woman with whom to dine.

In light of this, his aide and beloved nation could spot him an hour or two on his own.

"Do you know where you're going?" Jonathan dashed around the sofa to intercept Nathaniel in the foyer.

"Gladly, no." Nathaniel stepped around him and into the sunshine and freedom. He loved his country. Loved Brighton's low-cloud days that had a nip in the air, but he also loved the sun, the heat, and the endless blue sky of Georgia. "It's a small island. I'm sure I can manage my way round." He smiled at Jonathan, so serious and intense. The man took his duties as aide to the crown prince of Brighton most seriously.

"I'll go with you."

"Jonathan, I need a moment to myself." Nathaniel slipped behind the wheel. "To think."

"About what?"

"I don't know . . . life."

The man sighed, collapsing his thin shoulders. "You have your mobile?"

Nathaniel patted his trouser pocket, where he'd tucked the phone. "Go back to what you were doing, Jon. I'll not be gone long."

Pulling out of the drive, Nathaniel turned south on Ocean Boulevard and powered down all the windows.

The sun-baked July breeze filled the interior and blew his hair, the loose threads of his shirt, and the nagging thoughts on his heart.

Easing off the accelerator, Nathaniel jutted his elbow out the window, slid down in the seat, and steered the big machine through the dappled light where the brightness of the afternoon was giving way to the textured shadows of evening.

His tension began to ease at the sight of an old woman riding her bicycle on the dirt path next to the road.

Still, the news at home hadn't been good before he left. Dad's health was failing. Nathaniel half suspected he'd sent him on this junket not to please distant cousin Carlene Butler but because this might be Nathaniel's last excursion as a free man. At thirty-two, he thought he had years—decades—before becoming king.

But instead he had months. A year tops.

He steered the car around a curve with a sense of familiarity. He needed more time. To soak up Dad's wisdom. To amend his youthful rebellion and indiscretions.

"*You will be king within the year. Prepare yourself.*" Dad was so matter-of-fact. So true to form. King first, man second.

"*Dad, no, you're going to recover . . .*"

Nathaniel slowed for a traffic light, inhaling the scent of sweet jasmine. It brought memories of home. Of his youth summers with Dad, Mum, and little brother, Stephen, at Parrsons House.

When the light flashed green, Nathaniel urged the car forward, taking the roundabout along Frederica to Demere.

Surely this ride was what he needed. Fresh perspective. Life was changing, wasn't it? Too suddenly. Too quickly.

The pressure to choose a bride would increase the moment he returned to Brighton. From Mum first, then Dad. After that, the King's Office. Perhaps the prime minister would want to "have a word."

*Say, Nathaniel, what thoughts have you given to choosing a wife? The throne needs an heir.*

As of late, the media had begun to mimic their British and German cousins, printing salacious stories on the royal princes, trying to sell papers, casting aspersions about the crown prince's marriage intentions, reminding the populace of his youthful indiscretions, and that he'd not had a serious girlfriend in ten years. Fine that . . . a decade. Though he had been seen as of late with the beautiful Lady Genevieve Hawthorne.

Nathaniel took the Torras Causeway toward Brunswick, curving right or left as the road dictated, letting it lead him.

He turned a sharp, sudden right when his eye caught a street sign. Prince Street.

Slowing down, the SUV drifted through the shade under the live oaks, the breeze gentling past. Prince Street . . . The sign freed a bit of his hope, made him feel like everything would be all right. As if he might actually be in the right place at the right time. An unusual sensation for crown princes.

*Lord, am I ready . . .*

He was about to turn around when a strong feminine voice captured his attention. Nathaniel leaned over the wheel, squinting through the sun and shade. A woman walked 'round a car parked under an enormous, craggy old tree. A motley-looking man traipsed after her.

She stopped, wagged a metal rod or some such at him, and pointed down the road as if telling him to leave.

The man stepped forward with a wolfish grin. She swung at him. *Good going, girl.*

Nathaniel pulled his SUV under the tree, parking next to the small, green Cabrio and stepped out.

"Might I be of assistance?"

The woman whirled around, giving him a wide-eyed expression. The threads of light falling through the trees haloed her golden hair. "There you are. What took you so long?" She jammed the rod toward him. "I told this guy you were on your way . . . *darling.*" She made a face. "Can you believe it? Another flat tire." Her laugh carried no merriment. "The lug nuts are stuck tighter than a drum."

"Well, then, let's get them unstuck." Nathaniel took the cross wrench from the woman and examined it. He'd changed a few tires in his day. During his university years, racing over country roads had been a pastime for letting off steam.

He shifted his gaze to the pierced and tattooed man. He was thin, wearing tattered, soiled clothing, and Nathaniel felt sure he only wanted money. He was also sure the girl could've taken him if it had come to a brawl. "You can move on now."

"I only offered to help." The man stepped back.

"But I asked you to leave and you didn't." The woman bent toward him, hands on her hips, fire in her tone.

Nathaniel smiled. He liked her.

"Be on your way." Nathaniel slipped his hand into his pocket, pulling out the twenty-dollar bill he'd collected before going on his drive. Stepping around the blonde, he offered his hand to the man, pressing the bill into his gritty palm. "Have yourself a hot meal."

The man popped open the twenty and held it up, a hard glare in his eyes. "You rich folk think you can just do whatever you please, don't you?"

"And what do you *folk* think? You can continue pressing a lady when she asks you to leave?"

The man swore, tucked the money in his pocket, and walked off, talking to himself, filling the air with foul words.

"I could've done that." She turned a bit of her fire onto Nathaniel. "Given him money. You know he's going to buy booze or drugs, right?"

Nathaniel shrugged, watching her for a moment. She didn't seem to recognize him. But who would expect a real prince right here, right now? "Or he might buy a nice hot dinner. Seems the lad could use it." Nathaniel wrapped his fingers around the cool metal wrench. Something about her made him want to wrap his arms around her and assure her that he didn't care what the man did with the money, only that she was safe.

"Have we met before?" he asked, knowing he had not met this woman, but something about her seemed so familiar. Warm and perfect.

"No." She took the wrench from him. "Thanks for stopping. I appreciate it. But I can take it from here." Her voice wavered, and Nathaniel caught the glassy sheen of tears in her eyes before she glanced away.

"Are you sure? What of those tight lug nuts? I've changed lots of tires in my time." Nathaniel held out his hand, palm up. "What say we work at it together. Get you going straightaway."

"Straightaway to where? To what?" She fell against the car, exhaling, her wind-tangled ponytail falling over her shoulder. "What a stupid, rotten day."

Nathaniel sobered when she released a sharp sob.

"Ah, what's wrong? Can't be all that bad, can it?"

She swerved around, punishing the flat tire with a sharp kick. "Stupid, rotten day."

"It's just a flat tire."

She glared at him, a pink hue rimming her flooded blue eyes.

"We were supposed to be forever, you know? Twelve years . . . Who waits twelve years for a guy if it's not for forever?"

"Ah, lover's quarrel."

"Quarrel? No. Complete breakdown of what we thought we wanted in life, in our relationship." The first splash of tears hit her high, smooth cheeks. She brushed them away with the back of her hand, kicked the tire one last time, and passed behind Nathaniel toward the tree. "I don't know why I came here. I just got in the car and drove." She glanced back at the motor, making a face. "And I find myself here, at good ol' Lover's Oak."

"So this tree has a name and a tale?" Nathaniel came around the car, surveying the thick, curvy, Medusa-like limbs of the expansive oak.

"The tree is legend. Fabled to be nine hundred years old, a place where native braves met their maidens." She smoothed her hand along the curve of the lowest limb as if she might feel the tree's pulse, as if she might discern the stories of days gone by.

"Do you suppose it's true?" Nathaniel was acquainted with legends and fables, long tales of bravery, love, and courage. They were a part of Brighton. A part of his five-hundred-year-old family tree.

She peered over at him. "I wanted to get engaged under this tree. Soft white lights swinging from the branches. Maybe a string quartet playing over there." She pointed to the edge of the median. "Something special, romantic."

"But your lad had other intentions."

Tears filled the corners of her eyes. "I–I just . . . wanted . . ." She shook her head as she lowered her gaze. "I've been such a fool."

"I don't think anyone who freely gives her heart is a fool."

She sat down on the stump creasing the middle of the wide tree's base, face in her hands, weeping softly.

What was he to do? He didn't know the woman. And tears? He'd never been much good with tears.

"It's quite courageous. To give one's heart." What did he know? He'd failed at love once and never attempted it again.

She dried her face on the sleeve of her shirt. "I never expected much. Just love and devotion, you know? That he would do what he said he'd do . . . marry me. I lived my childhood not knowing what my parents were doing from one moment to the next. Kiss and make up or fire the dinner dishes at each other. I was fine with simple and slow, taking our time. We both went to college, started our careers." She inhaled a long, shaky breath. "He did four tours in Iraq and Afghanistan."

"A soldier."

"Marine. Captain."

"I served in the navy myself. Four years."

"Were you deployed?" She stood straighter.

How could he tell her? His birth status kept him from being deployed. That he presented more of a danger to his countrymen than the enemy. "I never shipped out to conflict zones."

"Are you from England?"

"Brighton Kingdom."

"Brighton. Beautiful gardens in Brighton."

"You know of our gardens?"

"Studied your Lecharran Garden in college. I'm a landscape architect—well, when I'm not serving up barbecue at the Rib Shack." Her eyes were clear, her gaze a strong blue when she looked at him. "I thought he was going to propose on the beach. Forget the tree, the twinkling lights, the quartet. We were finally moving forward." She smashed her fist against her palm, almost laughing.

"You *are* a beautiful woman. I'm sure there are a number of men?"

"Number of men? No, no . . . no. Look . . . What's your name?" Whatever process she was going through, it seemed to rebuke her sobs and energize her.

"Nate." He offered his hand. "Nate Kenneth." Parts of his name anyway. His traveling name.

"Susanna Truitt." She shook his hand, and he loved the feel of her grip.

"You were saying?"

"What? Yeah, you said . . ." Her eyes lingered on his face. Her hand remained in his. "Men. A number of men, right?" She slipped from his grasp.

His instinct was to reach for her again, but he curled his fingers into his palm instead.

"I don't want men. I want one man." She held up her finger. "One true love."

"There's only one?"

"Yes."

"How can you be so sure?"

She pressed her hand over her heart. "My heart tells me. There is *one* for me. Only one."

Her words vibrated through him—hot, exploding, bringing to life his own thoughts on love. "You almost convince me."

"Then you're as foolish as I am." She broke a dead twig from the tree and crumbled the leaves in her hand. "I thought I'd found him." Bits and pieces of dried brown leaves fluttered to the ground. "But I didn't." She breathed in a slow, quivering breath.

"Maybe he'll come 'round." If the man had half a wit. How could he walk away from her? From Susanna?

"He's met someone else." Her eyes glistened again, and the tip of her perfect nose reddened. "He said he found the right ring but not the right girl."

"Oh, he said that? He's an honest chap if not a bit brutal."

She shook her head, tapping her chest with her fingers. "The worst part of this is realizing I was so focused on him proposing one day I never imagined my answer. When he so honestly said he'd found the right ring but not the right girl, I was mad. Hoo boy, was I mad. But the more we talked, the more I realized . . . we were a high school romance plan gone wrong. Now all I can think is if he'd proposed"—she snapped another thin, dead twig from the tree—"I'm not sure I'd have said yes."

"You're not sure?" Nathaniel swallowed the *hurrah* pressing on his tongue. What right did the man have to this beauty if he'd break her heart with such a harsh confession?

"Argh. I don't know." Her gentle words bent and swayed with her Georgia accent. "I just hung on so tight . . ." She fisted the air. "He said I loved the plan more than him. But who does that? I told him he was crazy. But, Nate, he might just be right. I put all of my eggs in the marry-Adam-Peters basket and that was that. End of story."

"So you don't love him either?"

"Yes . . . no . . . I don't know." She squinted at him. "You're pushy for just having met me." Her laugh-cry escaped into the air between them. "Except I feel"—she fell against the wide, split base of the ancient tree—"peace. Something I've not felt in a long time. You know how you can hold on to something so tight . . . you're so close you can't even really see what you're clinging to anymore?"

Yes, he knew.

"Then you finally let go, only to see your hands are all rope burned and the pot of gold at the end of your rainbow turned out to be a pile of candy wrappers glinting in the sun."

Nathaniel snorted a light laugh but pulled it in, not sure she intended to be funny. "But now the future is yours to own, to mold."

She examined her palms as if she expected to find rope burns. "What a waste." She snapped her attention to him. "And look at me, telling all my woes to a complete stranger."

"Not so strange, I hope. Just new." Nathaniel had liked her a minute ago. He'd moved on to adoring her. "You've a career?"

"Not much going on in the landscape-architecture business

these days. People aren't redoing their grounds. They're saving money." She peered at the twilight sky, then held out her hand for the wrench. "I'm sure you have other things to do than talk to me. I can change the tire."

"It's been a pleasure to talk with you." Nathaniel walked to the flat and dropped to one knee. She'd kicked the old tire. He could kiss it. Because it had gone flat, he'd met the enchanting Susanna. "I envy you, Susanna. You have your life ahead of you, free to do whatever, start fresh, go wherever you want, do whatever you want."

"Keep talking, bubba. I might start believing you." She dropped the jack to the ground and shoved it under the car.

He loosened the lug nuts. "Consider some who have their lives planned for them from before they were born. No chance to make a change or go about as they please."

"I don't know anyone like that around here. Maybe Mose Watson, who's set to inherit his daddy's real estate business, but they're millionaires, and I don't hear Mose complaining."

"But if Mose wanted to leave, could he?"

"Technically. Though his old man might have a conniption."

She made him laugh. Inside and out. She made him forget the burden of having his future all planned, not just by his parents, but by five hundred years of history.

If he considered his destiny, in the deepest hours of night when he couldn't sleep, the burden nearly stole his breath.

But for now, Brighton Kingdom and his very orchestrated future didn't matter. Only the summer breeze slipping through Lover's Oak and assisting Susanna mattered.

Nathaniel removed the lug nuts and then worked the flat tire from the axle. "My mates and I used to let off steam in our university years racing cars down country roads." He let a memory rise in his soul and do the talking. "One of us always flattened a tire. But it was good to have a go at it with my mates."

"Sounds like you miss it." She peered at him through the golden wisps of her hair that had been freed from her ponytail.

"It was a different time. We were young and impetuous, thought we were invincible."

"And now?"

"I'm respectable and not so impetuous nor invincible."

"Is that bad?" She tugged the spare out of the trunk and dropped it next to Nathaniel.

"At the moment, not at all." He paused. "Not at all." For a sweet Southern moment, he let the light and life of Miss Susanna Truitt sink into the most secret place of his heart.

# THREE

By Saturday afternoon when Susanna had driven to the garage to get a new tire, half the island had heard about Adam finding "the right ring but not the right girl." By Monday morning, the whole island had heard. So it seemed.

Susanna half expected to see it on the front page of the paper. It would make the Glynn Academy alumni news for sure.

*Adam and Susanna, the couple most likely to be, aren't.*

Driving to Gage Stone Associates, Susanna wished she'd said nothing more to her parents than "we broke up."

But Mama . . . oh, Mama. She had her ways.

*"What's wrong? Mercy, Susanna. You look like who-shot-Liz."*

*"Thank you, Mama. That's what I was going for."*

Susanna had broken down this morning over a plate of scrambled eggs and toast, sitting in the Rib Shack's kitchen. She'd cried and confessed every word, every wounding, piercing word in her conversation with Adam. She felt raw and real, holding nothing about their exchange as sacred.

But then she met Nate. That news she kept to herself. He'd been the silver lining on her dark Friday afternoon. Perhaps a little tap on her shoulder from God.

*Don't despair.*

She'd skipped church Sunday. Adam's parents attended services at Christ Church, and Susanna couldn't bear the thought of running into them. Not this soon.

Sunday evening, the family dinner at the Rib Shack had taken place as usual, the restaurant brimming with laughter and music, with family, with warmth.

Susanna intended to hole up from that event too until baby sister Avery insisted she go. At seventeen, Avery was wise, young, and exuberant. And on occasion, a great persuader.

Grandparents, aunts and uncles, and all the cousins straight down the line to third cousin-once-removed showed up at the Shack the first Sunday of each month. Daddy closed down the restaurant for the family gathering. Wasn't hardly a soul who missed the ritual. Not even the Camdens, who might not actually be blood relatives of the Truitt-Franklin-Vogt clans. But they'd been around so long no one could remember.

Susanna had tucked her emotions behind her heart and hid in the shadows of the Shack's deck, letting the family flow of conversation, laughter, and music drown out her reality for a few barbecue sweetened hours.

Then Monday morning arrived with Susanna's alarm jolting her out of the best fifteen minutes' sleep she'd had all weekend. She'd stared at the clock's red numbers, working up an excuse to call in sick and stay in bed another day.

But she was out of Häagen-Dazs. And she was hungry for Mama's eggs and biscuits. So she let her heart wake up and face the day.

In the parking lot behind the Gage Stone offices, Susanna dropped her forehead to the steering wheel. As hard as she tried, she couldn't get the tenor of Adam's confession—"found the right ring but not the right girl"—out of her head.

Yes, she'd dialed him a dozen times, but she'd hung up before the call connected. What would she have said to him? "Take me back . . . Please change your mind, Adam." Or better, "Wait, I want to break up with you first. Ask me to marry you, go ahead. I'll say no."

Neither would make her feel better. Then Sunday at midnight, she went on a binge and purged everything from Adam on her phone, computer, and that crazy digital picture frame he gave her for Christmas two years ago.

Now that made her feel better. Much better. And she could finally sleep.

But the whole ordeal had caused a disturbance deep in her soul. Not about Adam, but about herself. How could she have been so blind? So foolish? Clinging to a man she didn't really love.

A soft rap against her car window caused her to look up. Aurora. "Suzy-Q, you all right?"

Susanna fumbled for the window's power button. "Aurora . . . hey."

"You good, girl?" The woman rested against the car door.

"Yeah, sure, I'm good."

"I heard." Deep creases marked the contours of her weathered but wise face. Her gray eyes, steady and clear, watched Susanna.

"Hasn't the whole island?" Susanna grabbed her satchel, popped open her door, and started for the office.

"Word gets 'round." Aurora fell in step with Susanna, her bare feet curling against the sharp gravel-and-sand parking lot.

"Aurora, where are your shoes?" Susanna pointed at the old woman's bright red toes.

"Gave them away." She hopped to the grass with an exhale. "My feet just aren't toughened up. I got soft wearing shoes. But I'll get them in shape." The homeless woman spoke with the cultured voice of one who had once lobbied Washington, DC, politicians. With great success. Brisk and to the point. "A gal came through the camp. She wasn't right." Aurora tapped her temple. "Didn't have any wherewithal."

Susanna paused on the sidewalk by Aurora. "So you gave her your shoes."

"Well, I certainly couldn't give her a pound of wherewithal." The woman chuckled. "Though don't think I didn't try."

"I have no doubt." Of all the women on St. Simons Island, Susanna felt sure Aurora possessed more wherewithal than all of them combined. "You need money for more shoes?"

"Nope. Got all the money I need."

The question was rhetorical. Susanna knew the woman had money. She just wanted her to spend a little to save her feet.

Aurora lived simply but wisely. Word was she'd amassed a small fortune before leaving DC to pitch a tent in the island woods.

*"Woke up one day with the Lord tapping on my shoulder. 'Really?' he said. 'This is what you want? To live with your boyfriend, drinking and drugging and lying?' Girl, back then I could spin a lie to perm your hair. The trappings I thought I possessed actually possessed me. So I cracked . . . but in all the right places."*

"Get a new pair of shoes, Aurora." Susanna smiled, swinging her black leather satchel at her feet. "You're going to ruin your pedicure."

"Don't despise me my pedicure, Suzy-Q. You can take the girl out of the city, but you can't take the city out of the girl. It's my one splurge. I don't think the Lord minds."

"I don't think he minds at all. Hey, get two pairs of shoes this time. One to wear, one to give away."

"Maybe." Aurora wore her gray hair in a ponytail. Loose ringlets adorned her neck and forehead. Ten years of living in the woods could not mask her classic, refined beauty. "He didn't break your heart, did he? That boy . . . I can see it in your eyes."

A brisk chill skirted along Susanna's scalp and down her back. "What are you doing nosing around in people's eyes?" Though she long suspected Aurora spent long days in her tent on her knees, hearing from God in ways others only dreamed of.

"Not nosing. But definitely seeing." She pointed from her eyes to Susanna's. "Got the gift, you know. It's why I had to leave Washington. God opened my eyes and I could see the lies, see the darkness. Not feel . . . but *see*. Couldn't take it anymore."

"You never saw the good?"

Aurora smiled. Her teeth were white and even, another remnant of her days in DC. "I'm looking at the good right now."

"I mean in Washington."

"I'm not in Washington. I'm in St. Simons looking at you."

More chills. Yet the fire of Aurora's intense gaze made Susanna's soul burn. "Is there something you have to say? Say it."

"Okay. Thank the Lord for this deal with Adam. Finally, you can get going on *your* way and stop fooling around, waiting on him." Aurora smacked her palms together, punctuating her declaration with such force Susanna jerked backward, squinting. "Know what your problem is, girl?"

"I only have one?"

Aurora's big laugh held no restraint. "Touché." She gripped Susanna's arms. "You just wouldn't break . . . wouldn't let go. You clung so tightly. I see a bit of myself in you, darling. I was bound so tight God couldn't even whisper my name lest I shatter. I had to let go. I had to crack." She wagged her finger under Susanna's nose. "That's what you need."

"I'm not sure I know how to crack. At least not in all the right places, Aurora."

"He does." She pointed toward the heavens. "And from what I can see, the first crack hit just right. Wasn't too painful, was it?"

"You're telling me God sent Adam to break up with me?"

"If he'd asked, would you have said yes?"

"No."

"See . . . you knew all along, girl. Just like I did. Back in the day, drugging and sleeping around, I thought I was all liberated and free, but I was nothing but bound." She gripped the air in front of her face. "But I held on. To my reputation, my career, my fancy home, my clothes and jewels, my expensive car."

"Your pedicures?" Aurora's intensity challenged Susanna's comfort and notion of God's role in her life. "How do I hang on to my goals and plans without being so . . ."

"Uptight? You let him figure the outcome. We make our plans, but God directs our steps."

"I have no plans, Aurora." Susanna glanced up at her second-story office window. "Zip, zero, nada. They vanished with Adam."

"Fantastic." Aurora danced a jig along the sidewalk. "Now he can come."

"Now who can come?"

"The one . . ." She covered her mouth with her long, slender hands and in an instant, the attitude and decorum of a DC lobbyist faded, and the innocent sweetness of a cracked woman emerged. "You only believe in 'the one,' don't you, Susanna?"

A divine disturbance rumbled through Susanna. She felt exposed and vulnerable. She'd never told anyone her belief in "the one true one." Well, until she blabbered it to Nate on Friday night.

"Aurora, what are you talking about?" *Please don't start talking nonsense.* Susanna ached to hear something good, profound. But Aurora straddled worlds, the natural, the supernatural, and the slightly nutty. At any given moment she slipped out of one into the other.

"One. Only one." Aurora flung wide her arms. "You're free, Suzy-Q. And now get ready." She tipped her face toward the heavens. "Believe. He's coming . . ." She sucked in a quick breath of surprise. "He's here, oh joy, he's already here." Aurora patted her hands together and danced a jig.

"All righty then." What had started out as an encouraging, sane conversation had gone cattywompus in the span of a sentence. "I'll see you, Aurora. Don't forget to buy shoes."

"I'll see you first, Suz. And get that Adam-boy the rest of the way out of your heart. Let go. Let *goooo*." She raised her hands and wiggled her fingers at Susanna. "God will fill your heart with wonders you never dared *dreeeaaam*."

"O–okay?" Dreams? Susanna couldn't conjure up one. Did she even have any? No, she had plans. Dreams were for fairy tales and romantics. She was practical, patient and . . . dreamless.

From her bag, her phone pinged. It was Gage's text tone.

Staff meeting in 5 minutes. You're late.

"Listen, Aurora, I need to run." She flashed the screen for her to see. "Do you need anything?"

"No, I'm right as rain." Aurora smiled, all perfect and sane, then hopped across the parking lot toward the woods, disappearing between the trees and brush.

"Aurora?" Susanna dashed after her, suddenly missing her divine confidence. "Get a pair of shoes, will you? Aurora?"

But she was gone.

"Aurora?"

How did she do that? Disappear in the mist.

Susanna's phone pinged again.

3 mins til meeting.

Gage. Like his staff meeting of five *had* to start at nine o'clock sharp. When Susanna made it to the second-floor landing, he was waiting for her.

"Well?" He folded his arms and searched her face.

"Well what?" She pushed past her boss—and friend— lowering her satchel to her desk.

"How'd it go?" Gage fell against the ornately carved door-frame, motioning toward her left hand. "How come I'm not blinded by bling?"

"I thought we had a meeting." Susanna reached for her University of Georgia mug sitting on the credenza. Time and use had faded the logo and the UGA looked more like IGI. And the bulldog mascot no longer had a nose.

"Yeah, we have a meeting but I wanted to see the bling. Adam came home, right? You left early Friday to meet him."

"I need coffee." Susanna slipped past Gage and down the stairs. She'd held herself together while talking to Aurora, but Gage's inquiry encroached on her emotional fortress. He'd been her friend, and Adam's, since the romance began and had been on the sidelines, watching, occasionally coaching, for twelve years.

"Suz, what happened?" Gage's steps thundered down the stairs after her.

"Nothing happened." Susanna ran into Myrna, the office manager, when she reached the bottom.

"Gage, leave the girl alone." Myrna smacked her gum and glanced at her clipboard schedule. "Susanna, your ten o'clock appointment cancelled."

"Glenn Cowger? No." Was it too late to join Aurora in the woods? "Did he say why?"

"Not a peep, darling. And I tried to get something out of him." She peered at Susanna. "You don't look half bad for a woman who got dumped."

Susanna made a face. "Yay me. So, did you ask Cowger to reschedule?"

"Shug, look who you're talking to. Me. Myrna." The woman with the henna-rinsed hair and the countenance of a marine on duty curled her lip. "Of course I asked him. Gave him ten ways to Sunday to reschedule, but he'd have none of it. Said he'd think on it, would call you later."

"Great." Susanna glanced at her boss. "Scratch Cowger Homes off our morning meeting."

"Let's not give up so easily," Gage said. "Get a plan together,

Suz. Myrna, pull files on the other architects in the region. Let's see if we can figure out who else Cowger is considering. Also, pull the city building permits. Wonder if he's run into a snag. Tell Clark and Alexis we're postponing the meeting for ten minutes."

Myrna went into action. "On it, boss. And, Suz, don't worry about Adam, he'll come around."

"Ugh, I'm so glad my personal life is out there for all to comment on." Susanna started for the kitchen. She really needed coffee. Gage trailed after her.

"Do you have any idea who Cowger—"

"Come on, Gage, he's clearly made another choice."

"We don't know what he's doing. There's a good chance he didn't get his building permit. So let's keep after him. Win him over." Gage cornered her in the kitchen. "I need your A game, Suz."

"How about my D-minus game?"

"No, I want the hotshot Atlanta landscape architect who won major jobs for Remington & Co."

"I had the Remington & Co. reputation behind me when I won those jobs." She let her expression and tone seal her implication. Gage Stone Associates was still building their company and reputation.

"Okay, fine. We've got a ways to go, but you had Cowger."

"And now I don't. Want my opinion? Your rates are too high, Gage." Susanna yanked the coffee carafe from the machine. Bone dry. She leaned toward the doorway and hollered into the hall. "All right, y'all. Who drank all the coffee and didn't make any more, huh? It's only nine o'clock."

"What do you mean my rates are too high?" he asked.

"It's not rocket science, Gage. You charge too much." Susanna opened the cabinet for the coffee. She popped the lid of the canister. Empty. She snorted, low, sardonic. "It's a conspiracy, I tell you." She tipped the empty canister at her boss. "I'm going to Starbucks."

"I need you at staff, Suz."

"I'll be back. But here's my big input for today. You want Cowger back? Lower your bids."

"My bids are competitive."

"Sure, if you're Remington & Co. You're building your rep, Gage. It's will-work-for-nothing time." Susanna pressed the plastic lid back on the canister. "I need coffee."

As she passed Gage, he snatched up her left hand. "So, Adam didn't propose?"

"No, and you must be the only person on the island who hasn't heard."

A crimson wash spread on his cheeks. "I did, but I wanted to hear it from you."

"So I could relive it all over again?" Nice.

"Did he really say he found the right ring but not the right girl?"

"Yep. Said we loved the plan more than each other."

"He's crazy. If any two people—"

"Needed a wake-up call, it was Adam and me. He's right, Gage. I just never wanted to see it." She headed for the stairs to get her purse. "I'll be back in time for the meeting."

"Are you okay?"

"I am." She gazed down at him from the bottom step, a wash of tears blurring her vision. "Sad but okay."

"You sure?"

"It's just going to take time to get used to the idea of Susanna with no Adam."

"He's crazy, you know, to let you go. Probably spent too much time in the desert."

"He seemed sane to me. Besides, he met someone else." The words sounded strange and formed an odd twist in her chest.

"Do you want to take the day off?" Gage said, soft and with sympathy.

"No. Work grounds me. Reminds me that life goes on. Reminds me this is the life I've always lived when he's been gone."

"Okay, but remember I need you tonight. If you need some time, take it during the day." Gage leaned against the banister, looking up at her, his gelled black hair catching the light falling from the second-floor windows. "The Butler benefit . . . for the hospital wing. Our chance to get the landscaping. Mrs. Butler is big on doing business with people she knows, and having you there will win points with the selection committee."

"That's tonight?" It would be black tie. She'd have to get dressed up, do something with her hair.

"Yes, tonight. We need this job, Suz. Word is the hospital committee will go with the architect Mrs. Butler recommends. And that's going to be us. A job like this will boost our resume."

Susanna stared down him. He was right. All hands on deck. And it wasn't Gage's fault she'd wasted twelve years with the wrong man.

"Of course I'll go." She forced a smile and punched the air. "Take one for the team."

"I'll pick you up at seven."

"I'll drive myself." Susanna dashed into her office and grabbed her bag, slinging the strap over her head.

"I'm picking you up. I want to make sure you get there."

Susanna headed back down the stairs. "Fine." Maybe a fancy benefit would be a good distraction, just like meeting Nate the other day. At the bottom of the steps she poked Gage in the chest. "You were the last one at the coffee pot, weren't you?"

"I'll send Myrna out for more coffee."

Susanna jangled her keys. "Be back in five."

"For what it's worth," he said, "Adam's a fool."

"Is he?" She paused in the doorway. "No, Gage, Adam's no fool. But me? I'm not so sure."

# FOUR

From the deck outside the leather-and-wood cottage library, Nathaniel watched a high, thin twilight bloom over the island. He tucked his hands into the silky pockets of his custom-tailored tux. The horizon reminded him of the purple and gold strata of a Brighton evening. It was fabled that if a man perched on top of Mount Braelor during a summer twilight, he could reach the Brighton sky, capture his destiny and make his fortune.

For Nathaniel, his destiny—and yes, his fortune—were already set. In the House of Stratton mountain. In the chiseled marble of his family tree. It all felt a bit claustrophobic at times. But these few days in Georgia had opened his heart some. Standing on the sultry shore reminded him the world was a grand, fruitful place. Made him believe anything was possible. Like finding true love. Or fully embracing his destiny.

Nathaniel returned to the library, locking the deck doors behind him. He scanned the documents and reports spread across his great-great-grandfather's desk, his mind's eye glazing over. So much law and legalese to wade through.

"You ready?" Jonathan stepped into the library, slipping on his tux jacket. "Liam's pulling the car 'round."

"Did you print my speech?" Nathaniel swept the documents into folders, stacked them so they aligned, and laid them on the desk.

Jonathan crossed the room, extending the white paper in his hand. "I read it over. Nicely done. It will satisfy Mrs. Butler."

"She said all she wanted was a quick word. Something about Great-Grandfather being so involved with the local hospital's expansion and improvements." When Great-Grandfather had made St. Simons a regular holiday spot, he'd donated sizable sums to the hospital. As did Nathaniel's grandfather and dad.

Nathaniel walked around the desk, scanning the words he'd penned with Jonathan.

. . . *we are honored to represent my father, the king, and all of Brighton Kingdom* . . .

. . . *dedicating a hospital wing in his honor* . . . *please accept our donation as the first fruits of good faith and health* . . .

He listened to the words flowing through his mind. His words. But with *her* accent. Susanna's. Lilting and bent with sweetness.

The beautiful girl from the lover's tree. Three days had passed since he'd helped change her tire, and still she flashed across his thoughts at random moments.

Like now, when he was reading over his speech. Or when he was running on the beach. Or in the exhaling moments as he was drifting off to sleep.

"Come across anything interesting?"

Nathaniel raised his attention to Jonathan, who'd moved to the desk and the stack of legal folders Nathaniel had been reading.

"Just what we know already. The Grand Duchy Hessenberg is to be given her independence from Brighton Kingdom if we find a royal heir." At the moment, finding a long-lost Hessenberg heir felt akin to Nathaniel finding true love. Impossible. "Otherwise, the Grand ol' Duchy becomes our province." The reality awakened fear in Nathaniel's heart. As one whose destiny was determined before he was born, his sympathies leaned toward Hessenberg. She deserved her independence if at all possible.

Freedom, independence, was of priceless worth. Not to mention the relationship between the two countries had become like feuding siblings. They were at odds with one another more often than not. And in the last decade, Hessenberg's economic woes had become a tangible leech on Brighton.

They could no longer afford to bail her out.

But the conditions of entail were ironclad. Heir or province.

"I can't image being King Nathaniel I and Prince Francis . . . negotiating an agreement while war loomed, doing the diplomatic dance with their royal cousins across Europe . . . the Kaiser, King George V, Tsar Nicolas II." Jonathan flipped through the entail pages copied from the original. "Russia flexing, Germany threatening, Hessenberg's southern and northern ports vulnerable to attack."

"What choice did Francis leave himself? He'd squandered Hessenberg's wealth and resources seeking pleasure, trying to get ahead in the industrial age with his wild inventions, building that exotic car, Starfire 89, that wooed kings but was entirely unaffordable for the people."

"A car worth millions now . . . if you can get hold of one." Jonathan closed the document and returned it to the desk. "This whole matter is complicated by the fact Francis was probably illiterate." He regarded his watch. "Liam's bringing the motor 'round. Are you ready?"

"Yes, yes, let's go." Nathaniel patted his jacket. Where were his notes? Ah, inside his breast pocket. "I don't envy them, facing war, crafting an entail that required complete surrender of land and authority, and all rights to the Hessenberg throne to protect the sovereignty of Brighton."

"Then be grateful you face the end of the entail, not the beginning."

"The end doesn't bring me much comfort either." Nathaniel pressed his palm on the stack of documents and diaries as he passed the desk. "I thought my biggest trial was finding true love."

Even if Dad's health stabilized, more than likely Nathaniel would be king in the years after Hessenberg became a Brighton province. A likely outcome since no heirs of the House of Augustine-Saxon had been heard from in sixty years.

"Love? Ah, looking for a woman fit to be queen of your heart and your country? Making sure the House of Stratton lives on?"

"You mock me, mate." Nathaniel patted his shoulder as he passed him on his way through the door.

"Mock you? No, I envy you. You have your pick of lovelies."

"Who want my crown not my heart."

"The least of which is Lady Genevieve." Jonathan's tone was teasing, leading.

"I see I was a fool to bring up the subject of love. Can we just get on with the evening?" Outside in the side driveway, Liam stood by the motorcar in his dark suit and shades. He looked like a movie character. It was one of the reasons Nathaniel liked the former special-forces major. He so looked the part, one could hardly believe he actually *was* a royal security officer.

Nathaniel rode to Mrs. Butler's in quiet contemplation as the pinkish lines of evening fell through the canopying oaks. Talk of his ancestors, of the 1914 Entailment, rattled the doubt resting in his bones. Was his calling to be king of Brighton man's idea or God's?

What choice did he have? What choice did God have? Nathaniel was the son of a king, who was the son of a king, who was a son of a king dating back five hundred years.

And what of his father's failing health? Would he be king

before he was ready? Where were the decades of time he thought he had to prepare?

As if his thoughts weren't tangled enough, he pictured *her*.

Susanna.

Jon peered around to the front seat. "You know what? Forget the entail. I think you're right. Your greatest challenge is to find a wife. You and Prince Stephen are the hope of the House of Stratton."

Was he telegraphing his thoughts? "I'd rather fight through the entail." He wanted to get married. But not because it fit his job description as a crown prince.

He wanted to marry for love.

Susanna remained in his thoughts until he corralled his image of her and sent it back to the dark recesses. Dreaming of her was a complete waste of time. He had a better chance of finding an heir to the Hessenberg throne than of marrying Susanna Truitt.

But oh, he wanted to see her again, practically yearned for it. So much so that on Sunday, Jon inquired about his grimace. Nathaniel quickly blamed heartburn from too much pizza.

On Sunday he took two five-mile runs—one in the morning, one in the evening—to distract his heart from her. Why go where he absolutely could not?

Then today, while attempting to read the ninety-nine-year-old entail, his mind rebelled, refusing to embrace another *wherewithin* and *hitherunto* so he could dream of a girl with cerulean-colored eyes and a smile that blinded his heart.

He'd come to the island on his father's business and a short holiday. No more. No less. To consider romance was foolhardy.

Because his name, his destiny, everything about him was for the king and Brighton Kingdom.

Right down to the beating of his heart.

# FIVE

*t six-thirty, Susanna slipped into the black sheath dress she kept in her closet for weddings and marine balls, along with a pair of matching heels.

Black. How fitting. In the aftermath of finding out *white* wasn't in her near or distant future, an elegant evening in a black gown, socializing with south Georgia's elite, almost mocked her. But instead, she chose to see it as a bit cathartic.

She fought the wash of sadness as she leaned toward her reflection in the bathroom mirror. "You're going to get over this, Suz. Adam did what you should've done long ago—speak the truth."

But twelve years? Ugh. It made her stomach knot and ring out all kinds of sour regret. Why had she remained silent when deep down . . . deep down, she knew? It made her question her integrity and discernment. Her courage.

But she'd been blinded by the safety of a life with the controlled and honorable Adam Peters. Sure, they had their quarrels and fights, but in the end, he was her safe and steady future. Someone she could count on.

A horn blast from the driveway below told her the time for reflection was over. She grabbed her silver clutch from the dresser and stuffed it with a twenty-dollar bill, lipstick, and her cell phone.

Time to move out—an Adam saying she'd adopted—and move on.

Gage met her at the door with a bouquet of flowers and shoved them at her with an awkward "here."

"O–okay." Her hand trembled as she gripped the plastic wrapping, the adrenaline and hope of moving on without Adam waning. She felt weak and watery. "Gage, I–I . . . Thank you for these."

The giving and getting of flowers had often been a source of contention with Adam. Gage knew that, or at least he used to know. He'd sided with Susanna once when Adam was home on leave.

*"Give the girl some flowers, Adam."*

The no-nonsense marine considered flowers a waste of money. Susanna agreed most of the time. Except for anniversaries, birthdays, and Valentine's Day. Especially when he'd been deployed most of the last six years. He missed all but one of her last seven birthdays.

"Yeah, forget it. I saw them at Publix. I like the orange flowers. Listen . . ." Gage tipped his head toward his car and offered his arm. "Here's how we ought to play tonight—"

"Gage, wait, maybe you should just go without me." Susanna stepped back inside the house, setting the bouquet on a table inside the door. She couldn't do this . . . she couldn't . . . The whole island knew.

*Found the right ring but not the right girl.*

"Come on, Suz. Let's win this one. This hospital gig will keep us in the black for a year."

"Us?"

"Yes, *us*. The firm." He offered his arm again, but Susanna descended the steps on her own. Handsome in his black tux and styled hair, Gage was just her boss. Just her *friend*.

At the Butlers', Gage pulled up to valet parking, checked his appearance in the rearview, and turned to Susanna before handing over his keys to the approaching red-vested man.

"Schmooze, schmooze, schmooze. That's our game plan. And oh, the event coordinator told me the hospital board members will be wearing red-ribbon pins."

"The event coordinator?" Susanna opened her car door.

"One can find out a lot over dinner and a boatload of compliments."

"Gage, it's a job. Don't sell your soul for it."

"We need this, Susanna. We. Need. This."

The Butler mansion was beautiful—cut from old river stone and inlaid with a marble foyer. A crystal chandelier hung above the hand-carved mahogany staircase and damask curtains adorned the twenty-foot windows.

Susanna had been inside once before, years ago, when Mrs. Butler had invited her to join the Debutants, a social service organization. Every spring, they'd plant flowers all over the island and hold a themed cotillion on a Saturday evening.

But the opulence and marbled wealth of the mansion, the grace and affluence of the other girls applying for the Debutants, sent Susanna back to herself. Her roots. To where she belonged— playing varsity volleyball and waiting tables at the Rib Shack, her surfboard leaning against the back kitchen wall.

Then, that summer, Adam came for dinner at the Shack with his parents. They left, but he waited for Susanna in the parking lot until closing so he could ask her to the movies.

"Let the schmoozing begin." Gage ushered her into the ballroom, alive with tuxedos and sequined gowns flowing over a gleaming walnut dance floor.

The warm air skirted around Susanna. She already wanted to leave. A passing server stuck a glass of wine in her hand, and she stepped farther into the Georgia aristocratic set, almost hankering for her surfboard and a whiff of barbecue.

Spotting a woman with a red-ribbon pin on the strap of her dress, Susanna inhaled deeply and worked her way through the crowd of guests. *Let the schmoozing begin.*

"Hello," Susanna said. There were three of them—spandexed into gowns cut too tight and too low.

"Hey there," they said, flickering glances toward Susanna.

"Do you *really* think he's coming?" This from a bouffant blonde wearing a blue strapless gown. It barely contained her *obvious* charms. "Carlene Butler has been claiming royal roots since Nixon was president. But I've never seen one ounce of proof." The woman downed the last of her wine and licked her lips. "Not one."

"Not just *roots*, sugar. She's *related* to the royal family." The brunette with the red-ribbon pin snickered into her glass. "I bet the royals have something to say about Carlene Butler's claims."

"Hush up, y'all." The rebuke came from a brilliant redhead in a canary-yellow gown. "Carlene is a fine, upstanding woman. Hold your gossip until we know for sure if *he's* here or not."

He who? Susanna set her wine on a passing tray of empty glasses. The last thing her bruised heart needed was the elixir of fermented grapes. She had to keep her wits about her.

The redhead bobbed her head toward Susanna. "Aren't you Glo Truitt's girl?"

"Yes, ma'am."

"Liz Cane." She switched her wine glass to her left hand and offered her right. "You remember me? I'm your Aunt Jen's friend. This here is Cybil and Babe." The blonde and brunette. "Anyway, shug. I *am* so sorry." The woman pressed her hand on Susanna's arm. "That Peters boy oughta be shot."

*Ho boy.* Embarrassment perspired across Susanna's forehead.

"Why? What'd he do?" Babe stepped close, her eyes glinting with a yearn for gossip.

"Nothing," Susanna said. This wasn't their business. But she was grateful that one person on the island didn't seem to know her personal woes.

"He told her he'd found the right ring but not the right girl."

Cybil and Babe gasped in unison and drew back, their hands pressed over their hearts.

"He did not." Cybil's eyes could not be wider with shock. "How in the world are you not in a million pieces?"

"Oh, my stars. I'd be *completely* gone . . . just gone." Babe inspected Susanna as if she might find a very obvious, exposing crack. "Him a decorated marine, a war hero and all?"

"He was being honest," Susanna blurted the confession, wishing it back because it invited more conversation. She wanted to schmooze the red-ribbon lady, Babe, about the hospital wing. Not discuss her broken love life.

"Honest?" Cybil scoffed and stopped a passing server for a fresh round of wine. She took two glasses and passed one to Babe. "There's honest, darling, then there's brutal."

"But I'm not the right girl." *Stop talking, Susanna.* These women were not worthy of her confession. They were strangers with a voyeuristic concern. "Babe, you're on the hospital wing committee?"

"Shug, don't even. We know you work for Gage Stone." Babe peered over the rim of her crystal glass. "What's he thinking bringing you out to kiss our grits while you're grieving such a love tragedy."

Oh, brother. Well, then. No flies on Babe. Susanna hunted the room for Gage and finally spied him standing with a regal, silver-haired woman wearing an elegant cream gown. Carlene Butler. He caught sight of her and waved her over.

"Excuse me." Susanna wove through the thick crowd. There had to be no less than three hundred people in the petite ballroom. "Pardon me." She drew up thin, trying to pass between small clusters of women.

Why were they congealing together instead of making way?

"Just let me through here . . ." She smiled at the backs of heads. Was something interesting happening by the entrance? Heat radiated from warm body to warm body. Susanna began to feel like she couldn't draw a pure breath.

*Have . . . to . . . get . . . out.*

"He's here."

"Where?"

"Is that him?"

"Oh, my . . ."

Her head pounded with the force of their whispers. Who's here? Finally, a sliver of an opening appeared amid the thicket of tuxes and gowns. Susanna broke free into a cool pocket just as three tall, dark-haired men with a palatable air of authority parted the awed guests. Susanna was pressed out of her free zone and back into the whispering heat.

"It's not him."

"Oh, such a shame. Are you sure?"

"By golly, it's him. Mercy a-mighty, he's here."

Yeah, well, she was out. Forget Gage and schmoozing, Susanna craved fresh air. It wasn't just the crowded hot ballroom, it was life, crowding in on her and pressing down. When her phone rang from her clutch, it was the perfect escape.

"Excuse me. Please, excuse me." Cutting east toward the ballroom's single-door exit, Susanna left the mysterious guests and the crowd behind. Besides, the special guests had captured everyone's attention and all schmoozing had temporarily stopped.

Gage should've made better use of his dinner and compliments with the event planner and found out about the special guests. But knowing him, the only information he wanted was the names of the power players on the hospital building committee.

"Hello?" Her voice echoed in the high, domed foyer as she exited the ballroom. Her heels clicked against the sleek floor.

"Suzy, w–where are you?" Avery.

"Out with Gage. At some benefit at the Butlers'. Aves, are you okay?" Susanna left the house and stepped into a hazy pink night. At seventeen, her baby sister was athletic, smart, popular, and a bit spoiled, but the pang in her voice was more than teen melodrama. "What's wrong?"

"It's Daddy. He was in the kitchen working . . . next thing I knew, he was on the floor, holding his arm."

"Call 9-1-1."

"Catfish already called, but Suz, Daddy says he won't go to the hospital, and Mama isn't here."

"Remind him that she'll come back sooner or later and—"

"Daddy." Avery's voice came muffled through the phone. "Suzy said Mama will come back sooner or later."

Susanna could hear her father speaking in the background.

"Okay, he'll go." Avery's voice buoyed with tangible relief.

"Call me when you get on the ambulance. I'm on my way to the hospital." She swung around to head toward the Butlers' massive double front doors. She needed to find Gage.

"Suz, I'm scared."

"It's going to be all right, Avery. Let the paramedics take care of him. You just stay calm."

"I will, but pray. Please pray."

Susanna leaned against a porch column and fixed her thoughts on the Healer. Her prayer was short but full of the wind from her own heart. *Heal Daddy.*

She could hear Avery crying and the wail of a siren through the phone.

"They're here."

"You go. Be with Daddy. I'll meet you at the hospital."

When Susanna entered the foyer again, guests were clapping, leaning and pushing forward to the front of the room.

*All right, Gage. Where are you?*

Smiles lit the warm faces of the guests and their dubious whispers were now filled with belief.

"Can you believe it? Right here on St. Simons Island."

"Such a marvelous speech."

"Brief and to the point. The way I like it." A microphone screech pierced the air causing the guests to ooh and angle back. "Dinner will be served in fifteen minutes. Please start making your way to the dining room."

Susanna shoved through the crowd to where she'd last seen Gage. The guests congealed at the very narrow dining hall doors. She was never going to find him in this mess.

She dialed his phone, but it went straight to voice mail.

Wait. What was she thinking? Gage's car and keys were with the valet. Surely he would concede her emergency and bring the car around.

Whirling for the front door, Susanna took one step before running into a wall of a man.

"Excuse me, I'm sorry, but I really need to—"

"Susanna?"

She peeked up at the chiseled face of Nate Kenneth. "Nate? Hey, what are you doing here?"

"I might ask the same of you." He smiled and bowed slightly. An electric sensation dashed through her belly. "I'm here to support the new hospital wing."

"I came with my boss. He's trying to win the expansion job." She glanced back toward the ballroom. One last chance to spot Gage before she borrowed his car. He'd be mad, but when he learned the truth, he'd understand. Completely. Right? Never mind his car was his first true love.

"You look troubled."

"I need to get to the hospital." *Come on, Gage. Where are you? I'm taking your car.* "My sister called . . ." She faced Nate, and his steady attention nearly made her knees wobble. "My father . . ."

"What are you doing standing here? Let's get you to the hospital. Come." He unbuttoned his tux jacket and offered her his hand. "I'll drive you."

"No, no. I can't ask you to do that, Nate. Thank you." She glanced around again. "I can take my boss's car. If the valet will give me his keys."

"My car is right this way." He grabbed her hand without waiting for her reply and drew her toward a dim, narrow hallway, slipping his phone from his jacket pocket. "Liam, come 'round to the car. A friend needs a ride to the hospital."

"Nate, I can't take you from this dinner." She had to stretch to keep in rhythm with his long strides. "Did you hear? There's some special, *royal* guest." The carpet pile caught the tip of her heel, and she fell against his arm.

He'd stopped. "A royal guest?"

"Yeah. At least that's what the spandex ladies were buzzing about. Some royal relative of Mrs. Butler's."

He moved forward again. "To whom do you think she was referring?"

"I don't know . . . Hey," she said low, "You're from Brighton. Wouldn't it be funny if you were their special guest?"

"Downright hilarious. Shall we get you to the hospital?"

"Never been much of a royal watcher anyway. Other than Kate Middleton, who marries a prince?"

"Precisely."

Nate guided her through a door tucked under the stairwell and they emerged into an interior garage.

"A secret garage?" Luxury cars were lined up, facing the closed bay doors. An attendant scurried toward them.

"Can I help you, sir?"

"Open the door quickly. We're off to the hospital."

"Yes, sir."

"Nate, are you sure . . . How did you get your car in here?"

"Ah, there's Liam."

A block of a man with stalwart features, appearing very uncomfortable in his tuxedo, marched toward them.

"Let's be quick, Liam." Nate opened the front passenger door for Susanna before climbing into the backseat behind her.

The big man said not a word but deftly shot backward out of the garage, then shifted into drive with only a passing glance at Susanna. "Southeast Medical?"

"Yes." Behind her Nate rested a hand on her shoulder, angling against his seat belt to watch the road.

The massive vehicle rumbled forward as Liam maneuvered through traffic.

"Thank you. Both." She had only a moment to absorb the vibe between the men. It was as if one *served* the other. But her phone chimed before she could finish her assessment.

"Avery?"

"It's a heart attack, Suz. He's so pale." Fear blurred her sister's words. "Are you on your way?"

"I'll be there in five minutes."

Nate reached around and took her hand, comforting her without a word, taking a small piece of her burden on himself.

# SIX

For a man trying to recover from a heart attack, Daddy was embroiled in chaos. His room flowed with aunts, uncles, and cousins.

Avery rested her head on the bed beside him, holding his hand in hers. But Susanna watched from the corner, smiling when Daddy's tired eyes met hers.

*Typical Truitt tumult.*

It's what he always said when the family descended upon them and Mama started bossing everyone around.

*"Are we eating or not?"*

*"Who wants to watch a movie?"*

*"Y'all, let's get a round of cards going. Start a tournament."*

A perpetual organizer. If she had to stop bossing, Susanna thought her mother might just lie down and die.

At the moment, she was shoving her clipboard at cousin Zack, telling him to note his shift at the Rib Shack.

"Aunt Glo, come on." He laughed. "I've not worked at the Rib Shack since my first summer in college."

Susanna smiled. Brave soul, Zack. Taking on Mama. A parks-and-recreation director, he surfed every morning and socialized every night. His white-blond hair, sky-blue eyes, and sun-roasted skin made him popular with the women of the island.

"Can you work a ladle?"

"Yeah, I'm not *stupid*."

"Then you can work the kitchen." Mama wrote on the clipboard schedule. "Come in Wednesday at six. Get your fish-frying legs back before the Friday rush."

"Aunt Glo . . ." Chuckle, snort, ha-ha, but Zack's face said it all. He was going down. "Look, I've got . . . stuff . . . to . . ." Mama's one-eyed glare cauterized his rebuttal. He shot Susanna a visual plea. *Help?*

"Don't look at me. I don't have the magic elixir." If she did, she wouldn't have given up a Christmas break trip to tour three of Europe's most beautiful gardens—Keukenhof in Holland, Mirabell in Germany, and the Lecharran in Brighton—her senior year of college to manage the restaurant while Mama surprised Daddy with a snowy Vermont getaway.

But Susanna had seen the miracle of their healed divorce, and it'd been years since they'd gotten away together, so she'd agreed to watch the Shack and Avery. Far be it from her not to lend love a hand when asked.

Zack exhaled and fell against the wall, running his hand through his hair.

"It's like the Borg." Silas, Zack's brother, popped him on the arm, laughing. "Resistance is futile."

But Silas's laugh was short lived.

"Silas." Mama shoved the clipboard at him. "I've got you down for Tuesday, Thursday, and Saturday."

"Me?" Eyes bulging, he pressed his hands to his chest. "Aunt Glo, I'm even less experienced than Zack. I haven't *stepped* into the kitchen since, like, tenth grade."

"Fine, then you can bus tables." Mama scribbled on her clipboard. "Your construction company isn't bringing in much work right now." Mama glared up at him. She knew everything. Even if she didn't, she made you think she did. "You start bringing in some cash, and maybe Hadley will give you a second chance."

Silas's cheeks beamed hot. "We weren't fighting over money."

"Nothing is sacred, Silas," Susanna said with a laugh. "You know that." Not even the brokenness of her own daughter. Already "I found the right ring but not the right girl" was halfway embedded into the family lore and lingo. All because of Mama.

Silas squinted at her. "You doing okay, cousin? Since the whole, you know, Adam thing?"

"I'm doing fine, Si." Zack and Silas were more like brothers to her than cousins. When she was little, their mama, Daddy's sister Linda, would keep Susanna for a day or two when Daddy and Mama got into a rip-roaring fight.

"Glo," Daddy raised his raspy voice. "Leave the boys alone. We've got plenty of staff to work the kitchen. Shoot, I'm only one man."

"One man who works like five." Mama leaned over his bed and smoothed her hand over his cheek. "It's what got you in here, Gib. We're lucky you only had a minor attack."

"Just take it easy on folks," Daddy whispered, his eyes fluttering shut.

"All right," Mama said, "everyone out. Let's give Gib some rest."

One by one, the family bid Daddy good night, promising to fill heaven with their prayers. Mama motioned for Avery to come around the bed.

"Come on, baby girl. Let's get you home. You've got school tomorrow."

"Bye, Daddy." Avery bent down to kiss him. "Sorry I called the ambulance."

Daddy's weak smile lit the room. "You did good, sweetie."

"She sure did." Mama tapped Avery on the behind as she left

the room. "I'll be back in the morning, Gib. Susanna, you too. Let's go."

"Stay." Daddy motioned to Susanna with a small finger wave. "Talk ... to ... you."

"Don't stay too long, Suz," Mama said, bending to kiss Daddy good night. "Get better, Gib. Hear me?" Mama. She who must be obeyed. Daddy couldn't dare do anything but return to one hundred percent.

The door swung softly closed behind Mama as she left, the tenderness in her voice lingering. Underneath all her gruffness, Mama was passionate about Daddy. About her family.

"She loves you," Susanna said, scooting into the chair Avery had vacated.

"She does. Bossy ol' gal."

"What would you do without her?" Susanna slipped her hand under Daddy's, careful not to disturb his IV.

"Have a moment of peace and quiet." He laughed then squeezed her hand. The heart monitor beeped, but when Susanna checked the screen, Daddy's heart rate held steady.

"You gave us a good scare." Susanna shifted in her chair, adjusting the constraints of her dress. The tight sheath was fine for standing and walking. Not so much for sitting.

"'Tain't nothing. Just a small blockage."

"You know we'd all be lost without you. Especially Mama." Susanna stroked her thumb over Daddy's hand, her eyes ripe with tears.

She could endure losing Adam and the idea of happily ever after, but she could not endure losing Daddy.

"Angioplasty in the morning. I'll be as good as new. Too stubborn to die. Only forty-eight. Planning on walking you down the aisle." In that moment, Daddy's eyes met hers with a clear focus. "I'm sorry about Adam, kitten. You always wanted the one true love, didn't you?"

"He wasn't it, I guess." Tears again. Susanna picked at the threads of the cotton hospital blanket with her free hand. "But you know, it was getting kind of silly. Waiting, not moving forward, acting more like friends than lovers." She reached for a tissue from the bedside table. "I can see it now. My fortieth birthday, and we're all sitting on the back deck of the Shack, and Aunt Jen says, 'Say, Suz, when you suppose Adam is going to propose? You're getting a bit long in the tooth.'"

Daddy's short laugh gave way to wheezing. Susanna rose up, ready to buzz the nurses as he fought for a good breath. "I guess . . . not so funny."

She sat back down, rolling the tissue over her finger and dabbing the water from her eyes. "But it is. Go ahead and laugh. We could use it." She cupped her hand under Daddy's. "What I care most about now is that you're okay."

"I'll be right as rain after tomorrow." Daddy closed his eyes with a slow, filling inhale. "So what's with your fancy duds?" He peeked at her through a one-eyed slit. "You look pretty."

"I was at some benefit with Gage. He's trying to get the job for the new hospital wing."

"Gage Stone. Good man. Industrious. Owns his own business—"

"Stop right there, Daddy."

His lips parted in a half smile. "You see right through me."

"I do." Susanna shredded the edge of her tissue. "Daddy, should I try to get Adam back?" She knew the answer. But she'd been committed for so long it seemed downright unholy to just let the relationship end so simply.

"Only you know, kitten."

"It smarts like the dickens, but . . ." Her voice waivered with truth. "I think he did us both a favor." The more she realized she didn't want to marry him either, the more she felt the fool. Best just to move on. Put it behind her.

The conversation settled, and Susanna watched Daddy resting, breathing. In his fighting years with Mama, Daddy would order Susanna to her room where she'd hide in her closet, shaking with fear. Now she was overwhelmed with love.

He became a very different Daddy after he remarried Mama when Susanna was twelve. He was gentle and kind, encouraging, supportive, and in his way, telling her he was sorry about her childhood. Over and over.

"What am I going to do with all that money?" he ventured through his medicated drowsiness, his eyes still closed, his breathing still a bit labored.

"What money?"

"The money I saved up for your wedding."

She laughed through a fresh start of tears. "Buy that yacht you've been threatening Mama with."

Wedding. Yacht. It didn't matter. There were no savings. Daddy and Mama sank all of their money into keeping the Rib Shack afloat. That was Daddy's yacht. Anchored in the red clay of Georgia.

"I blame myself. Well, your mama and me," he said, eyes open now. "We skewered you to the wall before you had a chance to duck."

"Stop it, Daddy. No need for this talk now." She caught a fast tear with her finger before it dripped from her chin onto his hand.

"You ain't protecting my feelings by pretending we were great parents."

"I'm not. You were rotten when I was little. But, Daddy, I can't blame you and Mama for my failed relationship with Adam."

"I always thought you were just settling with him."

"Really . . ." Susanna stretched back, eyes wide. "This is news."

"Well, you know. Love's a tricky business. You seemed to think he was the true love you always wanted. He was a nice, steady boy with a good career. But, kitten, there's something more for you. I can feel it. Something big."

"Now that's just the medication talking. All I want is for you to get better. That's my something big."

Daddy drifted off. In the quiet, Susanna realized how scared she had been on the way to the hospital, but Nate—

She jumped up. Nate. Goodness, she'd forgotten him. Left him in the waiting area.

The door eased open and two nurses entered.

"... he's been sitting there all night," said one of the nurses.

"I can't keep my eyes off of him. He's like a fine painting," said the nurse with the name tag that read *Kasey*. "Hey there, Mr. Truitt."

"He's sleeping," Susanna said. "Did you say a man was still sitting in the waiting room?"

"The handsome one." Kasey typed in notes on Daddy's bed-side computer. "Hasn't budged in the last hour. Said he was waiting for a woman." She arched her brow. "You that woman?"

"Of course not." Well, not *that* woman in *that* tone. Susanna gently kissed Daddy's cheek, then whispered, "I love you. You have all my prayers."

She hurried down the hall on tiptoe, trying not to disturb the patients with the click-clack of her heels against the tile. Her legs pushed against the constraints of her tight skirt. Her heart thumped against the confinement of her expectations.

Why had he waited so long?

Yet when she rounded the nurses' station, the chairs were empty. Susanna stopped cold. So he'd finally gone. Disappointment smarted as she slowly finished her route to the chairs.

Well, good for him. He shouldn't have hung around for so long.

But oh, it would've been nice to thank him. Again. Twice in four days he'd been her knight in shining armor.

Maybe she could contact Mrs. Butler's event coordinator, see if she'd release his phone number or address.

"Thanks, Nate," Susanna whispered to the cold waiting area as she sank down into the nearest chair, her thoughts drifting toward how she was going to get home.

"Susanna?"

She looked up into Nate's fine face. He stood over her with a cup of coffee in his hand.

"I thought you'd gone." She rose to meet him, hand pressed against her stomach as her heart splashed down. He *was* dashing, with his cocky grin and confident glint in his eyes.

"I'm still here. Just went for coffee." He hoisted his vending-machine cup. "Would you like some?"

"No, no. Thank you." She sank to the chair again, bone tired. "W–why did you stay?"

"To see how you—and your father—fared."

He took the seat next to her, feeling as if she were seeing him for the first time, seeing beyond his high, fine features, beyond the sense that he carried a hundred years of history in his bones.

He was handsome, yes, but *kind* was the first word that came to Susanna's mind when she thought of him—at Lover's Oak, leading her down the hall to the Butlers' secret garage. Comforting her on the drive to the hospital.

"I don't always need to be rescued," she said, out of the blue, out of her heart.

His smile challenged the waiting-room shadows. "Would it be bad if you did?"

She regarded him with wide eyes. "Do you know a man who wants a woman who always needs to be rescued?"

"Sometimes it does a chap's heart good to rescue a beautiful woman. Makes him remember why God rescued him." His velvet confession brushed her heart.

"You are a very interesting man, Nate Kenneth."

"You are a fascinating woman, Susanna Truitt." He sipped his coffee. "Tell me, how is your father?"

"Good. He's lucky. It's a mild blockage. They'll do an angioplasty in the morning."

"My father"—Nate settled back against the blue vinyl chair—"battles leukemia."

"Nate, I'm sorry." It was the first time she considered whether he had a father or parents.

"He's been failing the last few months." Emotion accented his eyes. "I quite regret all the years I fought him, believing I knew better, rebelled." He laughed at his comment. "I'm a brave man, am I not? To realize the errors of my youth just as my father is ailing?"

"Better than after he's gone."

Nate smiled, nodding. "It's what I love about you Americans. No fussing about. Just say it plain."

"Plain? I don't think I've been saying things very plain the past decade of my life." She slid back against the seat and rested her head against the back of the chair. "I'm too tired to go home."

"Then we'll just sit here and rest," Nate said.

With a slow breath out, Susanna released the tension of the night, of the day, of the weekend, and drew strength from Nate's calm company.

She'd nearly dozed off when his phone rang. The piercing sound jolted them forward in unison. "It's Liam." He answered, walking toward the window, then around the nurses' station, phone against one ear, hand over the other.

Susanna watched his straight back until he disappeared, deciding she liked him. Not because he showed up at the oddest, most-needed times, but because he appeared so genuine and down-to-earth. When she had more energy, she'd like to talk to him about Brighton, his family, what kind of work he did that required the likes of a Liam.

"Susanna! There you are . . ." Gage charged into the waiting area with the fierceness of a mad bull. "I've been looking all over for you."

"Daddy had a small heart attack."

"I spent all night apologizing to Mrs. Butler—"

"Excuse me, Gage, but Daddy had a *heart* attack." She was awake now, trembling with adrenaline.

"We're never going to get the job," Gage huffed, hands on his hips. "I took out a loan . . . made payroll . . . because I was so sure we'd—"

"Please do not imply we're not getting this job because of me. Please."

"No, not really." Gage dropped to the nearest chair. "She didn't even notice you'd gone. I'm just mad. Her guest speaker disappeared, and she was so frantic I couldn't get one word in about how Gage Stone Associates should be her architects of choice. I'm sure Hayes & Associates down in Savannah will get the job." His tone sank, despondent and weak. "We'll go under without this job. Do you hear me, Susanna? *Under.*"

"Know what, Gage?" Susanna faced him, reaching for her courage. "I'll make your burden a bit lighter. I quit." If she'd learned anything from the breakup with Adam, it was to let go. Open up her heart to new possibilities. Leap.

"Quit?" He mocked her resignation with a hard laugh. "Come on. Be real. Where are you going to go if you leave me?"

"I don't know, Gage. I don't know." She fortified herself with a big, cleansing breath. Exhaling all the gunk of having to live by *the plan.* "But for the first time in my life, I don't care."

# SEVEN

$\mathcal{N}$athaniel ran down the beach under a vanguard of seagulls. Images of Susanna soared through his mind. He'd woken up thinking of her and had yet to shake her from his thoughts.

He'd returned from his call with Liam to find her trembling, pacing, talking to herself. Her boss had come 'round, and she'd mustered the courage to quit her job. For what reason, Nathaniel did not know, nor did he inquire while driving her home. But he loved her spunk in the shadow of losing her would-be fiancé.

*"I quit."*

How incredibly freeing. Nathaniel had never in his life uttered those words. He'd resigned his naval commission. Stepped down as CEO of his communications company. All for the sake of the Crown.

But quit? He'd never been allowed. Or privileged to do so.

Quitting was a freedom most people took for granted. The chance to pull up an oar and row on the other side.

When the cottage came into view, Nathaniel sprinted up the beach path, shoving through the sea oats and overgrown palmettos. The sand slipped beneath his trainers, so he had to concentrate on each long stride.

A low stone wall hemmed in the St. Simons cottage, which

had been given to the Brighton royal family, to Great-Great-Grandfather Nathaniel I in 1902. Pre-war, the family annually made the voyage to America, to St. Simons Island. But in recent decades... The rusting hinges of the wrought-iron gate squeaked as Nathaniel pushed into the front garden.

He paused to take in his surroundings. The grounds were a bit of a mess and quite run down, distressed, untended.

Nathaniel hadn't been to the island in twenty years, but he remembered Dad's beautiful garden and lawn. Where weeds now grew, there'd been a rose bed. Along the lattice of the veranda, Dad had mulched beds of hedges and hibiscus. Nate only remembered because of the alliteration—hedges and hibiscus. Gardens were Dad's pastime. He said it helped him commune with God. Hours upon hours he'd kneel in the dirt, digging and planting, tending and pruning. Communing.

When he became ill, so did his gardens.

Nathaniel walked up the tattered path, pausing halfway to the house. He'd not inherited his father's skill with plants and flowers, but he knew of someone who might have an eye for restoring the garden's glory. Perhaps a beautiful landscape architect in need of employ.

Jonathan stepped onto the veranda from the kitchen, letting the screen door clack behind him.

"You're in the news." He held up his iPad.

"American or Brightonian?" Nathaniel joined his aide on the porch. A steady sea-salt breeze brushed under the eaves. With a final glance at the garden, he made up his mind. For his father's sake, he'd do something about the garden's abysmal state. It would warm the king's heart.

"Brightonian. We kept you out of the local paper here. Mrs. Butler kept her part of the bargain." Jonathan hooked a chair with his sandaled foot and sat as he began to read. "Though she was pretty upset at you for disappearing."

"Invite her to tea. I'll apologize." Nathaniel sat in the adjacent chair. He listened as Jon read aloud, tension building in his chest.

"' . . . with the king growing ill, is Prince Nathaniel ready to take on the kingdom and manage the end of the entail? He can't even seem to find love and a wife and secure the House of Stratton with an heir.'"

"Jon, seriously, are you making that up?"

"Reading straight off the *LibP*'s web page."

"The *Liberty Press*? And they call themselves a fine newspaper of record . . . Is there a point to all of this?"

"Yes, I'm getting to it." He scrolled down. "Ah, here 'tis. 'We have a suggestion for the prince—Lady Genevieve Hawthorne.'" Jonathan paused to peer at Nathaniel.

"Oh mercy. And who wrote this inspired piece?"

"Claudette Hein."

"Ah, of course." She was one of Ginny's best friends and a fiery, active Hessenberg reporter writing for Brighton's leading paper, the *Liberty Press*.

"And I should marry Ginny because she's a distant cousin to Prince Francis?"

Jonathan shifted forward, setting aside his iPad. "Naturally. She could make the end of the entail like a fairy tale. A Hessen princess, from the line of Prince Francis, giving the country independence, making them a sovereign nation again. It would earn you a lot of points with the people."

"What about this people?" Nathaniel tapped his chest. "I've to live with myself and the decisions I make."

He stood and leaned against the nearest porch post. Today, he didn't want to talk about entails and agreements or marrying out of duty. He wanted to imagine a lush garden and a beautiful woman in the midst. Susanna. But his thoughts were trapped in the discussion of the entail. "Ginny is not Hessenberg's solution. She's not in the grand duke's royal line, just a very distant cousin through a morganatic marriage a hundred and fifty years ago. The Hawthornes gave up their rights to the throne long before the entail."

"But the entail ends next year, Nathaniel. People are getting restless, looking for a solution. Is it possible for Hessenberg to be independent again? The EU has promised their financial support to help Hessenberg stand on her own."

"Yes and generous trade agreements are being discussed with the UK and Germany. But if it requires me to marry Ginny . . ." He'd have to consider it, wouldn't he? Could he just reject it out of hand?

"King Nathaniel I and Prince Francis must have had something in mind by requiring an heir at the end of the entail." Nathaniel determined to seek for it.

"Certainly, Hessenberg was the last autocrat. Prince Francis, well, the House of Augustine-Saxon practically owned all of Hessenberg."

"'Tis why they were in no shape for a war."

"A hundred years later, Nate"—Jonathan shook his head— "Ginny looks like heir enough."

"She's a noble. Not a royal. Prince Francis wanted Hessenberg to return to the royal family."

Judging from King Nathaniel I's diaries, Nathaniel knew his great-great-grandfather valued the role of kings in government and culture. It's why he agreed to aid Prince Francis in the first place. To save a nation. Now the end of the entail looked to fall to the next King Nathaniel. Him.

"It doesn't matter what they wanted, Nathaniel. It matters what you and your father want."

"But it does matter what they wanted. Maybe they are gone, but their will projects on us today. King Nathaniel I's blood flows through my veins." Nathaniel returned to his seat and reached for Jon's iPad. "I'll not marry a woman I don't love. I value freedom and independence, but I also value true love." He scrolled through the story. "Do you think Ginny knew about this piece? She and Claudette go back to university."

"Who knows? Does Ginny want to be the heir? If so, the only way for her to become a royal is to marry one. That's you, chap."

"There's my brother, the formidable Prince Stephen." Nathaniel handed back the iPad. He didn't want to read any more. It soured his thoughts of the garden and the girl. "That would be a train wreck."

"Something baffles me, Nathaniel," Jon said. "You've been friends with Ginny for years. Romantically linked in times past."

"We went on a few dates." Besides, he'd not yet met someone like Susanna.

"Why *not* marry her? She's a Brightonian icon. Olympic champion. Miss Brighton Universe. I don't think I need to remind you that she's hot, my friend. Unbelievably hot."

"There's more to a relationship than hot, Jon." There was Susanna. Beautiful in every way.

"Yes, but it's a fantastic start."

Nathaniel glared at his dignified aide. "*You* marry her then."

"Me? I'm not even titled. She's of higher rank than I am, technically speaking."

"Well, then, I'll take care of that straightaway when we return home. I'll have the king grant you knighthood. Sir Jonathan Oliver."

"Fine, but it buys Ginny nothing. She doesn't want a knight; she wants a crown prince."

"She'll grow gray waiting."

The notion of partnering with Genevieve ruffled Nathaniel to his core. The pressure to marry was always on the crown prince, but the pressure to marry someone specific was new and unwelcome.

"Come on, Nate." Jonathan locked his hands behind his head,

posturing himself as if they were discussing rugby scores instead of Nathaniel's life, his heart, the future of two nations. "Lady Genevieve may be an easy solution to a very emotional problem."

"Easy for whom?" No doubt Ginny was a Brightonian star. But not his star. Though Mum and most of the royal court seemed to love her. "The entailment requires a legitimate heir with rights to the throne. Ginny is not legitimate."

"Too bad you can't just style her as royal princess and be done with it."

"If the Crown styles her as a princess before the lease ends, we'll find ourselves before a European Union court. Not to mention the sanctions of our own Parliament. Or the fact it would appear as if a royal title can be bought. Sold to the highest bidder."

"So if not Ginny, who are you going to marry?"

"The woman I love." Nathaniel moved to the edge of the veranda and gazed over the lawn. "I'm thinking of redoing the garden. I think Dad would like that. What do you think?"

"We? As in you and me? I can't grow weeds, let alone real honest-to-goodness flowers."

"Susanna is a landscape architect."

"The girl who took you from Mrs. Butler's dinner?" Jonathan joined Nathaniel at the veranda steps. "Please don't tell me you fancy her."

"She's recently unemployed. A small, quick landscape hire might be just be the encouragement she needs."

"Avoidance equals a confession."

"I admit nothing."

"You've not even told me how you met her."

"Nor will I." He treasured the memory of meeting her under the tree. With the rest of his life spilling into Brighton and Hessenberg papers, he'd keep Susanna his secret. "I think she'd do a lovely job on the garden."

"If you want to redo the garden, I'll arrange for proposals from other landscapers and architects." Jon jogged down the steps and kicked at the lawn's brown, weedy edge.

"No need. Susanna is my choice." Nathaniel motioned to the small enclosed area. "It's one garden, Jon."

"You do fancy her." Jon stared over at him. "Nathaniel, what are you thinking? She knows who you are and—"

"She doesn't." Nathaniel reached for the green leaves swaying in the breeze from the end of a sagging tree branch. "I introduced myself as Nate Kenneth."

"What about your speech at the benefit?"

"She was outside on her mobile."

"How convenient."

"Yes, quite." Nathaniel made a face at Jonathan. "But I'm a prince, not a miracle worker. The call was purely coincidence."

"This is a waste of your time."

"Redoing the garden is a perfect use of my time."

"You know what I mean, Nathaniel."

"Shall you ring her for an appointment or shall I?"

"I'll arrange it." Jonathan retrieved his iPad.

"While you're at it, please call Mrs. Butler. Invite her to tea. I'll apologize for my absence last night."

"Already done. Scheduled for today at four."

"Good, good. Arrange for Susanna to come in the morning, will you?" Or tonight. Perhaps right now.

If he could, Nathaniel would spend every day of his holiday with her.

A garden project would be the perfect connection. And the perfect barrier. Intrigued by her, drawn to her, Nathaniel realized Jonathan's alarm was just. He must guard himself. He could never be anything more than friends with Susanna Truitt.

Tuesday morning, Susanna woke early, slipped on a pair of shorts and a top, gathered some boxes she'd left in the garage from her initial move back to the island, and headed to the office.

Gage was there, but he made himself scarce while she collected her stuff. Only Myrna tried to stop her.

"Suz, stay. He needs you. We all need you. You're the calm in the storm."

"Even if I wanted to, I can't, Myrna. I have to do this. I can't explain why. I just know I do."

Susanna carried her boxes to her car, exhilarated. She was free—really free—finishing what Adam had started. Kicking her plans and comfort zones out from under her.

Next she stopped by the hospital to sit with Daddy. He was out of surgery and recuperating in his room.

"Surgery went like a dream," Mama had whispered with emotion when Susanna had called earlier to check on him.

By noon, she was home again with a free afternoon stretching ahead of her. She'd never had a day of nothing before.

By two, she'd cleaned the kitchen cabinets and vacuumed and mopped the tile floor. After a second shower, she grabbed an orange and headed out to the backyard deck.

"Suz, you here?"

"Yeah, back deck." Susanna squinted over her shoulder through the sunbeams to see Gracie stroll toward her.

Best friends comforted the soul like none other.

Plopping down in the Adirondack chair beside Susanna, Gracie gathered her dark hair and piled it on top of her head. "Man, it's hot." She eyed Susanna's orange. "Are you going to eat that?"

"I *am* eating it." Susanna peeled off a slice for Gracie.

"So I have a question." Gracie shoved the piece into her mouth. "How come I had to hear about my best friend breaking up with her boyfriend from Mary Jo at the produce market?"

"I've been busy."

"Yeah? Doing what? You quit your job too."

Susanna looked askance. "How'd you find out?"

"Myna called me. You know she's thick as thieves with my Aunt Lisa."

"Sorry." She passed Gracie another orange slice. That ought to buy her an ounce of forgiveness. "I was going to call you but—"

"It's okay, Suz." Gracie lifted her face to the sun. "After fifteen years of friendship, I know you need time to process. But can I just say, wow, I'm proud of you. The girl with the plan, the girl who researches impulse buys, is freestyling it." Gracie held out her hand for another slice. "Remember that bicycle you wanted to buy a few years ago?"

"I'm never going to live that down, am I?" Susanna passed over more of her orange. "I just wanted to get the right bike. Make sure I would really use it."

"And you last rode it . . . when?" Gracie nodded at the yellow beach bike chained to the back porch.

"You think you're so funny. I *was* going to go for a ride tonight." Susanna made a face at her. "But Mama's got me running the Rib Shack while she sits with Daddy."

"If I didn't know your mama so well, I'd say that was a lousy excuse, working at the Shack. How's your dad, by the way? Which I forgive you for, for not calling me when he was rushed to the hospital." Gracie held out her hand and Susanna just handed over the rest of the orange.

"I was going to call you. And ride my bike." A ride through the island sunshine would be nice . . . a sweet breeze in her hair, sunshine on her shoulders, the sweet kiss of her freedom in her heart.

"So, really. How are you doing, Suz? Why'd you quit?"

"I don't know. I just . . . said it. Maybe it was my way of responding to Adam, you know? Taking control when I'd let him have the reins for so long."

"Did you get a picture? I'd love to have seen the look on Gage's face."

"Yeah, taking a picture was first on my mind when I said, 'I quit.' He stormed out so the shot would've been of the back of his head. I don't know, Gracie." Susanna started toward the edge of the lawn where the trimmed grass met the wild flowerbed she'd planted. "I jolted awake at three o'clock this morning wondering if I'd lost my mind. But when I packed up my office, it felt like the greatest moment of my life. Gage didn't have enough work for me anyway, truth be told. Landscape architecture is a luxury in this economy."

"What do you hear from Adam?"

"Silence." Susanna glanced back at her friend as she ate the last orange slice. "Which is fine. What's left to say? I feel relieved. Like I'd been holding my breath for a decade."

"I'm free to tell you now I never cared much for him." Gracie walked to the hose and twisted the nozzle.

"You big fat liar. You were green with envy when Adam and I started dating."

"That was high school. Every girl wanted to date Adam Peters."

"He's available now, if you're still interested." Susanna joined her friend at the hose, washing the orange stickiness from her hands when Gracie gave her a turn at the hose.

"Like I want your castoffs," Gracie said, walking back to her chair with dripping-wet hands. "But at least you had a lasting relationship, Suz. I have longer relationships with my shoes than the men in my life."

"Because you've decided every man out there is like your father." Susanna shut off the water and wrapped up the hose.

"No, I haven't," she said. "I've decided they're worse."

"You just need to get over that thinking." Susanna returned to her deck seat. "You have every man judged and condemned before you exchange names and numbers. You've got to let go, trust a little. Give a guy a chance." She eased against the back of the chair, tuning into the distant hum of a lawn mower and inhaling the aroma of fresh-cut, sunbaked grass.

"Let go a little? Ha! Said the pot to the kettle."

"What pot? There's no pot here. I stuck with same guy for twelve years."

"Because you had a plan."

"Now you sound like Adam." Susanna flopped her arm over the side of her chair and curled her toes over the edge of the deck, letting the sun soak into all of her hidden, cold places. "Enough about me. What happened to the sailor? The guy going around the world on his yacht?"

"Ethan? He's still around," she said casually. A bit too casually.

"Wonder of wonders. It's been what, two weeks?"

"Three."

"Ladies and gentlemen, I do believe we have a record here." Susanna sat forward, applauding her friend.

"Okay, smarty-pants, thank you. If you must know . . . I do like him. A lot."

Susanna stretched across the chair to squeeze Gracie's hand. "I'm happy for you."

"And what about you? What are you going to do?"

"Get past Adam, get some perspective." She considered confessing her fascination with her new friend, Nate Kenneth. But other than his coincidental rescues in her times of need, there wasn't much to tell. She hadn't yet put words to how he made her feel.

He'd dropped Susanna off at home Monday night. She'd expressed her thanks again and again. But by the time Liam turned into her drive, their relationship had reached its farthest bounds.

She was a recent relationship widow. And he was heading

home—four thousand miles away—in a week or so. What could become of her feelings for him?

"I'm glad you're in such a good frame of mind," Gracie said. "Because I got some sorta bad news. Aunt Rue called."

"Uh-oh. What?" Susanna sat up, brushing the sun's heat from her thighs. "She sold the house?"

"Worse. She's coming to the island in the fall." Gracie squeezed her shoulders toward her ears, wincing.

"And I have to move." Rue Prather, an Atlanta-based clothing designer, rented the house to Susanna by the month for little more than pennies. Her only caveat was if she wanted to spend a season on the island, Susanna had to find other digs.

*"Because I like to entertain."*

"October through March."

"Six months?"

"You know she won't stay that long, Suz. She'll get restless and leave. She'll hear of a new designer taking Atlanta by storm and skedaddle out of here. I bet she won't even show up until Thanksgiving. Then she'll be gone by Christmas."

"Either way, I can't move out for six months hoping it's only for a month. If she says she's coming in October, then I have to move in October. Which will be really super fun now that I am only pulling shifts at the Shack."

In five short days, everything stable and planned about her life went *poof.* Gone.

But in the quiet of her soul, Susanna believed something divine was transpiring. A holy shift was taking place. If she could just hold on long enough to see the outcome. Maybe Daddy was right. Something big was coming.

"You can live with me if you want."

"No, thank you. I love you too much." She'd lived with Gracie once. Right after she'd graduated from college. Never again. "I'd live with Aurora in her tent first."

"Oh, really, Suz. It wasn't that bad."

"Yeah, Gracie, it was."

Gracie lived broad and large. Boundaries were optional. She spread out all over the apartment. Susanna, on the other hand, thrived with boundaries. Everything in its place. Expected. Organized. Routine.

She moved out after a few months to save her sanity and their friendship.

"Fine, but just so you know, I'm not as messy as I used to be."

Their conversation shifted and settled into the easy rhythm that comes from being lifelong friends. Susanna didn't need to share with Gracie every detail of her heart. She knew. Just knew.

Gracie regaled Susanna with the latest news on her beauty salon and how her most recent stylist thought working when scheduled was optional. "She told me she got into hair because she heard she could make her own schedule."

Susanna laughed. "Isn't that why you got into hair?"

"Yes, but at least I had the decency to own my own shop first. Look, I gotta run." Her friend since sixth grade wrapped Susanna in her long, slender arms. "Need to run some errands before meeting sailor boy for dinner." She shot Susanna a backward glance as she started off the deck. "Want to come?"

"I'm on deck at the Rib Shack, remember? Plus, I have an errand to run myself."

"Okay . . . Suz, you all right?"

Alone again.

"As a matter of fact, yes, I am."

Susanna stayed on the deck thinking until the late afternoon shade cast long lines across the backyard.

# EIGHT

athaniel knew of Christ Church from his boyhood days on the island. He parked on the side of the road and sprinted across the lanes, dashing under the ivy-covered trellis onto the church grounds.

Two steps down the redbrick path, he slammed into a surprising, tangible Presence. Something divine. Awe swirled in his chest as he surveyed the green grounds and the white clapboard church.

Off the brick path, he cut through the light dripping through the live oaks and stood in the Presence as Spanish moss twisted above his head.

Tears gathered in his eyes as he fell prostrate on the luxurious lawn. As the leaves clattered overhead, Nathaniel sensed God reminding him that all of the earth was God's dwelling, including the finite heart of Prince Nathaniel.

The only other place on earth that made him feel so close to holiness was five-hundred-year-old St. Stephen's Chapel, which was just north of Brighton's capital, Cathedral City.

Nathaniel breathed life to his tears as he inhaled the earth beneath his face.

*What, Lord? What do you want?*

Waiting for another minute or two, Nathaniel felt the awe pass and pushed off the ground, dusting grass and dirt from his trousers. He had few moments before the Tuesday evening call to prayer.

Cutting a path to the petite vestibule, Nathaniel entered the long, rectangular sanctuary and took a middle-row pew.

The presence of the Lord intensified. This experience had nothing to do with him or his position on the earth as a prince, but everything to do with the goodness of God.

When the priest moved up the aisle and called out the first reading, Nathaniel pulled his handkerchief from his pocket, wiped his eyes, and opened the Book of Prayer.

> *The king rejoices in your strength, LORD*
> *How great is his joy in the victories you give!*
> *You have granted him his heart's desire*
> *and have not withheld the request of his lips.*

Psalm 21:1–2

King David's words shot like an arrow to Nathaniel's heart. He bent forward, resting his head on top of the pew in front of him, cradling the book in his hands.

"Lord, I need your wisdom," he whispered. "I'm not even sure of my heart's desire or the request of my lips." How did David do it? Rule God's nation? He didn't even have the blessing of a parliament. "I'd rather you heal Dad than put me in as king, if I must speak the truth. I'm not ready. Did you call me or did my forefathers?"

From the pulpit, the priest called the silent sanctuary into prayer. Nathaniel tried to focus on the next prayer, wanting to return to his connection with the Presence, but politics embroiled his thoughts.

Could he marry Genevieve for king and country? Make her heir to the Hessenberg House of Augustine-Saxon? Let her inherit Hessenberg? Even if he wanted to marry her, would the courts rule she satisfied the condition of being a true heir of the House of Augustine-Saxon? Nathaniel's peace began to evaporate. He needed to forget the entail and meditate on his Lord.

Closing his eyes, he exhaled his doubts and breathed in a sweet fragrance. A very familiar fragrance.

Nathaniel peeked around. More congregants had joined the prayer vigil, including Susanna Truitt. She sat all the way to the right on the pew in front of him.

He slid over a few inches and whispered, "Fancy meeting you here."

She kept her head bowed. "We have to stop meeting like this."

"I think you're stalking me."

He caught the edge of her smile. "Shhh." She pressed her finger to her lips.

Grinning, Nathaniel sat back and resumed his prayers, thanking God for leading him to the sanctuary tonight. When the priest concluded the service, Nathaniel slipped out of the pew and joined Susanna in the narrow aisle.

"Lovely evening."

"A bit warm, but yeah, it's nice." She smiled at him. Ah, she was equally pleased to see him.

They fell in line with the rest of the congregants bidding good night to the pastor at the vestibule door. When they stepped outside, the setting sun had painted a Monet-worthy scene. A visual prayer and for now, all was right in Nathaniel's world.

"Can I buy you a cup of coffee?" he said, trailing after Susanna.

"I'm on my way to work." She paused, pointing to the Rib Shack logo on her shirt. "Mama has had all hands on deck the past couple days to fill in for Daddy. I'm filling in for her so she can be at home. And, as you know, I'm unemployed."

"How is your father faring?"

"He's great." She started again down the brick path. "He'll probably outlive us all."

"Susanna, the cottage garden is in need of your services. Did a man named Jonathan contact you about the landscaping?"

"No." She moved aside for an elderly couple to pass. "Hey, Mr. and Mrs. Scott."

"Evening, Susanna," the woman replied. "It's been a while."

"Yes, ma'am."

"Sorry about you and Adam Peters."

"Thank you." Susanna peeked up at Nathaniel. "Live on a small island, everybody knows your business."

"Trust me, I know." Try being a prince of an island kingdom. So, Jon hadn't called her yet?

"Susanna, will you re-architect my father's garden?"

"How do you know you can afford me?"

"I don't." He loved that she answered with a question rather than a reply. "We can negotiate. Nine o'clock tomorrow morning? Come by the cottage. I'll give you a tour, then we'll dicker over the price." Nathaniel knew he'd pay whatever she asked. "Fair?"

"More than." She offered her hand, which he gladly took. "Ever get the feeling, Nate, that something is just around the corner, but you don't know what?"

Oh, if only it were possible. He hungered for such a feeling. But he had known every light and shadow around the corners of his life since he was a child. Though every once in a while . . . he encountered a surprise. Like the one standing before him.

"Tomorrow, then?" His hand felt empty and cold when she pulled hers away.

"Tomorrow. But right now, the Rib Shack awaits. It's like my own personal game of Monopoly. Return to Go. Return to the Rib Shack, Susanna, and start again."

Nathaniel laughed, walking with her toward her car. "Sometimes going back to the beginning is the only way."

"In my case, the only way. So, Nate, just what do you do in Brighton?" She walked under the Christ Church entry trellis and turned up the side of the road.

"I'm in government of sorts." Nathaniel's car was across the road and in the opposite direction, but he kept pace with Susanna.

"Politics?" She pulled her keys from her purse.

"Not if I can help it." He laughed. "I'm more of an advisor, if you will."

"A lobbyist?"

"No, no. Just a friend, a guiding light." *Say it, Nathaniel. Crown prince. King-in-waiting.* But he couldn't. It would change everything.

She stopped at the driver's side door of a green Cabrio. "Nine o'clock tomorrow, then?"

"Yes, 21 Ocean Boulevard." Nathaniel lurched forward, opening her door for her. "Suz, if your mum needs extra hands, may I offer mine?" He held them up, twisting them from back-to-front. "I pulled kitchen duty in the navy. Did a fair job of it."

She tossed her purse onto the passenger seat and regarded him for a moment "Sure, why not. Come on if you dare." She waved for him to follow. "Mama will love me forever for bringing extra help. Be warned—she only pays minimum wage to substitutes, plus a share of the tips."

"Money is no object." This was going to be fun. "Anything is better than sitting around with Jon and Liam."

"Hold that thought until you've worked a shift."

Nathaniel jogged to his SUV, and when Susanna passed, tooting her horn, he gunned into the lane behind her.

Once they pulled into the parking lot in the shadow of the island's grand lighthouse, Nathaniel rang Jon, glad to leave a message rather than debate how the crown prince of Brighton didn't need to bus tables or scrub floors.

Nathaniel's days on the island were limited, and he'd be jacked if he wasn't going to spend as many of them as he could near, around, in the presence of Susanna Truitt.

Wednesday morning, Susanna drove up Ocean Boulevard, hand out the window surfing the breeze.

What a great morning. Not in theory, but reality. Dawn's first light woke up with a sense of expectancy. So she shouted, "Joy!" in faith and powered up her iTunes, jamming to Bethel Live while getting ready.

How had she forgotten there were so many textured colors to the island morning? She had to get out more, pay attention to the beauty around her.

This is what freedom from fear did—opened up a girl's heart.

Memories from last night put a smile on her lips.

Mama had been packing to go be with Daddy when Susanna walked in with Nate. She'd lit up like a firefly, sized him up, and patted his shoulder. "You'll do right nicely."

Without one complaint, Nate had mopped floors, cleaned out the lowboy and the walk-in, carted in a truckload of supplies, and organized the storage room. For five full hours, Susanna had him running to and fro. He never flinched or let up. Not even when she sent him to clean the bathrooms after closing. He'd just picked up the mop bucket and headed off, whistling.

He was a lovely balm to her stinging heart. Just thinking of him made her laugh.

Susanna slowed down once she hit Ocean Boulevard. The houses sat back off the road, tucked in between oaks, pines, and palmettos. Addresses were hard to see, but she found Nate's house by the numbers tacked on the side of his mailbox.

At the end of a narrow, wooded drive, Susanna broke into a

clearing where a slate-gray beach cottage soaked in the morning sun. The blue edge of the quiet Atlantic rimmed green grounds.

Parking under a stand of trees, she stepped out of her car into the resonance of the morning tide, slinging her satchel over her shoulder.

For a moment, she felt like she owned the world. Her first job on her own. She should've started working for herself long ago.

About to start for the house, Susanna paused when she heard a twig snap behind her, followed by the crunch of dried, dead brush.

"Hello?" Susanna stepped around her car, angling toward the wooded roadside easement. "Nate?"

Aurora peeked out from behind a tree, clinging to her pink bicycle.

"Hey," Susanna said. "What are you doing here?" She smiled when she saw the woman's pristine red Keds.

"Riding my bike."

"In the woods?"

"Woods, road, beach." Aurora shrugged. "I see you made it."

"Made it where?" Surely Aurora didn't know about her appointment with Nate.

"Here." Aurora's loose T-shirt swung about her waist when she pointed at the cottage.

"Am I supposed to be here?" Susanna assessed her tent-dwelling friend. Aurora seemed clear, lucid, though she talked in riddles.

"Oh yes." Aurora walked her bike out from the trees and hopped on. "Most certainly." She began peddling. "Relax. He's got the whole world in his hand."

"Are you talking about God, Aurora?"

"Most certainly."

"Does he have *me* in his hand?" By faith, Susanna knew the Lord watched over her, but hearing someone else say it, even whacky Aurora, sealed the notion a bit deeper in her heart.

"Right here." Aurora shot her hand above her head, palm toward Susanna. "See you."

Susanna watched her ride away, envious of the woman's freedom, wondering if she could achieve the same while living in a brick-and-mortar structure and driving a car. Or did deep, abiding peace only come from giving up everything?

But there was no time to ponder. She was late. Susanna hurried to the house, shaking the sand and grit from her shoes as she landed on Nate's veranda and rang the bell.

The front door swooshed open. "You're late." Curt and formal, Jonathan stood aside for her to enter.

"Sorry. I had a moment with Aurora."

"Who?"

"Aurora." Forget it. Jonathan didn't know about Aurora. Besides that, he was walking off, and Susanna had to hurry to catch him.

The cottage was beautiful. The gray-shingled exterior hid the interior craftsman-style quality. Lunette windows, gleaming redwood, rounded archways, and the feeling that time rested here.

"Is this a craftsman house? They were popular at the turn of the twentieth century."

"You have a good eye. It was built in 1901 and given to the . . ." He reached the kitchen entry, pausing. " . . . the family a year later. It's one of the first craftsman homes built in the South." Jon led her outside to the white, airy veranda with its stone fireplace and stained concrete floor and Nate.

"Welcome," he said, rising, the same light in his eyes from last night. He looked different this morning in his crisp blue button-down and creased khaki shorts with his dark hair clean and loose about his forehead. A far cry from the aproned, hairnetted man who carried a ratty toothbrush into the bathrooms to scrub around the toilets.

Susanna released a low breath and steadied herself with

a hand on the back of a chair. "This place is beautiful." *He* was beautiful. Mercy...

She set her satchel on the table, her gaze flickering past Nate's. He was looking at her as though he could see right through her.

"So . . . this is the garden?" Moving to the edge of the porch, Susanna took in the withered shrubs and thriving weeds and the low stone wall.

"What do you think?" Nate stood next to her, hands tucked in his shorts pockets.

Oh, Nate . . . She stepped off the porch. *What are you doing to me?* He made her want to lean into him as if she'd arrived home after an aimless journey.

Rebound. That's all this was, rebound. Nate showed up just as Adam exited, and she was airing her feelings out on him. Thank goodness he was only here for a short holiday.

"You have tons of potential with this space." She walked a few feet down the path, focusing her thoughts on the reason Nate called her here in the first place. "What do you have in mind?"

"I've no idea, Suz." He'd started using her nickname steadily last night under the influence of Catfish, Bristol, Avery, and the rest of the crew. "You're the professional." Nate joined her on the path. "I had a grand time last night."

She laughed. "Grand time? Is this the Brighton form of politeness? You scrubbed toilets, Nate."

"There's nothing that cheers a man's heart like gleaming white porcelain."

"You're crazy." When she tapped his arm, he caught her hand in his.

"I could do with a dose of the crazies," he said, staring at her too long, holding on too long. "Shall we tour the garden? It's big, as you can see, but with plenty of beds and space to create."

"It's a blank canvas." His touch robbed her of breath. Why was he holding her hand? Why did she feel his heart against her palm? She took a giant step toward the ocean-side wall as if there were something important to inspect, dislodging her hand from his, easing his fuel from her pulse. "It's lovely, Nate. So very lovely."

"I see weeds. What do you see?"

Susanna cut across the lawn, smoothing her hands over her suit slacks. "Angles, textures, and ambiance. I see roses and foxglove, heather and perennials, perhaps a cobbled path and box hedges along the wall."

Like the Christ Church grounds, Nate's garden had a mystical aura, as if the flora and fauna understood gardens were for peace. For communing.

She could hide here. Find God here. Even among the barren beds. She stooped to run her hand over the cut blades of grass. "I could lie down and make a grass angel."

"Like a snow angel?"

"Exactly." She flopped on her back, pressed down into the grass and flapped her arms and legs, not caring about possible grass stains on her suit.

Nate bent over her. Did he know his smile was a potent elixir? "You look ridiculous."

"You should see this from my angle."

"Guess I'll have to fix that straightaway." He flopped down next to her, swinging his arms and legs over the grass. "Okay, on three, let's jump up and see our creations."

"One."

"Two."

"Three." She fired off the ground, twisting her ankle and tripping into Nate. He caught her, wrapping his arm about her waist, holding her to him.

"Well, what do you think?" He jutted his chin at their grassy, angelic impressions.

"I think, um, that my . . ." If he didn't let her go, her heart would rocket out of her chest on its way to the moon. "My angel has a rather large behind. Look at that." She bent down, moving out of his grasp, cupping her hands around the grassy impression of her derriere.

"Seems fine to me." He winked, and she almost swooned. "It's just where you pushed down to get up." He hovered his hand over the grass, a grin on his lips. "See?"

See? Oh, she was seeing . . .

Susanna pressed her palm against her forehead. "The garden . . . We should get back to the garden."

"The job is yours," he said, low, sincere.

"You don't know my price. You haven't seen any drawings."

"I don't have to know, Susanna. I trust you."

A pair of red birds flitted about in a black cherry tree while a couple of cherry-toting squirrels plunged their faces into the grass, storing up for the coming winter.

"You can't keep doing this, Nate." She sighed and headed for the veranda. Based on what she knew of the Ocean Boulevard homes, she'd worked up a rough estimate after work last night.

"Doing what?"

"Rescuing me."

"I protest." He followed her, arms wide. "I'm doing no such thing."

"You feel sorry for me." The truth escaped, smacking her heart.

"Sorry for you?" He dropped to a wicker chair. "No, Suz. Not for you." The sparkle faded from his eyes as he stared over the garden. "I don't feel sorry for you." He shifted his gaze to her. "I envy you."

"Envy me? You want to run the kitchen tonight while I tooth-brush bathroom tile?" How could he envy her?

"Tonight?" His countenance sparked.

"Oh, yeah." Susanna perched on the edge of her chair. "Mama called this morning. Said she'd put you on the schedule. I told her you were some kind of government official from Brighton and she had no right to schedule you just because you volunteered once."

"Volunteered? I was told I'd get a paycheck." He tapped the table. "I deserve it. I worked hard last night."

"Mama said government officials, of all people, need to see how hard a man works to get a decent wage."

"She's right. I'll be there."

"Okay, but be warned—she'll have you cleaning out the trash bins or Cloroxing mold from seedy, hidden places."

Nate leaned forward with arms on his thighs. "I'll scrub mold if you'll design my garden."

"Sorry, bubba, but working at the Shack isn't part of my negotiating. Besides, you don't even know if I'm a good architect, Nate." Truth nailed down some of her early morning excitement. "You barely know me."

"Then why do I feel as if I do?"

"Hero complex?" *Ha.* But he didn't laugh. He studied her as an easy breeze dropped by, scenting the porch with morning fragrances, and listened in on their words.

"I watched you work last night, Suz. You're the boss's daughter but you gave your all. You made everyone feel like a part of the team. Even me. You didn't ask them to do anything you weren't willing to do yourself. They respect you because you're a woman of integrity. That's how I know you'll design a lovely garden."

"You saw all of that on a five-hour shift?"

"It's amazing what we can see when we take the time to look." She surveyed the garden again, then Nate. "I'll do it."

He smiled. "Good. I knew you'd see reason."

"Whatever, wise guy." She took her sketch pad and pencils from her satchel. "But we're dickering over the price and signing a contract—the whole shooting match." She passed over the rough estimate she'd prepared.

Nate flipped back through the pages. "Are you sure you're charging enough?"

"Nate, I'm pretty sure you're supposed to dicker down, not up." Susanna positioned herself on the top porch step and made her first mark on the pristine page, noting the pockets of shade in contrast to the pockets of sun, imagining all the personalities of a southern Georgia, ocean-side garden.

Prayer.

Picnics.

Parties.

Politics.

She imagined the path of a pearly moon through the magnolias. A wisteria vine under which lovers might sit, holding hands, entwining their hearts.

She breathed in the scent of pine, palmetto, baked grass, sea salt. And the fresh scent of Nate's skin.

She glanced around to find him practically falling out of his seat to see her design.

"I'm just sketching . . ." She turned away.

"I'm just looking."

"Nathaniel, you've a call," Jonathan said from the kitchen door.

"Who is it?"

"Your father."

"Excuse me, Suz." Nate brushed his fingers over her hair as he left the porch.

"O–okay." His touch had produced chills on her hot skin. He had to stop touching her. Awakening something deep in her soul.

She tried to focus on the dry weeds and barren beds. But her heart yanked her thoughts back to his touch.

*Rebound. This is just rebound. A man gives you a bit of attention, and you're ready to hand over your heart . . .*

Back to the garden. What it needed was freedom. Space. A

subtle beauty. When she finished the sketch, she scripted a garden name across the top.

*A King's Garden.*

It helped her visualize the end design. Susanna wasn't sure Nate would find any connection to such a lofty-sounding name, but she did. Already "A King's Garden" took up a brilliant residence in her mind.

# NINE

"You fancy her," Jonathan said as he cleared the cups and cakes from Wednesday afternoon tea.

"That's out of the blue but if you're talking about Susanna, yes, I like her," Nathaniel said. "As a friend." Far be it from him to confess he hadn't been able to stop thinking about her since she left this morning with her sketch pad, excitement in her eyes.

Her design struck him. She'd sketched a near perfect replica of Dad's old garden, the one Nathaniel loved so much. It was as if she read life and color in the garden's fading shadows.

Simple. Spacious. But edged with blooming life.

"Friend? Nathaniel, I've not seen that look in your eye since Adel Gardner kissed you during the university autumn bash."

"Adel? Really? Jon, you've got to move on. University is over. Ten years over."

"Me move on? Who here has not fallen in love since our fourth year?" Jonathan's glare accented his sarcastic tone.

"At least I'm not like you. Falling in love every spring and out every fall. You're none the better for it, I'd say."

"At least I try."

"You don't have a big fat crown on your head either." Every

once in a while, Nathaniel felt justified to pull the crown prince card.

Jon laughed over the clatter of the dishes as he headed to the kitchen door. "True, I'll grant you, and I gather it's why you've not told your new friend that Nate Kenneth is really Prince Nathaniel Henry Kenneth Mark Stratton, future king of Brighton."

"She doesn't need to know."

"Perhaps *you* need to be reminded then. You fancy her. I see it in your eyes."

"I know who I am and the boundaries I have." How could he forget? Jonathan, Mum, Dad, the entire Brighton Parliament wouldn't let him forget. "Let Liam know I'll need the motorcar tonight, please."

"Where are you going? And wherever it is, Liam is tagging along."

"I can't have my security officer in tow when I pull a shift at the Rib Shack."

"Again?" Jon came around the kitchen island. "Whatever for?"

"Her mum put me on the schedule. They've been needing extra hands since her father has been in the hospital."

"Nathaniel, you're the crown prince. You don't need to wait tables at an American barbecue bistro."

"I'm not waiting tables." Nathaniel started for the stairs. "I'm scrubbing floors and cleaning toilets."

Jon swore blue. "The King's Office will have my job if they get wind of this."

"It's not your choice." Nathaniel stripped off his shirt as he made his way down the hall. Susanna and the rest of the crew wore shorts and Rib Shack T-shirts. He'd worn jeans last night and had sweat them through. Tonight he'd dress in the uniform—a pair of shorts he didn't mind soiling and a T-shirt.

"Then tell her who you are, Nate," Jon called after him.

"What for? To prove my superiority?" He paused on the first

landing, glancing over the rail at his aide. "Or to embarrass her and make her feel bad she asked a royal prince to scrub a dirty floor on his hands and knees?" Nathaniel jogged up the stairs. "I won't do it."

"What if she finds out on her own?" Jonathan followed Nathaniel up to his private quarters.

"And how would that happen? Will you tell her? Or Liam?"

"Three hundred people saw you give a speech Monday night, Nathaniel. I bet at least one or two of them enjoys a good barbecue meal now and again. What if a Brightonian or Hessen on holiday happens by the restaurant?"

"Then it's a good thing I'll be cleaning trash bins or some such out of sight. And you saw Mrs. Butler's social set. I daresay they won't be calling for reservations at the Rib Shack anytime soon."

Jon glared at him. "I said it once, I'll say it again. You *do* fancy her."

"Right now, I fancy you disappearing so I can change." Nathaniel pushed his aide out the door.

Yes, he fancied Susanna. A lot. And he'd flirted with her this morning, crossing over his own personal boundaries. Holding her hand, holding her waist, all the while concerned she'd mistake his heartbeat for distant thunder.

But it wasn't right nor fair for him to awaken a love that he could not return.

Scooping change into his pocket from the dresser, he sketched her face with his thoughts and stored it in a private room with signage—For Nathaniel Only.

Downstairs, Liam passed him the keys. "I'd feel better if you'd let me come along, sir."

"I'd feel better if you'd not go at all," Jon said. "You're a prince."

"I'm on holiday and this is my idea of fun. Don't wait up."

"Before you go, here's the latest from the *Liberty Press*." Jon offered Nathaniel his iPad.

Nathaniel opened the front door. Warm, glorious light flooded the foyer. "Unless it's a bomb scare or a catastrophe, I don't want to know."

"Define *catastrophe*," Jon said.

"A sudden widespread disaster. War. Terrorist attack."

"Does a headline suggesting you're engaged to Lady Genevieve Hawthorne qualify?"

"Engaged?" Nathaniel slammed the door shut, reaching for the tablet. He trusted Brighton's leading newspaper to confirm any royal engagement with the King's Office.

Prince Nathaniel's Marriage to Lady Genevieve Hawthorne Solves It All.

Bookmakers Give 3-to-1 Odds for End-of-Year Proposal.

"This is from the *Informant?*" Nathaniel scanned the article. Rubbish. Every word. The *Informant* was the gossip rag, purposefully inciting and salacious. But even this was below their standards.

"This is *Liberty Press*. *Informant*'s not jumped on this one."

The *LibP*? Nathaniel handed back Jon's tablet. "Something's not right."

"Every once in a while the *LibP* prints something outlandish. Remember when Prince Stephen failed to make the rugby team his first year at university?"

"Miserable. Humiliated my poor brother all the more when Dad asked the press corps to leave him alone."

Poor Stephen. He'd had photographers and reporters trailing him for weeks, recording his relentless effort to improve his game. They'd made all kinds of outlandish statements.

"Morris Alderman has Hessenberg ties. Not to mention his buddies in Brighton politics who want to cut Hessenberg free so we can save our own financial necks," Jon said, leaning against the back of the couch. "You've got pressure coming from all sides, chap. Alderman doesn't seem shy about forcing you into some kind of nineteenth-century arranged marriage for the sake of a nation."

"Bully for him. He can run his paper his way," Nathaniel said, taking his leave. "We all want Hessenberg's independence and a break in our financial quagmire."

King Nathaniel I and Prince Francis were not wise when it came to projecting the exchequer accounts of each country. "As for me, I'm going to work before I get docked for being late."

The emotional wrestling over the blasted entail darkened his heart. Couldn't he just forget it for a few days and soak in the sunshine of Susanna?

At five after eleven, Susanna peered into Mama's office as she tugged off her apron. "I don't know how Daddy does this night after night. We must have run twelve-hundred plates through the window tonight."

"More. Running the totals now." Mama motioned toward the back door. "Check on the Englishman. I sent him out with the trash."

"He's not English. He's Brightonian."

"Well, he sounds English." Mama's fingers flew over the keys as she added receipts. "I'm sure going to miss that boy when he goes home. Though I never saw a man cut up vegetables so slow. Mercy a-mighty."

Mama had about gone crazy on Nate when he'd only produced one container of sliced tomatoes after an hour at the prep table.

"But he's a master at the dishwasher, Mama. That counts for something."

"Yes, indeed it does. And after he spiffed up the bathroom, I plum-near put a place setting in there." The machine crunched Mama's final total, spitting out a long white tape.

Susanna reached for a towel and dried her hands. "I'll go check on him." She retrieved two Rib Shack tumblers, filled them with ice and soda, then pushed through the screen door.

The back deck faced the southern side of the inlet under the watchful eye of the St. Simons lighthouse.

Several customers lingered at their tables, listening to Mickey, the seasoned Irish singer who graced the Shack's back deck five nights a week.

Gracie was here with her man, Ethan-the-sailor, her head bent against his, enraptured, speaking low and intimately.

Susanna scanned the deck and beach, looking for Nate. Had it just been five days since she walked along the shore with Adam? Since she learned the life she'd been waiting for would never be?

At times, it felt like she'd been stuck in a really bad story, unaware that other books or stories existed.

Then someone—God—gave her a new book. One with creamy blank pages waiting for a new story to be told.

The image lingered in her heart as Nate emerged from the darkness, dusting his palms.

"I was getting worried." She offered him one of the tumblers of cold cola. "Wouldn't be the first time the Dumpster ate someone."

"Not to worry, I'm trained in defeating man-eating Dumpsters." He took a long sip of the cola. "I speared the beast into submission."

"Hurrah." Susanna pumped her fist in victory. "But where, O brave knight, is your sword?"

"In the belly of the beast, naturally." Nate cut a swath in the air, then held his palm over her eyes. "Don't look, fair maiden. It's a gruesome sight."

She snatched his hand away with a laugh. "Do you have a knight complex?"

"No, but I do have a prince complex."

"Then it's lucky you're not a prince."

"Isn't it, though?" He took a gulp from his tumbler, turning his attention to Mickey as he ended his song, the last note ringing out from his guitar.

"I love Mickey's music," Susanna said.

"Yes, he's quite good." Nate peered down at her, started to say something else but headed for the deck instead, taking a seat on the nearest picnic table.

Susanna followed and sat next to him, waiting for Mickey to start another song. Being with Nate was the nicest sensation she'd experienced in a really long time.

"I like it here," he said, glancing around the deck, then at her. "It's lovely. Most lovely."

*Lovely.* The confession sank through her, warm and silky, though at times she felt like he spoke in metaphors, challenging her to read between the lines.

"Come on, Nate, it's crazy around here, and you know it." She sipped her drink and scooted an inch away from him. *Remember you're in rebound mode, girl.*

"Why not work here, Suz?" Nate angled around to face her. "Take over the business?"

She shook her head. "When I was a kid . . ." Her tone was meant for him alone. "Mama and Daddy fought. Not little squabbles over disciplining me or balancing the checkbook but with fists flying and paint-peeling cursing. Daddy would yell at me to go to my room. I'd hide in my closet and pretend it was my secret garden. No one could get me because the closet had a magic door."

"So your love of gardens began."

"Pretty much. My safe place. By the time they healed their marriage when I was twelve, I'd read a hundred books about gardens.

Fiction, nonfiction. The garden section of the newspaper. I wanted to study horticulture and work in one of the world's great gardens—the Biltmore or the Brooklyn Botanical or the Claude Monet in Normandy. But Adam convinced me those jobs were few and far between, hard to get. He said architecture was the way to go."

"He may have been right." Nate stared right into her soul. "But he didn't hear your dream, did he?"

"I think he meant well." Forgotten remnants of her arguments with Adam elbowed forward. Her dreams versus his. A tug-of-war over when his season ended and hers, rather *theirs*, began. Dark moments she'd shoved aside for the sake of the relationship. The almighty plan. "I chose to believe Adam would do anything for me." The confession broke another thin shackle of her former life. "But it was my expectation, not his demonstration."

"A girl in love has a right to believe her man would lay down his life for her."

She gawked at him with bold skepticism. "Earth to Nate."

"What about your father? And his love for your mum?"

His soft suggestion inspired tears. How did he see so much so soon? "He's very devoted to Mama, but she demands it."

"And he freely gives it. He could walk away if he wanted. As he'd done in the past."

"I never saw it that way before," she said as Mickey rolled from one ballad to the next. This one had a minor-key melody that stirred Susanna's soul. "But yeah, Daddy would do just about anything for Mama."

"And she him."

Susanna peered at Nate. Maybe it was his accent or his Brighton birth or her crazy imagination or too many hours in the Rib Shack kitchen, but she felt as if she'd seen him before.

He caught her gaze and raised his hand as if he might stroke her face, but then pulled it away. "Can I ask you something?" he said.

"I'm twenty-nine," she answered without waiting for the question. He was getting to her. Too much. Too soon. So she moved another inch away from his intimate intonations by blocking his probing with a snide response. "And I won't tell you how much I weigh." She sipped from her soda, eyeing him over the rim of her tumbler.

He released his melodic, easy laugh. "Okay, I wasn't going to ask either of those, but good to know."

"How old are you?"

"Thirty-two. And nearly thirteen stone."

"Stones or pounds, I'm still not telling you how much I weigh."

"What made you stay with Adam for so long?"

Ah, a fair question. She shrugged. "The idea that I knew what tomorrow would bring. Adam. Eventually marriage. I didn't have to worry, you know? I liked things being secure and nailed down. By-product of the parental units fighting in my formative years. Can I ask you something?"

"I have a younger brother. I like dogs and cats, and I once had a pet mouse named Clint Eastwood." He turned toward Susanna, grinning, his arms spread wide.

She laughed. "Clint Eastwood? That's a mighty big name for a mouse."

"He wore it well."

"Why did you say you were envious of me earlier?"

"Because." He turned forward again and raised his tumbler to take a drink, covering his answer. "I just am. You have options. A blank diary in which to design your life."

How did he read her heart so well? "And you don't?"

"Sakes alive." Mama emerged from the back door with Mickey's complimentary plate of ribs and a broom. "What is all my help doing out here? Here you go, Mick. Nice singing tonight." She aimed the broom at Nate. "Dishwasher, no slacking off now. Just got you trained up right. Susanna, I'm going to head on home to tend to your daddy. Can you finish closing and lock up? Avery's got the front of the house all but done."

"It'll cost you overtime pay."

"How about I let you keep your job?"

"Say, Mama. Nate here hired me to design his daddy's garden." Susanna patted Nate's shoulders, letting her hand slip over the contours of his broad, firm back. Nate leaned ever so slightly into her touch.

"Did he now? Good for you. Get his money up front, Suz." The screen door banged as Mama returned to the kitchen, her voice filling every glorious pocket of the Shack. "Aves, shug, get finished up and come straight home. School tomorrow."

"Get his money up front?" Nate looked aghast. "Is she serious?"

"Mama never jokes about money." Susanna patted his shoulder one last time before pulling her hand away, the threads of his shirt releasing a subtle woodsy scent.

"By George, I do believe I'm offended."

"Well, it's a good thing you hired me to do the garden, not Mama." Susanna collected their empty tumblers. She'd prefer to sit on the deck talking to him all night, but it was time to get to work. "Listen, why don't you head on home? We're all done here except for the kitchen checklist and lock up."

"Are you sure? I can stay to help."

He was sweet. So very sweet. "Avery and I are old hands. We got it. Ten minutes and we're out. Go on." *Before I lean to kiss you.* "You worked hard tonight."

He removed his apron. "So the garden?"

"I'll start drawing up formal plans in the morning."

He slapped his hand to his chest. "Makes me glad." His smile stole another small chunk of her heart, and when he leaned in to hug her, she curled into his arms. "Good night, Susanna."

"'Night, Nate."

He passed Mickey, complimenting his music, digging change and a few loose bills from his pocket for the tip jar. "Puts me in mind of the old country."

Mickey acknowledged Nate with a nod, his mouth full of a meaty rib. He didn't bother to stop the barbecue sauce running down his chin.

"Good night again, Susanna." Nate stepped toward the front of the deck.

"Good night, Nate."

She waited on the deck until she heard the rumble of his SUV and saw the glow of taillights disappearing down the road.

And she missed him.

"You like him."

Susanna snapped around toward Mickey.

"We just met." She collected Mickey's plate of gnawed rib bones and pile of used napkins.

"So? You never liked a dude you just met before?" Mickey flicked his last bone onto the plate.

"Mick, I just broke up with Adam."

"You're full of excuses. Just admit it. Never saw you with Peters anyway."

"What is it with people?" Susanna snatched up his tumbler. "Twelve years with a man, and no one manages to tell me what they really think of him? He breaks up with me, and the whole island practically applauds. Do you want a refill?"

"Sweet tea." Mickey tore open a wet wipe with his teeth. "Oh, hey, take the change from the tip jar. Use it for the jukebox while you close up."

"I don't *like* him, Mickey. Not in the way you mean." Susanna set down the dirty dishes and reached into the jar, fishing out quarters. "Even if I did—which again, I don't—he lives four bazillion miles away. Across the Atlantic and halfway into the North Sea."

"So you know where he lives?"

Susanna banged into the kitchen, leaving Mickey and his amusing chuckle on the deck. What did he know? Old Irish-singing coot. He wasn't even really Irish, for crying out loud.

Placing the dishes by the dishwasher, Susanna checked on Avery and the front of the house. "You almost done?"

"Just have the foyer to mop," Avery said without looking up, moving the mop evenly across the stained concrete floor. "Then run down the checklist and take out the last of the trash."

"Mickey gave me change for the jukebox." Susanna walked to the music machine. "What do you want to hear?"

"Blake Shelton."

Okay, but first her old favorite. Susanna dropped the first quarter in and punched A10. Patsy Cline singing "Crazy."

Avery came up behind her and draped her long, slender arms around Susanna's shoulders. "You doing okay?"

*"Crazy, crazy for feeling so lonely . . ."*

"I'm more than okay." Susanna peered into her sister's brown eyes. So like Mama's. Intense but tempered with compassion. "Now tell me which Blake Shelton song."

"'God Gave Me You.'" Avery tucked a loose strand of hair behind her ear and tapped the glass.

Maybe it was the remains of Mickey's ballads or Patsy's evocative vocals, but Susanna knew in that moment how much she loved her sister. How baby Avery, the surprise child, had saved them all.

She planted a kiss on her sister's forehead.

"Hey, what was that for?" Avery raised her chin, pressing her fingers over Susanna's kiss.

"For being you."

"Ah, it's nothing." Avery flicked her hand and made a face. "It's easy to be me." She laughed. "You paved the way, you know."

"I'm sorry I wasn't really around for you, Aves." Regret had a certain timeless sting.

*"Crazy for feeling so lonely . . ."*

"You were in college, working."

"I was too focused on Adam."

"Well, if you want to make it up to me, I saw some great shoes in the mall."

Susanna laughed. "I bet you did. Here I am being gushy and sentimental, and you work it toward shopping."

"Whatever. It's your guilt." Avery returned to her mop bucket. "I was just giving you options."

Clever girl. Mama's daughter for sure. "How about this? You get to pick another song." Susanna flashed her the last quarter from the jar.

"I'd rather have the shoes."

"Pick a song."

"Miranda Lambert. 'The House That Built Me.'"

Patsy's voice faded as Susanna searched the song list for "The House That Built Me" and a song she wanted to hear. Maybe something from the eighties.

Blake's smooth tenor awoke the melody in Susanna's heart. She hummed along, whispering the lyrics.

She was about to drop the next quarter down the jukebox's gullet when she noticed something different about the silver piece.

Stepping into the recessed lighting, Susanna examined the coin. It was imprinted with a young man's profile. A profile she recognized. One she'd sat next to on the back deck ten minutes ago.

Blake sang, *"God gave me you for the ups and downs . . ."*

She flipped the coin over.

*Brighton Kingdom. Prince Nathaniel. Quarter pound sterling.*

Nate. She stared at the coin with cold realization. Prince Nathaniel? Nate Kenneth was Prince Nathaniel?

She glanced toward the bathrooms, the kitchen, and the man-eating Dumpster. She'd called him bubba. Mama'd had him Cloroxing toilets. Scrubbing grease traps.

"Suz, what's wrong?" Avery passed by with the mop and bucket. "You look sick."

"No, no, I'm . . . I'm just tired." She tucked the coin in her pocket. Why didn't he tell her? "Let's get finished up, okay?"

Susanna pushed through the kitchen doors, her steam rising. He'd said nothing. Not a word. Even when she scribbled "A King's Garden" on her sketch pad. When she asked him tonight if they'd met before.

Was he laughing at her? At the family and their countrified Southern ways?

But he was the man who'd come to her aid. Out of the blue. The one who'd run off a vagrant and changed her flat tire, who'd driven her to the hospital and waited all night. Nate had *volunteered* to be Mama's Rib Shack lackey. He'd asked her to design the cottage's garden.

It made no sense. What was a Brighton prince doing on St. Simons Island? Susanna finished closing down the kitchen and snapping off lights just as Blake rounded the chorus one last time.

*God gave me you . . .*

# TEN

## Brighton, Stratton Palace

*L*eo, please rest." Campbell slipped Friday morning's *Liberty Press* from her husband's limp grasp. The head-lines would only upset him.

Hessenberg's Entailment in the Crown Prince's Hand?
Brighton's Search for Hessenberg Royal Family a Weak Effort
Prince Nathaniel's American Girlfriend!

A dark, grainy picture taken through a stand of trees showed a man talking to a woman. It might be Nathaniel. The man bore his resemblance. But it very well might *not* be Nathaniel.

Campbell angled the paper toward the window's light. The couple in the picture sat on a table of some kind under trickles of light, talking. Nothing more.

But the story proposed that the crown prince was falling in love with an American and testing Brighton law.

Blasted *Liberty Press*. Such an inflammatory story. What had become of Brighton's noble paper of truth and record? This story was about nothing more than hearsay and rumor.

The *LibP*'s publisher, Morris Alderman, had protected the princes while they were young, attending school and university. The world barely knew of Brighton's young royals.

Except for Nathaniel's debacle with Lady Adel—which even Morris couldn't contain—the crown prince remained backstage on the world's tabloid theater.

Until recent months as Leo's health failed and the end of the entail neared.

From his couch, Leo stirred. "Campbell?"

"What is it, love?" She tucked away the paper and smoothed her hand over her husband's gaunt, pale expression. The effects of the chemotherapy were evident in his thinning white hair and in the mocking red circles around his once brilliant blue eyes.

"Read . . . the dailies . . ." Leo tried to raise his hand. Tried to point to his desk where the Parliament marshal deposited Leo's government reports each morning.

But in the past few weeks, he had not had the strength to read them.

"Leo, you don't need to concern yourself with the dailies. Please, dear, rest. Don't upset yourself." She'd been reading the dailies, and she knew the news outmanned her husband's strength.

"What's upsetting me is your resistance. Please, Campbell, I might be sick but I am still the king. Now retrieve them for me and read."

Campbell surrendered. As she knew she would. Her whole life was built around her husband, her king, her civic duty. But she offered one last protest.

"Henry is perfectly capable of tending to Brighton's business while you recuperate."

"Of course. This is why I called for him to be prime minister."

Leo tapped his thin chest. "But I am still the king. It is my duty . . ." His voice faltered with weariness and frustration. "To know what is happening . . . in Brighton Kingdom."

"As you wish." Campbell crossed the room and retrieved his beloved dailies. She supposed it steadied him. To continue his routines. To stay his hand on his duties.

Leukemia had withered the once vital man, but no disease could diminish his devotion to Brighton. Being King Leopold V was the very essence of his person.

"I'll read, but you drink your broth." Campbell pulled a chair around to the couch bed where Leo reclined. A wash of morning light brightened the room, and she was grateful July came to Brighton with more sun than rain. "You need to keep up your strength."

She examined the dailies folders, purposefully choosing the government's social diary rather than a report on the economy. Or worse, speculation on the end of the 1914 entailment with Hessenberg.

Leo supported a European Union court for upholding the entail when Hessenberg lawyers petitioned for it to be dissolved, despite the implications to Brighton's economy.

But he'd endured vicious slander in the papers. Now it was Nathaniel's turn.

Oh, what had Nathaniel I and Prince Francis been thinking when they orchestrated that requirement in the entail? That royal families would magically live on and on even if dispersed across Europe for a century?

Campbell shifted her glance briefly from the dailies to her dying husband. Oh, Leo . . . what would they all do without his wisdom? "Campbell? I'm eating my broth, but you are not reading."

"Yes, right, well, let's see." She scanned the briefings on the social daily. "The finalist for future G8 Summit locations has been announced. Well, isn't this grand . . . Cathedral City made the list." Campbell checked for Leo's reaction. But his eyes were closed. His breath was quick and shallow. And he'd fallen asleep.

Leo. The lion. The stalwart man who captured the people's hearts, and hers, with his charm and athleticism, his confidence and valor in diplomacy.

He was too young to die at fifty-eight. But, oh, he remained a roaring lion, this one.

*Rest, Leo.* Campbell gathered up the dailies, renewing her will to be strong. For Leo. For her boys. For Brighton.

After tuning the radio to the classical station, she walked through the palace apartment to her office. She'd read the dailies over tea.

The brightness of the Queen's Office on the south side of Stratton Palace cheered her. The modern décor with accents from the Old World and monuments to the queens before her was her own design.

This room, with her assistants aiding her in correspondence and her diary schedule, was more than home to her. It was where she found her purpose. Where she understood why she married Leo.

Campbell perched on a cushioned window seat and stared through the white sheers to the thin line where a blue heaven kissed the green earth.

That would all change soon. Not just when summer gave way to fall and fall to winter, but her place in it. She'd been "Her Royal Highness" for thirty-four years. The wife of the crown prince, then the king. Mother of princes. A champion for their customs, as well as for change and charity. She'd miss her public persona when he died. But above all, she'd miss growing old with the man she'd married. Once she'd committed to him, to the marriage, she'd given her whole heart. Never looking back.

But this summer, she knew her world teetered when Leo

refused their annual trip to the country house, Parrsons. He wasn't feeling "up to it." Seeing him retreat from life forced her to take stock of the days ahead.

When he died, she'd become the dowager queen. At fifty-six. The papers would write, "Dowager Queen Campbell Visited the Schools Today."

Yet she felt like a schoolgirl herself. A slow-moving one, with more aches and pains this year than the last, but a schoolgirl nonetheless.

"Campbell?" The prime minister pressed through her door.

"Henry?" She locked up her emotions in her heart and greeted him. "Please come in."

"How is he?" Henry shook her hand as he offered a slight bow.

"This last chemo treatment has taken all of his strength." Campbell motioned for Henry to take the seat next to her desk.

"We're prepared for whatever comes our way, Campbell." He waited for her to walk around her desk and sit before taking the chair she offered.

"We? Who is we, Henry? The government?" She fidgeted with the buttons on her jacket sleeve.

"Yes, the government. The King's Office. I daresay even the people."

"But I am not ready, Henry," she said, firing her words with precision. "I daresay neither is Nathaniel. Nor Stephen."

Henry remained steady. Calm. "Nathaniel is stronger than you know." He motioned to the copy of the *LibP* on her desk. "You've seen the story?"

"I have and it's nothing but rubbish. Nathaniel's not been gone a fortnight and the paper announces he's in love? Last week they wagered he'd be engaged to Lady Genevieve. This week, it's an American lass. Are they trying to paint him as unstable? Unable to ascend the throne?"

"Your Majesty," Henry began with a formal compassion,

"these stories are not about truth. They are about speculation. About casting aspersions. It sells papers. Of course, we can't discount Morris Alderman's editorials calling for an independent Hessenberg and the demand to free up Brighton from decades of bailing them out of their financial woes."

Campbell's raw emotions were displayed by her firm hand against the smooth grain of her two-hundred-year-old desk. "The entailment cannot be changed just because we don't like what our forefathers did. The European Court denied Hessenberg's petition for it to be abolished."

"Your Majesty, I'm on your side. Hessenberg's side. Brighton's side. Above all, the law's side."

"Please, Henry, call me Campbell." He'd been her friend long before she became queen. Now more than ever, she needed her friends. "So what do we do?"

"Nothing, really, other than to get the King's Office to make a statement about the crown prince's marriage intentions."

"I know his mum would like to know of his intentions." Marriage for a royal heir wasn't an option. It was a must. Leo's failing health highlighted more than ever the need for Nathaniel, or Stephen, to produce an heir. To carry on Leo's legacy.

Henry's exhale collapsed him against the back of his chair. "We might accomplish two feats in one, you realize. We can solve the end of the entail requirement for a descendant of Prince Francis to take the throne and Nathaniel's marriage question."

"You speak of Lady Genevieve?"

"She's a descendant of Prince Francis." Henry shrugged, casting his dignified features with indifference.

"But she's not royalty." Leo would never stand for it, Campbell felt certain.

"My dear Campbell, there is no one in the duchy's royal line at the moment. Genevieve is a noble. Daughter of a lord. A lady in her own right. Nathaniel marries her, styles her a royal princess, and like that"—he snapped his fingers—"she becomes a princess and a Hessen duchess."

Campbell exhaled, conceding Henry's point. Beautiful, educated Lady Genevieve *would* make an excellent wife for Nathaniel. An Olympic champion, she owned a successful public relations firm. She'd make a most excellent queen. As well as grand duchess of Hessenberg.

Brightonians loved her. Hessens loved her.

"Campbell? What are you thinking?"

"That Nathaniel must consider marrying Ginny. They've been friends for years. Perhaps even more than friends in one season or another. She would be a good match for him, don't you think? Keep him on his toes." Perhaps if Leo awoke from his nap feeling strong, she'd broach the subject with him.

"Yes, but it's up to him. Did you fancy someone telling you who to love? Whom to marry?" The blue glint in his eyes dimmed.

"I didn't see the wisdom at the time, no. But now?" She gripped her hands together at her waist. What right did Henry have to walk in here and bring up past history?

"It's the twenty-first century, Campbell. No one can tell the prince whom to marry. It's not good for the monarchy."

Campbell picked up the newspaper, turning the image of the supposed prince and his American date toward Henry. "But we can tell him whom not to marry."

"Let's reserve that judgment until we know more." Henry stood for a closer look. "I can't even say for certain it's the prince."

Campbell wanted to agree, but even in the shadows, she knew it was Nathaniel. But her son's heart was not so easily won. She took comfort in that notion. Genevieve certainly hadn't captured his fancy after years of friendship. Certainly this girl did not win his affection in mere days. She lowered the paper to her lap.

"Henry, can you believe our grandparents were babies, perhaps not even born, when the entailment was signed?"

"It's hard to imagine, isn't it?"

"And when the war ended, no one cared about leases and entailments. The two North Sea nations were happy to have survived, clinging to one another like twin cousins. Glowering at Britain and Germany for the suffering we endured."

"But now people do care. The EU cares." Henry pressed forward in his chair, his bold countenance bending, revealing his concern for the kingdom's position. "If we find no royal heir to Prince Francis, a nation disappears from the face of the earth. The end of an ancient nation. The Grand Duchy Hessenberg becomes Province Hessenberg of Brighton."

"Are you for it, Henry? The province?"

"It doesn't matter what I want, or you, or Leo, or the nation. It matters what the entail dictates. I fear repercussions if we try to modify the statutes through parliamentary procedure. It sets a bad legal precedent. Call me a coward, but I believe the entailment must play out as designed. An heir must be present for their independence even if Brighton struggles in the midst. I'm ready to lead us through this as prime minister. If we start meddling, Campbell . . . ," he sighed, "who knows what trouble we'll unearth." He held her glance for a moment. "We could lose the monarchy. Lose everything we know and love about Brighton, our way of life . . ."

"Henry, you make it sound as if we could be destroyed."

"From the inside out. Yes. We could end up with a very different government and a very different Brighton, Campbell."

"But you won't let that happen, will you?"

"I'm doing all I can to keep the ship moving forward without stalling in the political waters. But I need Nathaniel on deck, doing his part. His youth is over."

"You think he should marry Lady Genevieve?"

Henry sighed as he stood and walked over to the windows. "It would make things very smooth indeed. But I can't ask him to marry a woman he doesn't love." He glanced back at her, and Campbell glimpsed the burden Henry carried so graciously.

"Shall we call Nathaniel home? What do you need him to do? PR with Hessenberg? Speak of how they are and always will be a great people. How Brighton cares and will make the most of our permanent partnership?"

"No need. Leave him be. Like I said, his youth is ending. This may be his last carefree holiday for a while. We can expect more bawdy speculation in the press. More hearsay and rumors. News he's engaged to an American followed by a call to end the entail because the crown prince intends to break the Brighton marriage act. Bookmakers publishing odds of whom he'll marry and when. There will be stories about abolishing the monarchy, calling for a republic to be formed."

"It all seems so impossible, Henry."

"At times it feels impossible. But there's a solution. I know it. I must believe it." He stood with a glance at his watch. "I must run. But, Campbell, don't let the *LibP* get you down." Henry strode toward the door, pausing on his way out. "Strap in, Campbell, the fun is just beginning."

# ELEVEN

S usanna packed up her laptop with the intent of showing Nate her initial garden plans, tucked his Brighton coin in her pocket, and picked up the printout from Friday's edition of Brighton's newspaper.

Prince Nathaniel's American girlfriend!

The grainy image barely reflected people, let alone Nate and Susanna. Without the headline, those dark forms sitting on top of a picnic table could be anyone.

But Susanna recognized the back of the Rib Shack. Someone had been watching them.

The story under the photo was full of political fire she didn't quite understand, and the whole thing fortified her resolve to confront Nate. The prince who'd brought his lie to her family's doorstep.

Backing out of the driveway, she rehearsed her confrontation speech—so, you're a prince?—while she paused at Rue's birdhouse mailbox. She'd not bothered to check it in a couple of days, and sure enough, it was full of coupons and pizza fliers. And a perfumed letter from Aunt Rue.

Susanna idled on the edge of the driveway as she tore open the pink flap, releasing the fragrance of roses along with the note.

Dearest Susanna,

You know I love you dearly and you are the best tenant ever, but I am going to need my little ole St. Simons cottage by October. Did Gracie tell you?

Rue went on to explain when she would arrive and why she needed the cottage for the fall—she just had to get out of Atlanta for a while—and signed the note, *Love and smooches, Auntie Rue.*

Susanna tossed the letter on the passenger seat. She knew when she rented the cottage this could happen, though Gracie had assured her it never would. "Aunt Rue cannot tear herself away from the Atlanta fashion scene."

But it was happening, and the timing felt more than a little coincidental. It felt nearly divine.

First Adam's confession. Then Daddy's heart attack, which somehow inspired her to quit her job. An impulsive but freeing move. Now she was losing her home. *What's up, Jesus?*

Susanna shifted into gear and glanced in the rearview mirror to see her home fading away in the gauzy morning light.

At twenty-nine, her life was getting a redesign. Just like Nate's old garden.

Speaking of—she'd researched him when she came home Wednesday night.

On Brighton's royal website, she'd found his official biography. He was the thirtieth crown prince of Brighton, straight in the line of King Stephen I, who wrested Brighton from Britain's King Henry VIII in 1545 and freed the small island nation from serfdom.

No wonder she felt like she peered into history when she looked into his eyes.

Nate had run his own communications company until he

resigned last year. Speculation claimed his ill father was preparing him to be king.

But other than a few staid stories and photos of him at a state dinner or royal function or cheering on his brother, Stephen, who played rugby for the national team, Nathaniel kept a low media profile.

Susanna did find one raunchy story about him from ten years ago. Every European tabloid covered his disastrous public marriage proposal to someone named Lady Adel Gardner, a beautiful brunette.

Susanna read scads of corny headlines like "Adel, Adel, Ring the Prince's Bell."

Then time seemed to stop until he resigned and joined the "enterprise," as the newspaper *Liberty Press* called the royal family.

About the time he resigned from his company, a Hessenberg tabloid, the *Informant*, ran stories and photos of Nate escorting a raven-haired beauty with pearly skin and vivid blue eyes about Cathedral City, Lady Genevieve Hawthorne.

In one of the pictures with Genevieve, Nathaniel wore his naval uniform, adorned with ribbons and medals, his arm wrapped loosely around her waist. They were surrounded by photographers. The headline read:

When a Prince Falls in Love, Brighton's Future Appears Bright

The whole atmosphere in the picture felt mythical. A fairy tale. Prince Nathaniel and Lady Genevieve existed in a cosmic bubble where only the beautiful and talented were invited. Ordinary people were remanded to the earth, feet planted on the plain old ground. And she, Susanna Jean Truitt, was about as ordinary as they come.

But oh, he looked amazing in his uniform. Was that it? Was she a sucker for a man in uniform?

Maybe, but she'd never be a sucker for all those photographic eyes on her. How did Nate endure being watched? Critics dissecting his every move. Commenting with scrutiny and judgment.

Then she found a headline all but announcing Nathaniel's engagement.

Prince Nathaniel's Marriage to Lady Genevieve Hawthorn Solves It All
Bookmakers Give 3-to-1 for End-of-Year Proposal

She had clicked off the internet at that point. He was practically engaged?

Mama didn't schedule him to work Thursday night, but Susanna was kind of missing him when she got home so she brought up the royal website again. Her first glimpse of him in royal finery made her heart clutch.

Then she spotted a link to an early edition of Friday's *Liberty Press* and nearly fell out of her chair when the image of her with Nate splashed on her screen.

Susanna downshifted, circling the Frederica Road roundabout on this Friday morning, her windows powered down, bales of hot gusts tumbling through her car.

Who took the picture of them the other night?

And how did it get into a Brighton paper?

Whipping into Nate's place, she parked in the same spot she had the other day, under an oak canopy, and fired out of the car, bothered, ready to confront.

"Susanna, fair lass, good to see you." Nate watched her from the front porch, leaning against a white column, relaxed in his board shorts and bare feet.

"Y–you too." The sight of him—The sound of him—His casual but oh-so-larger-than-life confidence dissolved her steely resolve.

"Come, sit in my garden." He waved her to the veranda. "Or what will be my garden."

"I brought some plans for you. Well, a few rough ones." Her voice sounded cardboard and fake. *Just be yourself. What's changed really?*

Everything.

Gathering her things, she formed a strategy. Work first, royal truth second. He waited for her with a cute, quirky smile on his face that made her feel all gummy inside.

She stumbled up the steps.

"Careful there." He offered his hand.

"I got it." But she tripped up the last step and nearly stumbled to her knees. She grabbed for his hand.

"Steady now. You all right?"

Clinging to him, she righted herself with a deep inhale. "I'm fine, except you seem to constantly rescue me." Then she . . . *bobbed.* Down then up. A weak, broken curtsy.

"Susanna." Nate held on, keeping her steady. "Are you all right? What were you doing?"

"Tricky thing . . ." She patted her knee. "Old volleyball injury." He was a prince. A flipping *prince.*

"Trick knee? Really? Because for a moment, I don't know, it looked like you were trying to curtsy."

"Curtsy, why would I curtsy?" *Susanna, hello, open door. Walk through it.*

"I've seen enough bad curtsies to know."

Okay, now he was messing with her. "Why didn't you tell me?"

"How did you find out?"

"Why didn't you tell me?"

"How did you find out?"

"I started this. Why didn't you tell me?"

He sighed, dug his hands into his pockets, and looked out over the lawn. "Because people change. By the way, you're American. You're not required to curtsy."

"Required? People are required to curtsy?"

"Yes." He squinted at her, the wind running under the veranda eaves and tugging at his thick, dark hair emptied Susanna of her breath. "It's etiquette. Honor. Respect."

"Honor?" Her sense of awe waned, and Susanna found her good-ol'-girl courage. "Did you honor me by lying, telling me your name was Nate Kenneth when you're actually Prince Nathaniel Henry Kenneth Mark Stratton of the House of Stratton?" She stood toe-to-toe, eye-to-eye with him on the veranda.

"Hey, I don't make the rules; I just live by them." His calm, flirty demeanor hardened. "I use Nate Kenneth when on personal travel."

"Okay, fine, it's your code name. But why didn't you tell me?"

"When would I have told you?"

"When we met. When I said, 'My name is Susanna Truitt,' and you should've said—"

"Hello, my name is Prince Nathaniel? You can't be serious."

"I am serious. It's who you are, isn't it?"

"I am also Nate Kenneth." He motioned with a grimace to where she'd just curtsied. "I didn't tell you because I liked being a regular bloke around you. We got on well. If I say, 'Oh hey, Suz, I'm a prince,' it turns all weird between us." Nate, rather Nathaniel, brushed around her toward the front door, his stride determined and angry.

"It's weird between us because you *didn't* tell me."

At the door, she inched past Jon, who all but blocked her back with his scowl. "His Majesty went to the garden."

"Thank you." Obviously, Jon had the prince's back. Susanna found him on the veranda, angled forward in a porch chair, arms propped on his legs. "Nate?"

He stood at the sound of her voice. "I'm sorry, Susanna."

"Yeah, me too." She slipped her laptop to the table and sat in the chair next to Nate. "I had this whole scenario worked out in my head, which sounded nothing like what came out of my mouth."

"I sounded like an arrogant prig." He shook his head, regret in his tone, in his expression. "Susanna, I didn't lie to you. I am Nate Kenneth. I have been since university. Believe me, Prince Nathaniel is not a name you want on your school records." He held up his hands like reading a check list. "David, Misha, Prince Nathaniel . . ." His droll expression made Susanna laugh.

"Yeah, I guess that does throw things off a bit."

"Being Nate Kenneth put me on equal footing with all the other students. Now that I'm in the family enterprise, Nate Kenneth is fading under Prince Nathaniel's auspicious light. It's rare I keep company with anyone, man or woman, who isn't aware of who I am or who I am to be. With you, I was just a man on holiday with a few chaps. Forgive me if I didn't want to ruin my chances to spend time with a beautiful, charming woman."

Beautiful? Charming? Was she mad at him? In light of his compliment, hiding his identity didn't seem so bad. "I was more helpless than beautiful or charming." Susanna retrieved the Brighton coin from her pocket. "This was in Mickey's tip jar."

"Ah, I see." Nate took the coin from her. "I just grabbed the change off my bureau. Didn't realize this was in the mix."

"I was about to put it in the jukebox when I noticed something different."

"This was the coin for my twenty-first birthday." He set the silver piece on the table. "I regret you feel I dishonored you in any way, Susanna. That was never my intent."

"I just would've liked to have known before I called you bubba or made you clean toilets."

He laughed. "But that's what I loved. Just a mate doing a job. Please tell me you didn't out me to your mum."

"I didn't."

"Good." Nate smiled. "I'd like another shift at the Shack. And I find your mum charming."

"Charming? Yeah, well, she's a piece of work."

"But an interesting piece of work."

"She'd consider that a high compliment." Susanna angled around for her laptop bag, pulling out the *Liberty Press* story. "I found this too."

Nate reached for the printout. "Yeah, Jon showed this to me during breakfast. I'm so sorry, Susanna."

"I don't understand. Who took this picture?"

"Good question."

"Did Jon? Or Liam?"

Nathaniel recoiled. "I certainly hope not. Their jobs depend on trust and discretion. We wonder if it might not have been someone from the Butler benefit. The *LibP* invites readers to send in photographs and such."

"Am I safe? My family?"

"Yes, love, yes. You are perfectly safe. This is about me. But be assured the King's Office and security detail are investigating." He fluttered the printout onto the table, his demeanor hardening a bit. "I'm sorry for the invasion into your life, love."

"No, no, it's fine." She waved off his apology, liking the sound of *love* on his tongue. "I couldn't read the whole story without a subscription. What's this deal with the Grand Duchy Hessenberg?"

"The 1914 Entailment is coming to an end."

"The one where Hessenberg was given, or whatever, to Brighton for a hundred years?" Susanna had to do a mental dig into her high school history archives. "The Grand Duke spent all of Hessenberg's money, or something like that, and he wasn't ready for the coming war. So he aligned with Brighton for protection."

"Ah, the American knows her history. Brilliant." Nate sat forward, the shadows of his expression fleeing in a light of authority. "The agreement ends soon and is causing great political strain."

"Because . . ." Susanna propped her chin in her hand and leaned into the summer sun, listening, seeing pieces of the prince in the man as he spoke.

"My great-great-grandfather and Prince Francis were cousins."

"As were all European royalty."

"At that time, yes." Nate settled back, relaxed. At home. "He felt for Francis when he came to him for help. But he feared compromising Brighton's sovereignty if he left Francis on the throne as the Grand Duke. So he demanded the surrender of all land and resources and the rights to the throne."

"If I recall, the German Kaiser and the Russian Tsar—"

"Wilhelm II and Nicolas II—"

"—were ticked at Francis for making the deal."

"Extremely. So much so his life was threatened. He fled to Sweden while the rest of the royal family hid in Brighton and England."

"He never married, right?"

"He did not, so his brother's eldest daughter was the heir apparent."

"And the end of the entail needs *her* or one of her descendants to step up."

Nathaniel laughed softly. "By George, I think she's got it. 'Tis true, love, yes. But the House of Augustine-Saxon has not been heard from in sixty years."

"How do you lose an entire royal family?"

"Two world wars for starters. Prince Francis's brothers, nieces, and nephews fled during the first war. During the second, they seemed to disappear entirely. My father believes they might have changed their names to get a fresh start."

"What happens to Hessenberg if there is no heir?"

"They will cease to be an independent nation and become a permanent part of Brighton."

Susanna let the notion sink in, developing a mental picture to match his words. "Wow, that's pretty serious."

"Many in Brighton Kingdom and Hessenberg agree."

"And you?"

"I agree with them. Brighton and Hessenberg are like two sisters adrift at sea. When one struggles, she reaches out to the other, thus dragging her down. They struggle, fight for their lives, and one, usually Brighton, manages to keep her head above water and save her sister. Then, a few years pass and down goes one again, usually Hessenberg, and Brighton reaches down to pull her out of her troubles. But not without nearly drowning herself." He exhaled and gazed toward the white-tipped waves barely visible above the low stone wall. "The theory is that if Hessenberg becomes sovereign again, both economies will rebound. They'll be looked at as independent trade and revenue resources."

"So they really need their independence."

"And they'd have it if there were no heir clause in the entail."

"No way around it?"

"Around it? No, love, but there is a way through it. Though it just might come with a very high cost." He'd ceased talking to her and spoke to himself, to the wind and waves, to God. "Know what?" He brought his focus to her with a spreading smile. "I don't want to talk politics. I'd much rather see your drawings for the garden. Did you bring a contract?" Nate stepped toward the screen door. "Jon, bring 'round the checks, please."

He dragged his chair next to Susanna's as she booted up her MacBook. "Am I forgiven?"

"For not telling me . . . yes, of course." When she peered at him, he was staring at her and for a moment, she understood the burden he carried.

"Nate"—she pressed her hand on his arm—"whatever the cost, do it. Or help the people do it, whatever it is. Perhaps you were born for such a time as this. God knew you'd be born thirty-two years ago. He knew you'd be the crown prince right when this entail thing ended. That whatever solution was needed, you'd be the man." She gave his shoulder a playful punch.

"Then he also knew I'd meet you." His posture remained stiff and forward, his focus glued to the computer.

"Meet me?" His confession sent a fiery flutter through her heart. "W–what do you mean?"

"I mean . . ." He hesitated, motioning to her computer. "Let's see your grand design."

Susanna launched her design software and opened "A King's Garden Project," aware of Nate, aware of what he'd just confessed, aware she might never understand his implication, *God also knew I'd meet you.* "Here we go . . . now, remember, it's rough."

"I'm sure it's excellent." He glanced at her, a softer light in his eyes now, looking both rugged and boyish with his thick bangs arching over his forehead, flitting in the occasional breeze.

"I called it 'A King's Garden' before I knew." Susanna shoved the computer toward him, giving him a better angle on the design.

"'Tis a perfect name." He cleared his throat as he contemplated her drawing, a thin sheen in his eyes. After a minute, he said, "It's lovely, Susanna." He tapped his chest. "I can feel it."

Quiet fell between them. Susanna studied him, wrestling with the notion that the man who changed her tire, drove her to the hospital, cleaned toilets to Mama's pure satisfaction was a European royal prince.

A mental shiver ended her imaginings. Out of context, it seemed impossible. She preferred the man sitting next to her on a Georgia veranda, with his bare toes curled in a spotlight of sun, to a prince.

"Do you know Prince William?" A random thought became a random question.

Nate peeked over at her with a sly grin. "He's a good mate, yes."

"Wow . . ."

"Wow? I get a blessing out and Prince William gets a *wow?*" His laugh returned him to the Nate she'd come to know in the last week.

A week? When did six days turn into forever?

"You got a *wow* from Mama for your bathroom-cleaning superpowers," she offered with an arched brow and a laugh.

"That's right." He pointed at her. "I'd like to see Will do such a bang-up job, winning over the glorious Miss Glo." He used Mama's staff nickname as if he'd grown up with her. "Hey, are you working tonight?" He shoved back from the table.

"No, I actually have the night off. If you liked the garden, I planned to work on finishing the design, start making calls, and get a crew lined up."

"It's Friday, Suz." Nate spread his arms like powerful, muscled wings. "Work is for the week. As your new client, I say we oil up the old bikes Liam discovered in the garage and go riding. Show me your beautiful island."

"A bike ride? Really?" She'd been intending to do that for such a long time.

"As your ace number-one client—"

"My only client."

"I demand you take me on a biking tour. What do you think? Put our woes and concerns behind us."

"I don't know," she said, looking at her laptop. "I'd planned on working. If you want this garden done soon . . ."

"I want it done when it's done." He made a funny jig toward the garage. "A biking we will go, huh? Please?"

"No, really, I can't." She shook her head. Resist. Or fall.

"Susanna." Nate bent over, his hands propped on the arms of her chair, hemming her in. "Do me the honor of spending the day with me."

The man personified every imagining she'd had of Prince Charming. A most sincere Prince Charming. The *no*, knocking around her thoughts, found no open doors. Her heart utterly refused to answer. "I know the perfect place to have lunch."

"Grand." Nate jumped up, taking her with him and catching her up in his arms. He whirled her around with a merry laugh.

# TWELVE

*D*usk came to St. Simons Island like a celestial kaleido-
scope, the heavens turning from one vibrant color to
another.

But the most beautiful sight to Nathaniel was the flowing
gold of Susanna's hair as she challenged him to a race and sped
off before she hollered go.

She greeted everyone she met on the day's outing as if they
were true friends indeed. She introduced him as her friend,
Nate Kenneth. But if he had his way, he'd be more than a friend.
Much more.

When they stopped for ice cream, he lost one of his two
scoops in the dirt when he failed to maneuver his bike down the
road with any kind of schoolboy skill.

She laughed over the incident for the next mile, head back,
mouth wide, and Nathaniel had half a mind to do the trick all
over again just to hear that sound.

He liked the picture of her right now best of all, sitting on a
carpet of green beneath the live oaks of Christ Church.

"This was a good idea, prince." She'd started calling him
"prince" somewhere along the way, and he rather liked it. It felt
personal. Sincere.

With a sigh, she closed her eyes, stretched out her legs, reclined back, and locked her hands behind her head.

"I have my moments of brilliance." Nathaniel rested his arms on his drawn-up knees and averted his gaze. It'd be so easy . . . to bend down . . . kiss her. But he could not. He knew better. Any such action would be entirely selfish, awakening a possible love he could never satisfy. In himself or Susanna.

She opened her eyes. "I forget the beauty and history of the island. Started taking it all for granted. The lighthouse and museum, Fort Frederica, the historic buildings." She sat up. "Know what's weird?"

"That pi is a mathematical term as well as something delicious to eat?"

She laughed and swatted at him. He caught her hand and the silk of her touch challenged his resolve not to pull her into him for a kiss.

"Goofy. Pi, p-i and pie, p-i-e, are not the same. They only sound the same. I meant what's weird about today."

"Not a thing." He released her hand. So far, this day was at the top of his all-time, best-ever list.

"Every once in a while, it'd hit me—he's a prince. A real honest-to-goodness prince. Then you'd do something whacky, like circle the roundabout until you were dizzy or lose your ice cream in the dirt. Or run into a tree." She made a face. "I'm still trying to figure that one out."

*Staring at you.*

"You had me laughing so hard I'd forget you were anyone or anything other than plain ol' Nate."

He regarded her for a moment. "Don't take this wrong, Susanna. I'm most sincere when I say this, but I do believe that is the nicest thing anyone has ever said to me."

"Fine, whatever, you so lie, Nate Kenneth." Susanna tipped her face to catch the last drop of sunlight, gentle, easy, relaxed.

"Don't make me google you to prove nicer things have been said about you."

"About me? Yes. To me? No. And you can't find those words on the internet." Gone was the tentative woman on his porch this afternoon. She surged stronger with each hour in the sun, with each push of her bicycle pedal.

"Nate, don't you ever consider who you are and why God called you?" Susanna turned to him, sitting cross-legged, touching knees to knees. "I used to climb out of my bedroom window, sit on the roof and stare at the stars, thinking, 'I'm Susanna Truitt, born on St. Simons, for some purpose. I'm not an accident.'"

Her intensity disturbed his conviction that he wasn't chosen by God but rather by birth order and parentage.

"But *did* God call me? Or men? What choice did I have? The first born of a king. My forefathers, along with all the kings of Europe, thought they were God ordained, above it all. We know now, that's not the case."

"What? Of course you're called by God. I'm called by God. To do what, I don't know, but I'm just as called as you." He envied the confidence in her voice. He longed to drink from her well. "You are no accident. Isn't there some place in Brighton history where . . . I don't know . . . the family line took a turn? A second born became king? Or a nephew? Because the king had no children? Like that Grand Duke, Prince Francis."

"Several times. In the last two centuries it happened twice, landing my great-great-grandfather as heir."

"Nathaniel I?"

"What are you driving at, Susanna?"

"Your great-great-grandpa wasn't supposed to be king, but he was, and he orchestrated the entail with Hessenberg."

"And a hundred years later, here I am, the future King Nathaniel II, playing a pivotal role at the end of the agreement. I see what you're driving at, but—"

"It's no accident, Nate. You are in a position to impact two nations. To give independence to one of them. How incredible." She breathed out a soft chuckle as she plucked up blades of grass. "People will do the craziest things to have their names recorded in history."

"There are plenty of forgettable princes."

"But not you. Do you realize how selfless you can be? You have nothing to lose."

The conversation challenged him. Shoved him out of his well-worn, comfortable notion that he was the lowest of blokes because his high-ranking birth order denied him any choices.

"Susanna, we are all called to be selfless, to serve our fellow man, regardless of rank or birth order or where our names end up in history."

"True, but it takes a lifetime and, I daresay, a kiss from the Holy Spirit for most of us to gain that understanding. You were born knowing your destiny. Most people never know. So *what* is easy for you. Well, *easier.*"

He rocked a solid laugh. "Might I borrow your eyes and ears for a while? You mistake us for superheroes. Princes doubt their destiny as much as any human. We are just as subject to selfishness and doubt as anyone, if not more. Of wanting to make a mark in the world because of who he is as a man, not a prince. Not because of his family. He's afraid he'll never be completely sure of his calling. He's selfish of his time, his emotions, his talents because, blast it all, the government, the monarchy, the people want him, tug on him. He's afraid if he surrenders for one moment he'll never, ever get to be his true self again. If he's ever been his true self at all."

"Or, he can flip that all around in his head and realize being a prince is his true self. That he's got a leg up on knowing who he is and what he was born to do."

"So you stayed twelve years with a man who didn't love you because you thought it was your destiny?" His words fell to the ground like hot rocks. Too late to retrieve them now. She'd bothered him, poked at him, so he wanted to poke back. Yet she was being kind. He was perfectly rude. "Susanna, I'm sorry, my comment was over the line."

"But you're right." She sighed, turning away to stretch out on the lawn again. "I stayed because I wanted what you have. A sense of who I was and where I was going. Right or wrong, being Adam Peters's fiancée gave me a road map to follow." She stared at the stars. "Think of all the good you can do, Nate. How you can impact your people, the nations, for the Lord."

"I'm not sure God uses people like me. Men in high, visible places. He likes men and women most people can't see. Or haven't ever heard of."

"He'll use any humble, willing heart, Nate." She sat up. "Look at David and Solomon, your ancestor King Stephen. He went for God, didn't he? Maybe God doesn't use men like you because you're too busy trying to be someone else."

Mercy and all the saints, how did she do it? Crawled into his head, sorted through his thoughts, tossed away the rubbish, and polished the gems? "If he's looking for humble hearts, then he's found one in you, Susanna."

"Well, if humble means broken . . ." She picked at the grass blades, tossing a few to the wind. "I'm preaching to myself here. I've got to figure out where my life goes from here. Breaking up with Adam doesn't change who God is or his plan for me."

"Tell you what . . . Why don't we both tell God we are one hundred percent available to him?" He didn't wait for her to respond but slipped his hands under hers and scooted close.

She gripped her fingers with his, and already he knew he'd hate her letting go. "Susanna, you impacted a nation because you impacted me."

"Because *you* impacted me." She firmed her grasp around his. "Maybe it wasn't a coincidence we met that night at the tree."

"No, perhaps not." He released his heart to tumble headlong toward hers.

She looked up, checking the fading twilight. "Better get going soon. We'll be riding home in the dark."

"Might I pray? Or shall you?" Nathaniel had returned to his faith, to the Lord, last year, but praying aloud still proved a challenge.

"I'll do it." She inhaled. Exhaled. "Lord, here we are, Nate and me. One hundred percent available. We don't know what's ahead, but you do. Whatever it is, we'll love it because you love us. And you are good."

When her amen ended the prayer, a sweet breeze brushed between them. The tip of Susanna's hair fluttered over his arm with the scent of vanilla. Neither one of them moved to release their hands.

With her prayer and her touch, Nathaniel felt certain he'd just experienced a little bit of heaven on earth.

# THIRTEEN

He was full. In every way. The Rib Shack food satisfied his sun-and-surf-fed appetite. The laughter and storytelling around the table slaked his hunger for companions. The music, the lights, the lullaby of rain on the tin roof contented him so he thought he might just put down roots right where he sat.

Then Susanna passed by or brushed against him and fired up his longings and dreams.

It had been a week since their bicycle ride and prayer on the Christ Church grounds. He'd been with Susanna every day since. At church. At his cottage reviewing her updated garden plans. At the Rib Shack when he pulled an evening shift.

He was starting to know how it felt to be in love, though he'd never felt quite like this before. He'd experienced fluttering emotions, runaway thoughts, and numbed ambitions for anyone or anything but the girl of his eye, but this sense of peace and purpose, of clarity, of freedom to be himself, of selfless devotion was new to him.

And he loved it.

Yet it wasn't just Susanna that made him feel at home in this foreign place; it was her whole family. Gib, Glo, Avery. The multitudes of relatives and friends.

He'd been late to Sunday dinner with the family at the Rib Shack because Jonathan stopped him. "You're falling for her, mate. I can see it. You cannot continue to see her."

Yet when Nathaniel refused to stand her up or call to cancel, Jon demanded he tell Susanna the *whole* truth.

To what end? Was Jonathan concerned about Nathaniel's heart or Susanna's? Nathaniel reassured his aide that Susanna considered them no more than friends. Once he returned home, his heart was the only thing that would have to heal. Susanna was two weeks away from her breakup with Adam. She had no romantic interest in Nathaniel.

But as she sat beside him at the table, her arm against his, laughing with her friend Gracie and her cousin Kendall about a girl's-gone-bad shopping trip to New York City, he wondered if she did care for him. Perhaps just a wee bit.

Listening to her tale, Nathaniel decided he loved how Susanna found the silver thread in every story. How she saw the silver thread in him.

Peeking at her, scooping his wind-tangled hair from his forehead, he tried to envision how he would confess the whole truth, as Jon put it.

*There are certain expectations of future kings. I'm bound, you see, by law . . .*

At Nathaniel's back, thunder rumbled over the Atlantic. He could hear the southern Atlantic waves roaring toward the beach. And four thousand miles away, North Sea waves crashed against Brighton's shores, and it seemed like a different time and place.

He'd been disturbed all afternoon with the notion of returning home. As he tuned into the waves and thunder, he sensed a nagging urgency.

Up on Mickey's stage, Susanna's Uncle Hudson gathered his band to tune up, a fun but dissonant blend of a banjo, guitar, and fiddle.

He stepped up to the mic with a toothpick protruding from the side of his lips. "Let's make some music." Tapping his toe, he counted off—a one, two, three, four—and plucked a lively tune.

He sang about love and life with a nasal whine, his fingers flowing over the banjo strings. The guitar player found a sweet harmony, and a fourth man jumped up to clank a set of spoons against his thigh.

Susanna's grandparents two-stepped around the deck.

Nathaniel exhaled and reached to wrap Susanna in his arms when he pulled up short, realizing what he was doing. This place made him completely forget himself. Something he'd not done in a very long time. If ever.

He loved being part of the family, from the inside looking out, eating barbecue on Sunday nights, wearing shorts and flip-flops. He was in his first year of university before he'd dined without dressing. Jacket and tie.

A banjo player had never played at an evening meal. Spoons were used exclusively for sipping soup and digging out pudding. And the employees—the servants—never scooted up to the same table as the family.

But if he changed the course of his life, moved to St. Simons Island, home would never be the same. He'd be denying Dad and Mum, his grandparents, all he knew about life and himself. He'd be denying his destiny.

He cut a side glance at Susanna. How could he walk away from her, though? She'd challenged him, made him look at his life differently.

Two more men arrived with instrument cases and joined Uncle Hudson's banjo with an upright bass and a mandolin. With the full band going, cousin Silas dragged Susanna onto the dance floor, spinning her around to the music. She tipped her head back with a pitch-perfect yelp, her hair cascading over her shoulders like a sun-kissed waterfall.

*Oh, Susanna.*

When she forgot herself, Susanna was most beautiful. Because she laughed freely, spoke openly. Far too often she treaded with caution, peering at life with timidity. Afraid to let go.

Beneath his Oxford shirt, Nathaniel's heart thudded with love. Impossible love. If he chose her, he'd have to deny every other thing about himself. A larger and more daunting consequence than most sons who were poised to take over the family enterprise.

But if he chose his destiny, he denied himself of her. What an unbearable choice. The song ended, and Silas delivered Susanna back to the table, turning her around one last time so she dropped into Nathaniel's arms.

This time he didn't resist her. She fell against his chest, along with the perfume of fresh flowers, and he cradled her there, unwilling to let her go.

He'd come to Georgia with all his walls in place, but the blond American with wisdom in her soul hurdled over his barriers and caught him completely unaware.

Blast it all. Jon was right. He had to tell her. Tonight. If not tonight, soon. Very soon.

"Nate?" Glo put her plate down, wiped her hands on her napkin, and sashayed toward him. "Did you get enough to eat?" She pressed her hands on his shoulders. "How's my favorite dishwasher? The prince of suds."

Susanna glanced back, her eyes twinkling, then slipped away from him, gathering her hair off her neck.

"Ask her to dance, Nate." Avery dropped to the bench next to Susanna and squeezed into her so she fell against Nathaniel. "It's a rainy, romantic night." She leaned around him. "Play something slow, Uncle Hud."

"Aves, come on." Susanna shoved her back. "Ever hear of personal space?"

But the music started. A slow, gentle sound that matched the rain. "Susanna." Nathaniel offered her his hand. This might be his one and only chance. "Would you care to dance?"

When she took his hand, he turned her into him and lightly pressed his hand to her back. She fit with him, swaying easily to his steps.

"Having fun?" she asked, her chin resting on his shoulder.

"More than the prince of suds deserves."

She laughed. "I nearly spit when Mama said that."

"Does she know?"

"I've not said a word. Are you kidding? Mama would be the one sending pictures to the *Liberty Press*. 'Look at my daughter, y'all, friends with a prince.'"

"You are beautiful, Susanna." Nathaniel leaned down to see her face, tracing his finger over her warm check, sweeping aside wild strands of her hair caught in the breeze. His confession settled in her eyes just before she tucked her cheek against his shoulder. Nathaniel sighed and let the song take over.

When she exhaled against him, his heart trumpeted. *Tell her.* Any more of these intimate moments and Nathaniel would be completely defrauding her.

"M—might I talk with you in private?"

She studied his face. "Sure." She motioned toward the beach. "The rain's stopped. Want to walk?"

He took her hand and led her down the wet, glistening steps.

"You seem serious." Susanna bumped into him as they walked the soggy path to the beach, their faces set against the thick, salty air.

"Ah, no, love, I'm enjoying myself. Very much."

"Me too." She brushed her palm against an overgrown palmetto. Dew splashed on his hot skin.

When they hit the beach, Nathaniel released her hand. How did one tell a girl he could never love her?

"Susanna." He slowed with a glance back at the dancing, twinkling Rib Shack deck. "These two weeks … have been amazing for me."

"Me too. You really did rescue me. I'm not sure what I would've done without you. I'm not talking about flat tires and rides to the hospital either."

"Right, right …" He brushed his hands along the side seam of his shorts. "I–I want to talk to you … about something." Rubbish, how did he confess the constraints of his royal position without sounding like a royal prig? Straight up, but with kindness. "Susanna, there's a Brighton law … one for the many but that affects only a few."

She started down the beach, into the wind. "You do sound serious."

"More sad than serious." He fell in step with her.

"Okay, something has you all knotted up." She turned around, walked backward in front of him. "Out with it, Nate."

"You see, this law … it's been around for over two hundred years. It's to protect the monarchy, the people, though I tell you I think its true design is to harm the one in love."

"Love? What are you talking about? Don't make me look it up on the internet."

"Please, do. Then I don't have to tell you."

"Tell me what?" She faced forward again, faced the dew in the air.

"The Brighton Marriage Act of 1792." He came back to where she stood. "A royal in line to the throne cannot marry a foreigner. Royal spouses must be Brighton born and bred. Preferably of nobility. But commoners are welcome."

"What?" Her shrill response punctured the night. His barbecue dinner soured in his belly. "You brought me out here to tell me you can't *marry* me?"

"It's the law, Susanna. A two-hundred-year-old law."

"What in the world does it have to do with me?" She walked off, her long strides quickly taking her into the night shadows.

He saw this going entirely differently. "The Crown, you see, along with the Parliament enacted a law that restricted royals in line for the throne from marrying into the royal houses of Europe after a crown prince married the niece of King Louis XVI. She used her influence to send Brighton's army to help her uncle in the French Revolution and nearly destroyed our military."

His rushed words fell like stones to the sand. Nathaniel filled his lungs with the moist, saline air. He'd done his duty. Confessed. But it was no good for his soul.

He walked beside her, waiting. She said nothing.

"Susanna?"

"Shhh, I'm trying to take this all in. You dragged me out to the beach to tell me you couldn't marry me."

"Yes."

"Did I miss something? When did we ever talk about marriage?"

"I wanted to be honest."

"You've not wooed me or kissed me. I don't recall any confessions of love, a sure-fire requirement for marriage. You've flirted a little and maybe I flirted back, but I do *not* remember any talk of marriage."

"I guess I rather cut to the chase."

"Forget the chase, you started at the finish line." He let her rail because he deserved it. "So you confess to me something that's not even an issue? Are you trying to hurt me? Humiliate me?"

"Blast it, no. I thought my affection for you had become quite obvious. Since hiding my true identity didn't sit well with you, I decided I'd confess my romantic restrictions." Blast Jon, urging him to tell her the whole truth. What did he know?

"Romantic restrictions?"

"For lack of a better phrase, yes."

"Nate, meeting you has been the highlight of my summer. I needed you. And I think you might have needed me. But what's hitting me in the gut right now is that two weeks ago, on this very beach, the man I thought I was going to marry dumped me. Now, tonight, the man I had no intention of marrying *also* dumps me." She started down the beach. In the opposite direction. Just as the rain began again. "Perfect." She tipped her face to the heavens, arms wide.

"Susanna, what would you have me do. Not tell you?" Nathaniel ran after her, struggling for solid footing in the wet sand. "Let things go on, then just leave you without a word, have you read in the news I'm engaged to some other woman?"

"Nate, brother, you got yourself all knotted up here for nothing." Rain collected in the contours of her face and dripped from her chin. "It's going to snow on St. Simons before I fall in love again." She cupped her hands around her mouth. "Hear that, Lord? Snow. Send snow when it's time to fall in love, okay?" She peered at Nate, and he could see her glistening eyes in the refracted light from the Rib Shack deck. "So, see, Nate, you're off the hook. No snow. No love. It hasn't snowed in this part of Georgia for . . . well, almost a hundred years." She darted up the beach toward the Rib Shack, where the music made its way through the pines and palmettos.

"Susanna, wait. Please." He scooted around in front of her, running backward. "Were I not heir to the throne, I'd be saying different things to you right now. My feelings for you had to show, and I wanted you to understand why I could not pursue you." He reached for her, drawing her to a stop.

But she stared straight ahead, the rain soaking her hair, her skin, her clothes.

"Susanna?"

In the shadows, he couldn't see her face or read her expression.

Then a fast swat on his arm started him. "You're such a dork. Don't ever do that to me again."

"I'm a dork, yes. His Royal Highness, Prince Dork. And I'll never do that again. Ever." Relief flooded every hollow part of him.

"Thank you for telling me, but I expected you to go home and live your life. I never once imagined I'd be a part of it."

"Never once?" Her confession stung a bit more than he might have imagined. But she was wiser than her years.

"I'm getting soaked. Better get to the deck. It's really starting to come down now."

Together they dashed for the Rib Shack, Susanna on her side of the path, Nathaniel on his.

They were nearly to the music and the lights when his phone went off. Jonathan.

"Hello, lad—"

"Nathaniel, it's your father." The music faded. The lights dimmed. And his heart felt cold with the rain.

"Nate?" Susanna said when he ended the call.

"I've got to go, Susanna." He chose the path around the deck to the car park and the SUV. "That was Jon. My father has died."

Part Two

The Problem

# FOURTEEN

## December, St. Simons Island

*I* understand." Susanna held the phone beneath her chin so her discouraged exhale didn't echo in the man's ear. "I appreciate your time, Mr. Flynn. It was an honor to present you with a proposal."

She hung up and tossed her phone to her desk as she rocked back in the rickety old chair, pressing her hands over her eyes and resisting the urge to scream.

But when she couldn't contain her frustration any longer, she let loose a rebel yell and fired out of her chair, banging her shin against the side of the desk. Of course. How symbolic. Now she really wanted to scream. She hobbled to her office door and stepped out onto the fire escape.

"What in blazes is going on?"

The sun barely acknowledged her with a fast wink between two drifting clouds across a lofty blue perch. How was she ever going to get her life going if *nothing* ever came together?

She returned to the closet-sized office she rented from a group of lawyers, a square hovel that had once been an outside servants' entrance on the top floor of a refurbished antebellum. The room had one window—the narrow transom above the door.

Her drafting table and one small bookshelf barely fit in the ten-by-ten space. Using the bathroom required a trek down the fire escape, through the kitchen, past the senior lawyer's office, and down a long tiled hallway. Her heels resounded the entire trip, announcing her destination.

*Susanna's on her way to the bathroom.*

*Susanna's on her way to the bathroom.*

It was embarrassing. Worse, she paid eight hundred dollars a month for this box, which served as a boiler room in August and September and now was a freezer in December. How could a third-floor room on a Georgia island get so cold?

She wore a coat all day except between noon and two when the transom managed to capture the tail end of the sun and warm the place up.

Susanna turned her portable heater on and stretched her cold hands toward the first blast of heat. The initials days of December settled on St. Simons Island with a frost that refused to let go. But there were no snow predictions in the forecast. Thank goodness.

Yet the chill in the air congealed with the chill in her heart. Five months after Nate had left, she missed him. Her heart craved his warmth, his friendship, his presence.

She'd finished his garden. A framed and matted image of it hung on her wall. Sometimes on the slow afternoons when even her email didn't talk to her, she stared at her rendering of "A King's Garden" and mentally added two lovers to the garden bench.

*Oh, Nate, how did you get under my skin?*

He'd paid her in full, up front, and sent a bonus when the job was complete. It was the sum of two gardens, but when she tried to return the money, Jonathan refused to give her a wire transfer number.

The money afforded her this grand, opulent office (ha!) and new computer, but not one job had come her way since. She made ends meet by getting her hands dirty—working at the Rib Shack and taking on small landscaping jobs that required little to no technical design.

Yet the worst part of her life wasn't her career. It was missing him. Not Adam, the man she'd planned to marry, but Nate, the man she never planned to marry. Nor ever could.

After he left, she did her own research on the Brighton Marriage Act of 1792. Sure enough, the boy was telling the truth. No foreigners were allowed to marry into the line of the throne.

She fell against her desk. "God, I've got nothing. Nothing." A rush of tears came quickly, and she did nothing to stop them.

The depth of her nothingness even followed her as she went house hunting. Susanna had yet to find a new place. Aunt Rue had arrived in October as promised, graciously letting Susanna bunk with her for two months. But by the amount of Christmas baking and decorating Rue was doing, Susanna knew she'd need every inch of the cottage to quarter her holiday guests.

"I've got *nothing*." She eased down to the floor. All her plans had failed. "I–I'm one hundred percent available to you." She reconfirmed the offering she'd made to God that day on the Christ Church lawn with Nate. "W–who do you have like me? No husband or children, no career, no one needing or expecting me. Well, Mama, to run the back of the house, but shoot, she's got Catfish and Bristol to take my place. Gladly."

Susanna was, frankly, a girl who could go anywhere and do anything the Lord needed.

"Jesus, I have to believe you are so good, whatever you have me do, I'll love it." Susanna clung to the rise of peace that came with her surrender. "I have to believe . . ."

She drank of the peace, then hopped up and danced a little jig as she shimmied over to turn on the radio.

Powering it up to a Christmas station, she danced across the office, about to belt out "Hark the Herald," when Gage darkened her doorway.

"What are you doing here?" Wasn't this embarrassing? She cleared her throat and glanced at her desk, reaching for the mouse to minimize her Euchre game. She was losing anyway. Big surprise.

"Not having as much fun as you." He grinned and came the rest of the way into the office.

"You should know better than to sneak up on people." She sat at her desk, though she'd rather keep dancing. "What do you want?"

Gage had been after her for the last few months to work for him again. She'd resisted. Dread crept over her heart, mocking her joy. Was this God's answer to her surrender? Go to work for Gage? *Lord, wait now . . .*

"I just came by to let you know you're off the hook." He tipped his head to emphasize his point, then reached for the Super Ball she kept on top of her empty pencil canister. He bounced it against the dry, uneven hardwood.

"You hired someone else?" She *was* willing to work with him again. Wasn't she? If the Lord wanted. Sure. Because God was good and she trusted him. Besides, anything to get her career going, to move her life one inch down the road.

"I hired a landscape architect two weeks ago. She moved down from Charleston this weekend with a client in her hip pocket. We sealed the deal with them an hour ago. So"—he raised his hands to the tiny office—"blessings to you and your itty-bitty space." He kept the ball bouncing in an even rhythm. Thud against the floor. Smack against his palm.

Susanna came around and snatched the ball mid-bounce. "Just like that? You give up on me?"

"Hey, you're the one who quit. You're the one who put me off for months."

"But you didn't give me a chance to change my mind."

"I asked you a half-dozen times. Even sent you a couple of jobs. How'd they work out?"

She bounced the ball against the floor. "They decided to go in another direction."

"All of them?" Gage couldn't look more incredulous. "Suz, those jobs were shoo-ins."

"You sent me three friends of Mrs. Butler's. She still hates me from the summer, taking her prize guest away."

"You think I'm that big of a jack wagon? That I'd send you jobs she'd sabotage? Besides, she didn't know the prince left with you."

"She must know. I've run into her twice, and she gives me the evil eye." Susanna glared at him with a curled lip. "Trust me, I know the look. And if she does know, I'll never get a job on this island." What was she confessing? "Mrs. Butler has her nose in every garden and landscape project on the island, down to south Florida, up to north Georgia, to infinity and beyond." The thud and smack of the ball had a certain, soothing sound. *This* was why she had the Super Ball in the first place. To bounce off tension.

"You want me to talk to her?"

"No, yes . . ." She caught the ball and pointed at him. "Only if it comes up in natural conversation." She returned the Super Ball to the pencil canister. "I'm glad you hired someone. You deserve to have success."

Gage's stance softened. He was handsome in his white shirt, dark tie, and gelled hair. "Susanna, I've been thinking maybe you and I—"

The office door butted open, and Gracie tripped inside, along with a hearty gush of cold air and a large box in her hands. "Merry Christmas, Suz. Time to decorate this mousetrap you call an office . . . Gage . . ." Gracie gave him the once over as she dropped the box to the floor and took out a tiny Christmas tree. "What are you doing here?"

"Came to see Susanna."

"Again I ask, *what* are you doing here?" Gracie and Gage dated once in high school. He broke up with her one second before she was going to tell *him* "it's not working," and she'd never forgiven him. She slapped the plastic evergreen on the corner of Susanna's desk.

"Again, I *came* to see Susanna. What are *you* doing here?"

The thin, bare limbs of the fake tree trembled. A Charlie Brown tree. Just what this office needed. Hands on her waist, Gracie stood back to examine the tree, then she faced Susanna. "Did he tell you, huh? The big mouth. Couldn't wait... had to run over here and tell you."

"Gracie," Gage said, his tone low and warning as he gave her a familiar, knowing look. *What's with that?* "I came to talk to her about—"

"Yeah, he told me," Susanna said.

"He did? You don't look upset. I know you've been handling all this so well, but I expected you to be at least aggravated." Gracie peeled off a strip of duct tape and anchored the tree stand to the desk. "I got some fake snow to cover that up."

"Why would I be upset?" Susanna peered inside the Christmas box. Come to think of it, a bit of holiday decorating would cheer her up. She picked up a string of silver tinsel and wrapped it around her neck. "He tried to get me back but I refused. I don't blame him."

"What?" Gracie grabbed her arms, turning Susanna toward her. "When did he ever try to get you back?"

"Since the summer."

"Since the summer? Are you kidding me? You never said a word. Girl, I'm about to take away your best-friend card."

"What? I said a million words. You cheered me on. 'Go, girl, tell him no, girl.'"

"When did I ever?" Gracie glanced at her before retrieving cottony snow drape from the box.

"Gracie, think now before you—"

"Gage, shhhh." Gracie shot him a curled-lip look. "This is girl-friend talk. She never told me Adam tried to get her back."

"And there you go . . ." Gage stepped back, grinning, arms folded. "After this you can never call me a big mouth again."

"Adam?" Susanna twisted the tinsel around her fingers. "I'm talking about Gage trying to get me to work for him again. What are *you* talking about?"

"Yeah, Gracie, what *are* you talking about?" Gage shoved aside Susanna's pencil canister and collection of McDonald's toys to perch on the edge of her desk. "I came to tell her I'd finally hired a landscape architect."

"Oh." Gracie's cheeks flushed pink. A rare and unusual sight.

"Gracie, what's this about Adam?" Five minutes ago, Susanna was confident about throwing her life into God's hands. He had her back and she could do anything he called her to do. But news about Adam speared her confidence with doubt.

Gracie buried her attention in the Christmas box. "Won't these white lights brighten things up around here?"

"Gracie."

"You tell her." She shot up and cut a pleading glance toward Gage.

"No way. You started this."

"Oh, for crying out loud," Susanna said. "I don't care who started it, but someone had better finish it."

"Adam's getting married." Gracie and Gage. In harmony.

"Married?" Susanna unwound the tinsel and let it slither back into the box. "To Sheree?"

"Yeah, so you knew?" Gracie worked the knots from a string of lights.

"He told me about her when we broke up." Susanna motioned to the Christmas box. "Is that what this is about?"

"No, I really think this office needs some Christmas cheer."
Gracie dropped the lights. "I'm so sorry, Suz."

"Don't be. I'm glad you told me. I'd find out sooner or later."

So Adam was moving on. Getting married.

Susanna didn't have a place to live, but she'd surrendered her
last offering to the Lord. Her time. Her will. Her very heart. No
sense taking it back now. If all else failed, she knew of a good spot
in the woods next to Aurora.

# Brighton

Snow in early December put Nathaniel in a festive spirit, opened
his heart for the Christmas season, and for a moment allowed
him to forget the weight of preparing for his coronation.

He grieved his father still, wishing he could stride down the
hall to ask him questions, glean from his wisdom. He longed for
his strength and experience, his knowledge of the kingdom, of
the family, of the entail.

This time next month, Nathaniel would be king. Regent of the
Brighton Kingdom, the de facto Archduke of the Grand Duchy
Hessenberg, head of the state and constitutional monarchy.

Ten million citizens under his care. Ten million hearts fun-
neled into one—his. He must be an advocate for them all. Even
the rumbling Hessens whose demand for their independence
increased every day.

But they were all bound by the decisions of their forefathers
and the ironclad entail. One of the latest headlines declared
Brighton had stolen the rights to Hessenberg. Another declared
that the royal family from the House of Augustine-Saxon had been
murdered or exiled so far away they'd never be found again.

And yet, somehow, in the midst of the recent turmoil, the lovely Lady Genevieve came to the surface, a bright star willing to "save the day."

Recently, Nathaniel resolved, if it came down to it, he would sacrifice himself, his heart, for the welfare of Brighton and independence of Hessenberg and marry Ginny.

Shouts from the staff's children playing in the fresh snow beneath his window drew his attention from his worries. Gladly, Nathaniel shoved away from his desk for the window.

*Whoa* . . . Young Seamus Mackinder plastered pretty Sarah Warren with a fat snowball. She chased him 'round a tree, tackled him, and pushed his face beneath the snow.

*Atta, girl. Don't let the lads best you.*

He wanted to be out there with them, laughing and forgetting how alone he felt. He'd felt isolated on occasion. Distinctly different from his mates, as if he walked alongside them but on a different path.

Yet he never felt as if he were on the outside looking in. But since Dad's funeral, *that* brand of aloneness hit him. Along with a bit of fear.

He was the king. Walking in the giant footsteps of his father, grandfather, and every Stratton king back to King Stephen I.

Dad's death took living history with it. The people looked to Nathaniel as king. But to whom did he look? The pondering question overwhelmed him and more and more brought him to his knees.

Prayer was his saving grace.

The children jumped on their sleds and headed down the hill—just like Nathaniel and Stephen had done so many times.

But there was work to be done. Dailies to review, emails to read, newspapers to ignore.

Nathaniel sat at his desk, sipped his coffee, and scanned the *Daily Times* and *Hessen Today* headlines.

They were dry, more businesslike papers. Nathaniel had asked Jon to stop bringing him the *LibP* and the *Informant*.

The *LibP* read like a revolutionary propaganda sheet, and the *Informant* remained true to its tabloid origins, turning every little thing into a scandal.

By their assertions, Nathaniel and Lady Genevieve would be engaged, if not married, and their first child on the way by the end for the year. What was the term the *Informant* used? "Looking for an heir bump."

Horrid.

However, Jon informed him that the odds were now at fifty-to-one that Nathaniel would not propose to Lady Genevieve by Christmas. If he were a betting man, he'd take those odds.

The mantel clock chimed, and Nathaniel focused on the palace Christmas schedule, which required his approval.

Then he reviewed his weekly diary and answered a few emails before he shoved back from his desk, unable to shake the yearning to be out in the snow.

A good brisk walk ought to satisfy.

He headed for his private living quarters, knowing the subtle disturbance in his heart was about more than being king or wanting to play in the snow like a child.

Since he'd come home from St. Simons Island, he'd struggled with the quiet moments in his life.

Because that's when he thought of *her.* Five months had passed since he'd left her standing on the beach, soaking wet. And he could not get her out of his mind. Or his heart.

Susanna Truitt had taken up residence in his head and refused to vacate. The more time passed, the more prevalent she became in his thoughts.

Was he in love?

He had no idea. But what did it matter? He could *not* marry her. The Duke of Wabash, his great-grandfather's cousin, attempted to marry an English lady in the early nineteen hundreds and failed. If he'd married her, he would've lost his title, his inheritance, and his very way of life.

The duke gave up his intended. His love for her was not strong enough to endure a life without privilege.

Could Nathaniel give up everything for love? Or was he more devoted to duty? To his way of life? Title and privilege? Money?

But if God had placed him in Brighton at this moment in history, then surely he would help Nathaniel find love in the midst of it all.

Meanwhile, Jon informed him the *LibP* and *Informant* called for him to marry Lady Genevieve, saying it was the solution to both economies above all. But all the pressure to marry only made him want Susanna more.

In his day-to-day, he avoided marriage talk, preferring to give his heart and mind to becoming king. He'd fortified his emotional walls as best he could by eliminating all contact with Susanna.

When she completed "A King's Garden," Jonathan granted the final approval and sent the bonus check.

From the pictures, it appeared she had done a splendid job. Though he never doubted her. Nathaniel toyed with the idea of traveling to St. Simons Island to see the garden in person, but if he did, he'd feared his heart would never come home.

Arriving at his apartment, his butler Malcolm greeted him. "Your brother is in the living room."

"Good. He can join me outside." Nathaniel patted the elderly man on the shoulder. "Care to come, Malcolm? The snow is fresh."

"I prefer the fire, Your Majesty."

"Your choice. But at least put on a coat and step out on the balcony. It's a beautiful day. Christmas is in the air."

"Yes, sir," Malcolm said, bowing slightly. "I'll have tea and cakes waiting for your return."

"Stephen?" Nathaniel rounded the corner into the living quarters, a rectangular space with a southern wall of windows, hand-woven tapestries adorning the clean, cream-colored walls, and imported Italian carpets in the living areas. Polished marble in the walkways and kitchen. The design was his—crisp, clean, masculine. Simple.

His younger brother stood by the fireplace in his stocking feet while his muddy trainers left a brown puddle on the hearth. His rugby gear was wet and muddy. "We've a shot, Nate. To win the cup. Brighton Union is coming on strong."

"And with a prince as their star wing." Nathaniel raised his hand, his fingers forming the U of the Brighton Union sign. Stephen gave his all to making the national team, overcoming the stigma of being a rejected first-year player. "Want to go for a walk in the snow? The staff children inspired me."

"I just came from the snow." He offered up his cold red hands as proof. Stephen communicated with his entire being. His hands, his mannerisms, his movements. The way his dark hair stood on end made him look as if he were in a constant state of shock. But there wasn't a more steady, peaceful man.

Nathaniel crossed toward his room. "Have Malcolm bring 'round tea if you want. I'm going for a stroll outside."

"You can't ignore them." Stephen's voice trailed after him, giving advice to a notion Nathaniel never verbalized. "The call to marry Lady Genevieve."

"I can and I will." He turned back to his brother.

"Why don't you just address them?" Stephen dropped to the couch, tugging his rucksack to the cushion beside him. He dug around until he produced a plastic-wrapped sandwich of some sort. He took a big bite, then spread his arms across the back of the couch, glaring at Nathaniel and expecting an answer. And a darn good one.

"They'll draw me into the debate. Have me publicly announce

I don't love Lady Genevieve, and I won't marry her to save Hessenberg or our economy. Then the political pundits and factions will explode, calling me mean-spirited, selfish, only caring for myself. I have so much; they have so little. Though they themselves would not require this standard of themselves."

"What about the American girl?"

"What American girl?" He'd not talked to anyone but Jonathan about Susanna. Even then, only when she finished the garden. He believed his silence would help him forget her.

"The one in the *LibP* picture."

"From five months ago?"

Stephen shoved the corner of his sandwich into his mouth for another ravenous bite. "I don't know . . ." He spoke and chewed at the same time, like a rugby player rather than the man of manners Mum worked so hard to raise.

"If you're hungry, Stephen, I can ring for Malcolm."

He shook his head, finished his sandwich—in one bite, no less—and dusted crumbs from his fingers. "I've dinner plans." Still with his mouth full.

"Did you stop by just to see how I fared with the press?"

"That and to see if the jeweler delivered Mum's birthday gift."

"This morning." Nathaniel had one of Dad's pocket watches refurbished, the one he'd inherited from *his* grandfather, King Leopold IV. After Dad died, Mum said the ticking clocks reminded her of Dad's heart. Nathaniel thought the watch would bring her comfort.

"Did you give it to her? Did she cry?"

"In her way, yes. Wouldn't look at me for a few moments. You remember we're taking her to the symphony tomorrow night for her birthday celebration. Black tie. And no wild-colored cummerbunds."

"It's on my diary." Stephen reached into his rucksack and

tossed a velvet box toward Nathaniel. "Mum sent it over to me. Asked if I'd give it to you."

Nathaniel caught the box with one hand. He didn't have to ask what it was. He knew. Granny's engagement ring. "Mum already tried to give this to me a month ago, but I refused. I'm not getting engaged." About to toss the ring back to his brother, Nathaniel paused to lift the lid. A sparkling five-karat diamond rested in a bed of white velvet. Prisms of color splashed over Nathaniel's fingers. "Queen Anne-Marie's ring."

"Mum seems to think you need a bit of encouragement is all."

"Are you Mum's accomplice?" Nathaniel tossed the box back to his brother. "Conspiring to get me to marry Ginny?"

The ring had been in the family for over a century, but his paternal grandmother was the last to wear it. Grandfather King Stephen VII proposed marriage to Granny, Lady Isabelle, when she was a mere seventeen years old.

But exactly one hundred years before, Lord Thomas Winthrop had the ring made for Brighton's last reigning queen, Anne-Marie, in 1852.

"Don't shoot the messenger." Stephen caught the box and fired it back at Nathaniel as Malcolm entered the room with the tea cart. Stephen hopped up, aiming for the sweet cakes.

"I thought you were going to dinner." Nathaniel set the ring on the coffee table. He'd have Jon return it to the vault.

"A sweet cake is just what I need to hold me over." He shoved the whole thing in his mouth and reached for another. "Mum thinks Ginny would make a grand wife and future queen."

"Then you can marry her."

"Me? You're the heir. She's not in love with me."

"Nor is she in love with me." Nathaniel thought better of leaving the ring on the coffee table and placed it on the mantel behind the clock. A seventy-thousand-dollar ring was not to be tossed about like a football.

"Love? Do any of us ever know if we're really in love?"

Yes. "All your brilliant logic aside, Steve, I'm not marrying Lady Genevieve."

"You have to marry someone. All that jazz about heirs producing heirs, carrying on royal lines."

"You can produce an heir just as well as I can." The mantel clock chimed the hour. Four o'clock. He'd missed his moment to walk in the snow. Nathaniel peered at the window, the gray lines of the winter evening already shading the remains of the day. "Prince Francis had no children."

"He's your example? I daresay he's the reason why you're in this mess. All I'm saying is you should not count Ginny out so quickly."

Nathaniel watched Stephen go for a fourth, or was it his fifth, cake. Nathaniel didn't feel like having this conversation.

"Stephen, did Mum put you up to this? Or perhaps Morris Alderman?"

"Morris? You've lost your mind, man. The press? I avoid them."

"Ginny's spent more time wooing you and Mum, the King's Office, the prime minister, and the press than relating to me."

"How much time have you spent wooing her?" He was clearing the entire tea cart of sweet cakes.

"None." Nathaniel rammed his hands into his pockets—a habit he must break, since it was considered ill form to put his hands in his pocket during parliamentary meetings or government functions.

"If you marry her, the entail becomes a moot point. All is well."

Stephen must be reading the newspapers. "No, Stephen, it becomes more complicated. If I marry her and style her as Her Royal Highness queen of Brighton, she is no longer nobility but royalty. Then Parliament must decide whether she is a true enough descendant of Prince Francis to be his royal heir at the end of the entail agreement. She becomes the grand duchess of Hessenberg and the queen of Brighton. While I'll only be king of Brighton."

"Surely you're not jealous? 'I have one country and Ginny has two.' She won't stay the grand duchess. She calls forth a government, creates an independent Hessenberg, and resigns the throne. Returns to her place here."

"Are you so naïve? She'll never leave Hessenberg. Why would she? She'll have potential for enormous wealth."

He shrugged. "I don't know, but Hessenberg and Brighton will both be independent. What else is there to know?"

Politics was not Stephen's forte. "Plenty." This whole blooming thing made Nathaniel's head hurt. "But there is one true fact. I don't want to marry her."

Should he have a T-shirt made? Point to it when anyone asked?

"She's gorgeous, Nate. Smart, fun, popular. She'll rally the people no matter what happens with the entail." Stephen approached Nathaniel now that the sweet cakes were gone. "But I want you to know you're not in this alone. I'm here for you. Supporting you."

"Then start by ending this rush toward Ginny." Nathaniel clapped his hand on Stephen's shoulder, shaking him slightly, nabbing his full attention.

Three years apart, the brothers were the same height, but Nathaniel was broad and muscled like their father. Stephen was lean and wiry like Mum's father, strong with lightning moves. Nathaniel was deep and contemplative. Stephen lived on the surface with his emotions, quick and verbal.

"You're sure this has nothing to do with the American?"

"If you can give me a name. A real name. Not *the American*, I might give you an answer." Nathaniel poured himself a cup of tea. He bested his brother on this one. He had no idea—

"Susanna."

Nathaniel dropped a lump of sugar in his cup. "Jonathan told you?"

"Yes, if you promise not to fire him. Otherwise, no."

"He should mind his own business."

"He's concerned about you. You've changed since you came home from the States."

"Of course. Our father died, and I found myself king."

"Do you love her?"

"I don't know." But he did. The truth lived in the valleys of his heart and mind. He kept thinking that in time, he'd get over her. Find love in Brighton. "Even so, what does it matter?" Nathaniel sat with his tea. "Though I suppose I could abdicate, marry Susanna, hand you the Brighton throne and the entail mess. You could marry Ginny."

"Ha-ha, well played, old boy." Stephen pointed at him, smiling.

"You could finally convert the throne room to the bowling alley you always wanted."

Stephen laughed. "Dad would rise up out of his grave."

"With all the kings and queens of Brighton."

"Nate, would you? Abdicate over an American lass you knew for a fortnight?" Stephen sat on the coffee table in front of Nathaniel.

"Tempting, but no. I can't do it to Brighton. To Mum or the family. Besides, it would throw us into unbelievable turmoil."

"What of your own turmoil?"

"I'll shove it aside. Isn't that what kings do? Set aside their personal life for the good of all?"

"Certainly Dad did." Stephen jumped up when the mantel clock chimed again. "Need to run." He slung his rucksack over his shoulder. "Nate, would she be a good queen? The American?"

"I don't know. But I think, little brother, she would be good for the king."

Stephen stared away for a moment. "Odd how you seem to be a man who has it all, except you can't marry the woman you love."

"I can't even date her to see if I really do love her. It wouldn't be fair." Nathaniel sipped his tea and set it aside. It had grown cold.

"I have a few minutes, Nate." Stephen tossed his bag back to the couch. "Loan me some warmer clothes, and we can go out in the snow." He jumped to the window. "It's not too late. The children are still playing."

"I think I've lost my joy in the idea." Nathaniel peered out the window. A fresh snow had begun to fall, filling the sledding ruts of the south lawn with big flakes. The older kids had joined the younger ones, sledding, tossing snowballs.

"For Dad, Nate. For old times' sake."

Nathaniel glanced back at his brother. He was smiling, egging Nathaniel on with his expression. "All right, you're on." He craved the cold, a burst of icy wind to dismantle his warm feelings for Susanna.

Before the clock struck the half hour, Nathaniel and Stephen burst through the south entrance of the palace to the surprised glances of the staff and children.

With a shout, the smaller children left their sleds and ran to him. "It's Prince Nathaniel."

"King, silly, he's the king." One of the older girls ran after her brother and sister, stopping them just shy of Nathaniel to curtsy. "Begging your pardon, sir."

He bent down to her. "Not to worry."

Stephen chose that moment to interrupt with a wild-man yell and smacked Nathaniel in the side of the head with a snowball. "Snow wars!"

Oh, it was on. Nathaniel gathered a crew of two older boys, two little ones, and the youngest girls.

Stephen had the other kids—two older girls, a boy who was the size of two, and the remainder of the young ones.

White bombs flew through the air. Nathaniel aimed for Stephen, ducking his snowballs and taunting him.

At the doors and windows, the staff collected to watch. Cheering them on.

Nathaniel released his last snowball just as Stephen yelled, "Charge!" Ducking his head, Stephen hit him in the chest with his shoulder, knocking him to the ground.

Snow filled his ears and slipped down the collar of his coat. Oh, so cold. But so good. He laughed when Stephen let him up and the children charged them both this time. Nathaniel picked up little Ansley and spun her around.

The laughter, the cold and snow, the shouts of the children healed Nathaniel's sorrow over losing his dad. Over his lost boyhood, over memories of Stephen and his parents, over his life that changed forever the day Dad died. But most of all, he laughed for the future of Brighton and her children.

# FIFTEEN

$\mathcal{T}$he clock in the hall chimed midnight when Campbell entered her palace quarters, weary from the long but happy evening. If a woman had to turn fifty-seven, she must do it with her family and friends by her side, attending a Christmas symphony.

"Did you have a good evening, ma'am?" Megan, her lady's maid, met her at the door.

"I had a splendid time. You've not enjoyed a happy birthday song until a full orchestra has played it for you."

"I suppose not, ma'am." Megan took Campbell's coat, hat, and gloves. "Shall I draw you a bath?"

"No, thank you. I think I'll stay up awhile. I'm not quite sleepy. You may go."

The woman curtsied and backed out of the room.

A fire crackled in the fireplace. Christmas lights glowed from the tree and each windowsill.

Campbell eased around the living room, *feeling* this space she'd shared with Leo. When Nathaniel married, the apartment would become his. She would move to a smaller palace apartment.

She paused at the first window, missing Leo. Her friend and

companion. The one she leaned on to lead and guide the boys. To lead Brighton. To lead her.

Drawing aside the sheers, Campbell watched the midnight snowfall drift through the palace lights. Silent, peaceful, magical. Changing the world without a sound.

Could she do the same for her son? Guide him toward his future with a peaceful silence? With dutiful presence and love? Or would she need to be loud like Leo? Forceful and strong?

Nathaniel had not been the same since he returned from St. Simons. She saw it. Henry, Stephen, and the King's Office staff took notice as well. Even Jacque, his personal chef, inquired of the king's poor appetite and weight loss.

He was lovesick. She didn't need snow or prime ministers or chefs to figure that out. She'd been in love once, back when the very thought of a certain young man stole her breath.

But being crazy in love was not enough for her father. No, he felt Prince Leopold was a worthy husband, and he'd have his way, not even considering Campbell's love for another man.

There were many nights she soaked her pillow with tears, demanding her heart to surrender and please her father. But in the end, her true love made the decision for both of them. He withdrew his affection, and a year later, Campbell became Leo's bride.

It was Nathaniel's first birthday celebration when she realized she'd fallen in love with her husband. She watched Leo walk Nathaniel around the palace lawn on his first pony, and her heart felt one with him. She thanked God every day for his mercy.

With a sigh she left the window and reached for the TV remote and found a channel that played Christmas music. She slid off her heels and stretched out on the couch.

She drifted. Like the snow. Down, down, down, peaceful . . .

"Mum? You still awake?"

"I am." Campbell sat up, jerked from her slumber by her

youngest son's baritone. "Did you enjoy this evening?" She offered her cheek to Stephen's kiss.

"'Twas the symphony with my favorite gal. What's not to enjoy?" He plopped into Leo's leather easy chair and tugged at his tie. "You're the prettiest queen in Brighton."

Ruddy and regal in his tuxedo, there always seemed a bit of comedy about her youngest son with the way his hair stood tall and waved about of its own accord. But he looked and moved so much like her dignified, noble father.

"But I'm the only queen in Brighton," she said. "However, you might say I'm the prettiest *mum* in all of Brighton." Campbell picked up the remote to raise the volume of "Hark! The Herald Angels Sing." It was one of her favorite Christmas hymns.

"You *are* the prettiest mum in all of Brighton. But I'm one of only two chaps whose mum is also the prettiest queen."

"Then did you do as your queen asked? Did you give the ring to Nathaniel?"

"I did, but he's not going for it."

"He's stubborn like his father. He refused me too. What did he say?" Fully awake now, she gave her attention to Stephen. "Oh, Nathaniel . . ."

"He doesn't love her. But you know him, Mum. Mr. Perfection. It's my guess he chooses not to deal with love until this whole coronation business is over. Perhaps even to the end of the entail."

"End of the entail? It'll be too late. Lady Genevieve could be the answer. Brighton cannot bear any more of the financial burden."

"Or she could be more of the problem. Mum, she'd be queen of Brighton and grand duchess of Hessenberg." He fashioned a dubious face. "Quite sticky."

"But we will all be independent. I do believe I relish the notion."

"Nathaniel being the king married to the duchess of Hessenberg might mean we are more entangled than ever."

"Well, are we not in a fine mess."

"Mum, it's late and it's your birthday. Are you sure you want to talk politics?"

"Then tell me what you know about the American lass?"

Stephen shrugged out of his jacket and folded it over the arm of the adjacent chair. "He may or may not be in love with her."

"What a fine lot. What does that mean? He may or may not?"

"He loves her but knows he can't marry her. That's my conclusion. Never mind that she lives four thousand miles away."

Campbell stood, too restless now to sit. "Do you suppose four thousand miles make him love her all the more?"

"Who knows?" He lifted the crystal lid of the candy bowl on the table next to him, choosing a few chocolates. "I have a thought, Mum. What if we bring her here?"

"Here? To what end?" Campbell regarded him, hands clasped at her waist. "I like having an ocean between her heart and Nathaniel's."

"To what end? To burst his bubble. Let him discover he's not in love with her. He's in love with an idea, Mum. A fantasy. Let's bring her here and prove to him, show him, what it would really be like to an American folding into our customs and way of life. Not to mention Nathaniel's way of life. In his kingly day-to-day. He's not Nate Kenneth on holiday in Georgia, signing on to wash dishes or cart rubbish. He's the king of Brighton, and he'll see she's not right for him or us. He told me he wasn't sure he loved her, so let's help him be sure."

"What if he decides he loves her?"

"He won't, Mum, trust me. He's devoted to his duties first. He's too uptight and by-the-book to make waves. He'll come 'round to the proper way. Say what, let's bring the girl to the coronation festivities." Stephen gave Campbell a cocky grin and popped another chocolate in his mouth. His confidence was a mixture of his father's and hers.

"You want to amuse yourself at your brother's expense?"

"Never. But how else can we get him to see the truth? Once she arrives, Nathaniel will witness firsthand how awkward it is to have her here, how Brighton is more European than most of Europe. An American like Susanna will find our ways and customs awkward. Foreign. He'll see her next to Lady Genevieve and realize it's not love he feels for her, but how she reminded him of his freedoms. He won't have enough motivation to challenge the marriage act. At the same time, having Susanna around will kick Ginny in the boot. I daresay she spends too much of her affection winning over everyone but Nathaniel. She might just have to put her charms to good use on the king rather than the King's Office."

"She's being coy, Stephen. Waiting for him to show her a wee bit of affection. Spend some of *his* charm wooing *her*. She can't be seen chasing the king around." Campbell focused a moment on the music. A lovely quartet played "O Holy Night." Her faith had grown over the years of Leo's illness, but she felt so lacking when addressing the King of all kings.

"One snap of his fingers and she'd come running. But if she's jealous of another woman, she might use her Olympian efforts to convince Nathaniel she is the one he loves and needs."

"Does he love her?"

"He says he doesn't. He claims she doesn't love him either." Stephen approached the wet bar, which contained only diet fizzies and water. He twisted the cap from a water and took a long drink.

"Then we must believe him."

"Do you want grandchildren before you're too old to change their nappies?" Stephen came around the bar.

"Now you're being ruthless," Campbell said, retiring to her chair next to Leo's. "Besides, I believe I have *two* sons who could give me grandchildren. Even better, assure a Stratton heir to the throne."

Stephen spewed the gulp of water he'd been gurgling down. "Mum, please, if you've transferred your expectations to me, then you are in dire straits. All the more reason to bring Susanna over and shake things up. Besides, I've no use for romance."

Campbell gave Stephen the truth-eye she used when he was a boy to check his sincerity. "It would be a cruel trick if he fell in love with her all the more."

"It's a chance we'll have to take, but keeping her four thousand miles away, letting him pine, is not working either. Have you seen him? He's lost another stone."

The queen regarded her son. He made a sound argument but . . . would it backfire? Produce the opposite of what they desired? "All right, you win. Tell Jonathan to add her to the list. Allow her to bring a guest. Shall you tell Nathaniel, or shall I?"

"Neither, Mum. If he knows, he'll go all steely on us. He might tell Jon to remove her name from the list. We'll never get a true answer. Nor will he. Surprise is key."

Deception bothered her. But Stephen presented another good case. "If he asks me outright, I won't lie."

"Fine, Mum. Don't lie." Stephen reached for his jacket and wiggled his feet back into his shoes. "Where shall she stay? Parrsons House?"

"Absolutely not. She'll stay in a hotel. Parrsons is for family." The Stratton country home sat on the edge of Cathedral City, seventy kilometers north of the palace. "Besides, it's the place of the coronation ball."

Campbell had plans to stay there herself during the coronation week.

"Mum, we want him to resolve his feelings for her, not alert the tabs and paparazzi. The press will be mad over him coronation week. The world will be watching. The security risk will be too great if she's in the city. How will he see her in such a public place? Put her at Parrsons." Stephen exuded way too much energy for the late hour. Campbell tired merely listening to him.

"Then we must invite her to the ball. If she's at Parrsons, we can hardly hold a large dance under her nose and not invite her."

The Parrsons House ballroom was the largest of the royal ballrooms, added in 1890 by King Stephen VI in anticipation of his son's future coronation.

Stephen VI preferred living in the country and assumed his children and grandchildren would feel the same. But at the dawn of the twentieth century, the slow pace of country life seemed droll and backward compared to the excitement of an industrial city where motorcars and picture shows engaged the youth.

"Brilliant, Mum. Exactly. The Colors Coronation Ball will be a perfect place to reveal her to Nathaniel." Stephen came around the couch, giving her his best impish grin. "Let's blow this up King Leo style, what say? Put her on all the blue-book lists."

"Have her mingling among our friends, family, and royal guests?"

"If we want to prove she's not queen material, then yes, showcase her against our cultural elite, Mother."

Mother? He only called her Mother when he was dead serious. "All right, then, you must promise to pick up the debris."

"Done." He crossed his heart and kissed her good night. "I'll speak with Jon tomorrow and make arrangements for Susanna's travel and motor."

"You think this plan will work?"

"One way or the other."

Exactly what she feared. One way or the other. Nathaniel was not one to be trifled with. He cared deeply for truth and justice. It's what made him a good king. But a horrible one to manipulate. This plan could go against them as easily as for them.

The clock struck one. Campbell turned off the music, the gas lighting the fireplace, and the Christmas lights, and headed to bed, weary with the process of devising a plan to expose her son's heart.

"Mama, I'm going on break." Susanna tugged off her apron and wadded it up for the laundry hamper. Mama hated when she wore more than one apron per shift, but Catfish had tripped and sloshed barbecue sauce all over this one.

Heading out to the deck, Susanna snatched the newspaper from her locker. Aunt Rue was getting restless. Some of the gilt was coming off her Southern, overly sweet bloom.

*How's that house hunting going, Susanna?*

Aunt Rue had a bit of Aunt Shrew in her, leaving the classifieds on Susanna's pillow at night. This morning she *insisted* she *must* have her whole house to herself *as soon as possible* so she could have it painted, recarpeted, and Susanna's room fumigated by Christmas.

Okay, she didn't say fumigated, but she might as well have by the way she wrinkled her nose.

The way Susanna saw it, she had three choices.

Go for a cheap rental. One that a barbecue back-of-house manager could afford.

Move home. *Shudder.*

Buy a tent and pitch it next to Aurora's.

So far, she leaned toward the tent. Might be kind of freeing.

Choosing a table in the corner by the stage, Susanna popped open the paper but stared toward the beach instead of reading.

Sometimes when she had a free morning or evening, she would ride her bike to Christ Church, where she would park in the grass and stretch herself out over the blades to pray. She tried not to pick the same spot where she'd talked and prayed with Nate, but she did. Every time. Because God spoke to her there.

*Apart from me, you can do nothing.*

So there she was back to the "I got nothing" and "you can have all of me" prayer. What little remained of herself, her plans, her life. Maybe that was the point.

Out on the deck, she pulled her Sharpie from her hip pocket and scribbled "John 15" on the edge of the newspaper. She'd been reading the chapter before bed the last few nights. Much better reading than the For Rent classifieds. Sorry, Aunt Rue.

Beneath John 15 she wrote "abide, Jesus, fruit." She saw the message in the red words. She just wasn't clear on how to execute.

Begin with nothing? Check.

A December breeze skirted in from the ocean, cooling Susanna's kitchen-warmed skin. She capped her pen and hunched over the For Rent ads.

"Find anything?" The screen door slammed, and Mama stepped onto the deck, wiping her hands on a clean white dish towel.

"Looks like the same ads as yesterday." Susanna scanned the columns. "I might be living in my car." Car dwelling was an option. But down a ways on the list. Before living with Gracie but after camping with Aurora.

"Gracious girl, you are stubborn." Mama's sigh came from her heart. "Just come on home and live with your daddy, Avery, and me."

"Haven't I been humiliated enough this year?" She gazed up at Mama. "I'm already back working at the Shack. Moving home would seal the deal." She made a mock crowd cheer. "And the winner of Loser of the Year goes to—"

"Oh for crying out loud. You're so dramatic." Mama fluffed the dish towel, folding and unfolding it. "Lots of kids live at home with their parents."

"I'm not like other kids. I don't want to be a kid living at home. Shoot, you and Daddy married, divorced, and remarried by the time you were my age."

"I reckon you got a point." Mama sat on the bench next to Susanna. "I knew you were your own girl the moment you pushed your way into this world. Didn't make a peep. Just looked up at me with those big eyes like it was about time I let you out to see what was going on."

Susanna smiled. "How do you even remember that?" She tapped the paper with her pen. Lately, it seemed every conversation with Mama pierced her heart.

"I remember everything about you, baby girl." Mama sniffed and looked the other way. "Probably hard for you to believe, seeing how you came up, but I got a mental picture book of you that I glance through every day. You were the prettiest, sweetest thing. Everybody, and I do mean everybody, stopped me when I took you to the market or church, what have you. 'She's so beautiful,' they'd say. I had to start leaving you at home or my mama's if I wanted to get errands done quick. You had big blue eyes that watched everything as if you knew exactly what was going on. Rosy cheeks, cute bow lips, and perfect skin. And a mop of the thickest blond hair. I was nineteen and had my own real life baby doll." Mama dabbed her eyes with the dish towel. "Darn onions, still have my eyes leaking."

Susanna gave her a rapid kiss on her cheek. Okay, so they loved each other but were too proud, or too chicken, to look each other in the eye and say it.

"You know it's okay that you don't have a plan, Susanna. Sometimes it's good to let life just come and find you."

"Mama, you just described my worst nightmare." Susanna cut her a sideways glance and folded up the newspaper. "But at this point, I don't have much choice. At least I'm here with friends and family."

"What do you hear from ol' Nate?"

"Nothing. As it should be. He's got a life in Brighton." She stared ahead through the trees. She'd not confessed it out loud, but she'd googled him a few days ago. Just to see how he was faring.

She learned he was to be crowned on January 3 King Nathaniel II of the House of Stratton, Regent of the Brighton Kingdom, Archduke of the Grand Duchy Hessenberg—until and if they worked out an heir to the entail—and head of state and a constitutional monarchy.

Among his duties and allegiances was to be the Defender of the Faith. She liked that title the best. Defender of the Faith. Something the world needed now. A light in the midst of darkness.

She also discovered images of Lady Genevieve, whose beauty and poise were compared to Catherine, Duchess of Cambridge. Pretty Ginny, the press called her and urged the king to marry her.

"Susanna, are you hearing me?" Mama tapped Susanna's arm.

"Ummm . . . yes, 'Something will turn up.'"

Mama laughed. "Yes, something will turn up. Maybe you should go visit Nate, see what's going on over in Brighton. Aren't they famous for their Christmas gardens and shops, all lit up with old-fashioned carolers walking the streets, singing and what all?"

"Mama, I'm not going to see Nate." Never. Ever. She couldn't risk her heart. Besides, did one just walk up to the palace and ring the bell? Is Nate home? "I have better things to do with my money. Like buy a tent." Susanna hopped up from the table. "Time for dinner prep?"

"A tent. Susanna Jean, you are not living in a tent." Mama pressed her back down to the bench seat. "Sit a spell. I'll send out some dinner for you."

"Th–thanks, Mama."

The kitchen door clapped. Then a sound and a flash beyond the deck caught Susanna's attention. Pine needles and fall leaves crunched under invisible footsteps. Rising up, Susanna studied the space between the pines.

Sometimes diners came up to the Rib Shack from the beach side, but she couldn't see anyone. Heard no voices. Then she caught the tip of a bleach-blond head.

"Aurora?"

"You saw me." She popped out from behind a thick pine.

"Your hair . . . gave you away." Oh, to be as free as Aurora. "Are you playing hide-and-seek?"

"Watching. How are you?"

"Fair to middling." She held up the folded newspaper. "Do you have any room in your tent for a guest? I might need to bunk with you."

Aurora came from around the tree wearing a pair of khaki crops, a lime-green top, red Keds, and what appeared to be a pink cashmere sweater. "Small, small faith." She jabbed the air with her finger. "You're going to a palace."

"A palace?" So, this was an incoherent hour for Aurora. Though Susanna never counted out the supernatural—those moments when Aurora tapped into the unseen. She might seem a bit whacky-doodle, but seeing an angel or demon from time to time might do that to a girl. "I can't even afford a studio apartment."

"Small, small faith." Aurora hovered close to the deck, shivering when the wind blew.

"Come on up. Are you cold?"

The woman didn't move. "He's your prince."

"Who's my prince?" Susanna's pulse pushed a bit faster. "What are you talking about?" How could she know about Nate? Did she hear things when she rode her bike around the island and hid out in the woods?

Did she peek over the low stone wall and between the palmettos when Susanna landscaped the cottage garden?

"Don't forget the shoes."

"Shoes?" Susanna came down the steps and joined Aurora on the path. A reddish twilight flickered across the last blue hue of the December day, turning the sky a rich shade of purple. "Your shoes? My shoes?"

Aurora's hair needed a good comb, but it was clean and healthy, minus the nearly transparent shade of blond she chose.

"The shoes, Susanna. Remember to put on the shoes. I can't say it enough. Put on the shoes."

"What shoes?" Susanna flipped through her past conversations with the homeless ex-political savant. She couldn't remember any talk of shoes other than the July morning outside Gage's office.

"Shoes of peace. Shoes of joy. Shoes of . . ." Aurora spun around, flinging her arms wide, laughing, leaving a set of Keds treads in the sand.

"Aurora?" Mama returned to the porch. "Want some dinner?" She set Susanna's plate and a tall tumbler of tea on the table.

Aurora's expression softened and the intensity in her eyes faded. "That'd be fine, Glo. Can I have it to go? And some extra Gib rolls?" She wrinkled her nose at Susanna and stepped up to the deck. "I nuke them at the 7-11. Drives the cashiers crazy 'cause all the customers want to know what's cooking so they can buy some too."

"Gib will love hearing that, girl. Come on in, get your own tea while I prep your take-out. You want chicken or pork?"

"Beef." Aurora winked at Susanna as she passed by. "He's in control."

"Who? This prince you speak of or the Lord?"

"The Lord, of course. The prince is as muddled as you. Best remember you let go, told the Lord you was all for him. It'll work out all right."

A fiery fear shot down Susanna's spine. "How did you know that, Aurora?"

The woman closed her eyes and breathed deep. "I love me the smell of Georgia barbecue. There was a place up on K Street in DC"—Susanna suddenly faced a poised, whip-smart DC lobbyist—"that just made my mouth water every time I drove past. But I was all worried about being a size two back then. Never realized giving it all up would keep me at a lovely size six without any effort. Oh, but that barbecue wasn't nearly as good as your dad makes."

Susanna squeezed her friend's hand. It was cold and clammy, shivering. "Go on inside, get warm. Do you have enough blankets in your tent? I hear the temps are dropping tonight."

Not enough for snow, hallelujah, but down to the 50s.

"With some extra to share. I'm snug as a bug in a rug."

When Aurora went inside with her clichés, Susanna sat up to her dinner. She'd just taken a good bite of her chicken when Aurora came back out with her Rib Shack take-out and an extra brown bag of Daddy's rolls.

"See ya, Suz."

"'Night, Aurora."

Aurora cut across the lawn toward a stand of pines. Susanna doctored her baked potato, and when she looked up again, Aurora had disappeared.

Eerie, that woman. But intriguing. Susanna loved her. She took a swig of tea as Avery burst through the door with wild blue eyes and rushed at Susanna.

"Watch out, Aves. You almost made me spill my tea." She reached for her napkin and wiped the brownish splash from her hand. "I thought you were going to the movies with Mina."

She shook her head, gasping for breath, and shoved a thick linen envelope embossed in gold and red at Susanna.

"What is it?" Susanna reached for the envelope, but Avery hugged it to her chest while letting loose high, ear-busting squeals.

Susanna recoiled against the noise. "Avery, stop."

"We have to go ... We have to go." She bobbed up and down, waving the envelope. "In all my short little life ... I never, never, never."

Susanna made a face. Let's see. It wasn't homecoming or prom. In a week school would let out for Christmas, so there were parties to attend, but why did she think Susanna had to go?

"Suz, we're getting busy." Mama appeared in the doorway. "Hate to pull you from your dinner, but Christmas shoppers came early. Avery Mae, I thought you were going to the movies."

She released the same ear-busting squeal. "Mama, please, please, *please* let me go. Please . . . *pul-lease* . . . I'll clean the house, your car, do your laundry and ironing?"

"You hate ironing."

"—for the rest of your life."

"What about to infinity and beyond?" Susanna asked, grinning, taking up her plate and heading inside, grateful this teen episode was for Mama.

"Yes, yes, yes," Avery said. "To infinity and beyond. So, *please*, can I go?"

"Go where? Out with it. I got a restaurant to run. What's this all about? By the way, how was Daddy? Was he resting?"

"Yes, he's fine. Suz, wait, you can't go in yet." Avery intercepted her at the door, offering her the envelope with both hands. "Please . . . Susanna . . . please. If you love me at all . . . say yes."

Mama took Susanna's dishes and set them just inside the door. "Avery, did you open Susanna's mail?"

"I couldn't help it." She jumped. Jiggled. Jerked. "Look at the envelope flap. Oh, how did I not recognize him?" She conked her forehead with the heel of her hand then pointed at Mama. "You had him scrubbing grease traps with a toothbrush and Cloroxing toilets." Avery guffawed, slapping her knee.

"Hush, girl, are you talking about Nate?"

Susanna stared at the back flap, her lungs collapsing, shaken by a cocktail of nerves and anticipation. Pressed into the envelope's linen threads was a royal cipher—N II R—in a rich ruby red.

Avery soiled it by tapping the envelope with her finger. "Nathaniel II Regent."

"Avery." Susanna slapped away her finger. "Hush up now. Give me a minute. Please." Aurora's voice echoed in her head. *You're going to a palace.*

"Are you telling me our Nate, my dishwasher Nate, is a prince?"

"One and the same. Mama, he's the new king of Brighton. He left here like a shot because his father died."

"Susanna, you never said a word."

"I barely found out myself. I didn't think I'd ever hear from him again." Based on their last conversation on the beach.

"Open it, Suz."

Susanna gingerly opened the envelope. Her hand trembled as she removed the thick card inside.

On Behalf of Her Majesty the Queen,
The Prime Minister and Parliament of Brighton,
The Lord Chamberlain
Cordially Invites You to Attend
The Coronation and Celebration of His Royal Highness
Crown Prince Nathaniel Henry Kenneth Mark Stratton
Of the House of Stratton, Kingdom of Brighton
December 26th–January 3rd
RSVP

Oh my . . . Her heart beat wild and loud in her ears.

"Mama, if you let me go you won't have to buy me another present for Christmas or my birthday ever again."

"Would you stop all that forever talk?" Mama read over Susanna's shoulder, then exhaled hot and heavy against her skin. "Goodness, I don't know what to say."

"M–me neither."

"Say yes, Suz. Yes, we can go."

"Susanna?" Mama bent to see her face. "You've gone pale. I guess you didn't expect this."

"No." Every limb of her body weakened as she shoved the invitation back into the envelope. This didn't make sense. She'd not heard from him since he left in July. He'd put Jon in charge of approving the garden. She'd assumed he didn't want to talk to her.

"So, we can go? See, look." Avery fumbled through the contents of the envelope. "'Guest.' That's me. And here's one inviting you to stay at the Parrsons House as a guest of the queen." She clasped her hands together. "Oh my gosh, Suz, who gets an invitation to a coronation? No one! We *have* to go."

The edges and lights of the porch blended together in the cold breeze. But the idea of seeing him again warmed her all over.

*What are you doing, Nate?* How could she go? Why would she go? She couldn't even be sure he'd invited her, though she found it hard to imagine the disapproving Jonathan adding her name to the guest list.

"Suz, come on, we have to—"

"No, we don't, Avery." Susanna tapped the heavy invitation against her palm, then squeezed between Mama and her sister to head for the kitchen door. "I've got to prep for dinner. Mama, did Catfish bring the meat from the walk-in?"

"You can't be serious." Avery blocked Susanna's path to the door. "We don't have to go, but we *should* go. We'd be crazy not to, Suz. Crazy. Give me one good reason."

"I'll give you three. I can't afford it. I can't afford it. I can't afford it. I don't even have a place to live, Avery. I owe Blaine Jessup sixteen hundred dollars for my office rent, and the invoice for my new website arrived yesterday. And to be perfectly honest, I don't want to go. It's two weeks away, and we just now got the invitation? How rude. Clearly we are a second thought, or worse, and most likely, it's a joke."

Could this be from Mrs. Butler? Getting back at her for upstaging her benefit. Or from the person who took the picture of Susanna on the deck with Nate?

"Who cares about rude? Or being a joke? We're invited to the coronation of a European prince."

"Not if it's a joke, Avery." Susanna rapped lightly on the girl's forehead. "Hello, McFly."

"We're guests of Her Majesty, the queen. The *quueeenn*... How can you not want to go?" Avery spoke with her arms waving, her body jiggling and wiggling. "Mama, make her go."

"Don't rightly see how I can. Didn't work when she was three, and it certainly won't work now that she's grown." Mama's eyes met Susanna's. *Follow your heart.* "She doesn't want to go. I reckon she knows what she's doing. But it doesn't look like a joke to me, Susanna." Of course not. Because it wasn't. "Now come on, Avery, have you had your supper?" Mama shoved her youngest toward the kitchen. "If you're not going to the movies, I could use you around here."

"Suz, please, please . . ." Avery clung to her as Mama tried to guide her inside. "Think about it, okay?"

The melody of the Rib Shack, the music of the Atlantic, the songs of the island rose around her and moved her heart. The sounds of home. Of comfort. If she did nothing else with her life, if this was *all* God had for her, the Rib Shack, the folks, Avery, then so be it. Let her do it with her whole heart. With holy contentment.

Then the weight of the envelope became evident to her senses. There *was* more for her. She *felt* it, like a largeness in her spirit that she couldn't see or define or grasp with her hands, but it made her strive for something more.

Yet it began with having nothing at all. Total surrender.

She lightly traced Nathaniel's seal with her fingers. The largeness was something she had to see with her spiritual eyes. The answer would come when she hid herself in God. Not her closet garden. Not in a life with Adam. Not in her career or hometown. Not in Nate.

In God.

A tidal sob crashed her heart, breaking her will and strength to stand. Dropping to the picnic bench, she let tears of repentance surrender the last piece of her stubborn heart to the One who bought her with his own life.

*That one . . . she is mine.*

She heard rustlings in the kitchen and dabbed her cheeks with the back of her hand. If Mama or Avery caught her crying, there'd be twenty-times-twenty questions.

The breeze shuffled by, calling her out to the beach. Down the path with the treasure of the invitation in her hand and heart, Susanna reached the beach and headed north. The pinkish gold of the sunset on her left, the deep blue of evening on her right.

She passed the spot where Adam confessed he'd found the right ring but not the right girl. She passed where Nate admitted the legal and royal restrictions on his right to love whom he wanted.

She passed the Rib Shack's boundary lines and the edge of the angled deck lights.

Maybe the invitation wasn't about going to Brighton for a king's coronation, but about admitting she'd stuffed all her dreams into a relationship with a man instead of a relationship with Jesus.

He dreamed bigger dreams for her than she ever imagined. So why did she cling so tightly for so long?

A verse swirled in her thoughts, sinking deeper, her heart warmed by the Southern breeze.

> *How precious to me are your thoughts . . .*
> *How vast is the sum of them! . . .*
> *Outnumber the grains of sand.*

Susanna stared at the stars and curled her toes in the sand. She had no clue of God's thoughts toward her. But discovering one or two of them seemed like a worthy lifetime pursuit.

In the last edge of twilight, she gazed at the invitation. One thing she'd concluded about herself this summer was that she had to trust God, believing in the largeness, yet abandoning the outcome to him.

Yet, if she were honest, the invitation caused her to yearn for Nate and a very pleasing outcome. So how *could* she accept? It would make it all about her again.

Tipping her head back, she inhaled deep and made peace with the fact that God would have to boot her backside to Brighton with some kind of miracle. Why make it hard on herself? Make it hard on him. He was God after all.

As for Nate? King Nathaniel II? She made peace with him too. And the fact that when he rushed out of here last July, she'd seen him for the last time in her life.

# SIXTEEN

*B*lame it on the moon, but Susanna couldn't sleep. White light trumpeted through her bedroom window in the early hours of Wednesday.

Kicking back the covers, she decided to get up and shower. Her alarm clock would tell her to do it in an hour anyway.

For sure, she could get to work early now. Sneak an envelope with half of her rent money into Jessup's office.

Crossing her dark room, she cut through a stray thread of moonlight aimed at her dresser, accenting the royal invitation. She remained at peace about not going.

Though Avery bugged her every hour, on the hour, last night. "Please?"

"No."

Right now what Susanna needed was to get dressed and find coffee. Get to the office, follow up with prospective clients.

Plead with Jessup for more time on her rent. Dread, dread, dread.

Send her webmaster the pictures of "A King's Garden." He needed those today.

Christmas shop. Though it would be lean this year.

"Suz?" Gracie called from the living room.

"Gracie?" Susanna grabbed her shoes, hobbling them on as

she angled out her door. "What are you doing here? Is everything okay?" If the woman rolled out of bed before nine, she groused all day about how she had to wake up with the chickens.

"I brought Starbucks."

Coffee. Susanna raced down to the kitchen. A dejected-looking Gracie sat on an island stool. "I think I messed up."

"Oh, Gracie, don't tell me. Ethan?" Susanna reached for her coffee. She could be sympathetic while slurping caffeine. Besides, she'd been here many times with her friend. Lending an ear, listening and nodding. Wrecking relationships was Gracie's MO.

"Yes." Gracie dropped her fist against the countertop, shoving the bag of Danish pastries toward Susanna. "I think . . . I . . ."

"What's going on in here?" Aunt Rue arrived in the kitchen with her hair tied up in a sleeping turban and white plaster on her high, Botoxed cheeks. She stuck her nose in the Starbucks bag. "My nose sensed lattes. My ears heard girl talk."

Gracie raised her head, peered at her aunt, and moaned. "Oh, great, is this what I have to look forward to in my senior years?"

"Senior? Bite your tongue." Rue took a bold sip of Gracie's latte. "Where's mine?"

Gracie pushed her Danish and coffee cup toward her aunt. "I'm not hungry."

"Oh, you've done gone and fallen in love, haven't you?" Aunt Rue bit into the cheese Danish as if it were her last meal.

Susanna grinned. She was going to miss the ol' broad once she moved out.

"I didn't mean to. It just happened."

Susanna paused mid-sip. "You what?" Unheard of. Impossible. Alert the media.

Aunt Rue patted Gracie's arm. *There-there.* "Happened to me a hundred times. Don't worry, you'll get over it."

"That's just it, I don't want to get over it." Gracie stretched across the island and latched onto Susanna's arm, hanging on for dear life. "Tell me what to do."

"Are you serious? You're in love?"

"Completely."

"No, really?"

"Yes, really, and don't judge me. Suz, what am I going to do?" Gracie hammered her fist against the counter.

"Love him. Go for it."

"Love him? Go for it? That's all you got? How can I *love* him? It's only been five months. Who falls in love that fast? It's impossible. Right? What do you know about someone after a few months? You knew Adam for twelve years, and, well, here you are, having girl talk at six thirty in the morning with a dysfunctional hair stylist and an old lady in search of the fountain of youth."

"Elizabeth Grace, there is no need to insult me because you went and fell in love."

"Bear with me, Auntie, I'm in pain."

Susanna smacked her cup down to the counter. "Stop. Just stop. Melodrama doesn't become you. Gracie, trust your heart. Trust that God is watching over you, guiding your steps."

Could she preach a lesson she had barely learned herself? All these years she thought she and Gracie were polar opposites when it came to men. But they were exactly the same. Clinging to their fears instead of love.

Susanna with one man. Gracie with many. Neither one trusting. Neither one believing.

"But is he . . . watching over me?"

"God says he thinks so many thoughts about you, it's impossible to count them. So, yeah, I think you have to go with he's watching you. But don't go with me, ask him."

"Girls, it's *waaay* too early in the morning to be talking religion." Aunt Rue hooked her lip and shook her head, swatting the words from the air.

"I'm not talking religion, I'm talking faith, relationship, Jesus. Big diff," Susanna said. "Gracie, it's okay to let your heart love. You know Ethan is a good man."

"You thought Adam was a good man."

"He is, Gracie. Just because he realized he didn't want to marry me doesn't make him rotten." Susanna sighed with yet another heart revelation.

"What if Ethan decides the same thing?"

"Can you let yourself have a positive thought? Please? And you know Adam did what needed to be done. It actually makes him all the more noble. He put an end to a really bad habit for both of us."

"So . . . he was a hard habit to break?" Aunt Rue started swaying and singing. "I'm addicted to you baby . . ." Her voice faded when Susanna and Gracie stared at her. "I love the eighties and make no apologies."

"The eighties, the seventies, the sixties . . ."

"Keep it up and I'll return your Christmas present."

"Gracie." Susanna pried her friend's fingers from her arm. "Let go. Trust. If you love Ethan, stop sabotaging it. Does he love you?"

"He says he does." Such a sad face for admitting a man loved her.

"Then believe him. Why would he tell you he loves you if he doesn't? He's been hanging around for five months, putting off his own goal of sailing around the world even though you've still never told him you loved him back."

"I know, I know." Gracie flopped her head back with a moan. "Because the moment I do, it's game over. Remember Hap Medina? I told him I loved him and within two weeks he'd split. Poof. The chase was over. He had me."

"Love is not a game, Gracie."

"Chicago," Aunt Rue said with a bit of icing and Danish on the edge of her lip. "They sang that song. One of the great bands of the seventies and eighties, maybe of all time."

Gracie pointed at Susanna, remembering. "Keenan Kilpatrick . . . left the moment I told him I loved him."

"Gracie, he left when you confronted him about being married."

"That's even worse, Suz. How could I fall for a married man?"

Aunt Rue licked her fingers and continued to sing. The Botox had finally gone to her brain. "I'm not buying that the Beatles are the best band of all time."

"We know, Rue, you think it's the Rolling Stones," Gracie said. "But Mick Jagger? Please."

"He lied to you," Susanna said.

"Mick Jagger?" Rue gaped at her.

"No, Keenan."

"Mick Jagger lied to Keenan?"

"Oh my gosh, earth to Rue." Gracie snapped her finger at the woman.

"I nearly met Mick Jagger at a London fashion show. His wife was modeling and I was a young fashion intern."

Gracie made an "oh yeah" face at Susanna and mouthed, "Young?"

"I'm warning you, Gracie . . . coal in your stocking. Both of you." Aunt Rue sat, sipping her latte. "Ah, those were the days."

"Can we get back to *me* now? Suz, how do I know Ethan isn't lying to me? Huh? He lives on a boat. He could be a serial killer for all I know."

"You've met his family. His friends. It's not like he lives in a vacuum. Your other boyfriends refused to hang around with your family and friends. Is Ethan like that?"

"He golfs with Daddy. Loves Mama's cooking. She thinks he hung the moon."

"Gracie, you're making an argument for love."

A shy smile conquered her grimace. "He is pretty amazing."

"Then love him, Gracie. Sweetie, it's time to grow up."

Susanna grabbed her latte and the bag with her Danish. "I've got to go, girls. Need to beat Jessup to the office. Gracie, want to meet for lunch? We can talk more." She headed for the door. "And Rue, Led Zeppelin is the greatest band of all time."

"Zeppelin? Oh no, come on."

"Lunch is great, Suz. I've got clients until noon but after . . ."

"Call me. Rue, I'll be out by the end of the week."

"Oh, darling, no rush."

Susanna grinned. Sure, now that she was plied with sweets and caffeine. On the veranda, Susanna inhaled the clean Georgia morning and erased the emotion of the kitchen conversation. This was her favorite part of the day. Morning. Clean and fresh. Pregnant with expectation.

Susanna started for her car, stopping on the top step when she spotted a pair of glittering shoes poised together on the sidewalk. Bedazzled, gold-crystal, four-inch heels with red soles along with a white envelope.

Susanna pressed her hand over her heart. *Be still . . .*

She knew these shoes. A special design of Christian Louboutin's. She'd admired them online a few weeks ago when business was slow, and she spent most of the day surfing the web. She was just too embarrassed to arrive at work by nine and leave by ten thirty.

"Rue?" Susanna called toward the house, reaching around the back of the shoes for the envelope. "I think you have a present." Probably from a designer friend or a zealous up-and-coming designer who wanted to be her intern.

Bribery by Louboutin. It didn't stink.

But why were they on the sidewalk? Out of the box?

Susanna flipped to the front of the envelope, about to call for Rue one more time when she saw her name scrawled across the front.

She tore at the flap and pulled out a note written on the back of a bank receipt.

*Go! A.*

Susanna dashed into the yard. "Aurora?" She scanned the backyard tree line. "Aurora? Come out of the woods. I know you're there."

But the naked trees refused to give her up. Refused to give a glimpse of her white-blond hair.

Susanna read the note again. *Go!*

She'd just resolved *not* to go. She surrendered her will, her sense of largeness, with no plan of any outcome. This was real growth for her.

"Come on, God. Go? Really?"

Or was it God? Maybe this was all just crazy Aurora. But how did she know about the invitation? She'd left the Rib Shack before Avery showed up.

Susanna sat on the bottom step, kicked off her shoes, and gently slipped her foot into the Louboutins. Oh, Mama, never in her life . . . such shoe sweetness. They fit perfectly.

She raised her foot to admire the fit. Then stood. Oh, heaven, simply heaven. If she didn't know better, she'd believe they'd been custom made for her.

Susanna dropped back down to the step, carefully removed the shoe, and dug her phone from her bag.

"Avery," she said to voice mail. "We're going. Don't know how we can afford it, but we're going. Call me when you get out of school."

Pressing End, Susanna exhaled. With that call, there'd be no backing out now. She'd have to charge the airline tickets, indenture Avery to Mama for the rest of her life—which seemed like a fair exchange for a royal coronation—then work like crazy to get a few gardening or mulch-spreading jobs, but Susanna was saying yes.

Even if it was just a party in the street, there was no way she was going to miss dancing in those shoes at Nathaniel's coronation.

# SEVENTEEN

S now flurried in the crystal air as the uniformed driver scooted through the rapid traffic, honking, muttering, gesturing. "I say, the coronation festivities have made everyone a bit crazy."

He gunned the gas and zipped through the roundabout, slipping under a yellow light, threading his luxury sedan through Cathedral City.

He'd met them at the gate. Sent by someone. Nathaniel? Jon? Susanna didn't know. But there he was holding a sign with their names on it.

When she had RSVP'd to the Lord Chamberlain, Susanna had received an automatic response with details of the festivities. She fully expected to hail a taxi when they arrived, but this man was waiting for them.

Susanna gazed out her window. Avery pressed her nose against the other. Every few seconds, they sighed in harmony.

From the moment Mama and Daddy dropped them off in Atlanta, Susanna loved this journey.

A glitch in seating earned them an upgrade to first class.

A humorous flight attendant. Excellent food. Funny movie.

The fire in the clouds as the sun set over the Atlantic. Falling into a peaceful sleep.

It just felt like everything was going her way. As if she saw a piece of the largeness. Saw the beauty in believing apart from God she could do nothing.

Then there was Avery. Beautiful, bold, enthusiastic, embracing every moment of the journey with abandon.

For the first three hours of the flight, Susanna just listened to her sister talk. Smart and funny, Avery exuded wisdom beyond her seventeen years.

With twelve years between them, Susanna was always a bit big sister and a bit part-time mama. Just when Avery got interesting, Susanna was in college, then working in Atlanta, all the while tangled up with Adam.

She'd never spent much one-on-one time with her sister as a young woman until now. And she'd found a treasure she'd never realized before.

Was this the purpose of her invitation and royal journey? To see her sister in a new light? Susanna glanced across the car as a gust of cold air whipped around her. Avery had powered down the window and leaned out up to her waist. "Hello, Brighton! We're going to the coronation! Woohooooo!"

Well, there was this side of Avery too. The boisterous, slightly spoiled side. "Avery." Susanna tugged on her jeans. "Get in here. Sheath your Georgia redneck, will you?"

"I feel like I've walked into a real-life Disney fairy tale," she said for the hundredth time, squeezing Susanna's arm. "Thank you, thank you, thank you."

"The shoes were the real magic." A kiss from the Lord. Susanna had carried them on board with her and stored them under her seat. "What do you want to do first? Sightsee?"

"Shop." Daddy had handed both of them spending money at the airport.

"Don't feel like you can't get what you want," he said with his eyes watering. His emotions sat close to the surface since his heart attack.

"We could shop for ball gowns," Susanna said. There'd been no time to shop at home. Even if they knew what kind of gowns to buy. Besides, who wanted to wad up a beautiful gown into a suitcase for an eight-hour flight?

What she really wanted was to meld into the scene beyond her window. Into the gabled and turreted buildings. Into the cobbled streets and the aroma of open-air cafés.

She wanted to inspect the architecture and gardens. Brighton was as old as Britain, a blend of British, Prussian, German, and Russian art, thought, and design. Every structure seemed to tell a piece of the ancient island's story. Stone edifices with marble inlay—churches, courts of law, businesses. Then rows of plaster-and-beam buildings. Pubs, shops, and apartments.

Trees with bare, snowy limbs entwined with Christmas lights lining the avenues.

"This is the fashion district, ladies," the driver said, watching them in the rearview. "Do your shopping here."

Susanna looked close for dress shops. The day after Christmas, the fronts remained trimmed for Christmas as well as the coronation, and costumed carolers still strolled the streets. She opened her window to listen and was electrified by the unseen but tangible coronation excitement.

"This is amazing!" Avery slid from her side of the car into Susanna. "I want to eat at every restaurant and visit every shop."

Susanna lifted her face when she caught a whiff of baking bread. "We're only here five days. Let's pace ourselves."

"Pace ourselves? I'm going to burn the candle at both ends and every inch in between. Who needs sleep? We can sleep when we get home."

The scene changed as the car headed deeper into traffic. The avenues widened and the pedestrians had a business-like stroll, dressed in dark overcoats and galoshes. High lamps arched over the streets. Banners swayed from the poles.

N II R

Susanna fixed her eyes on his cipher and raised her hand to the nearest banner as the car slipped by. Her swirling emotions surprised her. The honor, the joy of being here for him. Even if she didn't get to see him in person.

*You go, Nate.*

"Look at the buildings, Suz." Avery peeked inside. "So old and cool. I love the turrets."

"Brighton dates back to ancient times," the driver said. "But five hundred years ago, good ol' King Stephen I wrenched the island jewel from King Henry VIII and gave us our little Brighton Kingdom. You'll enjoy the coronation celebration, ladies."

Avery shot forward, draping her arms over the back of his seat. "We're friends of the king's."

"Are you now? No wonder you're staying at the Parrsons House."

"Do you know if it has a dungeon?"

The driver laughed. "Don't know, lass, but I doubt it. Parrsons is the royal family's summer home. It's quite nice. Been a royal residence for two hundred years."

Avery chatted about Brighton and royalty with the driver. Susanna retreated to her thoughts, her heart, to the movement of the city.

She loved it here already. It felt like home. While she refused to imagine any kind of end result of this trip, every once in a while her stubborn thoughts reminded her that she and Avery were guests of the queen.

But weren't all the invitees and dignitaries guests of the

queen? It didn't mean anything, did it? Or that she'd have any access to Nate.

But there was a ball. The ball . . . she'd see him at the ball. Yet Susanna's only mental image of a royal ball was the Disney animated *Cinderella*. In her mental scenario, she and Avery were the clumsy Drizella and Anastasia Tremaine.

Obscurity might be the perfect option.

The driver surged through a changing light. Up ahead, a magnificent stone palace rose on the horizon.

"Is that Stratton Palace?"

"Yes, ma'am, where the king himself lives."

Banners waved from turret peaks, and golden lights illumined the paned windows. As the car drifted past, beneath, and through the palace shadow, the largeness feeling in her soul rested.

For a moment.

Then they left the city behind, sailing down narrow roads girded by stone fences, adorned with snowy white fields, sleeping farmhouses, and quaint countryside villages.

When the driver turned off the road and down a lane canopied with wintery trees, Susanna's nerves tapped her adrenaline.

Would she see Nate on the other side of the door? Why hadn't he contacted her about her RSVP? Her million questions lined up and saluted.

A clearing bloomed at the end of the lane, and a grand estate came into view.

"Oh, my gosh." Avery leaned out her open window for an unobstructed view.

Susanna leaned between the bucket seats for a closer look out the windshield. This was a country house? To her that meant small, quaint, a couple of bedrooms and a deck.

Parrsons was a palace, a massive brick-and-stone estate of classic design. Clean and simple with wings and turrets and a well-groomed, snow-covered ground.

"Quite a place," the driver said. "Over twenty thousand square feet, and that's not including the ballroom nor the royal mews." The driver eased to a stop by the front door.

Curved stone steps skirted down to the drive from an open, wide porch with a carved railing.

Avery aimed her iPhone, snapping pictures. "I'm going to run out of memory before the first day."

"Then take it easy," Susanna said, reaching for her bag.

Two young men in uniform wheeled a cart through the front door and scurried down the stairs, taking Susanna's bag without a word.

"Footmen. Wow," said Avery. Click, click.

With the women's bags on the cart, the footmen disappeared into the house, and the driver bid them good day.

Susanna reached for Avery's hand and faced the steps and the open door. "Ready?"

"Ready." She jerked and jiggled, stretching her arm to get a shot of the two of them.

"Okay, put that away." Susanna started forward. "Don't put anything on Facebook until we get home."

"Too late."

"Aves ... we don't know the protocol yet."

An older gentleman appeared in the doorway wearing a suit and high-collared shirt. "Pardon me, misses, I didn't mean to be tardy, but there was an emergency in the kitchen." He bowed, indicating they should come in. "I'm Rollins, the house manager. You are Susanna." He looked right at her. "And Avery."

"How did you know?" Avery curtsied.

"It is my job to know." He smiled. Susanna liked him immediately. He might be a good source of intel. *Who invited us?* "Welcome to Parrsons. No need to curtsy, miss. I'm the royal staff. Not a royal prince. Your suite is upstairs."

"Suite?" Avery looked at Susanna. Well, la-di-da. She engaged

Rollins in conversation while climbing the stairs like a Georgia tart, swinging her hips from side to side.

Susanna, on the other hand, realized how tired she was from the journey. The time difference, the long flight, the emotional challenge to keep her heart and head in check. The constant flittering hope that Nate would appear around a corner at any moment.

She paused halfway up the stairs and visually inhaled the main hall. Marble, teak, high domed ceiling, tapestries, damask draperies. The dramatic, bell-shaped staircase was fitted against the wall and arched around the foyer to the exposed second-floor landing.

She wanted to remember everything.

"Avery"—she ran up the stairs after her sister—"are you getting all this? On your phone?"

Avery whirled around, phone facing out. "Videoing."

"The house was built entirely from Brighton resources," Rollins said at the top of the landing. "The wood, the marble, the wool, the stone." He stopped at a gilded, carved door that reached to the ceiling. Eight feet if it was an inch. "Your quarters while you're guests of the queen. The American Suite."

"What?" Avery lowered her phone. "Can't we stay in a Brighton room?"

Rollins opened the door and led them in. He was perfect for speak-first, think-later Avery. "Presidents from Abraham Lincoln to George W. Bush have slept here. The queen thought you would enjoy it."

"Are you sure you don't need this room for the president?" Susanna eased into the room. It was like everything else she'd seen in Brighton. Bold. Beautiful. Historic.

"He has quarters in the city. I hope this suits you."

"This is hot-dog fantastic." Avery aimed her camera high and low, turning a slow circle.

"Rollins, please thank the queen for us."

"You'll have your chance, I'm sure. She'll be at Parrsons throughout the week, as will the other members of the royal family."

Others? What others? This adventure was starting to raise more questions than answers. She and Avery were staying at the royal summer house with members of the royal family? And she had yet to hear from Nate?

This made *no* sense.

She wrestled with her questions and fought burgeoning doubt as she followed Rollins through the suite. Living area. Two large bedrooms, each with a private bath. A library, kitchenette, and gabled balconies overlooking the grounds and the countryside.

"It's decided," Avery said as she leaned over the railing of the library balcony. "I'm never going home."

Rollins laughed. "Everyone becomes enchanted with Brighton when they see it for the first time. Especially from a Parrsons balcony."

"So, where's the dungeon?" Avery propped her elbow on the rail and peered at Rollins as if she were shooting the breeze at one of her teen hangouts. Rollins's lips twitched ever so slightly.

"We've no dungeon here, miss."

"Rats."

The wind was cold, and Susanna could tell Avery was actually fading, so she suggested going inside. Avery disappeared into one of the bedrooms. Good. She'd have to sleep a bit if she wanted to make the most of their trip.

Susanna walked with Rollins back to the living room. "Pardon me, Rollins, but do you know who invited us to the coronation?"

"I suppose Her Majesty."

"But I don't *know* Her Majesty." Susanna twisted her bottom lip. "Maybe *His* Majesty, King Nathaniel?"

"Highly possible, miss." Rollins made his way to the door, stopping by the desk in the corner, and handed Susanna a blue booklet with N II R on the spine. "Your coronation and festivities schedule. Everything you need to know is in this book. Please familiarize yourself with the events, the dress codes, and security requirements. The green events are for the general population in celebration of His Majesty."

Susanna flipped open to the middle pages.

"The yellow events are audiences with His Majesty for business and government leaders. Red for dignitaries."

"And the blue?"

"The blue events are private, invitation only."

"I see." She made note of the green events. There was a party tomorrow in the Violet Garden.

"Milady, you are free to attend any green event you desire, but you are expected at all of the blue." Rollins motioned for Susanna to turn to the back of the book. "You'll see the Colors Coronation Ball tomorrow evening at eight. 'Tis your first blue event. You are the queen's guests, so please make yourselves at home. Dinner is at seven o'clock sharp. The queen is not in residence, so dress is not required. Jeans and trainers will be suitable. If you wish to go into Cathedral City or into the village shops, which are quite nice, leave a note on the table in the foyer." Rollins moved into the hall and pointed over the banister rail to the high-gloss table by the main door. "I'll arrange a motor for you."

"Are you sure?" Susanna began to feel like an imposition.

"Yes, I'm to see to your needs." There was no tomfoolery in his voice. "This is the royal family's private country home. A very special place. The king died here, as did his father and grandfather before him. During this week, members of the extended family will lodge here for the celebration. The coronation ball honoring distinguished guests will be held here. You are free to roam the house—except the west wing." He stepped down the hall and pointed to a dark, right corridor. "That is the queen's private residence. You can't miss it. The king's cipher is on the wall."

"Thank you." Susanna smoothed her hand over the schedule. This would be going home with her as memorabilia. "We will need to go shopping for gowns."

"Will this afternoon work?" Rollins pulled out a small e-tablet. "Say three o'clock? Most of the village shops close at six. I'll arrange a motor for you in the morning as well."

"Thank you so much." Surreal. And utterly sublime.

"Don't forget, dinner at seven sharp. We're having rosemary lamb stew, warm bread, and apple pie."

"We wouldn't miss it."

Back in the room, Susanna clicked the door closed behind her. She had to agree with Avery in never wanting to leave.

Just then, the little fireball herself ran into the suite, jumping, spinning. "This is so awesome!"

"I thought you went to bed."

"Who can sleep?"

"Me." Susanna took the nearest chair and closed her eyes. "We're shopping at three."

"Really? Oh great. I need some hot, sexy gown." Avery's voice disappeared into another room. "I'm filming every room. Mama and Daddy are not going to believe this."

Susanna was drifting to sleep on a dreamy wave when she felt someone next to her.

"Do you like it here?"

Susanna opened her eyes. Avery knelt next to her, chin propped on Susanna's knee. "Yeah, I do. It feels like home."

"Same to me."

Susanna pushed up from her chair with a groan. "Unpack or nap?"

"Sightsee."

"Nap or *unpack*. We're shopping at three." Susanna pointed to the large grandfather clock in the corner. "We have five hours."

"Do you think we'll see Nate?"

"I don't know." She jerked up her bag and lugged it toward one of the bedrooms. "I'm not going to worry about it. I'm here with you, and I'm going to have fun."

"You'll see him, I mean, you *have* to see him, right?"

Susanna listened as Avery chatted while they unpacked—where did she get the energy?—ate cakes and cookies from the guest basket, turned on the telly, and flipped through the channels.

Susanna tried to lie down, but a maid brought up tea and cakes, which Avery announced by jumping on Susanna's bed.

So she showered, saying her prayers as the warm water refreshed her tired bones, believing in the Divine for the purpose of her trip.

She toured the suite again, brushing her fingers over the gold-embossed, leather-bound books in the cherry-stained shelves, then stepped onto the library balcony.

Leaning against the rail, she surveyed the landscape to the farthest point of the horizon. It was barren but white. Beautiful in the late-morning light. The sky was a low, hovering blue.

There was a lengthy red stable. Or what did the driver call it? The royal mews. A couple of men pulled up in a truck with a bale of hay and backed to the sliding side doors.

Beyond the mews were several walking paths to the forest's edge. Susanna spied a walled garden, nearer to the house, between the western and northern wings. A single wintery tree reached bare and silent above its stone enclosure. A lone but diligent sentry.

Susanna's heart yearned. She must see behind that wall. Was it a true garden or a pathway from the kitchen to the garbage? Was it a king's garden?

She loved the garden with a single tree. She understood such a garden, such a tree.

"Suz." Avery stuck her head through the glass doors. "There's a lady to see you." She made a face. "She's got something bad stuck in her craw."

"To see me?" Susanna came inside, shivering, unaware of how cold she'd become. "Who is it?" She locked the balcony doors behind her.

"I don't know but . . . *blech*." Avery cut through the library toward the bedrooms, avoiding the *blech* waiting for Susanna in the living room.

Susanna rounded the library corner to see a pinched-faced woman in a blue-green plaid tweed suit posing prim and proper in the middle of the room with her handbag dangling from her arm. Her dark hair trimmed her tapered face while a heavy fringe shaded her eyes.

"Can I help you?"

"I'm Lady Margaret Wiggins." She held her back stiff, her chin high. "You are the American?"

She turned *American* into a foul word. "I don't know about *the* American, but I'm from the States, yes."

"My husband, Lord Stanley, is Queen Campbell's cousin."

"Nice to meet you. Listen, my sister and I promise not to be in the family's way."

"Too late for that, I'm afraid."

"Excuse me?"

"You're the one who designed Leo's garden. In Georgia." She moved to the window and pulled back the sheer. Was she signaling someone? "His Majesty told me about it." Lady Margaret daggered a glance toward Susanna. Her heart lurched. "Yet I heard more love in his tone than garden talk. I won't have you ruining things for him. Or for us."

"Ruining things?" Susanna raised her arms. "I just got here." She batted the weariness from her thoughts. What was this woman talking about? And why did she keep looking out the window?

"I know what you're about."

"Good, then tell me because I sure don't." Forget standing. Susanna collapsed into the nearest chair.

Lady Margaret shoved the sheer wider and angled to see the snowy lawn below. "You're a ladder climber, a royal chaser, dreaming of some kind of fairy tale."

"Is that what Nathaniel told you?" Her words settled like hot coals in Susanna's soul.

"No, but I can read between the proverbial lines. Nathaniel is too kind. But I know what women like you are about."

"Because you're one?" She'd said it. Too late to retrieve it.

"How dare you—" Lady Margaret's gaze steamed.

"You need to leave, ma'am." Avery moved into the room and the conversation. "We were invited here. But not to be insulted by the likes of you."

"I don't know how you got an invitation but let me warn you, if you've set your sights on our new king, you will fail." Her eyes flickered with fiery flames. "We will see to it."

"We?" Avery was good-ol'-girl personified, hands locked on her hips, elbows wide, looking around the room with exaggeration. "I don't see no *we*. Just a snooty lady in an uptight suit."

"I don't have to put up with this." Lady Margaret rotated for the door.

"Neither do we." Avery ran around the furniture, arriving at the door before the lady, and jerked it open. "Don't let the doorknob hit you where the good Lord—"

"Avery!" Susanna fired to her feet. But she wanted to cry.

Lady Margaret paused with one last scouring glance. "You have no idea what is at stake if His Highness abdicates the throne."

"Abdicate? There's not going to be any abdicating. Not on my account. Believe me."

"So you don't love him?"

The question caught Susanna unaware. She tried to speak but no words formed. *No, just say no.*

"Just as I feared." Lady Margaret's expression drew taut. Susanna could bounce a quarter off her cheeks. "Watch yourself, miss. This is *way* bigger than you."

"No . . . no." Susanna ran after her and tried to open the door, but she trembled so hard she couldn't grip the knob. "I don't . . . love him."

"Suz." Avery's arms wrapped around her shoulders. "Don't listen to her."

"I'm not." But she did. She cradled her head against Avery's shoulder, weeping. For herself, for love found and love lost. For agreeing to the surrender of nothing.

She was so tired.

"It's okay if you do, you know." There was that seventeen-year-old profound wisdom.

"No, it's not." Susanna lifted her head and dried her face, glancing around for a tissue.

"Why not, Suz?" Avery curled up on the sofa. "I saw the way he looked at you last summer."

"He didn't look at me any way."

"Yeah, he did. Like he was completely and utterly in love."

"I'm telling Mama to get your eyes checked when you get home."

"Susanna, why not? He's amazing. You're amazing. Can you imagine being a queen? It could happen to you."

"He can't marry a foreigner. It's against the law."

"Huh, the people here can't marry foreigners?"

"No, not the people; just those in line for the throne."

"Nate."

"And he's not just in line, he's *on* the throne."

"Even if he was madly in love with you, he couldn't marry you?"

Tears had not been a part of her original agenda for this trip. "He can't. They have a law. People tried in the past to change it but failed."

"Why? Why the law?"

"To avoid divided loyalties among the royal houses of Europe. Some princess nearly depleted their army trying to help her Uncle Louis in the French Revolution."

"So Nate can't marry you in the twenty-first century?"

"I'm going to lie down until the car comes." But she didn't move. The confrontation with Lady Margaret had drained her.

"Suz, I'm sorry."

"Sorry for what?" She shrugged. "That I actually met a prince? And who says a girl has to marry the first prince she finds anyway?"

"Every fairy tale I read." Avery curled into her.

"Then it's a good thing I stopped reading fairy tales."

# EIGHTEEN

*B*rilliant-colored festoons swung from every point of the ballroom ceiling. Long ones, short ones, braided and woven ones, with every conceivable color.

The Parrsons House ballroom seemed to fly with the lauded and exported Brighton traditional festoons invented when Nathaniel's ancestor, King Mark IV, longed for something to battle his dark moods.

The musicians, affectionately called the Parrots for their fine feathers—detailed, colorful costumes—paraded around the grand, ornate hall in vivid array.

The Lord Chamberlain, Earl Browne, announced the guests at the Colors Coronation Ball as they arrived. Royals and dignitaries from seventy-five nations, decked in dashing black tie and beautiful, brilliant gowns, approached the dais where Nathaniel stood in royal array with Mum and Stephen.

Nathaniel welcomed each guest. Over six hundred for the coronation ball. This was his life from now on—standing and greeting, receptions and dinners. Diplomacy.

He was grateful to welcome old friends like Prince William and Kate, Prince Harry, and Prince Carl Phillip, where he dismissed formality and gave them exuberant hugs.

He was the first of his peers to become king. Tomorrow morning, seven thousand guests would file into Watchman Abbey for his coronation.

The Lord Chamberlain and the King's Office arranged for a live broadcast beyond Brighton Kingdom to the UK, the Americas, Africa, Asia, Australia, and the Middle East.

It would be King Nathaniel's first introduction to much of the world. Albert, in the King's Office, reported a viewership well into the billions.

But Nathaniel only wondered about one. Susanna Truitt. Would she wake up before dawn and turn on her telly?

The floor in front of the dais cleared as he finished greeting the guests. Lord Browne permitted the guests to enter twenty at a time, giving Nathaniel a breather before each cluster.

"Everyone okay?" Nathaniel peered at Mum, an old hand at receiving lines.

"Doing fine." Mum exchanged a glance with Stephen.

Nathaniel regarded each of them for a moment. Neither would look him square in the eye. They'd been acting strangely all day. "What's going on, you two?"

"Nothing."

"Nate, pay attention. Lord Browne is sending in the next group."

Lady Genevieve waited at the door in a rich, clinging red gown, which accented all her physical charms. Skilled and practiced at presenting herself, she posed in the soft light that floated down between the festoons. When the Lord Chamberlain announced her—"Lady Genevieve Hawthorne"—she commanded every eye in the room.

She moved with such poise she appeared to float. A small "oooh" ballooned across the ballroom.

Could she be his wife? The groundswell for him to marry her mounted with each passing day. Along with more news of Brighton and Hessenberg's struggling economies.

New odds were being set for him to propose by week's end. Never mind he'd not been seen with her in months. Not since the October state dinner. It had only fueled the press's romantic fires.

At the dais, she paused and offered her hand. A scholar, businesswoman, beauty queen, and skilled athlete, he could do worse. Much worse.

"Lady Genevieve." He bowed, knowing she expected him to step off the dais to greet her as was the tradition for the woman in the king's life.

But if he received her in such a manner, cameras would flash, speculation would rise, and the rumors would go viral. Odds would escalate. If he stepped off the dais for her, it meant she had the first and last dances of the evening. Tradition dictated it for unmarried princes and kings.

But Nathaniel didn't feel much like tradition tonight. So he shook Genevieve's hand after his bow, remained on the dais, and said, "Welcome to the Colors Coronation Ball."

Ginny barely refreshed her wilting smile before a photographer snapped her picture. As she passed the dais, she cast Nathaniel a hard, quizzical glance.

*Why didn't you receive me?*

"You're not dancing with Ginny first?" Mum asked.

Nathaniel glanced at her. "I thought I'd dance with you."

"Nonsense. There are too many beautiful women here for you to waste a tradition on me." Mum cast a coy side-glance to where Ginny waited in the shadow of the dais. "What was wrong with choosing Ginny?"

"Nothing." In theory. Nathaniel returned to greeting his guests.

Ginny captured his masculine eye—she was a vision no doubt—but she failed to capture his heart. Even if pieces of Susanna Truitt did not reside there, he cared not to make room for Ginny.

Seeing Ginny in the entryway, dressed in red, nearly gave him a cold sweat. There was something amiss about her. Something . . . disturbing. Could he marry her for Brighton, Hessenberg, and the entail's sake? He might convince himself. But the twist in his gut, the brake on his heart, warned him to wait.

The pipers played a rousing tune, passing by the dais. Nathaniel joined the clapping and tapping.

The Lord Chamberlain announced the prime minister, "His Lordship, Henry Montgomery, Prime Minister of Brighton Kingdom." He paraded past the dais alone.

"'Tis a grand night, Your Royal Highness."

"I believe so, Henry. Music, dancing, fair maidens, and gallant men."

"Or fair queens," the prime minister said with a glance at Mum.

*Ah, what have we here?* But Mum paid the prime minister no special attention.

When Henry passed on, Lady Genevieve intercepted him. A dark dread iced Nathaniel. She was up to something besides marrying him. He just couldn't figure out what.

The court parade continued until eight o'clock. Then the lights flickered and the orchestra finished their final tuning.

Nathaniel was ready to move, to dance, to sit, anything but stand. Stephen hopped off the dais to troll for his first dance. A cluster of eligible women eagerly gathered 'round. Even if he'd not been born a prince, his charm would make him a favorite of the ladies.

The lights flickered again, and Nathaniel glanced toward the Lord Chamberlain to see if he'd shut the expansive double doors to indicate the beginning of the evening. He had not closed them yet, so Nathaniel scanned the guests, considering his options for the first dance.

He caught the eye of Lady Hana, but she appeared to be

clinging to a strapping footballer. Truth was, few of the women wanted to dance with him. And fewer wanted to tether their lives to a husband who lived and died to serve the people. His life was not his own. His life did not belong to the one he loved. It was a daunting task to be wife of the king. So what made strong, independent Lady Genevieve so eager? Especially when she didn't love him? He watched her talk with members of Parliament.

*What are you up to, Ginny?*

He could ask her to dance, pry into her thoughts, see if she'd slip up and hint at her intentions. But no, he couldn't rouse himself to do it.

Mum? He turned to offer his hand, but she was knit together with Henry in what appeared to be a somber dialog.

The orchestra finished tuning, and the breath of the room held, waiting for the king to choose his dance partner.

Nathaniel checked with Lord Browne, his heart somewhat panicked at not having found a suitable partner. How fitting . . .

Lord Browne held the doors as he talked with late arrivals.

*Let them in, man.*

Nathaniel craned to see who tried to gain entrance. A woman in a pure white gown with long golden tresses and a second in a dark gown with burnished hair.

A whiff of familiarity pushed through his heart and lured him off the dais. Who was beyond the doors?

"Nathaniel? Where are you going?" Mum called, low and controlled.

"Pardon me," he muttered, squeezing through the guests gathered along the wall.

The crowd parted. "Your Majesty . . ."

As he arrived at the door, the Lord Chamberlain turned around. "Oh, Your Majesty. Begging your pardon. We've two more to announce. Then we shall begin."

*Susanna.*

Everything stopped. The voices, the orchestra hum . . . his heart. Beautiful, gracious Susanna. Along with lovely Avery.

"Susanna . . ." He wanted to scoop her up in his arms and whirl her around. Instead he curled his fingers into a fist and recognized her with a nod. What was she doing here?

She bounced down in her adorable, awkward curtsy, teetering to one side, and he smiled, remembering that day on the porch. "Your Majesty."

Avery gave a deep, practiced curtsy, and Nathaniel nearly burst with joy. Now he wanted to dance. To celebrate. But first . . .

"Do your duty, Lord Chamberlain." Nathaniel winked at Susanna before turning for the dais, cutting through the swath of black tuxedos and colorful ball gowns.

What a grand night this had turned out to be. How did she come to be here?

When he arrived at his post and faced the door, the Lord Chamberlain announced the last but most special guests.

"The Misses Susanna Truitt and Avery Truitt from St. Simons Island, Georgia, the United States of America."

*Come on, Suz. Enter with your head high.*

Susanna glided into the room, wearing a beautiful gown that fitted her in all the right places. Avery struck an elegant pose in her shimmery, beaded black gown, strutting proudly beside her sister.

Walking to the edge of the ballroom floor, Susanna stopped, not moving past the edge of the crowd.

The Lord Chamberlain whispered in her ear and ushered her forward. A glowing blush spread across her face and turned her blue eyes into summer pools as she moved toward the dais.

*Come on, show them who you are. Bold.*

"Who is that?" Mum stood beside Nathaniel.

"Susanna, my friend from America. I don't know how she came to be here, but I'm most glad."

"Ah, I see."

Every warm body froze with all eyes on the Truitt sisters. The orchestra hovered on the same single note, ready to explode into the opening waltz once Nathaniel greeted his final guests and chose a dance partner.

He cared not to hide his smile one minute more. He let it spring to life as he greeted his Susanna and Avery.

The ballroom doors closed, and Nathaniel stepped off the dais, took Susanna's hand, and peered into her eyes.

"May I have this dance?" He rose up to a hush of wonderment as he led her to the open, waiting floor. "The strings on those violins will pop if we don't let them play a song soon."

"I'd be honored." She gave him her hand. The music released the moment he swept her into his arms and swept her about the floor, feeling lighter than air and freer than a bird on the wing.

She wore the only white gown in a sea of color. She tried not to notice she'd missed the dress code as she turned about the floor—on gold Louboutin tip toe—in Nathaniel's arms. And everyone watched. Gawked.

Then there was Avery, dressed in a black sheath, watching and smiling with her nose in the air. A small cluster of young men had noticed her and started their approach.

Susanna's plan was to sneak into the ball well after the svelte Lady Genevieve had been introduced. After she'd captured every man's eye and sparked every woman's envy. After the first waltz had been danced.

But the movie-usher-looking dude at the door, the gentleman with the formal voice, saw them, and when she told him their names, he beckoned them inside, killing her plan to sneak inside.

"I can't believe you are here." Nathaniel finally spoke, guiding her through the dance.

"Am I not supposed to be wearing white?" She stayed on the

toes of her Louboutins and waltzed with the king to the melody of the music. "Because it feels like I should be wearing a vivid, colorful gown?"

"Susanna, how did you get here?"

"I received an invitation." His expression confirmed her suspicion. He didn't know. "You didn't send it, did you?"

"No, but I'll reward the person who did." His smile rivaled the stardust floating about the ballroom. "I wanted to call—"

"You don't owe me anything, Nate."

"I'm sorry for the way I left you on the beach."

"Your father had died, Nate, please, no apology. If you hadn't run off, I'd be worried about your soul."

He spun her with the music. "I apologize for the way I spoke about the marriage act." He drew her close, bending his cheek to her hair. "As if it were your problem, not mine."

"I'm glad you told me. Better than waiting twelve years . . ." She laughed, and he snatched her tighter, his own laugh rising as he spun her around.

The couples nearest them "oohed" and gave a wide berth.

"I look ridiculous, don't I? Spoiling the whole décor of the ball. How did I not think a colors ball required a colorful gown? Did I miss the asterisk in the blue book?"

"I don't know about any asterisk, but you look amazing." He'd not stopped making her feel treasured since they first said hello. "Color is not a requirement, just tradition. The Colors Coronation Ball started in the 1850s when everyone wore bright colors to King Mark IV's ball. I'm sure white is fine, though." He fixed his gaze on her. "It looks good in this room."

"Then I'm not sorry." Susanna couldn't resist him a moment longer. She closed her eyes and leaned against him. *Just be in the moment. No expected outcomes.*

The waltz ended and Nate gripped her hand, curling it to his chest. "Follow me."

He covered the dance floor in long strides, the marble pattern that of the Brighton flag. He ducked in and around the guests, leading her toward a dim exit.

They curved around a wall and into a lean crevice, which ended abruptly at a paneled wall.

Rapping on the top right corner, a wooden lever released. When Nate engaged the handle, a panel opened.

"A secret door? Ooh, a mystery."

"Watch your head." Nate patted the low doorway as he ducked inside.

"This isn't the tower, is it? Off with my head for wearing a white gown to the Colors Ball. Avery's going to be so jealous."

"It's not *the* tower." Nate pulled her into him. "I've missed you."

In the secret room, he held her in a way that made her feel a part of him.

"Me too."

"Susanna." He touched her chin to raise her face to his, but she broke out of his arms.

A kiss? He'd steal her heart for sure, and she feared she'd never get it back.

"So, what is this room?" They were in some kind of turret with arched windowpanes, bookshelves, and an eclectic arrangement of couches and chairs, floor lamps and tables. The amber lights from the grounds outside bounced against the glass and gave the round, dark room a romantic aura.

"Library. The architect designed it as a playroom for the king's children, but over time it became a library." Nathaniel hit a switch, and a fire ignited in the stone fireplace. A second switch engaged the fixtures moored in the ceiling recesses and spilled light down the walls.

"Oh, Nate." Susanna moved through the leather club chairs to the center of the room, her gold crystal Louboutins sinking into the plush carpet. "It's incredible."

Hanging on the wall between the bookcases was a portrait of a young man dressed in ornate robes, his hand on his sash, his right foot jutted forward. Waves of his dark hair drifted into his high, ruffled collar. Amusement adorned his expression.

"Who is this?"

"King Stephen I. At about twenty-five."

Susanna pressed her hand to her heart. His eyes seemed real, awake, as if they watched the room. Watched her. "Your ancestor," she whispered, stretching to brush her fingers over the tip of the sovereign's shoe. "You look like him."

"You think?" Nathaniel rattled the balcony doors. "Blooming thing sticks in winter. One would expect it to be easier to open when it's cold, but no, not in this old manse." A click sounded, and Nathaniel cheered himself as the doors swung open. "You can't beat me, you ol' door."

A fresh cold ushered the stale air from the room. The flames in the fireplace bent, fighting to stand.

Nathaniel stood behind her now, along with the lovely gust of cold, crystal air. She was happy. At peace. No matter how this trip ended, she already knew she was glad she came.

"So I look like him? I'd rather *be* like him," Nathaniel said. "The people of Brighton had just made him king after he freed them from British rule. Stephen I snuck into Brighton's north port with his merry band of twenty-five and captured three anchored ships. He sent a letter to Henry VIII demanding Brighton's freedom or he'd never see his men or ships again. Being as one of the captured admirals was in his court, Henry agreed. Brighton became a free nation. No more serfdom. A few years later, he assisted Hessenberg in gaining her freedom from Prussia."

"His blood runs in your veins."

"I fear it's been diluted through the ages." He laughed low, then encircled her in his arms, cradling her against his chest.

*Just be, Susanna.*

"Where are you staying?" he whispered in her ear, melting her.

"The Parrsons House." She arched back to see his face. "You really didn't know, did you?"

"Not a clue. They must have hid your name from me. I never saw you on the guest list." He released her, walking around her to face King Stephen I, hands in his pockets. "Tomorrow I'll be crowned because of this man's courage. Because he thought the Brightonians deserved freedom. To keep their own crops, their own wages."

"Are you nervous?" She was destined to love men who were duty bound, wasn't she?

"A bit. We've rehearsed plenty enough. If royals do anything well, it's rehearse ceremony." But when he turned to her, his thoughts about becoming king were not what she saw in his eyes. "Susanna—"

She moved away from him, her heart fluttering, and toward the portrait. "Your country values freedom, independence. All the way back to this man. He risked his own life to free people who were all but enslaved to King Henry VIII's feudal system."

"Yes, he did. Serving the people for their prosperity is part of the royal signature and pledge."

His voice, his presence whispered around her, wooing her. If she released her stiff posture, she'd fall into him.

"Susanna." His fingers grazed her neck, setting her on fire, as he brushed aside her hair.

"I'd better find Avery." She whirled around for the escape hatch, because if she didn't get out of here, no telling what crazy confession she'd make. *I love you. Marry me. I'll bear your children.* "What if she's looking for me? Poor Aves, all alone out there."

"Trust me, she's being tended to by any number of blokes."

"Still, I'd better go check."

Just before she reached for the door, he said, "I'm in love with you," and followed his words across the room.

"W–what?" She'd seen it in his eyes, but now she'd heard it. She reached for the nearest chair.

"I love you."

"Couldn't you leave well enough alone? Just dance with me, flirt with me, then send me on my way? No, you have to tell me you love me. To what end?" Vim and vigor took hold of her trembling limbs. "What am I supposed to do with that? Cart it home, tell it to my grandkids someday? 'Your grammy had the love of a prince?'"

"I'm sorry, Susanna, but it's true. I can't fight it anymore. What I feel for you is more real than his blood"—he pointed to King Stephen I—"flowing in my veins. I'm tired of holding it all together. You're on my mind constantly. Since the day I met you at the lover's tree."

"Lover's Oak." She dug her fingers into the upholstery.

"When you walked in tonight, I felt as if we'd never been apart. It almost seemed as if some part of me expected you to come."

"What about Lady Genevieve?"

"Lady Genev—ah, you've been reading the *LibP* online."

"They say you have to marry her . . . your economy depends on it." She walked over to the first king's portrait. "He slipped into a bay and captured ships to free Brighton. Surely you have that same kind of courage."

Why was she arguing against her own heart? The romantic glow of the room faded, and though the fire flickered, darkness edged the corners and a bit of Susanna's heart.

"You want me to marry her? I don't love her. I love you. Besides, Lady Genevieve barely qualifies as a relative of Prince Francis. I daresay *you* have more of King Stephen's blood in you than Ginny has of Prince Francis."

"But if you marry her, she becomes a royal and meets the requirement of the entail."

"I can't believe you want me to marry her when I just told you I love you." He sighed and sat on the arm of the courtier chair.

"Hey, I didn't mean to make it sound like I *wanted* you to marry Ginny." Susanna sat in the chair and rested her head against his back, feeling a bit of his burden. "I don't know what I'm talking about, Nate. I'm sorry."

He took her hand and drew her around to face him. The wind rattled the windows, peeking in to see if anyone was home. His gaze, his warmth, his touch . . .

She trembled right down to the tips of her Louboutins.

"It's cold." Susanna rubbed her arms. The heat of the fireplace stayed on the far side of the turret.

"Take my jacket." He shrugged out of his tuxedo then walked over to close the balcony doors. He remained there, gazing out. "I miss Dad. I'll be going about my day and remember something I meant to ask him but never got 'round to it."

"My granny used to say, 'You can't live life looking through the rearview mirror, shug.'"

His laugh bounced off the cold, amber-washed pane. "Wise woman."

"Do you feel you should marry her?"

"Your granny?" He glanced back when she laughed.

"Ginny."

"I lie awake at night wondering if I want it to be in the history books that on my watch I had it in my power to give a small duchy her freedom and my own country financial liberty but I refused because the solution involved marrying a woman I didn't love." He glanced down as he stamped the floor. "I can hear my ancestors rolling around in their graves."

"They would marry for political expediency?"

"Absolutely."

"But isn't that what the marriage act was all about? To stop the politics of royal marriages? Wouldn't marrying Ginny align Brighton with another country?"

He stared at her for a moment. "Yes, but remember the two adrift sisters? Hessens are not seen as foreigners."

Susanna motioned to King Stephen I. "Would he marry for freedom's sake?"

"I think King Stephen I would've preferred battle than marrying against his will," Nathaniel said, turning to the windowed doors again.

Susanna stood beside him, tugging on his sleeve. "Do what you have to do, Nate. Be courageous."

He gazed down at her, slipping his hand into hers. "When I look at you, I feel courageous. When I look at you, I see St. Simons Island in the summer." He reached up with his free hand and stroked her hair. "I see a beautiful woman that I was trying to forget until she showed up for my coronation."

"Should I have stayed home?" She stepped aside, freeing her hand from his.

"No, no . . ." His peering, blue eyes glistened. "I just wish it were July and I was driving by Lover's Oak."

"Would you stop again?" She smoothed her hand over her skirt, finding comfort in the silky sheen. "Knowing what you know now?"

"Certainly, only I'd not wait three days to see you again."

"We have two oceans and five hundred years of history separating us, Nate. My guess is if God meant me to be with you, I would've been born here. Even if Ginny and this Hessenberg mess weren't part of the problem, you legally couldn't marry me, right? Has that changed?" He shook his head. She steadied her voice. "And probably never will. I'd better go find Avery."

He didn't stop her this time as she ducked through the panel opening and moved down the narrow hall. The gold glitter of her shoes lit her through the deep shadows. Her jaw and neck hurt from holding back her tears.

When she heard the allegro tempo of the violins and rounded the secret passage into the grand ballroom, she fashioned a smile.

The sight was breathtaking. The trimmings, the music, the elegance of colorful dancers. She glanced down the hall one last time. No Nate.

It was for the best. She could not come between a man and his country. If it were even possible. Then she spotted Avery, laughing and dancing with an astute, regal-looking young man.

That image alone was worth the trip. Avery lost in a fairy tale.

Susanna paused on the edge of the dance floor, suddenly aware of sharp, scornful glances. She scanned the shadows along the back wall, looking for a place to hide and figure out her heart.

She loved Nate. Of that she was certain. Yet his confession about Brighton, Hessenberg, and Lady Genevieve gave her a glimpse into his world. And it didn't revolve around her.

A familiar hand took hold of hers. Nate stepped in front of her. "Maybe we can't have everything we want in this relationship, Susanna." He bent his lips to her ears and whispered, "But we have this ball and tonight, you are my queen."

The firebrand of chills burned up any possible refusal. She let him lead her to the dance floor and take her into his arms, swirling again through the stardust to the music of their own hearts.

# NINETEEN

*A* little before one in the morning, Nathaniel knocked on his mum's door. She answered in her royal blue evening gown, every strand of her sculptured dark hair in place under her diamond-studded tiara.

"I thought you might come." She turned toward the room, expecting him to follow. "I made some tea."

Nathaniel settled his jacket on the coat rack by the door and tugged at his tie. "Who invited her?"

"The American?" Mum passed him a gold-trimmed cup. "Or Lady Margaret? You heard of her altercation with Lady Keri in the powder room?" Mum took up her own tea, shaking her head, clinking her spoon against the thin porcelain. "She and Stan do come from the underbelly of the family. She can be brusque. Though you danced with her twice tonight."

"Mum, seriously, Lady Margaret? You think I'd knock on your door at this hour to talk about that old mare? Susanna, Mum— who invited her?"

Mum twisted her lip. She was caught. "If you must know"— stiff, defensive—"Stephen and I did." She sat with a silent huff in her posture and avoided eye contact.

"You and Stephen?" Nathaniel sat, her confession disarming

him. Jonathan, maybe. Or Albert from the King's Office, but Mum and his brother? "How could you invite her without telling me?"

"'Twas for your own good." Mum took refuge behind her teacup just as the door slammed and Stephen entered, his polka-dot tie hanging loose, his jet-black hair electrified.

"Great ball, Nate. Lots of pretty women." He tumbled over the back of the couch and stretched out on the cushions.

"He wants to know why we invited Susanna." Mum poured Stephen a cup of tea without asking and passed it to him. He cast Nathaniel a sly glance, said nothing, sat forward, and doctored Mum's brew with whatever concoction he had in his pocket flask.

"Because she was under your skin," he said. "You didn't know if you loved her or not. So we brought her here for you to find out."

"Stephen noticed that Ginny gave more attention to your friends and family, to your prime minister, than to you, so we thought Susanna's presence might give her a good jolt. Make her realize she must capture your heart before ours."

"You assume I've captured Ginny's, Mum."

"Susanna doesn't belong here, Nate." Stephen aimed the remote at the telly and powered it on. "She's lovely and sweet, we grant you. But an American as queen of Brighton? Chap, it can't happen. Think of Brighton, the monarchy. Think of me and the sort of lifestyle I have." Stephen gulped his tea this time. "I can't be a king, nor risk a revolt should you abdicate."

"Abdication? Your lifestyle?" Nathaniel stood, tea in his hand. But he didn't have the stomach for cordial tea so he set it on the tea cart. "That's your big care, Stephen? At the moment Susanna believes in me more than my own family. Did you think how she might feel when she learns of your trick? Or me? Bringing her over here to use her? To what end? We have real, live, beating hearts in our chests. We're not pawns in your worried little royal games."

"Son, we didn't mean—"

"Of course not, Mum, but you did." Nathaniel paced around the back of the couch, his emotions twisting in his chest.

Stephen muted the television and turned to Nathaniel. "You said yourself you didn't know if you loved her."

"So you concoct a scheme and drag Mum into it?" Tired, frustrated, and aware that he had an early morning motor coming to take him to Watchman Abbey, Nathaniel wanted to wring his brother's neck. "You can't just tamper with my private feelings, Steve. If I love Susanna, that's my issue. Not yours. Nor Mum's. My whole life is going to be onstage beginning tomorrow. Except for what's in here." He motioned to the triangle of space between him, Mum, and Stephen. "Your plan backfired, by the way."

At that, Stephen shut off the telly. Mum's cup clattered against the saucer.

"Before I wasn't sure I loved her. Now I know I do. And . . ." Should he confess? "I–I told her."

Mum moaned. "You didn't."

"Good for you, Nate," Stephen said with a cockeyed smile, revealing he'd had entirely too much doctored tea this evening. "Really, good for you. Way to go and bravo."

"You're drunk." Nathaniel snatched the cup and saucer from Stephen's hand and set it on the cart. "You best be bright-eyed and spot-on in the morning."

"Nathaniel." Stephen worked to command his words. "Our plan was to wake you up. Stop dragging your feet with Genevieve, nursing some schoolboy crush over this American girl. It's Lady Adel all over."

"Ah, there it is." Nathaniel dropped to the couch. Mum listened humbly from her chair.

"You've not fallen in love since," Stephen said.

"Adel was ten years ago. I was an idiot university man. Susanna is nothing like Adel. Nor is our relationship. If you must know, I've not spoken to her since I left Georgia in July. Until tonight . . . thanks to you. I came home focused on my business here and getting over her."

"We believed if you met Susanna on your terms, in your home, you'd see your vast differences. That she's not right for you. Nathaniel, you're more than a king, you're a beacon for all Brighton's tomorrows. The hope of the monarchy." Mum set down her tea. "If you marry for the monarchy, for Brighton and her future, then you will do well. Time will prove you right. You will be following in the footsteps of many who've gone before you. Love is a choice. Choose to love what is right for Brighton."

"Gone before? Like who? You, Mum?" Nathaniel spilt his words without considering the consequences. His frustration and the late hour made this conversation unwise.

"What are you saying, Nate?" Stephen asked. "Mum, did you marry Dad for Brighton?"

"We are not talking about me." She made her way to the tea cart without her cup and saucer. "Get this American out of your system, Nathaniel, and propose to Ginny. Let's solve your queen, heir, and political situation in one joyous celebration. Find a way to love her. Woo her. Make her love you. In a few hours you will be anointed as king. It won't be a week before the papers, the bookmakers, the gossips, our friends and foes will be begging for a royal wedding. Will we have an heir? Will the House of Stratton live on?" Mum's steely, stubborn side surfaced. "Our foes would like nothing more than for our reign to at least crumble. Though our friends, who are many, cheer us on."

"I'm only thirty-two. There's time to marry."

"Do you intend to abdicate? I want to know."

"Mum, I've been working for five months, preparing for the coronation. Why would I abdicate?"

"You know if you leave things to Stephen he'll have the

throne room converted into a bowling alley before his coronation confetti has been swept from the streets."

Stephen cut Mum a wry smile. "Sweet, Mum, you remembered."

Mum sighed. "Nathaniel, we're sorry." She walked over to
him and took hold of him. "But it's untrue that we don't believe
in you. We do. You are our king."

When Nathaniel returned to his quarters, Ginny waited for him.

"I hope it's not too late." She stood as he entered, still in her
ball gown. "Malcolm let me in."

"What do you want, Ginny?" Nathaniel tossed his keys to the
lamp table, still steaming from his confrontation with Mum and
Stephen.

She regarded him with tired green eyes. Ringlets of her
black hair had fallen loose from her hairdo and curled about
her neck.

"Why did you humiliate me like that tonight? The first
dance? With her? My stars, Nathaniel, she disrespected the
guests, the Crown, the ball, and all of Brighton when she dragged
you off, away from your guests."

"She did no such thing. I took her off." He sighed as he slipped
his tie from around his neck. "This is what you want to talk about
at nearly two in the morning? The first dance?" He motioned to
the clock. "I have to be up in six hours, fresh and alert for my
coronation. If you don't mind . . ." He pointed to the door.

"Yes, I do mind." She crossed her arms, standing firm. "Let's
just get this out. How do you feel about me?"

Pretty Ginny. Gutsy Ginny.

"Why don't you tell me how you feel?" He was really too
weary for this, but she was here now, might as well go 'round.

"You know how I feel." She fixed her pearly smile on him and shifted her pose. Ginny used her assets well. "Nathaniel, you're tying yourself up in knots over this when the solution is so simple. I know this girl was your friend in America. I understand she's different, exciting, fresh. But I'm your kind. I'm Brightonian. I'm the solution to the entail."

"Excuse me, but I thought we were talking about love. Not a business deal." Nathaniel looked for a place to sit that didn't have him crossing Ginny's path. But she stood between him and his favorite chair.

Had he confessed to Susanna just hours before that he loved her? The whole exchange in the turret library was beginning to feel like a dream.

She laughed. "Darling, remember the year I studied abroad and fell in love with the French ambassador? I was so sure he was my destiny, but you and Jon knew better. You flew all the way to Paris to snatch me out of his clutches."

"He was a schemer and a lothario." Nathaniel pulled a nearby King Mark chair forward and sat. "He'd have taken every shilling of your father's money."

"But you showed me the light. Now it's my turn. We're a good team, Nathaniel. We cover all the bases. You're a military officer and businessman, an ambassador, a bright star in Brighton, handsome, smart, athletic. I'm a businesswoman, a scholar, an athlete, a beauty queen. We have a common history. I am Brightonian with Hessen roots. Our partnership will put us in the halls of great European monarchies. We can't lose."

"You don't know that, Ginny. You as grand duchess only gets Hessenberg back to being a sovereign nation. Are you prepared to help guide them through their floundering economy?"

"I've read for my business master's, Nathaniel. I run a successful company—"

"And we've not even discussed the implications of the grand

duchess being married to the king of Brighton. What kind of turmoil might that create?"

"Details, love. Details we can manage along with our governments. But the goal of a sovereign Hessenberg will be achieved."

"With *you* as their monarch?"

"Yes, with me as their duchess." Ginny stood in front of him, arms out to her sides. "Nathaniel, I'm offering myself as wife, lover, partner."

When he was weary, his senses, his reasoning broke down. Ginny's offer wasn't really about tomorrow, but about tonight. Right now. His bed more than his heart. The weight of revelation and responsibility caused his soul to ache.

"Nathaniel?"

A thread of pain crept up the back of his neck, around his ears, and up to his temple. "I don't know, Ginny."

"What don't you know?" She knelt beside him, placed her hand on his knee. He shifted his leg away. "Know what I think? The people of Brighton and Hessenberg will embrace us." She rose up, leaning into him and smoothing her hands over his shoulders. "It will be a win for all, love." He felt like he was drowning. Suffocating. He unlocked Ginny's arms from around his neck.

"You're willing to marry a man you don't love? Who doesn't love you? A man who loves someone else?"

"What is love, really?" Ginny slipped her hands from his shoulders down to his chest. "It's friendship, commitment, a decision. I can love you, Nathaniel."

The exact words a man likes to hear from the woman he might marry. *I can love you.*

He gazed toward the window, where snow drifted through the outside lights. Perhaps he'd change clothes and take a walk, be one with the snowy silence.

"You won't be happy, Ginny. Not unless you're married to a

man who loves you with an intense passion." He looked at her. "'Twill be a long life, waking up every day with your heart empty of things I just cannot give you."

"My dear Nathaniel, do you not know me at all?" She flashed a tiger grin and it frightened him a bit. "I'm so confident in our match that we will be lovers by day's end. Make no mistake." She slinked against him as if to give him a taste of her hidden talents.

He shoved her away. Space. He needed space. "Are you the one behind the *LibP* articles?"

"What? I can't believe you'd ask me such a thing." She rose up, turning away with a pout. "Morris fancies me, but he's just running those stories to sell papers."

"Just to sell papers?" He leaned toward her. "What did you promise him if I actually married you?"

"You're tired. I'm not going to dignify that with an answer."

"Stop evading, Ginny." Nathaniel grabbed her hand as she started away. "What deal did you strike with him?"

"Nathaniel, listen to you. You're suspicious and testy. But if you must know, I bring the power of the press and media with me. You want the monarchy to survive the twenty-first century? Then you need me. You *want* me with you." *Ah, the she-devil surfaces.* "But you abdicate to marry this woman or force the law to change or linger too long in bachelorhood, the press will turn on you. Hessenberg won't be independent, and she will turn on you. The Crown will be all but lost. The legacy of Brighton's great kings will end in disgrace with you standing watch."

"I see you have it all worked out. What's in it for you?"

Her laugh rang wicked in his ears. "Royalty, Nathaniel. Royalty. It's the closest thing to immortality."

"But if I don't marry you the press will hunt me down? Murder my reign in a slow agonizing newsprint and cyber-space death?"

Ginny bent over him, hemming him in with her hands on

the arms of his chair. "You've a year." She lurched back, grabbed her bag and coat and headed for the door. "One year."

"Are you threatening me?"

"Certainly not. How unproductive to threaten the king. I'm merely informing you, Your Majesty. The press will give you a honeymoon for your glorious inaugural year. Just in time for the entail to end." She slammed the door as she left.

A cold breeze cut through the room. Numb, Nathaniel collapsed forward, face in his hands.

*Lord, give me wisdom.*

Malcolm made his presence known.

"Your quarters are ready, sir."

"Thank you." Nathaniel unbuttoned his shirt, making his way to his room, his thoughts entangled, catching in his own heartstrings.

He loved Susanna.

He loved Brighton.

He disdained Ginny.

More than ever, he needed the presence and grace of the Almighty.

An usher escorted Susanna and Avery down the nave toward the altar of the breathtaking, ancient Watchman Abbey.

"This place is amazing, Suz," Avery said, aiming her smartphone.

"Amazing in its purest definition." Susanna examined the ribbed vaulting and flying buttresses cut from polished stone, the high-gloss wood accents, and the arched windows that were stained with religious scenes and Brighton's history. From the resurrection of Christ to King Stephen I's coronation to the Battle of Shores in World War II.

More and more she realized the sacredness of the day.

*Nathaniel was a king on the earth.* Largeness pinged in her spirit. The extraordinary God was in attendance. The Divine was tangibly touching earth.

Susanna fluttered away her tears as prune-like Lady Margaret, along with her peckish husband, Lord Stanley, joined them in the row and scowled at her.

Susanna grabbed a pinch of Avery's arm. "Let's move to the back."

"Nothing doing. These are great seats."

"We're not at the movies."

"Even more reason to sit here. When are we going to be this close to a coronation again?"

Susanna made a face. She batted away tears. She thought more about her own sense of largeness while Aves took her seat like she sat front row at a Michael Bublé concert. Thrilling, sure, but not *quite* the same.

The coronation combined all that was good about life, church, weddings, babies, first kisses, and yes, front row at Bublé.

"Aves." Susanna pinched her again with a viral whisper.

"Stop doing that." Avery jerked her arm across her torso.

"Do you recognize these people? They're the nobles and royals, dignitaries from the ball. Good grief." Susanna pointed discreetly to the left corner pew. "That's our president."

"OMG, where?" Avery rose up, then sat down, grinning, and wedged herself against the polished pew. "We're sitting among princes and presidents. You're going to have to blast me out of this seat."

"Lady Margaret is sitting just to the right of me." Susanna tipped her head slightly, cupping her hand to the side of her face. "How's that for dynamite?"

Avery had groused again last night on their way up to their suite after the ball about how the lady introduced herself to Susanna with such a rude confrontation.

But Susanna only heard every hundredth word or so. She was reliving her evening with Nathaniel.

Avery angled a sharp look at Lady M., as she liked to call her. "I'm still not leaving. We danced all night among these people. They love us."

"You're too much like your mama." Susanna cut a glance at Lady M. She stared straight ahead. Fine, they could sit together in silence.

"Thank you. She'll be proud to hear it."

Susanna sighed. Aves was right. They had blended beautifully with these people last night. She opened the embossed coronation program, but scenes from last evening paraded across the scripted pages.

Nathaniel kept to his confession and treated her like a queen, *his* queen, all night. Susanna felt treasured and special. He left her a few times to dance with others, but when he did, he secured Susanna a dance with a prince, duke, or lord. But when they danced, he held her as if she were meant to be in his arms. They shared private laughs and tingling whispers.

He introduced her to his mates with his arm around her. She curtsied her wobbly curtsy before Prince William and Kate but, by gum, held her own during the conversation. She'd even made the duchess laugh, touch her arm, and declare, "I'm with Susanna."

Surreal. Magical. Out of this world. And *over*. Done.

Last night they could pretend they had a forever, but the light of morning brought truth and reality. She was *the* American. A commoner's commoner. Unworthy of a royal prince.

In three days, she was getting on the plane for home and never looking back. She could not, before God, interfere with Nathaniel's destiny.

Besides, what did she have to bring to the royal table? Her extraordinary landscaping design skills? Her sharp people skills? How she stayed with a man she didn't love for twelve years? With a somewhat alarming amount of contentment. Her ability to make a plan.

Or her waitressing and back-of-house skills she'd honed at the Rib Shack?

*Need a baby with sweet, side fries, greens, and cinn apples.*

"There's Prince Colin." Avery cracked Susanna in the ribs with her elbow, rising up to wave at the twenty-something prince, cousin to the king, a lower-ranking member of the House of Stratton, sitting in the forward pews.

Lean, aristocratic with an outdoorsman ruddiness, he nearly made Susanna swoon when he winked at Avery.

"Let me never wake up," baby sister said, fainting back down to the pew, fanning herself.

"Wake up? I thought you never wanted to sleep."

"Quiet," Lady Margaret hissed, pointedly touching the brim of her hat. "The coronation is underway."

Susanna scooted down an inch, ducking under the rebuke and the sea of hats in which she and Avery sat—remembering they were bareheaded.

No one said anything about hats! Susanna only hoped they weren't offending the hallowed abbey or Nate's family.

When the car arrived at Parrsons this morning at ten sharp to pick them up for the coronation, Rollins met Susanna at the bottom of the stairs with a look of bewilderment.

"What's wrong?" In two short days, he'd become something of a confidant.

He cleared his throat and tilted his head toward Lady Margaret's sprawling feathered chapeau. They needed hats? Panic. But with no time to shop, off they went to the coronation, rude and bareheaded.

Yet comfortable-in-her-own-skin Avery barely noticed. The difference in their upbringing surfaced in times like these.

Susanna was purposeful, watchful, as if on constant guard.

Avery was spirited, confident, passionate, and deeply trusting. Beautiful. A low Georgia moon on a steamy night.

So here Susanna sat, bareheaded under an ornate hemispherical dome painted with images of holy life, a boys choir began to sing "Jesu, Joy of Man's Desiring," and a royal guard marched with precision toward the altar, carrying Brighton banners of chivalry.

Chills raced over her skin, over her heart. The power of the organ and the crescendo of pitch-perfect voices awakened her heart.

Forget hats. Or how baby sister Avery was raised by the same parents but in a different *house*. Forget the beauty of a low Georgia moon.

She was here to witness a man being crowned king before men and God. All else paled. She closed her eyes. *Be with Nate, Jesus.*

The song ended, a celestial crown of notes and lyrics dripped gently from the hand of God, anointing them all.

The quiet stirred the air. The narthex doors opened and the congregation rose. Led by the archbishop and priests, Nathaniel entered dressed in simple white slacks and a button-down shirt. His eyes were intent and fixed straight ahead.

Susanna's heart turned over in her chest.

"This is so sobering," Avery whispered, linking her arm with Susanna's.

"I know, I can hardly breathe."

The archbishop took his place beside the throne and stood over a kneeling Nathaniel. From the side of the abbey, remote-control cameras drifted slowly, silently, over the congregation.

Susanna glanced at the ceremony program as they were instructed to sit. A procession of nobles dressed in blue robes entered from the side of the abbey carrying the regalia and artifacts of Brighton's ancient coronation ritual.

Susanna watched Nate, her heart fluttering, her thoughts

churning. What was he feeling? Or thinking? Her veins pulsed with anxiety and excitement for him. What a divine privilege to stand with the kings of the earth.

Nathaniel rose at the archbishop's beckoning. In a strong, steady voice, he repeated his vows, pledging his life and loyalty to the people of Brighton and Hessenberg.

He vowed to uphold and defend Brighton's laws, traditions, and antiquities, to defend her against enemies both foreign and domestic, to seek the good of all, to defend the faith and serve the Lord in all his ways, spoke his troth to honor King Stephen I, who dedicated the kingdom to the Lord and his Christ.

Her tears soaked the plains and valleys of her heart. *Oh, Nathaniel, you are called to be Brighton's regent.* Gladness filled her. He had to run this kingly race. He must finish well. Even if it meant she'd never be a part of his life.

The archbishop uttered words in Latin and Greek, read scriptures, and prayed for the king, with booming sincerity, to follow in the ways of God, the church, and Brighton law.

When his voice felt silent, he placed a robe on Nathaniel's shoulders. "The mantle of kings." Then he set the tall, heavy, gold and gem-encrusted crown on his head. The archbishop called for the assembly to declare with joy, "Long live Nathaniel, king of Brighton Kingdom."

Susanna raised her voice with all the people. "Long live Nathaniel, king of Brighton Kingdom."

"Let us join together for a prayer of ascent." The archbishop raised his hands to the congregation, inviting them to pay homage to the Lord by kneeling and praying for Nathaniel. The abbey itself seemed to bow as the guests lowered to their knees. Susanna meant to kneel along with them but she stood instead.

With the hats and heads out of her way, she had a clear, unobstructed view of King Nathaniel II in all of his glory. In his bejeweled crown and brilliant royal robes.

He stole her breath. He was a king among men. A king in heaven. She *felt* his destiny, and it seemed to awaken yet comfort her own destiny yearnings.

Just as he bowed to pray, Nathaniel shifted his stance and looked out over the abbey. In that split second, his eyes found hers and invited her into the moment with him.

She pressed her hand over her heart. *I'm with you.* A very faint smiled tugged on the edge of his lips as he bowed in prayer. Just in time for the archbishop's first somber words, "O, Lord of heaven and earth..."

"Suz, why are you standing?" Avery said in a hoarse whisper, jerking on Susanna's hand. "Kneel."

She dropped to the kneeler, her heart cooling. Being swept away by the splendor and fairy-tale likeness of last night and today was foolish. Fantasy and dreams would not be her friend once she returned home.

Had she not learned her lesson with Adam?

But she prayed for Nathaniel, putting her prayers in the bowls of heaven along with the archbishop's and the rest of the coronation guests.

But oh, she couldn't help herself. She peeked at Nate again. He was on his knees, bent forward with his head to the altar carpet, his crown removed and on the floor beside him. Another robed bishop came to the pulpit to pray, casting Nate a curious glance, but the king never lifted his head.

When the prayers ended, the guests returned to their seats and joined in the choir's hymn. The archbishop stooped over and tapped Nathaniel on the shoulder. For a tense moment, he didn't move, then rose up, somber, with a posture that seemed to unnerve the holy man. He moved to the pulpit and read Psalm 21 as the bishop returned the crown to Nathaniel's head.

"The king rejoices in your strength, Lord. How great is his joy in the victories you give!"

Next came the pledges of allegiance from the dowager queen

and HRH Prince Stephen. They knelt and swore their loyalty to King Nathaniel II.

One by one, the prime minister, the leaders of the House of Senators and House of Commons pledged their loyalty to the king, followed by other members of the royal family and the leaders of Brighton's noble houses, then by the governor and leaders of Hessenberg.

When the final scripture was read and the closing prayer uttered, the abbey erupted with a fanfare of trumpets and a shout. "Here we have Nathaniel II, king of Brighton Kingdom!"

The *Hallelujah Chorus* exploded in the abbey. In Susanna. Glorious!

From in the back, the sanctuary's gilded doors swung open, flooding the nave with light. The archbishop led King Nathaniel, his mum, and his brother through the cheering and shouting down the long aisle and into the waiting day.

"God save King Nathaniel and all his descendants."

Susanna mentally and emotionally clung to every moment, savoring every detail, scribbling, painting, breathing in the textures, sights, and sounds.

She whirled around to Avery. "Are you taking pictures?"

She flung her arm around Susanna's shoulders and turned her phone camera on the two of them. "We're at Nate's coronation. Woo-hoo!"

See, Avery was a low moon on a steaming Georgia night. She just existed in every moment, free from constraint.

The guests made their way out of the abbey, laughing and chatting, making celebration plans for the rest of the day.

Susanna had hoped Nate would give her a visual as he left, but he remained focused, looking ahead.

All for the best. Really. She had to reckon with truth. There was nowhere to go from here but sightseeing with Avery and then home.

She'd also learned of another coronation schedule color code today—thanks to Rollins. Purple, to which she was not invited. A private luncheon followed by an evening performance by the Brighton Royal Symphony.

Susanna wiped away a small kiss of disappointment. It was fine. She and Avery had gobs of plans. A tour of Cathedral City and at least three of the green-labeled coronation street parties with food and live bands, which looked amazing.

One featured a singer Avery adored. Christina Jensen.

Down the aisle, Susanna and Avery finally pushed into the crisp Brighton sunshine. Prince Colin shoved away from the abbey wall where he'd been waiting. His smile flashed the moment he saw Avery.

"You free? I thought I might tour you 'round Brighton. If your sister doesn't mind."

"She doesn't." Avery whirled to Susanna, her heart fluttering in her eyes. "Do you?"

"No, no, of course not." The company of a handsome young man trumped the plans of a sister every time. At least this time. Colin watched Avery like a very thirsty man. "Take care of her, please. She's my daddy's baby." Susanna tried to give him the parental eye.

"Yes, ma'am. On my honor." He blushed a bit, then jerked a crossing motion over his heart. And off they went, planning, first driving Avery to Parrsons to change her clothes, then to meet Colin's mates for tea.

Perhaps it was Avery who came to Brighton to be with a prince. Not Susanna. Watching her sister go, her auburn tresses catching the sun, Susanna wanted the world for her. A prince if God willed it. But she still wanted Nathaniel for herself.

Avery paused at the bottom of the steps and looked back. She smiled and waved, but a subtle concern marked her expression. *You okay?*

*I'm fine.* Susanna shooed her on with a flick of her hands.

The abbey steps were empty now of all but a few stragglers. With an exhale, Susanna realized she was starving.

Perhaps she could raid Parrsons' kitchen. The staff had the morning off to enjoy the coronation, but she'd heard finger food was being prepared. She relished the idea of being alone at Parrsons to think and catalog her memories. Maybe she'd go exploring, try to find what existed behind the garden wall besides the solo tree.

"Miss Truitt?" A young man appeared off her right shoulder with a bow, offering her a sealed envelope. "From His Majesty."

"His Majesty? Nathaniel?"

"Yes, ma'am, His Majesty King Nathaniel."

The envelope burned in her hand and Susanna ached to open it, but she waited until her car arrived and was maneuvered through pockets of celebration before gently tearing away the flap. If she was going to cry or be disappointed further, she wanted to be hidden behind smoke-tinted windows.

Her fingers trembled as she read a brief handwritten note.

*Nine o'clock tonight. Be ready.*

She smiled, slid against the leather seats, and pressed Nate's note to her heart.

# TWENTY

*P*arrsons House sat still and quiet under a clear, very cold full moon. A fresh snow fell while she shopped then napped in the afternoon, the wind turning delicate snow hills into soft powder mountains.

Peeking out of her room, Susanna worked the buttons on her new red wool coat and scanned the hallway. The coast was clear. No Lady Margaret. She'd returned from lunch with Lord Stan-the-man, grousing how they'd not been invited to the luncheon, parliamentary reception, or symphony.

If she caught Susanna sneaking out, Lady M. might demand to know where she was going, and Susanna failed lying in kindergarten. It wasn't even close to one of her superpowers.

She'd crack. Confess. Spill all. *Meeting Nate.*

Susanna half suspected the woman would find a way to blame her for being excluded from whatever royal events took place this afternoon. That's what bitter people did. Pointed the finger and blamed others. Obfuscation was a way of hiding from their own shortcomings and wounds.

Closing the suite door behind her with one last scout for Lady M., Susanna tiptoed down the hall under the regal gold light of the wall sconces.

Avery had called earlier, waking Susanna from her nap. Thank goodness. She'd not set her phone alarm and slept into her getting-ready time. Nate would be here in a few minutes.

Anyway, because of the snow, Colin had taken Avery to his family's home for dinner. He put his mum, Princess Louisa, on the phone to assure Susanna that her little sister was in safe hands. There was music and laughter behind her voice.

Susanna imagined that God himself took time to make this a special week for Avery. God was like that, wasn't he? Dreaming big dreams for those he loved.

But what did he dream for Susanna? And did it have anything to do with why she was sneaking down the stairs to meet Nate?

Susanna gripped the banister still entwined with Christmas trimmings—fragrant pine garlands and red bows. She figured she would wait for Nate in the foyer or parlor, watching out the window.

When she descended the last step, she spotted a note on the mahogany table.

Susanna, His Highness is delayed thirty minutes. He sends his apologies.

Oh, okay. Well, then … She glanced around, tucking the note in her coat pocket, hoping Lady M. hadn't already spotted this gem.

Digging her hands into the silky pockets of her coat, Susanna roamed from the foyer to the dining room, catching the fragrance of steeping tea and cinnamon swirling from the kitchen.

Her stomach rumbled. She followed the sound of voices and clattering of pots.

"Evening, miss." Rollins slipped from the stool where he sat, removing the napkin from his shirt collar. "Would you care for dinner?"

The cook and maids paused in their work, eyes on her, waiting for her answer. Rumbling stomach aside, she couldn't eat with people watching her, waiting on her. She *was* the waitress, the architect serving a client.

"No, no, please . . . I'm fine. I heard voices?"

Rollins exhaled, returning to his stool. The others went back to their work. "We're just back from a celebration in the village. Agatha was telling us about the latest reality show on the telly. Are you sure you won't have a bit to eat, ma'am?"

"The muffins *do* smell good."

The cook came alive, snatching up the muffin tin, cutting through the ancient redbrick kitchen toward Susanna, passing what appeared to be the original wood-burning oven that now housed high-end stainless steel.

"Here you go, miss." She curtsied, offering the tin along with a plate. "Rollins speaks well of you."

"Rollins has been very kind to my sister and me." She smiled at the blushing butler, wrapping up a muffin in a napkin. "These smell delicious."

"I'm Agatha."

"Agatha, nice to meet you." She motioned to the door. "I wanted to explore. Would it be all right?"

"Certainly, ma'am." Rollins opened the door for her, smiling, his expression tender.

Down the hall, Susanna bit into the warm, sweet, cinnamon-laced muffin and peeked into the laundry room, then the library.

Parrsons House was a maze of nooks and pinwheel passageways. She found a small corridor, entered it, and came out on the other side, facing the king's cipher on the doorpost: L V R.

Rollins expressly warned her this area was private. But what was down the hall? Susanna suspected the way to the walled garden.

*Turn around. Respect the rules.* But just as she turned, a cold breeze tunneled through and she noticed a beam of light where a door stood ajar.

She shoved the last of the muffin in her mouth and crept along the stone passage. She fastened her coat's top button and toed open the door, shushing the hinges when they creaked.

The garden. The secret garden.

Ducking through the door, Susanna inhaled the view. Hauntingly beautiful under the round white moon, the snow-covered, barren landscape possessed her heart. Like all of Brighton, she felt as if she'd been here before. An icy blast dropped over the wall and moaned through the snow-laden tree limbs, shaking snow to the ground.

Despite a small inner voice of caution—*You're not supposed to be here*—Susanna's wonderment moved her further inside the garden, and she crossed a swath of the moon's glow into the night's shadows. Other than the snow and white drifts against the wall, the garden appeared empty and unattended.

A stone bench rested under the tree as if waiting for a companion, and Susanna recognized the Spirit whirling about her. The same one she experienced at Christ Church. Serene. Holy.

She sat on the bench and ran her bare hand over the tree's winter bark. Was it like Lover's Oak, ancient and fabled? Was it anxious for spring? For love to bloom under its leaves again?

With a sigh, she reclined against the trunk and warmed her hands in her coat pockets while the breeze stung her face and tugged the ends of her loose hair. She loved a locked garden. She understood the meaning of this walled place. Secret and intended for only one.

The tree.

This was how it should be with the Lord. Walled. Locked. Intended for only One. The Tree. But she'd let other things, foreign things, come and plant in her garden. The cares of life.

Trying to make her entire world secure and safe, planned, when in fact there were no real guarantees.

Except one.

"I'm sorry, Lord. I've made it all about me and what I want—"

"Excuse me, what are you doing here?"

Susanna jolted forward, her resting heart startled. The queen stood at the opening of the narrow, low garden door.

"Ma'am." She curtsied then retraced her snowy path toward the door. "I'm sorry, I was waiting for Nate . . . Nathaniel . . . the king." She fumbled, stuttered, and found no comfort in tucking her hands in her pockets. "The door . . . was ajar. I'd never have seen it otherwise. I didn't realize anyone else was here."

"This is a private garden."

"I didn't mean to intrude." She wanted to escape but couldn't. She was walled in and the queen blocked the only way out.

"I invited you. To the coronation." The queen moved forward, her footsteps kicking up a small tuft of snow. She wore jeans and a heavy knit turtleneck along with a pair of knee boots with fur trim rolling over the tops. She appeared relaxed and casual. "I wanted Nathaniel to see you are not right for Brighton, for him."

"I never said I was, ma'am."

"Why did you come then? I had my reasons for inviting you. You must have had your reasons for coming."

"Believe it or not, the same as yours. Prove to myself Brighton wasn't for me. Not that I thought a lot about it, but I wanted to put Nate, er, I mean—"

"Nathaniel."

"Yes, Nathaniel, behind me. I didn't think I was in love with him . . ." *Shut up.* But it was too late. The queen's expression hardened. Susanna had said too much. "And . . . my little sister . . ." Did the garden get a sudden blast of warm air? Heat blazed under her coat, across her torso and up her neck. "Avery begged to come . . . she'd have never forgiven me . . . if I passed this up."

"You didn't think you were in love with him?"

"No, yes, right . . ." Could she be dismissed? Susanna guessed that a mad dash for the door, which would require her to slam the queen of Brighton against a stone wall, might be frowned upon. "I'm not. Right."

"You're not?"

"No." She shook her head. "Definitely . . . *not.*" She was lying to the queen. "I'm sorry, Your Majesty. I just lied to you. I do love him." The truth straightened her rounded shoulders. "I do."

"I see. And does he know?"

Susanna shook her head. "I didn't see the point."

"Wise woman. You know, even if the law allowed Nathaniel to marry a foreigner, I'd not approve of you. Nor would the prime minister."

Susanna regarded the woman a moment, ascertaining her tone, her intent. She welcomed the cold air again, snapping against her legs. "If the law allowed it, I think it'd be up to Nathaniel to choose who to love."

The queen smiled and brushed the chill off her arms. Or perhaps she brushed away Susanna's tart reply. "You know my son, don't you. He's very decisive, yes. He'll choose his own bride. And he has a perfect choice right here in Brighton."

"Lady Genevieve."

"Ah, so you know of her then. I'm sure he'll propose to her within a fortnight now that the coronation is over."

"When I met Nathaniel, I didn't even know he was a prince. He was just an amazing, kind man who kept showing up whenever I needed someone. When he volunteered to help out at our restaurant, I still didn't know he was a crown prince. Then I saw his face on a coin."

"He's a chameleon, that one." The queen's smile dallied with the moonlight. "Loves to roll up his sleeves and work with the people. That's what will make him a great king."

"That and his character," Susanna said. "I saw it today, ma'am, at the coronation. He was born for this. It's his destiny."

The queen's stance relaxed a bit. "Then you know what's at stake here. If he—"

"Hello?" Nathaniel's handsome face appeared through the opening and Susanna rooted her heels into the cold ground to keep from running to him. He looked sporty and sexy, dressed in a field jacket, boots, and jeans. "Do I even want to know what you two are doing out here?" He glanced at his mother, then at Susanna.

"Why aren't you at the symphony?"

"I left. Took my escape during intermission." Nathaniel peered at Susanna, and her heart blazed. "We've three more days of celebration. No need to weary myself. Besides, I wanted to visit with my friend from America." He stepped around his mum to greet Susanna, lightly kissing her cheek. "I see you found Dad's garden."

"It's incredible. Doesn't it remind you of the Christ Church grounds?"

"So it does." He scanned the perimeter. "Dad's old garden. The first King's Garden."

"What do you mean the *first* King's Garden?" the queen asked.

"Susanna named the garden on St. Simons 'A King's Garden'— before she knew anything of my royal business." Nathaniel took Susanna's hand. "Mum, have a good evening."

"Where are you two going? Nathaniel, where's Liam?" The queen's inquiry trailed them down the corridor and into the bright, warm main hall.

"Taking a much needed night off." Nathaniel led Susanna out of the house to an idling compact sports convertible with the top down.

"You have other protection officers. Nathaniel, you shan't go out alone."

"Don't worry, Mum." Nathaniel opened Susanna's door. "I can see to myself." Then he leaned and whispered in Susanna's ear, "I haven't stopped thinking of you all day."

She smiled all over as he clapped her door closed. She was definitely heading in the wrong direction. But for now, she just couldn't make herself care. Being alone with Nathaniel was all that mattered.

Susanna snuggled down in the two-seater, wrapped in a coach blanket, riding in wistful silence next to Nathaniel.

He reached for her hand. "You cold? This was the closest thing I had to a open carriage ride without disturbing the mews. I wanted you to see the countryside in the light of the stars."

"I'm good." She snuggled deeper under the blanket, her eyes heavy with peace. The night air skimmed her hair, twisting the ends in an arctic rush.

"Don't fall asleep on me now."

"Peaceful." Susanna peeked at him through low eye slits.

His heart rumbled. Love. He was falling deeper by the minute.

Squeezing her hand, Nathaniel released her and gripped the steering wheel, surging the motor forward, hugging the pebbled berm of the country bend. The sports car sailed about the curve, over the rise and fall of the road.

He loved racing free over Brighton's countryside, directed only by the truth in his heart. No King's Office. No prime minister. No entailment. No paparazzi. No TV cameras. No political entanglements. No coronation parties or dissonant symphonies. Just the wind whistling through the stars and the woman he loved by his side. He cut a glance at Susanna. The greenish-gold glow from the dash accented her facial contours. She reclined as if she'd ridden next to him a hundred times.

Not once did she ask, "Where are we going?" She trusted him. Until now he never calculated how much trust mattered to him. Trust *of* the woman he loved. Trust *in* the woman he loved.

From the cubby above the gearshift box, his phone rang, lighting the small space between the dashboard and seats. He peeked at the screen. Mum. Probably calling to pick up her cause. The phone went silent and dark. Then immediately rang again. Susanna reached forward and offered it to Nathaniel.

"Answer it," she said, soft, low. "You're the king, Nathaniel. Act like it."

He took the phone, and she ducked her hand back under the blanket. "Busting my chops, I see." Honest. He needed a woman who was honest.

Nathaniel tapped the screen with his thumb. "Hello." It was the prime minister taking up Mum's protection-officer cause and bringing political news.

"There was a small riot in Strauberg. Rejecting the king and calling for the independence of Hessenberg regardless of the entail."

"Was anyone hurt?"

"People no, some property, yes."

"Is my presence required?"

"No, but—"

"Can we discuss this in the morning?"

"All right."

"Thank you, Henry."

The phone went dark and silent. For all of ten seconds. Then Jonathan rang.

"Where are you?"

"Taking personal time."

"With Susanna? Nathaniel, if this gets out—"

"It won't." Nathaniel ended the call and tossed his phone to the dashboard. He felt like he just denied her, and it didn't sit well with him. "There are days technology is a complete bother."

"But if you want to dance, you got to pay the piper."

He looked at her then laughed. "How profound. You have a way of cutting through the mess, don't you?"

"Of others, yes. Not my own so much."

"'Tis always the case. It's easy to see the speck in our brother's eye while missing the beam in our own." Nathaniel downshifted as the village light bloomed over the dark horizon.

Susanna sat forward, inhaling deep, drawing the blanket to her chin. "Hmm, that smells wonderful. What is it?"

"Puffs. Something like an American pastry but very light." Nathaniel rolled slowly down the quiet, deserted street. "I'm sorry the shops are all closed, though the bakers are hard at work."

"I'm coming here tomorrow for a puff."

The town lights faded in the rearview, and Nathaniel continued north, shifting through the gears, riding the asphalt wave, cutting through snowy white meadows. His heart hummed in harmony with the motor when Susanna's hand covered his.

"I saw it today, Nate. You are the right man for the job of king. God has called you, not man."

Nathaniel raised her hand to his lips. "This is why I need you with me."

"You don't need me. The Lord has given you everything you need to succeed."

"But you remind me like no one else."

"Then you have me. Right here. Right now."

A shadow of reality darkened Nathaniel's joy in the evening. Right here, right now, but not for long. That's what she was whispering to his soul. In a few days' time, she'd be gone and he'd be king without her.

His heart refused the idea. He must figure out a remedy. But what if he did and she refused to come to Brighton? Moving would require enormous change and uprooting.

When a rustic building with a high, narrow steeple came into view, he slowed, took the bend left, and aimed the sports car for the gravel driveway. The tires crunched over the rocks. Susanna tossed off the blanket and fingered the tangles from her hair.

"Where are we?"

"St. Stephen's Chapel. Named for the saint, not the king. But it was built by Stephen I in 1550." Nathaniel parked beside the thick trunk of a high-reaching tree with snow balancing on the limbs.

"I feel like I've been in a state of wonder ever since I got here." Susanna started to step out of the car.

"Wait, wait . . ." Nathaniel scurried around the back of the car, his feet sliding on the snow-covered ice. He loped sideways, banging his side against the car's boot.

"Are you okay?" Susanna angled around to see him.

"Other than my pride, yes." He took a careful step forward. Then another. His foot slid but he balanced by putting his hand down above the taillight. "Slippery mess tonight."

"Kind of prophetic, don't you think?"

He glared at her. "Yes, and now I'm depressed." He laughed low, reaching for the door handle. "Milady."

She took his hand and curtsied. "Milord."

He snatched up the blanket she'd been using and led her to the chapel.

In the small foyer, Nathaniel hunted for the candles. "They used to be right . . . here . . . in the cabinet under the usher's bench." His fingers curved around the thick tapers. "Ah, here they are."

"There's no electricity?" she asked.

"Not for the last four hundred and fifty years." Nathaniel passed three candles to Susanna then took three for himself. He struck a match and touched the flame to each used wick.

The flickering flames devoured the darkness, and he could see Susanna's eyes. He loved her eyes. They spoke to him more than words. He wanted to hold her, kiss her, but he'd promised himself he'd keep the evening very chaste.

Though the scent of her skin perfuming the entryway did his thudding heart no good. If he closed the millimeter distance between them, he could bend to taste her lips and blame his surrender on their tight quarters, the candlelight, perhaps the cold or the moonbeams streaming through the stained glass.

She smiled.

*Oh, Susanna.* His hungry heart rumbled.

He cleared his throat. "Shall we?" He led her with her three flickering flames through the door, no wider than the frame of a large man, into the sanctuary.

He momentarily regretted his decision to bring her here alone. Letting her face and form awaken a love that a mere friendship could not slake.

Susanna raised her candles and turned a small circle to see the simple, rustic structure with rough-hewn pews and dry, wide floorboards.

"Beautiful, beautiful."

Nathaniel surveyed the chapel through her eyes. Time had worn down the exterior stone and timber, but the fragrance of incense offered to the King of all kings lingered in the rafter beams and preserved the sanctuary.

"King Stephen I was married here," he said, spreading out the blanket at the altar, his breath billowing against the candlelight. "Dedicated his children here." He patted the flat, unadorned horizontal beam that crossed the kneeler. "With his noble men and women in attendance."

"I feel like just sitting and listening, see if the room will whisper its secrets." Susanna stepped up the altar to the short platform and faced forward. Raising her candles higher, she examined the beams and the windows, the seats for the bishops and king, the loft for the choir. "It's like their songs and prayers still hover here."

"Perhaps that's why I love this place so much." Nathaniel

anchored his candles in the wooden and wax-stained stands closest to Susanna. "Come 'round here." He sat on the blanket, adjusting the altar cushion to brace their backs.

She plopped down next to him with a contented sigh.

"Are you glad you came?"

"Yes." She gave him a blue glance. "But I have to go too."

"Don't remind me. I'm having fun." Daylight, candlelight, ballroom light, she captivated him. "You were beautiful today in the abbey, standing while everyone bowed, so confident of yourself. You were a beacon to me." He shrugged. "When I saw you, I knew what *it* was about. Not just echoing hollow words kings recited before me, but accepting what I was born to do, for God, for the people."

"It's about time, Nate."

"You helped me see the truth."

"You knew it. You just didn't want to accept it. I didn't mean to stand today. I was just so caught up in the moment."

"I nearly smiled."

"I know." She smacked her hand against the hardwood floor. "I'm glad you didn't. I might have cracked up. There was such joy in that place to be so somber."

He said nothing but pressed his hand over hers.

"You looked great up there, you know," she said, "all regal and stately. Exactly where you were supposed to be."

He resituated to face her. "So if I'm to be Brighton's king—I know it, you know it—then why am I so madly in love with you?"

"You're crazy—" She laughed but her voice quivered and faltered.

"I'm serious, Susanna."

"Oh, by the way, Daddy, Mama, and everyone back home send their love." She deftly changed the subject, rose to her feet, and paced away. "I think Mama's going to hang a plaque, 'King Nathaniel II of Brighton Cleaned Toilets Here.'"

He laughed. "I'm honored. How grand. I miss them. How is your father healing?"

"Back at work. But Catfish took over a lot of his duties. All Mama lets him do is make sauce and rolls."

"Very worthy endeavors. I still want his sweet-sauce recipe. And Gracie? What's going on with her sailor?" Talk of her home settled him. He thought it settled her too.

"She's in love. Can you believe it?" She perched on the edge of a front-row pew.

"I only saw the sailor a few times but he seemed determined to win her heart."

"She was just as determined not to let him."

"But she failed?"

Susanna smiled, nodding. "Best kind of failure. Not to want to fall in love, but then . . ." The light in her eyes dimmed. "We're talking about love again."

"Are you going to be like Gracie? Refuse to fall in love?"

"There's nothing to refuse, Nate. We had a few moments in Georgia, two people in the midst of big change. One stepping back, one moving forward. Did it ever occur to you that you have feelings for me simply because you can't have me?"

"I know that feeling. It's obsessive. Consuming. Blinding. That's not how I feel about you." He joined her on the pew. "For five months, I forced myself not to contact you. Tried not to think about you. I wanted to move on. But no matter what I do, the truth demands to be recognized. I love you."

"Nate, that is both blinding and consuming." Susanna walked toward one of the moon-haloed windows. "Adam said he and I liked the idea of each other more than each other. He was right. I'm not sure the same isn't happening here."

"Not to be rude, but don't try Adam's advice on me. And by the way, you think rather highly of yourself if you think I love you just because I can't have you."

"Highly of myself?" She crossed back over to him, her heels hard against the plank floor. "Who's the one who announced to a girl he'd known for two weeks he couldn't marry her?"

"I did. I don't deny it. I felt you should know."

"Talk about thinking highly of oneself."

"Jon urged me. He thought you might get the wrong impression."

"Because I'm a dishrag who falls for any handsome man who gives her a bit of a flirt?"

This wasn't going at all like he'd pictured.

"He knew I fancied you."

Her breath misted the sanctuary's chilled air. "Want a newsflash, Nate? I'm not interested in marrying you. You're pretty cool, and I like hanging out with you, but marriage? Living in Brighton? It's freezing here. And all this snow? I'd miss the heat and the beach."

"I'm glad we had this little talk. This exchange will help me get my heart in line." The candles flickered, breaking up the shadows moving about them.

"Good." She backed away from him, returning to the blanket. "You're kind of self-focused, you know."

"As are you. The wounded woman thing doesn't play well with you. You're hiding your strength. I suppose you owe that to Adam."

"Hey, leave him out of this."

"Simply making an observation." Nathaniel joined her on the blanket, his heart awake and burning in his chest.

"Back at you, bub. This whole 'Ooh, I don't think I can be king' crock has got to go. I saw you up there this morning, and you looked like you'd been king for years. Completely comfortable. Like you were born to do this."

"Why are you still in St. Simons trying to start a business? Why don't you get out of there? Go back to Atlanta or Birmingham or New York? You're a talented architect. What about your dream to work in one of the world's great gardens?"

"Too late."

"Only if you give up."

She folded her arms across her torso and closed herself off. "I'll think about it." Then she peered at him. "You should think about marrying Lady Genevieve. Might be the best for everyone."

"Leave her out of this."

"Just saying."

"Fine, Susanna, I get it. You're mad because I told you I love you." But he didn't wish back his words. He'd say them again right now if he didn't know without a doubt she'd belt him.

"I'm mad because you told me, fully aware you can't do anything about it."

"And if I could? You made your stand clear. You'd not marry me anyway."

"Glad we cleared that up." She brushed a bit of nothing from her jeans, then tugged the edge of the blanket over her.

In the silence, the tension between them ebbed. Nathaniel rested his head against the altar rail. Should he take her back to Parrsons? Forget spending time with her?

"Is it pretty awesome to be a royal?" When he looked over at her, she was peering at him with the faint candlelight flickering in her eyes.

"Awesome?" He'd not fielded such a question in a while. "I don't know . . . yeah, I guess. I've never know anything else. But I see the privilege and wealth. It affords me good things. I also live under weighty expectations and centuries of history. It's both comforting and unsettling to know where I come from and where I'm going. Where my children and their children will go."

"Will you still be Nate Kenneth?"

"When I travel, I'm sure. Yes."

"Will you introduce yourself to potential dates as Nate or King Nathaniel?"

Did she really want to talk about this? "Depends. If she's under an oak tree with a flat tire?"

"Don't . . . I'm serious here."

"Marrying a king is not an easy life. Constantly in the public eye. Every move watched and scrutinized. Did you know companies build royal purchase power into their annual budgets?"

"Oh, I couldn't handle it." She faced him, sitting cross-legged, her attitude firing.

"Of course you could." He smiled, grateful the conversation had changed, relieving the tension between them. "One year I fancied a certain brand of sweaters and the company went worldwide. The wife of the king will wield the same power. Not to mention the pressure and expectation to produce an heir."

"Now *that's* pressure." Susanna tugged the edge of the blanket about her shoulders.

"But most of all, the people want their king happy and in love. It encourages marriage and family, love and commitment, in the fabric of society."

"I'll pray for you. I will."

"We're in St. Stephen's Chapel. Can you pray now?" Her prayers for them on the Christ Church grounds still resonated with him. "Next week I'm in a series of meetings about Hessenberg and the entail. And the pressure to marry will intensify."

"S–sure." Susanna touched her hand to his knee. Nathaniel closed his eyes and focused heavenward though every part of him wanted to hold her.

Susanna began a slow, clear, whispering song.

> *Yes, he loves us,*
> *oh, how he loves us.*

Nathaniel blended his voice with hers, singing to the true King of Brighton, the One who is Lord of Heaven and Earth.

# TWENTY-ONE

*A* bright light fell over Nathaniel. He stirred, cold and stiff but cozy, still wanting to sleep. A warm body pressed in against him. He reached round behind him, resting his hand on the high curve of a feminine hip.

Susanna. He bolted upright. "Suz."

They'd talked long into the night—about life and love, about being royal and being Southern. The two factions weren't so far apart. "Suz." He gently shook her shoulder.

She bolted upright, bonking her head on the altar. "Ouch . . . for crying out loud." She punished the time-darkened wood with a slap of her hand, then scrambled to untangle her feet from the blanket. "Let go, you stupid thing." Her words created crystal billows in the frigid air.

"I take it you're not a morning person." He sat up and smoothed his every-which-way hair into place.

"No, but I'm also not so fond of hitting my head." She glanced at the morning light shining palely through the window. "What time is it? Did we fall asleep? We did. We fell asleep. We've got to go. Your mama is going to hate me."

"Susanna, I'm a grown man. I can do as I please." He smoothed his hair into place and picked up the blanket. "She's not going to hate you."

All but one of the candles had burned out, and wax stalactites hung from the wooden holders. Nathaniel leaned forward and doused the last remaining flame with a thin, cold puff.

"Do as you please? Are you kidding me?" A fierce blue intensified her eyes. "You can't just run off and not tell people where you are, Nate. How did we fall asleep all night? We've got to go . . . you've got to go." She charged up the aisle, her hair snapping behind her as if to say, "Yeah, what she said."

"I'll just call Jon." Nathaniel tucked the blanket under his arm and raced after her. Oh, his keys. He ran back and snatched them from the altar railing. "'Tis fine. Everything is fine. Don't worry, love."

She stopped in the foyer doorway. "How can you be so calm? They'll be looking for you. 'King disappears on his coronation night.' It looks like we . . . you know . . ." Her expression paled as she motioned to their altar bed. "Slept together."

"Slept. Yes. Nothing more. You fret so, Suz." He'd laugh if she weren't so darn serious. And cute. "If I was needed, or they were concerned, they would've called. No one called. I'll prove it to you." He patted his pockets for his phone. "Bugger, where's my phone?"

"Well?" She waited, arms folded, tapping her toe.

"I must have left it in the car." He shoved past her and out the door, his concern mounting. "I thought no one rang up because they wanted to leave me be."

"We're dead."

Nathaniel paused just outside the door. "We are *not* dead. I didn't take you to be such a pessimist." His eyes searched hers. "But if we were to die, would it be so bad? We had a lovely evening."

She shoved him on out the door. "Go, get your phone."

"I'm glad we came up here," he said, trying to shake off his frustration—first by leaving his phone in the car, second by the sense Susanna was restricting his access to her heart. "This is my favorite place in all of Brighton."

"I'm glad we came too. It's a beautiful chapel."

A swirl of white confronted Nathaniel when he started for his motorcar. "It's snowing again."

Susanna slipped on the bottom step and stumbled down to the gravel path.

Nathaniel reached back, catching her in his arms, steadied himself, and held her close.

"Susanna?"

"Nate, we're not alone." She pointed behind him, and he whirled 'round just as an army, yea a battalion, of photographers emerged from a motorcade of black SUVs and motor scooters. Their cameras fired a rat-a-tat-tat as Nathaniel stood in freeze-frame with Susanna still in his arms.

"How did they find us?" She shoved away from him.

"Get in my car." Nathaniel grabbed her hand, shielding her from the digital firing squad. How could he have forgotten? His much ballyhooed antique MG was given to him by his grandfather when he was sixteen. He used to present it at antique motor shows.

"Your Majesty, is this the American girl? The one who didn't kneel in the abbey?"

"Are you two in love?"

"What about the marriage law?"

"Does Lady Genevieve know you've taken a mistress already?"

"Mistress?" Susanna stepped toward the photographers. "Hey, I'm not any man's mistress."

"Susanna, please." He took hold of her arm. "Don't feed the jackals."

"I'm not going to let them believe a lie." She faced them again. "I'm only a friend."

"A friend?" They cackled. Every man of them. "A friend for

a one-nighter? Last hurrah before heading home so you can tell your friends you shagged the Brighton king?"

"No!" Against the pale morning, her cheeks beamed a brilliant red.

"Get in the car, Suz. Don't encourage them." But the small sports motor was buried in snow. Nathaniel started scraping and shoveling away the mounds of snow.

"But they're making stuff up."

"Susanna. Please." She must listen to him. "Defending yourself only fans their flames."

"I'm a friend, just a friend. Which is more than I can say for any of you."

"Susanna . . . shovel, please." Nathaniel was grateful the snow was soft and powderlike. He'd have put the top up last night if he'd known he was going to fall asleep and spend the night.

"We spent the night in prayer and worship."

"Prayer and worship?" Laughter burst from among the congregation of photographers. "You're serious? You expect us to believe he *prayed* with you?"

Susanna began clearing the snow from the car with vigor. "Bunch of meanies."

"I told you not to engage them." Nathaniel shoveled faster, the motion warming away the cold but awakening his anxieties.

He'd not been very public with his renewed faith yet. These men would find it hard to believe Nathaniel spent the night with anyone in prayer and worship, let alone a beautiful woman.

"Your Majesty, do you have a word on the explosions this morning?"

He stopped shoveling. "This morning?"

"You've not heard?" A red-cheeked man peered from around his camera.

"No, not yet." *Again?* Nate jerked open the driver-side door, plopped into his seat, and fired up the engine. "Get in."

Susanna's seat was still mostly covered in snow but she jumped in, slamming her door as Nathaniel shot in reverse toward the road, scattering the photographers like wild chickens.

With the road clear, Nathaniel sped toward Parrsons, the wind biting as it dipped down over the windshield.

He glanced at his phone. "Thirty missed calls."

"I'm sorry, Nate."

"It's not your fault."

"It will be to them. This is why they don't want Brighton kings marrying foreign women. They steal their affections."

He peered at her. She was right. She'd stolen his affections. "Those chaps don't care a whit about my affections." When he covered the major curves in the road and hit a straight stretch, Nathaniel dialed Jonathan.

"I'm on my way to Parrsons."

"No, don't. Parrsons is swarming with press. Where've you been? The Royal Guard is on alert."

"What? Mum knew I was with Susanna."

"But where? You never returned."

"Blast it man, the photographers found me. You mean my own security detail couldn't? I was at St. Stephen's."

"The *LibP* came out with an entire front page photo, half you, half Susanna. Looks as if you were making hot-eyes at each other during the coronation prayers. What was she doing standing?"

"What's this about another explosion?" He glanced over at Susanna. She sat stiff and pale. He needed to get her to warmth and safety.

"A small bomb. Blew out an empty building. We got a message a few minutes after from a free Hessenberg group, demanding the end to the entail. There's all kinds of wild speculation in the press this morning. Everything from you purposefully ignoring Lady Genevieve to deny Hessenberg's independence. Others calling for a revolt. Some saying you're going to abdicate."

"Meet me at my office in an hour. And tell the guards to stand down." He ended the call just as the first small village popped up on the horizon.

"I'm going to drop you off here, Susanna. The press is all over Parrsons."

Her eyes glistened. "O–okay."

"This isn't your fault." Nathaniel took the first right at cruising speed, then the first left, arriving in a service alley. He idled the MG behind the loading dock of the Horch Bakery, secure from the probing eyes of the press. "This is just the media being the media. Nothing we can't handle."

"Were people hurt?" She got out, shivering, shaking the snow from her coat.

"Jon will brief me, but I don't think so. Henry said not last night. Suzanna, this has nothing to do with me disappearing for a night. Dissenters are just looking for ways to break the entail. To free themselves from the monarchy."

"It'll be worse when the pictures of us go live." The color of cold and emotion shaded her cheeks.

"Let them do their worst. We did nothing wrong."

"But we gave the appearance of wrong. The people depend on you to do what's right. To put aside your own desires and will. That's just for everyday situations. But you have a political entanglement that requires you do what's right for millions of people. If you've lost their trust, you've lost them. You've lost your ability to influence. So yeah, we did do something wrong."

He exhaled at her frank truth. "I should have you on my privy council."

"You should get going." She walked around the back of the car. "Am I going in here?" She pointed to the bakery's back door.

"You'll be safe here. Horch makes the best puffs in Brighton." Nathaniel reached for the door. "I'll alert Rollins to send a car when things die down."

"You think Avery's all right?"

"If she's with Aunt Louisa, yes. I'll have Rollins check in on her." He stepped inside the warm, fragrant bakery. The place was empty except for the puffy-faced proprietor behind the counter.

"Two coffees and whatever fresh puffs you have," Nate said. "My friend will be staying for a while." He passed the man several sterling notes. "Please see to it that she's taken care of properly. If she owes more, I'll settle when the car arrives to collect her."

The proprietor waved off Nathaniel's money. "It's an honor, Your Majesty. I'm glad to know you're all right. I heard on the news you were missing." The baker cut a glance toward Susanna. "I'll see to your friend."

"Discretion is a virtue, Mr. Horch."

"Yes, sir." He bent beneath the counter and came up with a folded *Liberty Press*.

Susanna angled around Nathaniel. The front page was split into two pictures. In the top left, Nathaniel peeking out from under his crown with a wee hint of a smile on his lips. Then a diagonal line and Susanna's image on the bottom right of the page, standing, gazing intent and blue toward the altar, her golden hair falling about her shoulders from her bare head, the congregation kneeling around her.

She looked enraptured. Captured.

"'Tis you, miss?"

"Yes," Susanna said, weak, resigned.

The bold block headline all but incited the readers:

The House of Stratton Falling to Foreign Loves

The sidebar story asked,

Could This Woman Topple the Dynasty?

"Oh my gosh . . . Nate, that's ridiculous." Susanna spun away, hand to her forehead. "I've never so much as toppled an anthill, let alone a royal dynasty."

Nathaniel snapped the paper shut and handed it over the counter. "There's a Civil Honor Medal in it for you if you keep the photographers out."

Mr. Horch bristled as he passed the coffee and bag of puffs to Nathaniel, flattening his round chin into his neck. "Medal or not, Your Highness, she's safe with me."

"I meant no insult, Mr. Horch." Nathaniel passed one of the coffees to Susanna. "I've got to go." He scurried around for the back door, then paused. "I hate leaving you here like this."

"I'm fine." She waved him on. "Go."

He hesitated, itching to take her in his arms and kiss her. Blast it, if he was being accused of an indiscretion he might as well taste of its fruits, no?

Instead he nodded to Horch. "Good day."

Outside, he scraped the last of the snow from his seat and settled in, revving the engine and blasting the heat. He crept to the end of the alley, anxious to be on his way. Braking at the end of the low row of shops, he took a sip of his coffee and shifted into gear.

The road was clear. Nathaniel shot onto the road, aiming for Cathedral City, leaving a chunk of his heart behind in the rich fragrance of the Horch Bakery.

Campbell discarded the *Liberty Press* to the pile of newspapers by her chair. A fine first day in the press for her son, the king. His somber, dignified crowning moment ruined by the bareheaded American who did not kneel when called upon, but stood, gaping at Nathaniel like a schoolgirl at a youth dance.

The queen studied the image one last time. It hadn't helped that the morning light had fallen through the abbey windows, illuminating the American as if she were some kind of earth angel.

The *LibP* all but accused the Crown of conspiring to break the law. The *Informant's* headline merely speculated.

The King's Angel. Who Is This Woman?

With a steady hand, Campbell tipped the royal-blue, gilt-edged porcelain teapot and filled the matching cup. It had been many years, but Nathaniel was no stranger to scandal or tabloid headlines.

Adding a small lump of sugar and dollop of cream, Campbell rose and moved to the window, cup and saucer in hand. How many cups of tea had aided her life's musings? Thousands? She glanced down at the royal china set that served centuries of House of Stratton queens.

*What wisdom have you, teacup?*

"Leo, are you watching from above?" Campbell longed for a glimpse of sunlight to break through the cold, slate sky. "He's in love, Leo. But he can't have her. If you could ask the good Lord to give him wisdom . . ." Her slight laugh steamed the cold pane.

So bold and in control, she often teased her husband about his arrival in heaven.

*Leo, are you going to ask the good Lord to get up from his throne when you finally arrive at your judgment, thanking him kindly for keeping it warm for you all these centuries?*

*I just might, Campbell, I just might.*

If she'd known then what she knew now about love, marriage, and sharing a life with a crown prince, a king, she'd . . .

Do it all over again. Even the first years of turmoil and heartache, when she literally had to patch together her heart piece by piece, discovering how to love a man by choice and not by feelings.

"Nathaniel is not you, Leo. Nor is he me." Campbell circled around the couch to the fireplace. "He's his own man, living in a very different age than you and I. It's as if Brighton leapt a hundred years forward since your father approached mine and asked for my hand for his son."

A soft knock sounded at her door, and Rollins appeared. "Lady Genevieve to see you, ma'am."

"This is a pleasant surprise." Campbell faced the door, nodding to Lady Genevieve's curtsy. "Tea?"

"Please." Ginny tugged off her gloves and shrugged out of her coat, as well as any pretense at decorum.

Campbell watched her as she poured her tea. A tiger lady, that one. Knew how to play the game, get her way.

"You saw the paper?" Ginny motioned to the one on top of the pile. "She's insulting the monarchy, Campbell. Showing up to the coronation improperly dressed, standing when all else are kneeling." She snatched up the paper. "Flirting with the king during prayers. It's scandalous. Could they make her look any more like a fairy from Grimm?"

"You seem a bit ruffled by it all." Campbell passed Ginny her tea then took to her chair. "Surely you're not jealous."

"Jealous? Whatever for?" she scoffed, dropping the *LibP* back to the pile and taking the adjacent seat. "She's no threat to me."

"Then why haven't you convinced him?"

"Convinced him of what? To marry me? Have you ever known Nathaniel to do anything that the rest of the world wanted him to? No worry, I've got everything under control. We chatted the other night . . . after the ball."

"Chatted?" Campbell had also chatted with him after the ball. "About what?"

"Let's just say we came to an understanding."

Well then. Campbell sat back, smiling. "How long before I have grandchildren?"

"Two years, tops."

Campbell arched her brow. "Two years?" If he proposed today, it'd take six months to plan the wedding, another one or two to conceive a child, if Ginny were as good at getting pregnant as she was at everything else. "Don't you dare get pregnant outside of wedlock."

"I'd never. It's my name, my crown, my reputation, as much as his and the House of Stratton's." Ginny sipped her tea. "Have you seen the news shows this morning?"

"Only the papers." Did she want this woman for her son? As a daughter-in-law? She seemed so self-aware. So self-absorbed.

"A group of photographers spotted Nathaniel's car this morning up at St. Stephen's. They waited for him to emerge. Which he did. With her. She's already being labeled his American mistress."

"Mercy." Campbell lost her breath. Her hand trembled when she set her teacup on the table beside her. "What in the world?"

"Not to worry, I've got it covered." Ginny's smile garnered no confidence from the queen. "Morris and the lot turned to me when the pictures started coming in. I assured them Susanna was only his friend, a girl of no import, and no threat to Brighton or Hessenberg. The king and I are on a fine, steady footing."

"But you're not on a fine, steady footing. And who authorized you to speak for the king? The King's Office is to deal with the media."

"Campbell, the media came to me. Who better to cover for Nathaniel's romantic foolishness than me?" When Ginny stood, Campbell did also. "The entail depends on me becoming queen. Everyone knows it."

"The entail depends on a descendant of the grand duke's royal line."

"I am the closest thing." She offered a high, twittery laugh.

"The others renounced the throne and scattered across Europe. Marrying me is the perfect solution. You know it's true, Campbell."

"It's a solution though I daresay not perfect. And it's *Your Majesty* or *ma'am* to you, my good woman. Don't come into my home impertinent and arrogant. I have lived to serve Brighton my whole life, and I am keen on every aspect of her laws, her alliances, and her responsibilities."

"I didn't mean to imply—"

"Then just what did you mean to imply? Next time the newspapers contact you instead of the King's Office, kindly decline to comment."

"They know me, Camp—ma'am. I've spent years building a relationship with Morris and the like."

"When you were crawling around in your stinky nappies, I was taking tea with Morris Alderman." Campbell's suspicions rose. She'd not noticed this side of the lady before. "What have you done, Ginny? What have you said to the media?"

"What have I done? Ensured your monarchy, that's what. Your foolish son tramped off with an American commoner. She'll ruin us all. So I ran interference with the press. I did it for you, for Nathaniel."

"You mean for you."

"Yes, for me as well. So what? I'm right for queen. After all, you married to be queen one day, did you not?" Ginny had mastered sly and slithery.

Ire sparked Campbell to her senses. Such an ugly side to the beautiful Lady Genevieve. "Don't count my marriage to Leo as part of your manipulation strategy. You know nothing of what you're talking about."

"This I do know, ma'am." Ginny set down her tea. "We do not live in a time when royalty is as revered. The respect of the people must be earned. The palace must be a PR firm every bit as much as a monarchy. With Nathaniel's charm and leadership and my popularity and PR experience we can make the House of Stratton one of the strongest monarchies in Europe. We can rule Brighton *and* Hessenberg. So what if I did a bit of meddling? You'd do the same. It was for the good of all. Tell me, what will you do when this foreigner comes 'round saying she's pregnant with Nathaniel's child and scandalizes the whole country?"

Campbell gasped. Ginny's brazenness broached permanent offense.

"Don't be naïve, Your Majesty. Brace yourself, because such a claim will be the first death peal of the Crown."

"But last I knew one had to have sex to be pregnant." A voice crossed the room from the doorway. "So claiming his love child will be impossible."

Campbell aimed her focus on the door as Ginny whirled around. "Excuse me, but this is a private conversation."

Rollins stood in the doorway with Susanna. "Ma'am, she asked to speak with you. I took the liberty of escorting her to your quarters."

"Thank you, Rollins. Susanna, do come in." Campbell stepped around the chairs to greet her new guest. Step aside, *Lady* Ginny.

"Thank you, but I don't mean to interrupt. I was . . ." She looked down. "I'm sorry about all the mess."

Her humble posture moved Campbell. She looked in need of a shower and fresh clothes. "Please, come sit for tea. You look absolutely chilled."

"Thank you, ma'am, but no. I need to get . . . cleaned up. Have you seen my sister, Avery?"

"No, I've not."

"I'll see if Rollins can call Colin." Susanna motioned behind her, toward the door. "Ma'am, I want to thank you for inviting us. It's been a true honor. We'll never forget it."

"I imagine you won't," Ginny said. "Look at all the trouble you've—"

"Lady Genevieve," Campbell said. "Be quiet." The woman took too much liberty. Dared to insult a guest of Parrsons House and the queen.

"I never meant any disrespect or harm. Nate and I . . . I never meant to cause any trouble for the family." Susanna curtsied and backed toward the door. "I just . . . just wanted to . . ."

"Oh my stars." Ginny thundered toward her. "You're in love with him, aren't you?"

Infernal Ginny. She could take a few lessons from this girl on humility.

Susanna looked up. "Are you?" she asked, strong and steady, despite her quivering chin.

"I hardly see it as your business." Ginny mocked her with a conciliatory glance at Campbell as if they were on the same team.

And suddenly, they were not. Campbell abandoned her passion to see Lady Genevieve as her future queen. The woman had no concern for her son, for the House of Stratton, nor for her country. She cared only for herself.

"Then neither are my feelings your business," Susanna said.

Campbell chortled. Ginny's glare iced.

"When shall we hear you are expecting his child?"

"Ginny!" Campbell burned with embarrassment. For herself, for her countrywoman.

"Hey." Susanna forced herself into Ginny's space. "If you knew Nate at all, you'd know better than to make such an assumption." *Good show, Susanna, tell her.* "You claim to know him, but you don't. You claim you want to marry him, but—"

"What do you know of my *claims*?" Ginny flared and fired.

"You blab it all over the press."

Campbell laughed outright as she took her seat. She'd never seen Lady Genevieve speechless and red faced. This was better than an evening at the royal theater. *Go on, Susanna, take this lady to school.*

"If you spent half as much energy proving to Nathaniel that you care about him, he just might not have to hold his nose if he decided to propose." Susanna stepped back, pinching her lips under a sheepish expression.

"What do you know, silly girl?" Ginny crossed to stand in front of Susanna and nearly grabbed a fistful of her coat collar.

But the American didn't back down. Campbell all but shouted, "Touché."

Susanna inched toward Ginny. "I know he's a man of honor, and he'll do what's right. But what about you?"

Ginny eased, smiling, crossing her arms. "I won't be drawn into this debate."

Campbell angled forward in her chair, teacup gripped in her fingers, waiting for Susanna's parlay.

But she said no more, merely turned to Campbell and curtsied. "Ma'am, I won't apologize for saying yes to the invitation, but I am sorry for the trouble my presence has caused. I didn't mean to stand when everyone else was kneeling. And that hat thing?"

"Dear Susanna," Campbell said, "you were refreshing."

"Refreshing?" Ginny screeched.

"I'm not here to trap Nathaniel or to embarrass the royal family."

"No, no, of course not." Campbell rose to her feet, setting her tea aside.

"Yet you trolley off with him last evening, stealing him from his peers," Ginny said. "From his people."

Susanna glanced at Ginny over her shoulder. "Excuse me, but I'm talking to Her Majesty the queen."

Campbell tapped her fingertips to her lips, suppressing her smile. So this is why Nathaniel loved her.

"Like I said, it was just an honor to be invited." Susanna looked Campbell straight on. "You should be proud of him, ma'am."

"Yes, I believe I am."

As Susanna exited, closing the door softly behind her, a flicker of recognition pinged through Campbell's mind. She reminded her of a woman she knew long ago. More than thirty years ago. A woman lost to her until now.

Herself.

"You may go, Ginny."

"You can't seriously side with that woman."

"You may *go*." Campbell picked up her tea and wandered to the window. She might just have to do some gardening today. Not among the frozen palace walls, but among the old, ivy-covered walls of her very own heart.

# TWENTY-TWO

*L*et's just have it on the table. Henry? Seamus?" Nathaniel stood in the center of the Parliament's debate box, an anterior room to the Parliament chambers where fighting factions adjourned to hash out their issues with leaders of the senate and commons.

"I say, Your Majesty, one night with the American undid hours of diplomatic meetings." Hessenberg's governor, Seamus Fitzsimmons, chewed on the tip of his highly polished pipe.

"She's a *friend*." For the hundredth time. Nathaniel paced the masculine room, dark with paneled walls, leather seating, a billiard table, and liquor cabinets. "That's all."

He should be celebrating his coronation today. Instead, he was in the hotbox with his prime minister and the Hessenberg governor, defending his name.

"Did you see Morris Alderman's piece on the Marriage Act?" Sir George, leader of the House of Senators, held up the *LibP*. "Asserting it's a fine law, served us well for two hundred years. He gives a good argument for the importance of the monarchs marrying only Brightonians. Also makes a case if you marry your longtime love—his words not mine, Nathaniel—Lady Genevieve, Hessenberg has their required royal to execute the end of the entail."

"I read it." Nathaniel rubbed his hands over his eyes. He'd bet his last quid that Ginny was behind all of this. After he'd read the piece, he had stood in front of the mirror and practiced proposing to her.

*Ginny, would you do me the honor?*

*Lady Genevieve, will you marry me?*

*Hey, let's just do this, get it over with?*

But he couldn't do it. His love for Susanna sat too close to the surface. Despite her declaration she'd never marry him, he still loved her. His strategy now was to give himself time to get over her.

It'd been ten hours since he'd walked out of St. Stephen's Chapel into the camera firing squad, embroiled in gossip, speculation, and political debate. But it felt like weeks.

Nathaniel pressed his hand against his chest where the ache of missing her persisted.

"We're fortunate the explosion last night and this morning harmed no one," Henry said, "and the people are carrying on with their celebrations. We've doubled your security to walk the streets this evening, Nathaniel."

"It's just the free Hessenberg nationals." Seamus shifted his pipe from one side of his mouth to the other. "Feeling their oats, ol' boy."

"What do you propose?"

"Stay away from the American, Nathaniel." Henry capped the bourbon bottle.

"Seriously? You think avoiding Susanna Truitt will appease the faction that blows up bombs?"

"Rebels, gossips . . ." Henry came 'round to face him. "Whatever. This is about the future government of both countries. A hundred years of pent-up emotions are rising to the fore. There's going to be more trouble." He glanced at Seamus. "Let's minimize what we can."

"Hessenberg becoming a part of Brighton is not new. We've known for at least sixty years we'd lost track of Prince Francis's family. And despite the ongoing economic strain to us, they'd in all likelihood become a province."

"But in the last ten years, a hundred-year-old entail feels old-fashioned, unnecessary." Henry loved to counterpoint and debate.

"Tell that to the EU court."

"She's a rich land, Nathaniel." Seamus puffed on his pipe so smoke encircled his head. He looked like a tweed St. Nicholas. "If we can just get her back on track."

"Yes, but she keeps falling into financial trouble, which harms Brighton's economy."

"Either way, Your Majesty"—Henry arched his brow—"we must prepare for Hessenberg to become a permanent province. The EU will downgrade our credit rating again if we combine our treasuries."

"We may not have a choice, Henry." Nathaniel braced for one of the men to push the conversation toward Ginny. It's what they all wanted . . . two nations.

"Well if you're going to be king, then *be* a king. Lead. Don't be wishy-washy." Henry's admonition surprised Nathaniel. "No one likes wishy-washy royals."

"All right. You want decisiveness? Announce Hessenberg will become a province."

Henry arched his brow. "Let's not be hasty."

Ah finally, his true colors. "You want me to marry Ginny, then?"

Seamus frowned and lowered his pipe.

"Something wrong, Seamus?" Nathaniel said. An old-guard Hessen, the man's years in Brighton-Hessenberg politics had softened him to the province cause. But faced with its reality . . .

"I never believed you should marry Lady Genevieve to save

the entail." He tapped his pipe on a crystal ashtray. "I always thought someone would come 'round to save us. But now that Henry's indicated his opinion, I might change my mind."

In that moment, Nathaniel's thoughts and feelings cleared and aligned. No more dallying with the idea he might marry Ginny. "I'm sorry. I hinted I was willing to marry Ginny, but alas, I'm not."

Seamus sighed, his large chest rising then falling.

Nathaniel decided to meet with Jonathan and discuss one last heroic effort to find a niece or nephew of Prince Francis. Somewhere in the world one must exist.

In the meantime . . .

"What can we do about changing the Marriage Act?" asked Nathaniel.

"What?" The question caught Henry completely unaware.

"We can do nothing." Seamus returned to puffing his pipe. A human chimney. In a room with no windows.

"Seamus, please, your pipe." Nathaniel batted away the smoke.

"Sorry, Your Majesty, but I can't think without it."

"Nathaniel, you go after the Marriage Act and the press will serve you for tea," Henry said.

"Talk about old laws that make no sense. We're all for abolishing an ironclad hundred-year-old entail, but squeamish on examining a two-hundred-year-old marriage act. The world has changed more since 1792 than 1914."

"The press will call it treason, my good lad," Seamus said.

Henry added, "Or worse. Call for the end of the monarchy."

"Henry, who's going to call for the end of the monarchy because we change a law that only impacts me and mine? Let the royal heirs marry who they will as long as there is no formidable objection."

"Some saying marrying a foreigner is objection enough," Seamus said.

"Then let them speak up when and if it happens."

"When and if?" Henry arched his brow and sat in the nearest leather chair. The worn material creaked and moaned. "Whom you marry impacts Brighton, Nathaniel. It's why the law came into being in the first place. You cannot marry someone who might cause potential harm to our sovereignty."

"And I'm quite sure Hessenberg will see it as an end-run, Nathaniel," Seamus said. "It will only fuel the dissidents. Brighton changes laws to suit themselves but not Hessenberg."

"It will appear to be an abuse of power," Henry said. "The rest of *us* poor common folks must obey the law, seek out representatives to plead our case, but not the royals."

"Are you sure you cannot see your way to marry Lady Genevieve?" Seamus cleared his throat and again moved his pipe from one side of his mouth to the other.

"Open your eyes. She's scheming, plotting. She's behind most of the rubbish in the press."

"She'd make a fine queen," Seamus said, unmasking his support for Ginny.

"Really? A schemer and plotter?"

"You'd not be the first Stratton to marry for the kingdom." Henry poured another shot in his glass.

"Oh? What does that mean?"

Henry glanced at Seamus, then to Sir George, who had been listening in quiet contemplation. "It means love for the kingdom overcomes love of the heart."

Nathaniel eyed Henry as he took a shot of the liquor in his glass. The prime minster was brilliant, layered and nuanced.

"I cannot do it."

"Nathaniel, despite these small protests, your coronation has stirred a lot of goodwill," Sir George said. "I support your notion to adjust the marriage act, but let's wait awhile before the king marches down to parliament with his own Order of Council."

"Wait for what?"

"End of the entail."

"End of the entail? That's a year off, Sir George." Plenty of time for Ginny to do her worst. Nathaniel paced to the end of the long, rectangular room. Why were there no blasted windows?

"Nathaniel, would this American even marry you if you asked her?" Henry asked, removing the cloak from their conversation.

He faced the painting of his father and grandfather. "She said she would not."

"Then why cause all this needless fuss?"

Because he didn't believe Susanna. Because he wanted a chance to woo her and change her mind. "Because I want my children, should I have any, to marry whom they love."

"She's thinking of Brighton even if you're not," Sir George said.

"It's a grave thing to let a nation disappear from the face of the earth, Nathaniel." Seamus continued to shed his congenial politician persona. "The history books will remember us, remember *you*, for giving Hessenberg her independence. Allowing her to remain a sovereign nation."

"I'll say it now. I won't marry Ginny. Even if I can't pursue Susanna. I don't love her."

"What does love have to do with freeing a nation?" Seamus, so casual, so practical. Because his heart wasn't on the line. Perhaps Ginny had wooed him too. Like Henry and Mum. And promised him a lofty reward should she become the grand duchess.

"Love has everything to do with freeing a nation, Seamus."

The room fell silent. The arguments had been mounted and failed.

"Thank you, gentlemen, for your council." Nathaniel made his way to the door, tired, ready for luncheon. "It *is* a grave thing to let a nation disappear from the earth, Seamus. I grant you it will be a sad day in Hessenberg. But it's an even graver thing to ask a man to disappear from his own heart."

Out the door and down the hall, his heels tapped the marble

mezzanine and echoed between the crystal chandeliers. Liam fell in step behind him.

Jogging down the sweeping staircase, Nathaniel checked the time. Six-ten. Rollins had sent a car 'round for Susanna by now. She was back at Parrsons, but he'd not be able to see her before the evening stroll through the street parties.

He'd have to arrange a way to see her later tonight. He nearly ached to see her.

At the bottom of the stairs, Jon waited with a knowing grin. "Nathaniel, I received an interesting call this afternoon from Tanner Burkhard." Jonathan fell into step with Nathaniel, heading for the Parliament House main doors. "It has to do with the entail."

"Go on." Tanner was Hessenberg's Minister of Culture and a former university mate of Nathaniel's and Jonathan's.

"Tanner Burkhard studied the entail at the law college the same year as I. It kind of became a hobby for him. Anyway, in his pursuit of entail trivia, he came across an old navy chaplain, Yardley Prather."

"Yardley Prather. Didn't he perform services on campus when we were in university?" Nathaniel hurried toward the waiting SUV. The street stroll began in an hour, and he wanted to dine first. "He was old then. He must be nearing a hundred now."

"He's ninety-four, and Nathaniel," Jonathan said, pausing by the passenger door of the motor, "his older brother Otto witnessed the signing of the entail."

Nathaniel stood aside as Liam opened his door, regarding Jon with a suspicious gaze. "And we're just now hearing of it? Come on, man, is Tanner serious?"

"Apparently the old chap was sworn to secrecy, but he hinted at something when Tanner interviewed him on the anniversary of D-Day about life in Brighton right after World War I. Yardley kind of drifted on him and said something about the 'entail' and 'the secret princess.'"

"The princess? You think he might really know something?" Nathaniel asked. "Can we talk to him? Is he around? Of sane mind?"

"He's living in a senior home on the north end of the County Haybryer. I've an appointment with him in the morning. He's sharp, Nathaniel." Jonathan's eyes lit. "Told me his older brother Otto was sworn to secrecy by Nathaniel I and Prince Francis. But he got into his father's bourbon one Festive Day and confessed something to Yardley, swearing him to secrecy. The old man has never told a soul. But with the end drawing near, he's ready to tell his tale."

"I'm going with you." Nathaniel clapped his hand on Jonathan's shoulder, his hope rising.

"You can't, your diary is full tomorrow, Nathaniel. It's the last day of the coronation celebration. Tanner and the entail barrister are going with me."

Why the governments hadn't done this research before was beyond Nathaniel. A task lost in translation? Lost in *transition*? It was right and fitting to find the true heir to Prince Francis, not settle for a counterfeit who was doing her level best to manipulate the king of Brighton.

Outside Parliament, the retiring day pulled the night shade over Cathedral City. This was not how Nathaniel planned to spend his first day as king, but the overnight in St. Stephen's and the bomb ignited a media storm.

As he climbed into the motorcar, firecrackers popped in the distance. A band began to play. The glow of a central city party pushed back the darkness. Another night of coronation celebrations awaited.

"Liam, can we send a security detail to Parrsons, pick up Susanna and Avery later this evening?" Nathaniel asked. "Jon, how is she? She returned to Parrsons safely, I presume."

Jon and Liam exchanged a look.

"What? Don't hide anything from me."

Jonathan turned around in his seat, facing Nathaniel. "She's gone," he said. "Rollins called. Susanna and Avery left for the airport this afternoon."

"Liam"—Nathaniel tapped the big man's shoulder—"to the airport."

"Nathaniel," Jon said, concern making his eyes appear sadder than usual. "Let her go. Let this whole mess go. She's most likely gone by now."

"Then I have to see for myself. Liam, to the airport."

"She's leaving without saying good-bye to you, Nathaniel. What does that tell you? Don't do this . . . another Lady—"

"Adel?"

"—all over again. Don't scoff . . . you know I'm right."

"No, you are not right," Nathaniel huffed, crashing back against his seat, staring out his window at the night sky. Was Jon right? Was Susanna just this decade's Lady Adel? Was he doomed always to lose his heart to a woman who didn't love him? And make a fool of himself in the midst of it?

"Nathaniel, it's a security risk for you to go to the airport. Liam?"

"I have to agree."

"She did leave without a word to me. I suppose that says more than a thousand words." Nathaniel frowned at his aide, his heart heavy and sad. "You're right too often these days."

Jon faced forward, shaking his head. "Sorry, Nathaniel. I know she meant a great deal to you."

Yeah, whatever. He closed his eyes, breathed deep and tried to focus on the night ahead, his responsibility, his duty to Brighton. "Stratton Palace, Liam. I'd like to dine and change before the street stroll."

As Liam motored through the crowded, festive city toward home, Nathaniel watched the celebrations from his window.

Pints were being raised in his honor. Music and dancing cele-brated him. But it all seemed stars and moons away.

Did they know, under the banner of their merriment, his heart was breaking?

Tomorrow evening would be the Grand Coronation Parade. He'd ride in a gilded white horse-drawn carriage—alone—toward the palace through a city overflowing with citizens wishing him well.

The day after that, life would return to normal, and Nathaniel would settle into his duties. Settle into a life without Susanna Truitt.

# TWENTY-THREE

Susanna wore the gold Louboutins out of Parrsons House and into the taxi, through airport security, and down the long thoroughfare to their gate for home.

Brighton to Atlanta. Nine hours. All while wearing the magic, *stupid* shoes. A reminder never to believe in fairy tales, nor the wild musings of a half-sane homeless woman. Even if she was a millionaire.

"You look ridiculous." Avery pointed at the shoes, her elbows propped on her knee.

"Do I look like I care?" Susanna crossed her legs, exposing her right shoe in all of its crystal and glitter glory, pumping her leg up and down as she flipped through a magazine.

"What if someone recognizes you?"

Susanna tugged the brim of the wide hat she'd purchased at a souvenir shop in the airport. "They won't be expecting me under a hat."

"I can't believe this." Avery stood, flapping her hands against her thighs. "Colin said he'd bring us around when the flight actually left. But no, we have to sit here all day like a couple of jack wagons."

"I'm sorry, but we have to get out of here before it gets

worse." While packing, Susanna had turned on the television to discover she was the topic of a TV show. *Madeline & Hyacinth* went on and on about "the American," playing the coronation video where Susanna stood instead of kneeling and popping up pictures of her this morning at St. Stephen's in Nathaniel's arms.

"He was going to take me riding." Avery pouted, kicking at Susanna's chair.

"You don't ride."

"If I can stand on a board and ride an unpredictable wave, I think I can manage a horse."

"Aves." Susanna flipped the magazine closed. "We're going home. Stop complaining."

With a sigh, Avery flopped back down to her seat and peered at Susanna through a reddish sheen of her chestnut hair. "We were living a fairy tale, weren't we? Just for a moment."

"For a moment," Susanna said, "though I never wanted the fairy tale thing or to be a princess. I just wanted true love. The one."

"You just happened to find a real prince."

"But not true love. Not *the* one."

Avery sat up and gripped Susanna's forearm with her hands. "You are such a liar. You do so love him."

"I don't, and I told him I'd never marry him."

"You did not . . . Susanna, come on, he loves you."

"What difference does it make, Avery?" Susanna leaned right up to her ear. "He can't marry me." The tears she'd been bottling up fizzed and hissed. "I've told God I'd go anywhere, do anything, be anyone he wanted. But I'm not staying here to make a mess of things. Make fun of me if you want but not of him." She dabbed her cheeks with the back of her hand. "He doesn't deserve it."

"Oh, Suz." Avery dropped her arm around Susanna and rested her cheek against her shoulder. "You do love him, don't you?"

"And not because he's a prince."

"King."

"Whatever."

A commotion a few gates away interrupted the sisters' conversation. Susanna peered down the thoroughfare. A cluster of men with cameras scurried toward her gate, elbowing each other for first place, flowing against a stream of travelers heading for alternate gates and baggage claim.

"Paparazzi," Avery said.

Susanna tugged on her hat. "Get your stuff. Slowly. No quick moves. Put your hood up."

She'd just settled her backpack on her shoulders when she heard the shout, "There she is!"

A chorus of clomping shoes echoed in the thoroughfare as the troop of photographers charged, the lead man toppling a woman and her carry-ons.

"Aves, go, go, go." Susanna held onto her hat and sprinted, her body moving twice the speed of her slick-soled Louboutins.

"There's the elevator." Avery ran ahead, dashing through a cluster of kids dressed in matching royal-blue T-shirts.

"Suz, come on." She pinched between the closing elevator doors and pried them open.

Susanna slipped inside and collapsed against the elevator's handrail, gasping, catching her breath.

Slowly, ever so slowly, the doors . . . slid . . . closed.

"Susanna?" A photographer raised his camera, and the shutter whirred just as the doors closed.

"Oh my stars." Susanna sank down the wall, her quivering legs refusing to hold her up. "I can't breathe."

The elevator stopped with a ding, and before she could collect herself, the doors opened to another battalion of photographers.

Avery pressed the Close button, then held her palm toward the photographers, belting out a deep "Leave us alone." Then she knelt next to Susanna. "Know what? We're going back to our gate. Forget them. What can they do to you? Besides, you can't run from everything, Suz."

"Run? Me? Ha." She was coming to life now. "When do I run? I'm the one who stays. Remember? Adam? Twelve years?"

"He was all about you running from your past, your fears of growing up with Mama and Daddy fighting."

Susanna made a face. "Where did you get such a cockamamie idea?"

Avery tapped her temple. "Right here. I'm right and you know it."

"I'm not running from Nate. I'm just going home. He can't be with me anyway, and I'm complicating things for him by being here."

"You're complicating things by running." The elevator jerked to a stop, returning Susanna and Avery to the beginning of their escape.

As much as she believed she was a control freak who hated change, Susanna also hated confrontation. She hated pain. She ran. Hid under covers. In dark, small closets that transformed into magical gardens.

Avery grabbed her hand as the elevator stopped. "Ready?"

"Ready." Susanna squeezed her sister's fingers. "Thank you."

"By the time we get home, I'll be the most popular girl in school, maybe all of south Georgia, thanks to Facebook."

"Might as well do this right." Susanna whipped off her hat, fluffed her hair, and stepped off the elevator as the doors opened.

The photographers swarmed.

"Susanna, are you in love with the king?"

"Did you spend the night together, Susanna?"

"Are you having his love child?"

With Avery, Susanna cut a swath toward their abandoned seats. The photographers continued to digitally document the event, shouting questions.

"Will you be back, Susanna?"

"Suz, is that your nickname?"

"What do you think of Lady Genevieve?"

But Susanna sat where she'd left her bags and didn't answer. She had learned from this morning. *Don't feed the jackals.*

"Susanna, how about a smile?"

Enough. Susanna stood in her chair, towering over the photographers. "Please, we just want to wait for our flight in peace."

"When will you see the king again?"

"Is he coming to say good-bye to you?"

"How did you two meet?"

"Psst." The woman waiting in the chair next to Susanna tugged on her jeans. "Who are you anyway?"

Yeah, just *who* was she anyway? Nobody. A small-town south Georgia girl. Loving Jesus. Loving Nate Kenneth.

Her fifteen minutes of fame ended right now.

"Okay, y'all . . ." The cameras whizzed and clicked, flashing. "First of all, thank you for giving my sister and me a heart attack. Have you ever tried to run in Louboutin spikes?"

The photographers laughed. Passengers slowed and added to the crowd.

"I'm no one of acclaim or interest. I was your king's landscape architect on his father's garden on St. Simons Island. We became friends. His mother and brother invited me to the coronation. I came. I saw. I'm going home. End of story."

Susanna tugged on her hat and dropped down to her seat. Now, if they would shoo, leave her alone. She was tired, drained, and ready to go home.

"One last question, Suz." A skinny photographer bent toward her with a friendly smile. "What did you think of our great sapphire isle?"

She sighed. That question was easy. "It's one of the most beautiful places I've ever seen." She peered toward the window, lit with the golden edge of the Cathedral City lights. "It felt like home."

Part Three

The Proposal

# TWENTY-FOUR

The world was quiet except for the sound of the surf roaring in Susanna's ears as she rode her board toward the shore. A southern storm off the coast churned the Atlantic, exhorting the waves. She'd been home from Brighton for two hours, arriving in Atlanta from New York in the early morning.

Avery hugged Daddy and Mama, talked a mile a minute, and then passed out on the couch midsentence.

But Susanna was restless. Burdened. She donned her wetsuit and grabbed her board. She'd not slept a wink on the flight, but she knew if she lay down, she'd only stare wide-eyed at the ceiling and wonder what *he* was doing.

The long journey home branded an excruciating question on her heart: Did she leave too soon? Should she have waited to say good-bye?

The wave beneath her softened, breaking as it carried Susanna toward the beach. She fished the board with the flow of the current, staying erect until at last she sank through the shallow, cold water to the slippery ocean floor.

She climbed back up on the board, sitting and bobbing with the lap of the waves, paddling the board around to face the northeast. To face Brighton.

In retrospect, she felt like some sort of drama queen—pun on queen intended—skedaddling out of there at the first sign of controversy.

But what would she have done differently? She replayed the morning at St. Stephens in her mind until her head ached and came to the same conclusion each time. She'd have done nothing differently. Besides, after he dropped her off at the puff shop, she never heard from him again.

So why bemoan her own quick departure?

She scooped up a handful of water and washed away the heat of doubt. The water ran into her eyes, and she blinked back the burn. But the salty sting wasn't from the ocean but her own tears.

She surfed until the tide began to change and the tempest eased in the waves. It was time to go home. Time to move on. Time to eat dinner and begin the first day of the rest of her life. New year. Fresh start.

A recommitment to "I got nothing, Lord. I'm a hundred percent available to you."

Mama met her in the kitchen when she came home. Avery remained passed out on the sunroom sofa, her burnished tresses flowing over the brown microfiber fabric like molten lava.

"Made some spaghetti. Hungry?" Mama said.

Susanna wandered through the kitchen, lifted the skillet lid, sniffed, then reached for a plate. "Who's watching the Shack?"

"Daddy, Catfish, and Bristol. How was surfing?" Mama moved in gently behind her. "Go sit, let me fix this for you."

Pulling out the counter stool, Susanna perched on the edge, chin propped in her hands, eyes drifting to half-mast.

"I'm sorry, Susanna. For what it's worth." Mama set the plate in front of her, then passed over a fork. "I have some Italian bread warming."

"Sounds good." She picked up the fork and stabbed at her

pile of spaghetti. "I knew the score when I went over. Nate is king. He's married to a nation."

"I didn't mean about Nate, Suz, though I am sorry about him too." Mama set a glass of tea in front of her, then took a long loaf of bread from the oven. "I meant I'm sorry for how you had to grow up."

"Mama, please—"

"Your daddy and I were so young, thought we knew each other, but we didn't."

"Okay, fine. It's in the past." Susanna gulped down her tea. Didn't she have enough on her heart without digging up her past to find a place to bury Mama's burden?

"I know it's in the past, but it doesn't release me from saying I'm sorry. Asking your forgiveness." Mama cut a thick slice of bread and passed it to Susanna along with the butter. "We did you wrong. Never did make up for it. Then Miss Thing over there on the couch arrived, and we felt like we had a chance to start over."

Susanna rubbed her hand over her face. Surfing had drained the last ounce of her energy. "Do we have to talk about this now?" Or ever?

"I know that's why you stayed with Adam for so long. A steady guy, good-looking, smart, caring, dependable. One of the few good men."

"Mama, what started all this introspection?" Susanna twisted the thin spaghetti around her fork and shoved it into her mouth.

"Because... well, I did me some thinking while you girls were gone. I never told you I was sorry, Susanna. My pride, I guess. Hard to look at your child and admit you done them wrong, but I'm saying it now. I done you wrong. I wasn't a good mama when my girl needed me the most, and it breaks my heart."

The salty burn in Susanna's eyes was even more annoying sitting in Mama's kitchen than on the surfboard. "It's okay."

"I loved you from the moment I set eyes on you. So did your daddy. Our problems were never about you."

"I know." She did. Honest. But the walls she'd built while hiding in the closet were set in time-proven, emotional cement.

"So, you can let go now. Hear me?"

"Let go?" Susanna cut a pat of butter and spread it over the warm bread. "Of what? Adam? My one-legged business?" She wiggled her fingers in the air. "Poof, be gone."

"Let go of *you*. You're safe. Stop holding back."

"What are you talking about?" She was too exhausted to deal with Mama-come-clean. Not to mention it was a bit freaky.

"Did you tell that prince you love him?"

"The king? No. Nor did I tell him when he was a prince. Why would I do that?"

"Because you do love him."

"He lives four thousand miles away, and he can't legally ... oh, forget it. Mama, Nathaniel's a nice memory from the past. Over. Done. Can we not talk about it for a while. For like . . . twenty, thirty years. And please"—Susanna sighed as she looked up at her mama—"don't go creating family lore out of this. Or hang a sign in the restaurant, 'King Nathaniel II cleaned toilets here.'"

"Oh, please, I'd never. Not about toilets anyway." Mama perched on the stool next to Susanna. "Does he love you?"

"Can we go back to how you wronged me as a kid? What happened to that conversation?"

"This is the same conversation. You shut your heart up good when you were little and now I'm asking you to open it up."

"I loved Adam. What do you call that?"

"Safety, the high-school-quarterback syndrome. You loved the first boy who looked your way, and by George"—Mama gripped the air and shook her fists—"you were going to hang on. Come what may."

"So I let go." Susanna held up her open palm. "I think I

recovered nicely from 'I found the right ring but not the right girl.'"

"You did and I'm proud. Just make sure you're opening your heart all the way." Mama reached for Susanna's other hand and uncurled her fingers. "You still feel so tense to me. If you love Nate, you got to confess it to yourself before you can ever move on or heal."

Tears splashed her cheeks. *Oh, Mama.*

"You're beautiful, Susanna. Before you can lay hold of all God's got for you, you must forgive your ol' mama and daddy, and confess to yourself you love Nate. Even more, that Jesus loves you."

"Mama—"

"You sure are beautiful to your daddy and me. We used to get you out of your crib at night and put you in the bed between us just so we could stare at you." Mama brushed her hand over Susanna's hair. Something Susanna watched her do to Avery a thousand times but had no memory of Mama ever doing it to her. "I sure saw how Nate looked at you. He loves you."

Susanna fell against her and broke, letting the forgiveness out and the truth in.

"I–I forgive you, Mama. And Daddy. Did a long time ago."

"I needed to hear it. You needed to say it." Mama's voice weakened with her own weepy confession.

"And Jesus loves me."

"That he does. And Nathaniel."

"Yes, I love him." Susanna wrapped tight around Mama and buried her burden in her mama's bosom for the first time in her life. "I do love him. I do. It just hurts so much."

Locked. Susanna twisted her office doorknob and tried the key again. But it no longer fit. She banged the door with her fist. "Hello?"

Down the outside stairs, she rounded the bottom step to the back door. The kitchen smelled of fresh-brewed coffee and something cinnamon. In the hall toward Jessup's office, Bonnie, his assistant, intercepted her.

"He's in a meeting."

"I just saw him walk in from the parking lot, Bonnie."

"What can I help you with, Susanna?"

"I'm locked out of my office." She held up her key. "What's going on?"

"The lock has been changed."

"Because?"

"You were sixty days late on your rent."

"Impossible. I paid a week before Christmas." A last-minute contract had come in, along with a deposit check.

Bonnie opened her middle desk drawer. "Your payment bounced." She passed Susanna an envelope. "The notice is inside with a copy of the check."

"Bounced?" Susanna's gumption sank like an anchored bolder. "How could it bounce?"

"Susanna, I don't know how you run your business, but we pay our bills on time around here, and we expect others to do likewise." Bonnie sat at her desk, a haughty expression on her skinny, overly made-up face. "We work on integrity and honor." She shuffled her pencil can to the other side of her vase of faux flowers.

"Integrity and honor? Ah, I see." Susanna tapped the rubber check notification against her fingertips. "Is that what you and Jessup are working on late at night? Honor and integrity? When his wife thinks he's burning the midnight oil on a case?"

A bomb exploded behind Bonnie's eyes. She bounded to her feet, her lean, prissy face a red ball of fire. "Get out." She pointed toward the door, her lips pressed into a tight, red line.

"I need my office equipment, my computer." Maybe she

should've kept her observation to herself. "Bonnie, um, I shouldn't have said what I said." She had no truth or facts, just suspicions and her own bitterness to sweeten it. "I'm just . . . Look, sorry."

"It's all right. Guess everyone has a bad day." Bonnie's tight-lipped expression eased up.

"Or a bad year."

"Your stuff is in the storeroom by the kitchen."

Sure enough, her entire office was crammed into the triangle-shaped closet. Susanna found her desk folded up, her chair rammed into a narrow space, perching precariously over her new, not-yet-paid-for iMac.

A lifetime had passed in the five days she'd been away, and suddenly she was back to the broken days of running on ice, trying to figure out how the Lord planned to use a girl who had nothing.

Dropping to the floor, Susanna pulled her keyboard from a box jammed with other stuff, muttering to herself.

She logged into her bank account. Sure enough, there were red flags all over the place. What happened to the check she deposited? Susanna launched email to see if JacDel Homes sent word of what happened on their end.

The stale storeroom air clung to her damp cheeks. Stretching out her foot, Susanna shoved the door the rest of the way open, letting light in and the hot air out.

The explanation came a few emails down the list. From JacDel Homes.

*Susanna, we decided to go in a different direction. We're canceling our contract and stopping payment. We'll send another check with the kill fee.*

She cracked her head against the back of the wall. A different direction? It made no sense. JacDel came to her. Offered her the job with a set price, and she accepted.

"Hey, Jesus, your girl down here doesn't understand what's going on."

Climbing off the floor, she headed back down the hall to Jessup's office, once again stopped by Bonnie. "If I have the money to him by tonight, can I have my office back?" She'd have to break down and ask Mama and Daddy.

"I'm afraid not." Bonnie could trademark her smirk. Best in all of St. Simons Island. "He's already rented it to his nephew. Also a landscape architect."

Perfect. Susanna started back down the hall. All this day needed was—

"Adam?"

He stood in the foyer, neat and pristine in his fatigues, cap in his hands.

"Hey, Suz." He smiled shy and tentative. "Your mama said I'd find you here."

"How are you?"

"Good, good. Can we talk?" He motioned toward the exit. "Maybe grab a coffee?"

"I'm in the middle of something." She pointed toward the storage closet. "Got to get to work." On the floor. Of a closet.

"Can I help?" Adam stepped forward, leaning for a look. His woodsy-spicy fragrance wafted up from his olive skin, coloring in her fading memories of him. Of them.

"I think I fell in love with you because you always smelled so good." She laughed low.

Adam stepped back, made a face, then broke into a grin. "You should've been with me in the trenches of Afghanistan."

She leaned against the wall, arms folded. "I heard you're engaged."

"Yeah, Sheree." He studied the hardwood, nodding. "Do you hate me?"

"Hate you? No." She started to her closet and he followed. "But you do have twelve years of my life." Stopping at the storage closet, she pointed at him. "Treat them kind."

"I never meant to hurt you, Suz. I should've called after you left the beach. But you always liked your space."

"Help me carry this stuff out to my car, will you?" She swung wide the door.

"You moving out?"

"Something like that." Susanna picked up the box of supplies and whatnot and peered at Adam, who reached for the chair. "You look happy."

He bobbed his head. "I am." A red blush stained his cheeks.

"It's okay, bubba, you can be happy about the woman you're going to marry." Susanna kicked open the kitchen door. Know what? She was happy for him. Really.

They loaded her car with her office equipment, wrangling the desk chair into the backseat somehow. Then she leaned with him against the green driver's side door and let the breeze tangle her hair and unwind her heart.

"You will always be special to me. Always," he said.

"Adam, when you broke up with me, I knew you were right. I just didn't want to admit it." She peered into his eyes. "I know it was hard for you to tell me."

"I felt sick for a month."

"But free."

"Yeah, free." He kicked a clump of sandy soil. "Who told you I was getting married?"

"Gage and Gracie."

"Ah, of course." Adam laughed, his perfect skin pulling taut over his perfect features. "Can't keep a secret with those two."

"I met someone too."

"Really?" Adam regarded her for a moment. "He's a lucky son-of-a-gun."

"But he lives in Europe and—" She inhaled, fortifying her heart. "It's a long, complicated story."

"You always wanted to work in Europe's gardens. There's

nothing holding you here." Adam nudged her with his words, with a sharp jab of his elbow to her ribs. "Why not go?"

"Yeah, true." She sighed, tears rising and burning. She always believed she'd lift her wings and fly away.

"Mom and Dad are throwing a little party for Sheree and me tonight. I'd love it if you'd come by the house. Say hi. Meet Sheree."

Susanna peered up at him. "Sounds lovely. I'd love to meet her." Honest. She would.

"Good, good." He took a step back, hesitated, then strode forward and kissed her on the cheek. "You look good."

"So do you. S–see you, Adam." Susanna headed back inside, rounded the kitchen corner toward the storeroom, and pulled the door closed behind her.

Sinking down to the floor, she drew her legs to her chest and let her sobs push her forehead to her knees. For the past, the present, the unknown future.

For Adam. For Nate. For losing her office. For letting go and admitting the truth—she loved Nathaniel. For the courage to discover a part of herself she never knew before.

A light tap on the door stirred her to look up. "Yeah?" She dabbed her face with the back of her hand. "Who is it?"

When no one answered, Susanna twisted the knob, cracking open the door. A cold Diet Coke, a glass of ice, and a chocolate bar sat on a small tray. With a laugh, she pulled in the comfort and closed the door.

"You're all right, Bonnie," she whispered, twisting the cap off the bottle and taking a swig. "You're all right."

# TWENTY-FIVE

## Two Months Later, March

*D*id you see this morning's paper?" Jon tossed a copy of the *LibP* onto the desk, the colorful newsprint slicing through the nine o'clock sun beaming through the windows.

Nathaniel looked up from his dailies. The headline speculated, "Lady Genevieve Hawthorn, a Duchess of the People," over a crisp, beautiful image of Ginny in a tailored blue suit, wooing schoolchildren in Hessenberg's capital city, Strauberg.

"I've got to give her credit. She's working this like a champ."

"She's on with *Madeline & Hyacinth Live!* today at four."

"If I were so inclined to marry her, doesn't she realize how difficult all this campaigning makes it?" Nathaniel pushed away from his desk.

"Then it's a good thing you're not planning to marry her."

"You were pushing for it a few months back."

"Before she showed her dark underbelly."

Nathaniel regarded his aide. "We've known of her dark, controlling, manipulative side since university. Don't act surprised."

"But she never used her evil against us, Nathaniel."

"By the way, we found out how the *LibP* got a picture of you and Susanna." Jon took a seat and shoved a brown dossier toward Nathaniel. "You were tagged on Facebook."

"I have a Facebook?" Nathaniel asked, surprised.

"You have a fan page. We follow it just to see what people are posting. You're quite popular. The owner is a Brighton woman. Married with kids. It's all innocent enough. But a woman at the Butler benefit found the page and posted the picture of you and Susanna. She and her family were at the Rib Shack the night you two sat on the deck."

"Where can I see this page?" Nathaniel sat at his computer and launched a browser.

"Nathaniel, I have news." He glanced around to see Jon leaning forward, tapping the dossier. "There's a Hessenberg heir."

"There's a—" Nathaniel snapped up the dossier. "Really, chap? There's an heir? Who?" He flipped through the pages, weighing the revelation.

A few months ago he had hope after reading the initial interview Jonathan and Tanner did with Yardley Prather, but finding an heir proved to be tedious and tangled with international red tape.

Yardley's older brother had been in attendance at the entail signing. Prince Francis was more given to parties than military strategy, but the crafty grand duke knew enough about entails to require his own heir, whoever he or she may be, to inherit back the land at the expiration of the entail.

"Jon, there's nothing new here," Nathaniel said, scanning the old information, searching for the new.

"Keep reading."

Prince Francis fled to Sweden where he died in 1944 at the age of seventy-six.

Yardley Prather believed he died of a broken heart.

What remained of the House of Augustine-Saxon crumbled

under the weight of two world wars. Artifacts and records had been destroyed by World War II German surface-to-surface missiles.

"So where is this heir?" Nathaniel skimmed the report pages.

Jonathan took the dossier, leafed to the last page, and set it in front of him. "Here." He handed the dossier back to Nathaniel. "Lady Alice Stephanie Regina."

"Moved to New York after the war. British flyer she married … killed in '45." Nathaniel shook his head. "This family certainly knew tragedy."

"Alice had enough of war and skipped the pond to America."

For the first time in two months, Nathaniel allowed his heart to hope. Really hope. "How sure are we about all of this?"

"I've had the staff rooting around in files locked in rooms we'd forgotten about, calling over to London, checking marriage certificates and birth notices, death notices in London and New York. The American law firm we hired found record of an Alice Edmunds arriving in New York, August 13, 1946, but that's where the trail ends."

"Good job." Nathaniel's smile ballooned over his white clouds of hope. "I knew it, chap. I knew it. We're going to find an heir."

"Don't get ahead of yourself. We may not find anyone of the grand duke's line. Alice may have died or never remarried."

"Don't say it. We're going to find her great-granddaughter." He popped his hands together, grinning. "Let's have Lady Genevieve to tea when we tell her."

"We? You. I don't want to be in that firestorm."

"Firestorm? It'll be a bright, happy day, Jon. Come on. Don't tell me you're afraid of Ginny."

"Terrified. Now that I know her true colors."

Nathaniel regarded his aide and friend. "What do you think of Susanna now?"

The man gathered up the dossier. "That I wish she'd been born in Brighton."

Nathaniel returned to his apartment and inhaled the glorious smells of Jacque's cooking.

"Malcolm, are those dumplings I smell?"

"Your Majesty's favorite." Nate's butler bobbed out of the kitchen. "They're calling for a fresh snow tonight, sir. I thought warm dumplings would cheer you. Jacque agreed."

"You're too good to me." Nathaniel turned when he heard the knock on the door. He reached for the handle, motioning to Malcolm to attend to his duties.

Ginny stood on the other side. "Hello, Nathaniel." She crossed the threshold with one long, stiletto-heeled stride.

Malcolm ducked back into the kitchen.

"Ginny. What brings you 'round?" Nathaniel loosened his tie. Dad honored the king's office by wearing one every day, but Nathaniel had arrived to work his first day as king with an open collar. Then he sat behind the desk where the kings before him—his forefathers—sat. He rang Jonathan straightaway to bring him a tie.

"It's been two months. I think I've proven I'm the people's choice." Ginny walked from the foyer to the living room and draped herself in a chair in a way that allowed her sheer blouse to hint at her womanly features.

"I didn't realize there was a contest."

"Nathaniel, you're not thinking." She spoke like a CEO rather than an intended lover. "We can be a powerhouse, spearheading a strong, enduring monarchy."

"I think I can do that without you."

"Think?"

"Know."

"Know? Do you hear yourself? You have no confidence. You need me to assure you, remind you of who you are."

"You want to see confidence?"

"Yes, in all of blazes, yes." She walked over to him and leaned in, her sweet perfume belying her true identity. "Show me some courage. Marry me."

"There's no courage in marrying a woman I don't love and who doesn't love me. Sounds rather cowardly."

"Nathaniel." She stepped into him, powering up her wiles. Her long, sleek hair flowed like rich oil over her shoulders. Nathaniel stepped out of her reach. "Here's how this plays out. You marry me, style me as Queen Genevieve of Brighton and grand duchess of Hessenberg. Right before the entail ends, we'll divorce."

"Divorce?"

"Yes, darling, the nasty, ugly D-word."

"I'm not marrying you with the intention of divorcing you. I'm head of the church, the defender of the faith, Ginny. Not to mention it's a stupid idea."

"Listen to me. This is a win-win-win-win. Just before the entail ends, we'll have a horrible row. In public. I might even be willing to succumb to an affair and let you toss me out on my ear." She flailed her arms about with dramatic flair. "You demand a divorce. The press will agree." She lowered her voice. "I know I can get the *LibP* to agree. The other papers will follow. And off I go. You strip me of my HRH Queen Genevieve title, but I'll retain the one of grand duchess because when the entail ends, I'll be the legitimate royal heir, inheriting the land of my ancestors. It'll be all nice and legal. I'll ask the governor, Seamus Fitzsimmons, to be prime minister and form a government." Ah, so she did woo Seamus. Prime minister, eh?

"How long have you been planning this one?"

"What is wrong with you, Nathaniel?" Desperation exploded in her voice. "The plan is perfect. Everyone gets what they want. An independent Hessenberg and Brighton free from her economy."

"And you get to be a royal."

"Yes, I get to be a royal. So sue me."

"You know we can't divorce unless the archbishop and the Parliament approve."

"They won't force you to stay with an adulteress."

"You have this all worked out, don't you?" He moved from anger to pity. "You factor everyone into your schemes and think we'll all play along. But I can't lie to myself or to the people. I most certainly cannot stand before God and make a vow I don't intend to keep."

The desperation in her eyes rose to a roaring fire. "A grand duchess. Me. Her Royal Highness, Queen Genevieve, grand duchess of Hessenberg. By some fluke of history, war, and the destroyed records of my dear departed distant cousin, Prince Francis, I am in line to be a woman standing on the stage of the world's leaders. A grand duchess when there is rarely such a thing anymore."

"Are you that fixated on titles? Ginny, you can change the world where you stand. One person at a time. With your family, your company, your charities. You don't need to be grand duchess. It's not a power grab. You won't be ruler, empress, queen, potentate, commander of all. You'll be a servant to millions of people. It's daunting, I tell you."

"They'll love me." Something otherworldly flared in her eyes, and it chilled Nathaniel to the bone. His spirit churned.

"Ginny, if the Lord called you to the throne in Brighton, he'll put you there. But it's not going to be through me." Nathaniel walked to the door and held it open for his departing guest. "Have a good day."

She reared back, stiff, hostile, eyes narrowed with anger. "I warned you."

"And I am warning you." Calm. Steady. Confident. He locked his eyes on her and she broke.

"You're a fool, Nathaniel." She snatched up her bag and stormed out the door, upbraiding him with one final glance.

"A fool, you say? Then why would you want to marry me? A fool."

She released a small, frustrated scream and barged down the hall. Nathaniel eased the door closed, then collapsed in his favorite chair. That exchange felt kind of good. Empowering. It was way better to confront a Jezebel than to kowtow to one.

He slipped his phone from his pocket and dialed Henry. The confrontation with Ginny sparked his courage. If he was going to become the king he wanted to be, then it must begin with becoming the man he wanted to be.

# TWENTY-SIX

## St. Simons Island

The chiffon rays of the March sun stretched down from an azure sky, dropping gold on the Spanish moss dangling from the knotted oak shading Granddaddy's old garage, a detached building with a sliding door and oil stains from his old Plymouth.

The afternoon light and all its warmth barely reached the edge of the concrete floor. In the shadow, Susanna worked at her computer to the hum of a creaking ceiling fan.

Daddy had strung an internet cable from her grandparents' house, out the back porch, through the grass like a skinny blue snake, across the end of the driveway, through the seeped-in oil stains on the garage concrete, and into the back of her iMac.

"Craig Hobbs, please," Susanna said into the phone, propping her elbows on the desk, studying the pegboard walls.

She'd played in here as a kid, climbing behind the big steering wheel of Granddaddy's car, pretending to drive down Ocean Boulevard with the wind in her hair, making motor sounds in her throat. She'd felt safe in the old garage, away from the fighting and screaming at home. Behind the big wheel, she was free, commanding her own destiny.

"Yes, Mr. Hobbs." She sat up straight when the president of Drapper Clothing answered. "My name's Susanna Truitt. I'm a landscape architect on St. Simons Island, Georgia."

"If you're calling about the landscape project, the bidding closed two days ago."

"Yes sir, I realize that, but I'd heard Remington had withdrawn, so I thought—"

"Do you know how many bids we received? One less will expedite our decision."

Susanna jumped to her feet, pushing her chair into the rusty, old deep cooler circa 1960. "I'll do it pro bono."

"Pro bono?" He laughed. But not the kind that warmed a desperate girl's heart. "Have you seen the plans? We're building a multimillion-dollar factory and offices."

"Yes sir." Her friend from the Atlanta-based Remington & Co. had called last night with a tip on the job with the words "multi-million-dollar project." No more. No less. "The design work I'll do pro bono. I'll bring a top-notch crew up to Atlanta and get the project done in half the time of most firms. You pay labor for the crew and materials."

Silence. Then a long sigh. "Why would we hire you, Miss—"

"Truitt. Susanna Truitt."

"—when we can afford the best?"

"I'm the best, sir, if you don't mind me saying. You just don't know it yet." Oh, wow, hello bold and brash, pull up a chair and join the conversation. Desperation made a confident business partner.

"I'm not sure I know how to respond, Miss Truitt." No laughter this time. No amusement.

"Mr. Hobbs, listen, I can do this. I don't mind working for free to prove myself to you. I know you have plans for another factory." *Thank you*, Forbes. "With plans for a few brick-and-mortar stores. I want to be your landscape architect."

"Miss Truitt, I admire your spirit, but we have a formal process in place to choose our vendors. I think I'll stick with the plan for now."

"Mr. Hobbs, I totally understand." Susanna walked to the edge of the garage and stuck her flip-flopped foot into the edge of the sun. "I'm a by-the-plan girl myself. But I've recently learned life is rather dull if we don't leap, take a chance once in a while. Trust our gut."

"How'd that work for you, Miss Truitt?"

"If you must know, stinky. I got my heart broken twice in five months, but if I had to do it again, I would. And that's a monumental confession for me. Join me, Mr. Hobbs, let go, change the plan"—she lowered the receiver below her chin and steadied her voice—"discovering what else is out there, even if it's just a new piece of you, is worth it."

He didn't answer, but sighed. Susanna leaned against the faded, barn-red wall of the garage, hooking her fingers into her jeans pockets. *Come on, Mr. Hobbs. Take a chance.*

She pictured the founder and CEO at his desk, angled back in his chair, decked out in a pullover and khakis, his fingers pressed to the bridge of his nose, asking himself why his assistant passed along a call from a crazy lady. "Like I said, Miss Truitt. I admire your spirit. But—"

The most humiliating word in the human language. *But.*

"Our processes and plans work fine for us. We're a growing company. I can't start leaping without looking now."

"But isn't that how you got to where you are now? Leaping? Taking chances?"

"Yes, but there's a time and place. Hiring an overeager landscape architect right now is not one of them." He added a few kind words about hanging in there, how a girl with her gumption was sure to go far. When he said good-bye, Susanna returned to her desk with the wind chasing her, flitting her papers and twisting her hair.

She pressed her fingers against her eyes and shoved the bubbles of tears back into their bottle.

"Can I buy you a Diet Coke?"

Susanna raised her eyes to see Gage walking through the wide garage door, a cold soda bottle swinging from his hand.

"Didn't your mama teach you not to sneak up on people?" She took the offered Coke and twisted off the cap.

"Sneak? The garage door is wide open. Didn't you hear my truck?" Gage pointed to his vehicle parked in a glob of light as he walked behind her desk to perch on the old cooler.

"I was busy. Working." Susanna stooped to pick up the papers the wind rustled off her desk.

"I can see." Gage motioned to her screen. "Solitaire is time consuming."

"Did you come here to torment me? Isn't there a kitten to harass somewhere?"

"How long have you been in these luxury quarters?"

"Two months."

He whistled. "Any business?"

"Noneya."

"Noneya?" His laugh drew her smile to the surface. "What are we, in third grade?" He swigged his co-cola with casual swagger. "None ya business?"

"Mrs. Caller. Okay . . . I took a job with Mrs. Caller."

Gage guffawed, slapped his thigh with his free hand, then covered his laugh with his fist. "I didn't realize you were that destitute."

"Destitute? She's a fine, good paying—" Oh who was she kidding? Susanna laughed, then moaned, cradling her head in her hands. "I've changed her spring garden plans ten times. Ten times. In two weeks. I've already lost money and we've not even started."

"Ten times? Girl, I'm impressed. There was a time when even one change sent you up the wall. And now look at you . . . set up in this fancy office . . . your own internet cable . . ." He angled back to tap the blue cable hooked to her computer.

She smacked his hand. "Leave it alone. I just got it all working." Then she rocked back in her chair with another moan. "I'm trying here, Gage."

"What happened to the prince?"

"He became a king."

Once Avery posted her entire coronation adventure on Facebook, all of the island knew the truth about Nate Kenneth. The paper ran a story quoting the indomitable Mrs. Butler, "Unlike the Truitt girls, I was trying to be discreet. Let my dear cousin visit the island in peace."

*Dear cousin, my eye* . . . She wanted him all to herself.

She peered into Gage's mahogany eyes. So very different from Nathaniel's light blue irises that matched the hue of the winter mountaintops.

"And?" he said.

"There's no *and*, Gage. He became king, went on with his life. I'm going on with mine."

He bent to see her face, his gaze narrowed at her. "With Mrs. Caller?"

"Yes, with Mrs. Caller." Susanna's stomach rumbled, and she had a sudden urge for chocolate. "She's going to give me an extra hundred dollars for all my troubles."

Gage laughed way too easily, way too loud. "Susanna, end this misery and come back to work for me."

"You have that fancy landscape architect, remember. Miss La-di-da."

"I fired her."

"You're kidding." It was her turn to down her co-cola with a casual swagger. "We're a mess, you and me."

"Yep, you and me." A pink hue tinted his high, lean cheeks. "I was thinking we could be a mess together. At work." He walked to the cooler, pretending to be interested in the rusty old thing. "Outside of work." He rapped on the cooler lid. "This thing work?"

"It's full of Diet Coke and barbecue sauce." *Outside of work?* She regarded him from under her tipped brow. "I–I d–don't know. I–I mean, Daddy went to all the trouble to string the internet cable across the lawn. I got a fan." She pointed overhead. "And the fridge."

He stared at the daylight framed by the garage door. "You'll start at your old salary plus ten percent. I'll give you a bonus on all jobs you do. You can have fifty percent of any clients you bring in as long as you make a profit." He finally looked back at her.

"If I could bring in clients, I wouldn't need to work for you, Gage."

"I have the reputation. Well, building one. You just need to get some jobs going, Suz. Build some momentum. You'll be in high demand." He picked at the wrapping on his soda bottle. "As for the other thing, we can take it slow, you know, see how it goes. Adam's moved on, the prince is a king, and suddenly I'm the luckiest guy in the world to have the prettiest girl I've ever known sitting in front of me. Available." He held her gaze for only a moment. "She makes me think of a field after a spring rain."

"Gage." That was the nicest thing he'd ever said to her. And by far the most poetic. She didn't know he had it in him. And she sympathized with him in that moment, putting himself out there, laying his heart on the line. She admired him for it. But she was powerless to do anything about it. "I can't work for you *and* date you."

"Then you're fired."

"I'm not even hired yet." She walked over, gave his arm a friendly tug. "I think I'd best just stay here in my old garage." *Hear what I'm saying, friend.*

"I'll treat you right."

"I remember in eleventh grade you brought flowers to Willa Lund every day until she said yes to your homecoming invitation. You were persistent." Susanna patted his shoulder. "Every girl wanted to be your girlfriend."

"But I wanted you. Before Adam even knew you existed."

She peered up at him. "You never said a word."

He shrugged. "Too chicken to talk to you, let alone ask you out. What would I do if you said no?" Gage snatched her hand. "Come work for me. We'll be Stone & Truitt, powerhouse Southern firm. All business, above board, strictly professional. If, over time, something more happens, then"—he skipped his booted foot over the cracked concrete floor—"we'll see where that leads. You're a great landscape architect. But no one is going to find that out as long as you're working in an old garage."

This wasn't *the* plan. Broken heart. Detached garage office. Faltered career. Ex-boyfriend. Prince. King. Gage Stone. "Let me think about it, okay? I'll call you."

He gave her a somber nod, then smiled. "Don't let Mrs. Caller make too many changes. She's just lonely, Susanna. Rich, but lonely."

"I know." She liked Mrs. Caller. Susanna had a lot in common with the old Georgia belle.

She walked Gage to the edge of the garage, then waved as he fired up his truck and backed down the drive. "Don't drive over my cable."

Back at her desk, Susanna finished her Diet Coke and fielded his invitation, rather invitations plural, tossing them around in her heart.

Could she date Gage? It had been two months since the

coronation, and she'd not heard boo from Nate. But she thought of him every day.

She was waiting for a ripple of news that he'd proposed to Lady Genevieve or some Brighton lady. Or news that a resolution to the entail had been discovered.

Reaching to her track pad, she surfed the web for the Brighton papers. Last time she looked, Lady Genevieve was wooing Hessenberg schoolchildren. Predictions of a royal wedding flourished.

Gage's offer of love reminded her how much she missed Nathaniel. How she loved him. Heaven help her, she loved a man who lived four thousand miles away.

She played their few private moments together over and over in her mind like humming a favorite song. But the images had begun to wear thin, lose their impact on her heart. Her memory of his fine, pristine voice was starting to fade and on occasion sound a lot like Daddy's Southern twang.

When the *Liberty Press* unfolded on her screen, Susanna braced herself as she forayed into Brighton's world.

She half closed her eyes and clenched her stomach, expecting to see a big ol' honking headline:

ENGAGED!

Then, *then*, she could truly let go and convince her heart it was time to move on. He wasn't coming for her. They were the wrong people at the wrong time. Or maybe the right people at the wrong time. But *wrong* definitely factored into the whole equation.

But there was no *ENGAGED!* headline. She exhaled, then heated with frustration. *Come on, Nate, get it over with. Propose already.*

But why was she thinking of Nate? A man, a nice man, a handsome man, a successful man wanted her. She didn't love Gage, but she could learn to love him, right? After all, love was a choice, wasn't it?

Susanna shoved away from her desk and pressed the heel of her hands to her forehead. Eight months after she'd prayed with Nathaniel on Christ Church grounds, she still had nothing.

"Lord, is this what you have for me? Gage? Do I move? Stay on the island? Can you please get Nathaniel out of my heart?"

She mimed pulling him out of her chest. Mimed tossing away the largeness sensation she carried with her every day.

She thought of the green lawn of Christ Church. God had something for her. She just knew it. So how was she to stumble upon it? How did she live day-to-day trusting him to be in charge of the outcome?

Grabbing her purse, she started for her car. She stopped and gasped when she saw the gold Louboutins she'd tossed to the back of her closet when she returned from Brighton sitting on the edge of the garage floor, glittering in the sunlight.

"Aurora!" Susanna picked up the shoes and ran onto the lawn. "Where are you? Aurora. Come back here. You've got to stop this. How did you get into my closet?" Mama! She probably let her in.

The homeless woman streaked across the lawn from the back porch toward the woods behind the house, waving her hands in the air. "The prince is coming."

"Aurora, please, stop bringing me . . ."—Susanna offered the Louboutins to the breeze—"shoes. No more talk of princes."

"The prince is coming." She paused on the edge of the woods, her bleached hair glinting like spun silk.

"Come back here. I know you're not crazy. Tell me what you're talking about."

"He's coming. Chase no other loves. Chase no other loves."

"Oh my gosh, you make no sense. Aurora, he's not coming. He's not. It's been too long. He doesn't love me." The words rang out, hard, cold, frozen in the warm island air and for a fast instant, her heart's eye could see the words. Feel the reality.

Maybe *now* she could move on with her life.

# May

He was nervous. More than any time he could remember in the past. More than on his January coronation day when a surreal calm steadied him the entire time.

But this? If he crashed and burned, he'd not get another chance.

Most days, his confidence rode high. After all, he walked in his destiny, one he'd accepted as ordained by God. Not men.

But today, he presented the Senate House and Commons House his own Order of Council. The first brought by a sitting royal in a hundred and two years.

Waiting for Henry in the briefing quarters, he tapped his jacket pocket. The small box bounced against his hip. Queen Anne-Marie's ring.

Dashing out this morning, he remembered he'd tucked it away on his fireplace mantel and snatched it up, slipping it into his pocket. Lord Thomas Winthrop, who had designed the ring, was known for his devotion to Queen Anne-Marie. Nathaniel wanted to carry *that* heritage with him into the chamber. Then, perchance, on his way to the car, he remembered the queen's formal name.

*HRH Queen Anne-Marie Victoria Karoline Susanna.*

He was smiling when Henry entered. "Well, you look confident."

"Actually, I'm a bit nervous. I was smiling at something I

remembered . . . a bit of serendipity. Otherwise, I'm turning with nerves." He flicked his gaze toward the sounds beyond the ornate paneled room. With no windows, he'd lost track of the minutes passing.

"You'll do fine. They're coming in now for the joint session." Henry paused at the bourbon cabinet. "Care for a nip?" He raised a glass.

"When have you ever seen me take a nip?"

Henry chuckled. "Well said, Your Majesty." He glanced at his hands. "No notes?"

"I memorized it. I didn't want to come off stuffy." He shook off his nervous tension through his fingertips. "I want to be sincere."

Nathaniel's presentation today would not only impact him but the generations to come. Generations over which he would have no control. Just as his forefathers had no control over him but trusted their king, yes, *theirs*, to make correct decisions during his hour in Brighton history.

"You are always sincere, Nathaniel. You'll do fine. You've made dozens of speeches in your short career."

"None so important as this one." Now he wished he had printed out his speech for today's session. This one meant so much. What if he fumbled his points? He turned to Henry. "Do you have the official Order of Council prepared?"

"I do." Henry finished his shot of bourbon and set his glass on a service tray. "Nathaniel, the members understand the Crown does not take this privilege lightly."

"I'd feel better if this were not solely for my own gain. If I were bringing some kind of passion before them on behalf of the people. Instead I want something that only regards me and mine."

"Then give it your all." Henry patted him on the shoulder. "Your ancestors and the Parliament didn't seem bothered by restricting you and yours two hundred years ago when they imposed the Marriage Act."

"You've never said if you agree."

"I'm quite sure I don't." So, his prime minster did not agree with him. "It could leave the monarchy vulnerable."

"Which is why we've written in conditions and stipulations," Nathaniel said.

"Then let the order go to the vote," Henry said. "Are you ready to accept whatever comes?"

"I am. I've not spoken to Susanna since she left. I've no guarantee that if the law is changed she'd even speak to me, let alone marry me. She told me straight to my face she didn't want to marry me. I'm not an easy guy for a girl to commit to. I come with a kingdom on my shoulders."

"If she loves you—"

"She never said she loved me either."

"And you're still going through with this?"

"Yes." It'd become his conviction to do so.

"Love is not for the weary or faint of heart, is it?"

"Henry, do you love my mother?" Nathaniel asked, quick, without much thought.

"Excuse me, Your Majesty?" He reached for his bourbon glass on the service tray, then thought better of it and set it down.

"Do you love my mother? Simple question."

"Rather personal and straightforward as well." Henry stared at Nathaniel then away, glancing about the debate box, walking around the chairs, trying to choose on which to sit.

"Do you?"

"Yes. For a long time now."

"You were her first love? Before my father?" Nathaniel relaxed a bit, dipped his hands into his pockets, and leaned against the mahogany wall.

"She told you, then?"

"Not directly. I put the pieces together."

"We met after university. Your mum, quite a rebel in her day.

Shunning the social season to work at a rug factory, refusing to debut. I admired her, followed her to one of her poetry readings. We read a lot of poetry in the seventies. I fell in love. It took her a few months, but she . . . well, we planned to marry. But her parents had other plans. A prince, not a blue-collar lad with solicitor aspirations."

"You have my blessing, as her son and as your king, to pursue her."

The prime minister of Brighton blushed. "Perhaps, when my term is up."

"Why wait?" Nathaniel asked. "If you still love her after all these years, why must you wait? It's a gift. Take it."

"I do believe you're preaching to yourself a good deal more than me, Nathaniel," Henry said.

He laughed, his nerves rising again, and reached into his pocket for his handkerchief, patting the perspiration from his forehead. "How do you think Hessenberg will respond to the order?"

"Their representatives will hear your argument and the order, then vote accordingly. No need to try to predict their response."

Nathaniel glanced at his phone. "Best get to the robe room."

Henry nodded. "See you in the chamber."

Down the hall, Nathaniel peeked into the murmur of the chamber over the mezzanine banister. The members were arriving, taking their seats.

But where was Jon? He'd promised to be here at half past. He was late. The information he bore would uphold the first half of Nathaniel's speech. Information Nathaniel had not even told Henry about.

Jon's team of investigators had discovered a woman in Florida who appeared to be a true descendant of Prince Francis. His great-great-niece.

Though it seemed odd. A Hessen royal living in America unawares? But she was the great-granddaughter of Alice Edmunds.

In the robe room, Nathaniel found Jon waiting for him. He jumped to his feet when Nathaniel entered. "Regina Beswick. Or shall I say Princess Regina Beswick." He passed Nathaniel the brown dossier, much thicker now with two months of reports and information.

"Beswick? Her name is Beswick?" He skimmed the last page of the dossier before handing it back to Jonathan. The robe-room steward seemed rather miffed over Jon's interfering with his duties.

"Still investigating the details, but I'm pretty sure we have the princess."

Nathaniel punched the air with his fist. "I knew an heir was out there." He listened to Jon's briefing as the steward aided Nathaniel into his robes and crown.

A bit of courage, a lot of prayers, and the heir to Hessenberg had been found. It was a good moment to be king. And a fine day to fight for the right to marry the woman he loved.

The spotlight over the podium beamed down on Nathaniel. His hands steadied as he surveyed the long, narrow room of posh leather, cherry wood, and Brighton-quarried stone.

"You all look as terrified as I feel," he began, and the chamber filled with a tempered laugh. A feathery touch brushed over Nathaniel's head. A sensation he'd experienced since childhood. One he believed to be the tip of God's wing.

"Ladies and gentlemen of the chamber, members of the Senators House and the Commons House, thank you for this audience today.

"The Marriage Act of 1792 came about when royals ruled

Europe. When our forefathers and mothers were united in marriage for the sake of power and possession.

"Your predecessors, along with mine, took matters in hand and instituted the Marriage Act when Princess Paulette of Lorraine nearly destroyed our military by helping her Uncle Louis fight Napoleon. Our Parliament, along with the Crown, decreed no royal could marry outside Brighton as long as the ruling royal, the archbishop, prime minister, and privy council did not object.

"So our way has been for over two hundred years."

The chamber gave a united, quick "hurrah" as was their tradition when they agreed with a speaker.

"As it should be." A lone but powerful voice pierced the "hurrah."

Beading sweat popped out on Nathaniel's brow. "Yet history has changed." His voice held steady as he scanned the chamber for a visual barometer. "Europe's royal houses have fallen. Republics and democracies have taken their place.

"But we hold to our constitutional-monarchical government as a way of checks and balances on the law of the land and our way of life.

"We work hand-in-hand, you and I, the Crown and the Parliament. We are partners. Servants of the people.

"But you, ladies and gentlemen, are free to choose your own life. Especially when it comes to love.

"I won't stand here and tell you what a sad life I lead because I am king."

Laughter rippled toward him.

"But perhaps I might gain your sympathies over the notion I am not free to marry whom I love. I've pledged my life and heart to Brighton Kingdom. I'll serve her as she wills. But my good friends, I'm here today to ask for the Marriage Act to be amended."

Several "boos" haunted the room.

Nathaniel gripped the side of the podium. Did he not expect opposition? "I'm asking for myself and for those who follow me. I submit to you Order of Council HRC 143 that the crown prince or princess may marry whom they love, domestic or foreign.

"Your monarchs will serve better when serving with one they love. I ask you, my countrymen, not to abolish the Marriage Act of 1792, but to amend it. Let's write a new covenant of love. One where the good of Brighton and the Crown come together."

Nathaniel raised his chin and regarded again the room. Were they with him? Smiling faces turned stony, and the buoyancy of having the king in the room sank.

To his right, a contingent of representatives shifted. Spoke low to one another.

"On a final note, I received a good word before coming into this hallowed chamber that an heir of Prince Francis has been discovered in the state of Florida." The room rumbled. "My staff has worked tirelessly for the last few months, following every lead until they discovered the grand duke's niece. We will contact her and inform her that a deserving nation awaits her destiny." He paused, smiling. Hessenberg representatives were on their feet, fixed and focused. "I'm sure she'll need our most ardent prayers."

He thanked them, bowed, and backed away from the speaker's podium. His heart thundered as he exited the chamber. In silence.

He'd done what he came to do. And for the first time since he determined to propose this change, Parliament's response did not matter.

He'd leave the matter to the God he trusted.

Jon fell in step with him as he headed for the robe room. "Well done, sir, well done."

"We shall see."

Then he heard it. The rumble, the shaking, the shouts and stomping feet. And an earth shattering, one-chorus, "Hurrah!"

There was a reason she had left the gardening to Leo. He knew what the blazes he was doing. She did not.

Campbell sat back on her heels, shoved her sun hat off of her damp forehead, and considered the mess she'd made with her spade. The spring forget-me-nots she'd planted in Leo's honor were ... well, forgettable.

She'd consulted the royal gardener, Sir Pine, who offered to travel out to Parrsons and care for the walled garden himself, but Campbell insisted she needed to attend to this task herself.

This was Leo's garden, his private refuge, and she didn't want to turn it over to a mere custodian. It needed care. Her care.

Besides, she needed a distraction. Especially today. Nathaniel presented his order to the parliament today. The first one in a hundred and two years. She was nervous for him.

Did she agree with his actions? Campbell wasn't sure. The old law made her feel safe. Protected from foreign influence through marriage. Yet her mother's heart wanted her son happy. She liked Susanna. Admired her. Given any other circumstances, she'd praise Nathaniel's choice.

So perhaps she should let go of fear and distrust.

Rising off her knees, Campbell sat on the stone bench under the tree and slipped off her gloves and hat, cooling off in the spring breeze drifting down through the branches.

With the coronation over and the first anniversary of Leo's death approaching, she felt restless. As if life were calling but she wasn't sure to where or what.

"Taking a rest, I see?"

Campbell smiled at Henry. He was a welcome sight. "I can't go on torturing these poor forget-me-nots."

"Rollins said you were here." Henry sat next to her on the stone bench and covered her hand with his. "You can be proud of your son. He did splendidly."

Despite the strangeness of his intimate touch, she did not pull away.

"And?"

"The order passed."

"Oh, Henry!" She tightened her grip around his hand. Joy! "Is he off then, to see her?"

"He received the news rather calmly. Looked to Jon and said, 'See you at my office.' So I have no idea of his plans. He claims she said she'd not marry him. Never said she loved him. But things are changing in Brighton, Campbell. It's a new era, a new day."

"It is at that, isn't it?" Campbell watched a pair of robins bounce from limb to limb, twittering after one another. "She'll be a grand queen, won't she? If she accepts Nathaniel."

"I think we have a fine queen." Henry squeezed her hand. Did he mean to look at her so intently? She blushed under his stare. "But the American?"

"Susanna."

"Yes, of course . . . Susanna will be a grand wife for our king, if as you say, she'll have him. If he pursues her."

"I'm not *the* queen anymore, Henry."

"Yes, I know." Henry's eyes remained so intently on her. "We didn't get our day when we were young, Campbell."

"Henry . . ." She withdrew her hand, stood, and paced out of the shade into the sun. "Do you know anything about forget-me-nots?" She squinted up at the beaming light. "I believe there's too much sun."

"The only forget-me-nots I care about is that after thirty-five years I cannot forget you." Henry reached for her and she felt weak. "Campbell Stratton, ma'am, what are you doing the rest of your life?"

She pressed her trembling hand over her quivering lips, her heart jumbling up her words, not resisting him when he tugged her back to the bench and curled his arms about her.

"Will you have me?"

"I–I don't know." She'd spent years burying her memories of her first love. Of giving her heart, her all, to Leo.

"I don't know?" He chuckled low. "That's fair enough for me." He kissed her cheek and stood. "Campbell Stratton, what are you doing for dinner, then?"

"I've no specific plans."

"Would you dine with me?"

"That would be lovely."

He bowed and backed away. "I'll come 'round at seven."

She stood to watch him go in the shifting morning shade. Indeed things were changing in Brighton. Changing in her.

With another peek at the forget-me-nots, she dropped to her knees and began to work the soil, watering them with her own teardrops.

# TWENTY-SEVEN

S orry I'm late, Mama." Susanna scooted into the Rib Shack, the heels of her pumps crunching sand from the parking lot against the kitchen floor. She stuffed her briefcase inside her locker and slipped off her suit jacket. "We had a client cancel, but we were able to squeeze in another one. I think this one's going to hire us. Gage gets so mad when I offer my services pro bono, but I think that's just the best way to build a client base."

"Got a window full of tickets. Get the lead out." Mama didn't look up from her work at the lowboy prep station.

In the two-by-four kitchen bathroom, Susanna changed from one uniform to the next. Corporate world to service world. After a week of partnering with Gage, she was kind of falling into a groove. One she felt like she might be able to live with the rest of her life.

Okay, *not* for the rest of her life. For the next year. Just a year. Build her resume and then see. She'd begun to curb her appetite for long-term plans.

She'd promised herself, and Jesus, she'd commit to nothing and let him design the outcome of the garden of her life, determine the fruit of the largeness she still felt in her heart.

Reverend Smith called such a plan being "poor in spirit." Being humble yet expectant of Jesus.

Susanna burst from the bathroom, leaving her work clothes swinging from a hanger, and took up Mama's place at the window.

"It's family barbecue night . . . let's go, people." Bossing the back of house took the edge off all the rebuttals she swallowed during the day. Oh, if Gage only knew how many times she wanted to object to his plans.

Dating would never work for them. Even if she were to ever have romantic feelings for him. Which she did not.

Susanna grabbed the tickets waiting in the window and went to work. "Catfish, I need two family pulled-pork-barbecue platters and one chicken. Let's go, we're backing up here. Daddy, are those fries hot? I don't want cold fries going out my window."

"Hotter than the sand in July, baby girl." Daddy winked at her. "I'm sure going to miss you."

She stared at him. "Miss me? Why? Where are you going? Catfish, we need a Caesar and a house. Daddy, are you finally taking Mama on that African safari she's always talking about?" She took a plate from Catfish and added two biscuits. "Table nine, up. Let's go, Bristol."

"Good grief, girl, you think she'd go if I booked it? She still talks of Vermont as if it happened yesterday. That woman is a vacation camel." Daddy swept his shoulder against his misty gray eyes.

"Daddy? What's wrong?" She hurried around the lowboy for a good look-see. "Are you okay? It's not your heart, is it?"

"I'm fine." He tapped his chest. "My ticker's right as rain. In fact, it's downright happy."

"Then what's going on?" Susanna looked at Mama. Something was up because Mama wasn't bossing Daddy and he wasn't bossing back. "What are y'all not telling me?"

"Get to work, Susanna. I don't know what that old man is going on about. Gib, how them biscuits coming? They won't make themselves."

"I'm on it, woman. Just leave me be. I can make these in my sleep."

"Then get to napping." Mama refused to look at Susanna.

"Mama?"

"Suz, if that window backs up, I'm going to let you deal with all the complaints." She sorted paid tickets on a lowboy. "I'll be in the office."

Susanna had just caught up on the orders and restocked the salad bins when Bristol came around and announced she was taking over the window.

"You're on break."

"What break?" Susanna didn't budge when Bristol tried to move her from her spot. "I got this, Bristol. Get back out front."

"You're on break." Bristol hip butted Susanna and fired her clear to the edge of the lowboy. She packed a powerful punch for being nothing but skin and bones.

Susanna peered toward the office. "I'm on break?"

"I guess so." Mama's hand flew over the ten key, adding up tickets.

But what didn't add up was being on break an hour after she'd punched in, having Mama say, "I guess so," and the fact that the woman had yet to look her in the eye.

"Mama, what's going on?"

"Suz, go on break. You bother me like a two-year-old asking why."

"Suz?" Avery burst through the back door, breathless and windblown, her voice shrill.

"Aves." Susanna mimicked her high tone. "Are you working the deck? I thought Tina was out there."

"Come on, we got to go." Avery covered the space between them in one-two-three steps and linked her arm through Susanna's.

"Go? Where?" Dang girl had not been the same since returning home from Brighton. Prince Colin had sent her the most beautiful bouquet of flowers—to school no less—on her birthday. The gesture made her a princess in the eyes of everyone and sealed her heart from any overtures a mere mortal boy might offer.

"You have to see something."

"Another bouquet from Prince Colin?"

"Hush." Out the back door, down the deck steps toward the beach. Susanna jogged alongside her sister, her heart kicking up soul dust, her thoughts aiming down a dark corridor.

*Nathaniel? Was he here? No, of course not. Why would he . . .*

A jolt of anticipation fired Susanna through the sea oats and palmettos onto the beach. "Nathan . . ." She stopped. "Colin. Hello." The energy in her veins collapsed, leaving her weak. She braced her legs to keep from crumbling to the sand.

"Susanna, hello." Colin offered a steadying hand. His voice was so much like Nathaniel's.

"Surprise," Avery said, arms high and wide. "Aren't you surprised, Suz? We wanted to surprise you."

"Very much, yes . . . surprised." Trembling, she tried to stand on her own but the shifting sand beneath her feet made it difficult. "W–what brings you here, Colin?"

"Holiday from university. I thought I'd inspect the island, see what splendor captured Uncle Leo and Nathaniel." He motioned to Avery. "And to see this miss, discover what she was up to these days."

"Are you staying at the cottage?"

"Yes, it's quite nice. Your garden . . ." He whistled. Clearly overpaying his compliment. "Beautiful. Aunt Campbell would adore it."

"She should come with you next time." Susanna drew a long breath of the spring air, but nothing seemed to cool her disappointment that Nathaniel was not at the end of the path.

But she'd made herself clear that night at St. Stephen's. She'd not marry him. She left without saying good-bye and she'd never declared her love.

"Colin, let's go meet Daddy and Mama. Then, please, can I show you off to my friends?" Avery checked with Susanna as she tugged her prince up the path to the Rib Shack deck.

"Only if you ply me with some of your father's famous barbecue sauce," he said, also visually checking with Susanna. "Every meal we shared in Brighton she went on and on about your father's famous sauce."

"Have the pulled pork tonight," Susanna said, watching them go. "It's really tender and juicy."

"But first, how about we tour the island?" Colin spread his arms as if he'd stumbled onto a wild, fun idea. "I'm not terribly starved." He patted his stomach. "We can dine later." He scanned the deck. "It seems rather crowded, Aves-love."

*Aves-love?* A pet name. Susanna's heart yearned. *Down, jealousy, that's your baby sister hand-in-hand with a prince who loves her.*

"Yeah, what a good idea." Avery stopped tugging Colin up the path. "Suz, can you take me and Colin around the island? Put the top down on your car and—"

"My keys are in my locker." Susanna started for the deck. She had work to do.

Doubt knocked softly on her heart. Was she right to tell Nathaniel "no way, no how"? Should she have left without a good-bye?

Entrenched behind the service window, she could tear up some if she wanted and do a lot of emotional mulling while barking, "Pick up."

"Please, Susanna, come with us," Colin said.

No, no, no. Susanna exhaled, closed her eyes. She'd been doing so well with her "nothing" plan until Colin arrived.

"Three's a crowd, Colin," she said. "You two go on. Have fun." Mrs. Caller waved to Susanna from the far corner of the deck. Just today, she'd approved the seventeenth draft of her garden plans.

"Yeah, Suz, come with. You know the island history way

better than I do." Avery ran up the deck steps and cut off Susanna's path to the kitchen.

"Avery, I'm working. I can't go. We're slammed tonight."

"I'll get your car keys. Colin, do you want something to drink? A Coke or tea?"

"Tea sounds grand."

"Southern sweet, of course." Avery flirted. *Brother* ...

"If you fix it for me, it will have all the sweetness I need."

"Oh, please." Susanna rolled her eyes and exhaled. "I think I just got a cavity." She shifted Avery out of the way. "I'll get the keys. You go in there, Mama will see you, and you won't come out."

In reality, Susanna wanted to duck into the bathroom and cry into a wad of toilet paper. Colin's presence awakened all of her buried, impossible feelings for Nathaniel.

"You think I don't know how to sneak in without her seeing me?" *Pffpppt.* "Stay here, Suz. I'll be right back." Avery bolted for the kitchen and returned with Susanna's handbag, not one ripple or "hey there" from Mama. "Aves, I'm not going." Susanna dug out her keys, certain Mama would be at the door any minute, looking for her if not Aves, wondering what in tarnation happened to her help and adding something about docking pay. "Here." She slapped her keys against Avery's palm just as Mickey arrived with his banjo and guitar case.

"Susanna."

"Mickey."

Avery shoved the keys back at Susanna. "Come on, you're wasting daylight. It's going to be dark soon."

"Susanna, please, for me?" Prince Colin used his sultry, princely voice. Entirely unfair.

She relented. "Mama's going to flip."

"I'll go tell her." Off Avery dashed. Again.

Was it a full moon tonight? Susanna ducked to see beneath

the deck roof and scanned twilight threads through the budding tree branches for a hint of the moon.

"She has a lot of energy," Colin said to Susanna with affection in his words.

"Yes, she does."

Any minute now Mama would loom large in the doorway. No way was she dismissing Susanna tonight.

"Let's go." Avery marched out big as you please with two tumblers in her hand. One for Colin. One for herself.

"You're kidding. Mama's letting me go?" Had the world gone crazy? Daddy with his misty eyes. Mama with her avoidance. Now excusing both of her girls from Friday-night duty. "Okay, whoa, what's going on?"

"Um, Colin's here. That's what's going on." Avery was too bright, too cheery. "He wants to see the sights."

"Are you leaving before tomorrow, Colin? Because if you're not, we can do this tomorrow. It's supposed to be a beautiful day. We can see all of south Georgia if you want."

"He wants to see Lover's Oak." Avery threaded her fingers through Susanna's and pulled her toward the car.

"Lover's Oak?" All this cajoling was getting on her nerves. "Colin, you really want to see Lover's Oak?" This made no sense. Susanna aimed the remote entry key and unlocked the car. She moved in numb submission, her fractured thoughts trying to figure out what was going on.

"Grab that latch there, Colin," Avery said. "Pull down. Yep. Good, now shove the top back."

"A nine-hundred-year-old tree?" he said to Susanna. "Yes, I'd love to see it."

"And how do you know about Lover's Oak?" Pinpricks of revelation began to fire across her spirit. Something was up. Definitely up.

*Don't imagine what, Suz. Don't . . .*

"Avery told me about it. When she was in Brighton."

"And you want to see it? Now?"

"Why not? Let's see this infamous tree." Colin smiled all bright and overly cheery.

"Well, okay." Susanna walked around to the driver's side, ignoring the knot in her stomach. Colin was here. She should relax and enjoy his company. Just seeing Avery's joy was worth any pain to her own heart.

Her sister was going to be a princess. The idea fluttered large in Susanna's heart.

She was about to get behind the wheel when Avery came up behind her, reaching for the keys.

"How about I drive? You can be the backseat tour guide. We'll chauffeur you around."

Colin stepped up and pushed the seat for Susanna to crawl in the back. "Milady."

"Backseat tour guide. You best go where I tell you to go. Turn when I tell you to turn." She dropped to the seat with a sigh. If she had her wits about her at all, she'd pop out of the car the moment Avery backed out of the parking slot and go back to work. To the hustling insanity. To normal. "Aves, why am I going if I'm not driving?"

"Because you're tour guiding." Avery, really. So insufferable at times.

"And our chaperone."

Susanna arched her brow and leaned between the seats for a good look at Colin. "You need a chaperone?"

*Lord, you can't ask me to do this.* Lover's Oak? On the surface, it seemed so simple. Take a couple of kids around the island, then to see an ancient tree fabled to hold the secrets of its lovers.

But it was her tree. Where she met Nate Kenneth. King Nathaniel. Anticipation beaded over her skin, thriving under the cool current of the spring breeze. When Avery whizzed toward Christ Church, Susanna tapped her shoulder.

"Pull over." She needed to think, to pray, to go face down on the grass and strangle every last living hope of Nate coming for her.

That's what bothered her. The realization she'd been holding her breath since January wondering if he'd come for her.

Before Avery cut the car engine, Susanna hopped out over the back, her limbs weak and rickety. Just inside the stone wall, she ran across the smooth, cool grass, collapsing on the lawn, forehead to the ground.

Stretched out, arms over her head, sharp grass blades pricking her eyelids and the tip of her nose, she spilled it.

"I thought it was Nathaniel waiting on the beach. I did. I really did. I imagined an outcome and I was wrong. *Soooo* wrong. But, Lord, I miss him." She hammered her fists into the grass. "I love him."

The confession bounced from her lips to the ground and into her own heart. It was the first time she'd ever heard her own true confession.

"I love him, Lord. I do."

A thick tear dripped down on the nearest grass blade, but with each breath, peace filled her. The wind rustled through the trees. In the distance a car door slammed. Voices. Footsteps crunching on the redbrick path.

Was that what God was waiting for? To hear her confession? What if the answer to "Lord, I've got nothing. I'll do whatever you want" was loving Nathaniel?

But how impossible? To love a man who could never love her.

"Suz?" Avery's small voice reminded her of when she was a girl, sneaking into her room at night, begging to sleep with her.

"Yeah?" The grass muffled her tone.

"Are you all right? We don't have to go. I didn't mean to upset you. It's Nate, isn't it? You miss him." Avery smoothed her hand over the crown of Susanna's head.

"I do." Susanna pushed up from the ground. "I'm fine. Just needed to deal." Avery and Colin peered at her with concern. "Prince Colin, welcome to St. Simons. I'm delighted to be your tour guide."

"Susanna, sincerely, Avery's right. We can go tomorrow. Perhaps you're right. In the light of day and all." He peered at Susanna. "Aves-love, we've only been thinking of ourselves."

"Yeah, I know. Suz, let's go back to the Shack."

"Are you kidding? Mama let us both off? This is a monumental moment. Besides, the island is beautiful at sunset. Tonight's the night." Susanna trumpeted her arm in the air. "To Lover's Oak. Where all true lovers find their way." She wiggled her eyebrows at Avery. "Who knows what awaits you, my dear sister."

The teen's face flashed a delicious shade of apple red. "Suuuzz!"

"Prince Street." Avery pointed to the street sign as she turned, slowing the car. "Here you go, Colin. Your street."

"And the tree? Straight ahead?"

"Just down there a bit." Avery glanced back at Susanna. "You doing okay back there?"

"Peachy keen." Susanna had finally relaxed and joined Avery's fun, helping her shine in front of Prince Colin. After a short tour of the southern tip of the island and a climb to the top of the lighthouse, they crossed the causeway and headed for the old Brunswick tree. "My hair looks like I got hit by a wind tunnel, but ah, what the heck."

Who was she, Susanna Truitt, to determine which sister won the prince? The coronation royal affair landed *one* of the Truitt girls in a fairy tale. The better of the two at that.

"Y–you want a brush or something?" Avery rose up to see her in the rearview.

"A brush? It'll just tangle up on the way home." Susanna tapped Colin's shoulder. "There's the tree"—why was it glowing? She reached for the roll bar and pulled herself up—"with all of those white lights."

Hundreds of them. Thousands. Glittering against the velvet night.

The Cabrio inched into a pocket of air filled with the music of a string quartet.

A sand-bag candle path began halfway down Prince Street, lining the street to the corner of Albany and the tree.

Susanna gripped Avery's shoulder as she crept along the avenue.

"Avery?"

"Yeah?"

"What's going on?"

Silence.

"Colin?"

Ditto silence.

Susanna sat on the collapsed rooftop and slid over the back of the car. Jogging alongside, she peered through the flickering angles of light toward the tree.

She had no thoughts. No conclusion. Just a powerful urge to move toward the lights, toward the fullness of the oak tree.

Then *he* stepped around the craggy old trunk. Handsome and regal in his pressed white shirt and blue jeans, his dark hair loose about his face.

"Nathaniel." She broke into a full run, the heels of her worn work clogs soft against the hard pavement. "Nathaniel." When she reached the tree, she launched into his arms.

"Susanna." He swept her around, holding her so tight she couldn't feel where she ended and he began.

"I missed you so much."

"I missed you." He cupped her face in his hands, brushing his thumbs over her lips. "I'm so sorry for my silence, so sorry."

"No, no, it's okay. Of course you were silent. I left without a word. I told you I wouldn't marry you. But I was wrong. I would, I would. If you could. I'm so glad you're here." She threw her arms around his neck and wept against his shoulder. "I love you. I do. I can't help it. No matter what, I do love you even if you can't—"

"Hey, love, hey." He freed her arms and stepped back, holding her face in his hands, joy in his glistening eyes. "You just made my quest much easier."

"What quest?" She didn't bother with her tears or wet cheeks.

"To see you. But I had to take time to arrange things."

"What things?" Had she not just been lying face down in the grass telling the Lord she was letting go? Was *this* the fruit of letting go? Seeing Nathaniel stirred the silt of her soul where she'd hoped her prayers had settled.

"This." Nathaniel skipped back toward the tree and pulled a scroll from a leather bag.

With great pomp and circumstance, he unfurled the scroll, cleared his voice, and read in his best bass. "'We, the Parliament of Brighton Kingdom'"—he leaned toward her—"this is my version because the official one is full of barrister speak, but I assure you it's all valid and official."

"Official?" The stammering of her heart vibrated in her words.

"'Along with the Crown and House of Stratton, decree a new covenant of love in the Marriage Act of 1792 and hereby grant rights to King Nathaniel II and his descendants hitherto and hereafter to marry whomever they choose as long as the Crown, the prime minister, and the privy council don't disapprove.'"

Tremors anchored Susanna to where she stood and shook her breath.

"'In so being, we decree our high approval of Miss Susanna Truitt'—they really said that, Susanna, I didn't add that part—'of St. Simons Island, of Georgia, of America.'" Nathaniel lowered the scroll and peered at her. "Of Nathaniel's mind." He lowered to one knee. "Of Nathaniel's heart."

"Nathaniel, w–what are you doing?" The quartet, in portable chairs on the left side of the Prince and Albany intersection, raised their bows. Neighbors came out of their houses, stepped from their porches.

"Susanna Truitt, I don't know truly how you feel. Or if you'd fancy marrying a king. But I love you, I can't stop thinking of you, and I want to spend my life with you." He pulled a wooden ring box from his jeans pocket. "It's unfair to ask you to leave your home, your friends and family, your country, your right to privacy, and your own career and desires, but I'm asking anyway. Will you marry me?"

What did he say? The breeze moving through Lover's Oak must have twisted his words.

*"Will you marry me?"*

She covered her mouth and took a step back, her world quaking.

"No man will love you more. I can't be a good king without the woman I love. Without you. Once you said if we were meant to be you'd have been born in Brighton, or I'd have been born in America, but I respectfully decline your theory, Susanna. We are meant to be. You are right for me, for Brighton. God expands the boundaries of nations, changes their DNA, by giving us sincere souls like you. By the love of a king's heart. Brighton needs you. I need you. But the lingering question is, am I right for you? Do you need and want me?"

Susanna dropped to her knees and searched his gaze. "I do. I can't get you out of my heart. I've tried, oh, I've tried." Words watered with the sweetness of tears were the best. "I'm terrified of all of this. But I love you." She laughed low, suddenly realizing how wild she must look. She patted down her wind-matted hair. "Now I know why Avery asked me if I wanted to brush my hair."

"He went to Parliament, Susanna." Jonathan came from the other side of a dark SUV that was merged with the shadows. "He implored them to change the Marriage Act. Risked his reputation, his credibility. First time a king brought an Order of Council before the Parliament in over a century."

"Jon, please, chap, I think I can woo her on my own."

Jonathan grinned with a slight bow. "His love for you changed our nation, Susanna. Changed me."

"Susanna." Nathaniel opened the ring box. The jewel inside caught the tiny white lights and created a rainbow over Susanna and the base of Lover's Oak. It captured her breath, her heart. "This belonged to Brighton's last reigning queen, Anne-Marie."

"I–I couldn't . . . It's . . . incredible." She'd never seen anything like it. An oval center pink diamond surrounded by smaller diamonds, sapphires, and rubies.

"Lord Thomas Winthrop designed it for her. They were known in Brighton for their love. Then my grandfather gave it to my Granny, Isabella." Nathaniel reached for her hand. "But I think Queen Anne-Marie Victoria Karoline Susanna would love for you to have it."

"Susanna?"

"Yes, and you've not given me your answer. Will you marry me? Be my queen?"

"Marry you?" She didn't mean to repeat the question but it felt so overwhelming.

"Marry me."

"Marry you?" She couldn't stop trembling.

"Susanna Jean." A sharp but very familiar voice hit her in the back of the head. "Stop stalling. Say yes."

"Mama?" Susanna jumped to her feet and whirled around to see Daddy, Mama, Avery, Colin, Gracie, and Ethan sitting on car hoods and truck gates. "Are you tailgating my engagement?"

"Oh, my stars-a-mighty." Mama surrendered her hands. "Pay attention to the man on his knees."

"Suz"—Nathaniel grabbed her hand and rose to his feet—"if you want to think for a while, I understand. It's all quite sudden."

"Do you think I can do it? Marry you, be a . . . a . . . *queen*?" The word tumbled awkwardly from her tongue. "Can I do what's required?"

"I have no doubt. I'd not be here otherwise. I need you, Suz. Brighton needs you. I'd not put you in this position if I didn't believe in you."

"What about Hessenberg, Lady Genevieve, the entail?"

"Goodness, you ask a lot of questions when a man's heart is beating against his chest." He kissed her forehead. "We found an heir to Prince Francis."

"Really?"

"An American. Regina Beswick."

"An American?" She grinned. "Seems America will be invading the nations of the North Sea."

"What are you saying?"

Susanna loved the look of realization in Nathaniel's eyes. She tugged at his button-down shirt. Might as well have some fun of her own. "I would say yes, Nate, but I told God it'd have to be a snowy day in Georgia before I ever fell in love again. Or at least admitted to it." She tipped her head toward the night and offered up her palms. "Sixty degrees and no snow."

"So, that's it? No snow, no engagement?" He backed toward the tree, somber, serious.

Susanna regarded him a moment, wondering how far she could push this bit. "Yes, that's it. No snow, no engagement." She glanced back at her family. Were they eating popcorn? Oh, mercy . . . back at Nathaniel, she crossed her arms. "Yeah, chap, it has to snow."

"I wasn't sure you'd reduce me to this, but . . ." He pulled a cord and smiled as a delicate cloud of Styrofoam snow drifted down from the highest limbs of Lover's Oak.

"Oh my . . ." She held up her hands as she turned slowly in the swirling white flakes. They covered her hair, her shoulders, the edge of her eyelashes, and filled her with tears.

"You never said it had to be real snow, milady."

"No, I guess I didn't." She peered at him, love spilling over her heart into her mind, will, and emotions. He did this for her, to win her heart.

She didn't need fake snow or a proposal beneath an ancient tree to know God had brought this man into her life.

The morning she'd confessed to God she had nothing and he could set her on any journey he deemed necessary. Susanna understood completely now the Lord had Nathaniel in mind all along.

"Susanna Truitt, please, you're killing me. Will you marry me? How many times must a king ask?"

"Yes, Nathaniel II of the House of Stratton"—she laced her arms about his neck—"I will most definitely, certainly, one hundred percent marry you and be your snow queen."

"Thank goodness." He exhaled, then scooped her up, whirled her around as the last of the fake snow whispered down over their true love.

The tailgaters erupted with cheers and whistles.

"I love you, Susanna-babe."

"I love you too, Nathaniel. I love you too."

He set her down and held her face in his hands, smoothing his thumbs over her cheeks, and sealed the moment with their first kiss. Tender but passionate.

Susanna had never believed much in fairy tales or charming princes, or knights on white steeds, but she'd always believed in the one true love.

And tonight, and forever, he held her in his arms.

# READING GROUP GUIDE

1. In the opening of the story, Susanna had a plan. One she stuck to for far too long. Is it possible to cling to an idea or want too long? Discuss areas of your life where you might need to let go.

2. Nathaniel's life is about to change. He doesn't feel ready to be king. He hopes it's later rather than sooner. Discuss ways to embrace life's changes. If change is hard for you, how can you embrace it with a more willing heart?

3. In the beginning we see Susanna wants what she wants. Adam and living on St. Simons Island. There's little consideration of God's plan. Our plans and wants can muddy up our ability to seek God's desires. How can we clear the waters and tap into his heart for us?

4. Aurora restructured her life to engage God. Would you be willing to give up something that meant a great deal to you if it meant you had a constant sense of God's presence?

5. Susanna says Aurora is the most free of them all. Is she? How can we be "tent dwellers" in our daily lives?

6. Often there are clues directing us into the Lord's will but we can't see them or grasp them. The gold shoes are that

for Susanna. She misses the clue but doesn't give up on seeking understanding. What clues have you received that were indicators of God's direction for your life?

7. Nathaniel is locked into duty to his country but he loves Susanna even though he can't marry her. Have you ever surrendered your will for the sake of a greater cause? If not, how would you respond if faced with such a challenge?

8. When Prince Stephen and Queen Campbell conspire to bring Susanna to the coronation, did you see it as manipulative or something for the greater good?

9. Was Susanna right to leave early? Was she being a coward or trying to get out of Nathaniel's way? Is it sometimes best to get out of the way of another person's destiny even if it hurts our own wants?

10. Nathaniel changed a nation because of love. Is it possible to change our families, our relationship, our communities, even our nation with the pure love of Jesus? How can you be both bold and humble in truth and love?

11. Nathaniel remembered the snow. Was there a time in your life when you remembered something special about someone and filled a need? Did someone do that for you?

12. An engagement tailgate party! Share a story from your life when you were surprised by friends, family, or your spouse.

# ACKNOWLEDGMENTS

W hen my alarm went off at 5:00 a.m. the morning Prince William married Catherine Middleton, my first thought was, "Do I really want to do this? It's so early!" But I love watching history in the making. I love a good romantic ending to any relationship.

Twenty-nine years earlier I'd watched Prince Charles marry Lady Diana. How could I miss the nuptials of their son?

So I rolled out of bed, hopped online, and watched the wedding of the century. The new Duchess of Cambridge captured me, and the rest of the world, with her poise and confidence.

She was . . . like me. An ordinary girl marrying the man she loved, living her dream. My imagination took hold. What if an American girl was invited to a royal wedding? Wouldn't that be cool? What if she met a prince and fell in love? What if she didn't know he was a prince?

Through several iterations, brainstorming, writing, and rewriting, Susanna and Nathaniel's story came to life. Thank you to Catherine, Duchess of Cambridge, for inspiring us all.

The countries used in this story are fictional—a blend of English and German culture, rooted in the history of European royalty. The characters reflect no real persons or ruling families. They are entirely of my imagination. Terminology and setting, and the political situation, is also solely of my creation, though I relied on real historical facts to build my royal world.

That being said, a novel is written in solitude but with the support of many. My debt of love and thanks goes to:

Brainstorm partners Debbie Macomber, DiAnn Mills, and Karen Young.

My agent, Chip MacGregor, for loving this idea and lending it his support. I really appreciate you!

My editor, Sue Brower, and the Zondervan team for seeing the merit of a royal story. Sue, your phone call and honest, real conversation won my heart.

Bob Hudson for your wise insight and skilled copy edits.

Authors Beth K. Vogt and Lisa Jordan for reading the synopsis and giving me your input.

My writing partner, Susan May Warren, who continually carves time out of her busy life to sound out story ideas and plot points with me. Who said without hesitation when I called with a "new" idea for a big, smashing ending, "No terrorist attacks in a prince story!" Thank you, friend. I'm so grateful to the Lord for you.

Ellen Tarver for reading and editing at the last minute. Amy Simpson, my real-life princess model. Thanks for loaning my imagination your beauty.

My husband and very own prince, who is a constant encouragement and intellectual resource. He makes me laugh and reminds me who I'm writing for and why. He exhorts me to chase God and the things he's called me to do with liberty. He is my best friend. "Love you, babe!"

All the royal watchers and biographers who blog and write about Europe's kings, queens, and royal families, especially the folks on the Royal Forums.

And to you, the readers, who give your precious time to my stories! You bless me way more than you can ever know.

Jesus! Thanks be to God who leads me into triumph! What an honor to know you and write for you.

# A Note from the Author

Finding Lover's Oak during my research was a bit of serendipity—a piece of the Gospel message hidden amid the story. Jesus is the Tree of Life, the "Lover's Oak" of our hearts. The Cross is often called "the tree." It was on a tree that Jesus died for love. For you and me. If we have Jesus, we don't need a Lover's Oak in Brunswick, Georgia. We have unending love in our hearts. We have the Tree of Life. Reach out for him.

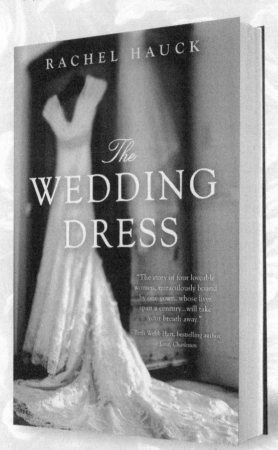